Apricots
A Novel of Saint Domingue

By

Sally Christie

ISBN: 978-1-7359246-1-8

For John & Sylvia

In 1789, tremors of unrest from the start of the French Revolution traveled across the Atlantic to Saint Domingue, France's star colony and known as *The Pearl of the Antilles*. Tension built until August 1791 when the colony was shaken by the largest slave insurrection the world had ever seen: one thousand plantations burned and two thousand whites massacred before tenuous order was restored, savagery answered with even greater savagery. It was as if nature's prophecy, the one foretold by the stark, bare numbers—more than four hundred thousand slaves against forty thousand whites and thirty thousand "free people of color"—had finally, and inevitably, been fulfilled.

A year later, slave rebels still control most of the northern plains and unrest is spreading throughout the colony. Certain pockets, including the remote southwest region known as the Grand'Anse, remain seemingly free of strife and life continues on, uncertain yet familiar.

BOOK ONE

DAWN

The Gardens
5 am

Her husband leans over and brushes her cheek, gently, and Rose turns towards him. Suddenly he is backing away, and just as she reaches for him, a tremor breaks the walls apart.

Rose escapes and jerks awake, her heart pounding.

She touches the wall by her bed. Solid. Just another nightmare, or the best of dreams. Her husband died two years ago and Rose treasures these nights when he appears to her. She lies until the world settles into a more familiar rhythm, then rises and pulls on a shift. She steps onto the veranda and into the silvery stillness of the early dawn: her favorite time of day, when all is quiet and cool, before the heat scorches everything, before the silence is broken and real life intrudes.

Rose settles on the top step of the stairs that lead down to the garden. The plantation house—the *gran caze*—is built on a hillside to capture the sea breezes and overlooks a flower garden. The delicate roses she once hopefully planted are long since dead, but bougainvillea, poinsettias and hibiscus all flourish with tremendous abandon.

A statue of Venus, carved decades ago by a slave, stands sentinel in the middle of the tangle of bush and flowers. Every time Rose sees the tarred wood in half-shadows, for a sliver of a second before her mind catches up with her eyes, she always thinks it a slave—one of *them,* inside her sacred space. I should get it moved, she thinks in irritation, as she thinks almost every day. Resolutely she looks past it down the hillside to the sea below, lavender with white caps cresting in the first light of dawn.

Her stomach tightens at the sight of a small boat in the bay. Docked there since yesterday, waiting to transport her coffee to the port at Jérémie where the *Marie Celeste,* bound for Baltimore, waits with its cavernous cargo mouth. Rose has four days to get all her dried coffee sorted, milled, into sacks and loaded onto the boat—an impossible task while she has two fields of bushes begging to be picked before the cherries, as the unpicked beans are known, ferment on the branches; they are horribly behind in all pursuits. But there are so few ships these days and if she misses the *Marie Celeste,* her bags of milled coffee will have to be warehoused, subject to theft and rats and the rotting effects of humidity.

No, decides Rose in sudden resolution. She'll worry about all that later. The sun is not even in the sky and the day—and its incessant demands—is not begun. For now, she will enjoy the peace and solitude.

Sheba and Rex round the veranda, their nails clipping on the wooden slats. They sniff at her, delicately, and she gives Rex a half-pat. They are tall, brutish dogs, well-trained to chase slaves or wild boars. They share the morning stillness with her briefly before setting off to explore the remains of the night. A kestrel circles overhead and cries out, breaking the silence, then disappears into the mountains behind. Around Rose, the hillsides start to come alive, the chirping of the birds mounting in a symphony to herald the coming day.

This week there are guests in the house, the intruders like a physical presence itching her skin. Last week, Rose watched in disbelief as an unheralded carriage that she recognized as belonging to her cousin pulled up to the house and disgorged a plump man with a white wig, followed—most unexpectedly—by an elderly woman.

"Madame, may I present myself—I am Philibert Theophile de Moran de Thoreau," said the man, bowing extravagantly and presenting Rose with a well-thumbed introductory letter from the *Académie Nationale des Arts et des Sciences de Bordeaux.* Rose noticed the man's fingernails were buffed and white, and her overall impression was that of a tatty peacock, faded but trying desperately to be brilliant. "Your cousin in Corail assured me you would be happy to receive us, and support my efforts."

"We are honored," replied Rose, trying not to scowl. Why had her cousin not sent warning? Then she might have sent word back that she was unwell, or away. These days she has no inclination for the little miseries of manners that society entails. Life, once full of visits and guests, has shrunk considerably since her husband's death.

"On a mission of great importance and delicacy," her guest continued, and soon revealed that he was in Saint Domingue to study the ways in which horse and cattle breeding techniques, and animal husbandry in general, might be applied to improve the slaves' abysmal birth and child mortality rates.

Rose nodded politely but thought it a fool's mission: many had tried and failed on that account.

On top of Thoreau and his elderly sister, the Englishman Plunkett is here to deliver his monthly week of lessons to her children. Usually free to roam the countryside, Charles and Aimée are cooped up inside the house, adding to the sense of a world bursting at the seams. The house is in chaos, the guest rooms all full and Plunkett reduced to sleeping on the dining room table, his nightshirt draped over a chair even during meals. Books everywhere, Charles endlessly proclaiming his Latin verbs, Aimée sulking and banging away on the piano. Monsieur Thoreau running around brandishing a tape measure, spouting off about scientific methods and fertility, while his sister Mathilde, as silent as her brother is voluble, seems to appear whenever Rose turns around— she is beginning to think the woman is *stalking* her.

And Rose mustn't forget, though she often does, her sister-in-law Julienne who spends her days lying in bed, sometimes shouting, sometimes silent, her mind addled beyond repair.

So many people, so many demands, when all Rose wants is peace.

At the bottom of the garden the dogs are circling something. Rose squints through the half-light. A log? A dead pig, feral from the mountains? Or perhaps one of hers, stolen and now returned as an omen or a warning. A few weeks ago on the back steps Rose found a disemboweled lizard, its entrails arranged in an 'X.' Or was that just the way the cat left it?

Since the great slave revolt in the north last August, nothing has been the same and everything is worse. The uprising took more than just property or lives; it took away the very surety with which the whites of the colony lived their lives. It imbued every crackle of leaf, every half-formed shadow and every dead lizard with menace. Now the colony is spiraling out of control, unrest pockmarking the island, the horrors coming closer. The tension of life in Saint Domingue—so apparent to Rose when she first arrived, yet gradually lost beneath the calming rhythms of everyday life—has returned with a vengeance.

Rose sees it isn't an animal the dogs are circling in the garden.

It's a man.

Lying on his side, clad in a green coat and breeches. Rose's mouth tightens in disgust: Plunkett, the children's tutor. She recalls boisterous voices floating through the walls of the house last night. Plunkett and the guest Thoreau, arguing about… about what, she can't remember. Politics and the interests of men, no doubt. *Economic rights*, she remembers Plunkett shouting: *Economic rights must equal political rights!*

Rose was careful to leave her guests only one bottle of rum but now there he is, passed out at the bottom of the garden. Disgraceful. Though the tutor's visits are necessary, there is much to dislike about him: an Englishman with bad breath and a reputation for thievery, living like a buccaneer down in the town of Apricots with his slave wife and bastards.

Rose picks her way over the mossy cobbles of the garden path and past the statue of the black Venus, her breath quick with anger. Such a disgrace. She can't have him in front of the children if liquor is still leaking from his pores. She decides she'll send him away early. Next month Charles, already fourteen, will leave for France to complete his education and Rose doubts she'll keep his services for her daughter.

Rose reaches Plunkett, face down in the mud, his left arm oddly akimbo. She prods him with her bare toe but it feels wrong—too intimate—to be touching him like that. Then roosters call out in quick, angry succession, followed immediately by the shrill hoot of the plantation conch—the peace of the dawn shattered, the wheels of another day set in motion.

Rex gives the man's arm a tentative lick but Sheba whines fearfully against her. But what to do about Plunkett? A thick gray mud, like that found near the old indigo vats, covers his shoes and extends up his breeches. What is he doing in the garden? There is nothing out here for a drunken man, especially for one as debauched as Plunkett. Rose feels a chill coming from the forest behind her, still dark and secret at this time of the morning. Sheba whines once more and the world stops, briefly.

"Get away, Rex," Rose says, pushing at the dog now vigorously nuzzling the man's neck.

Plunkett isn't drunk, or asleep.

He is dead.

The Slave Houses
6 am

The bellow of the conch rips through the dawn. Appollon rolls over. He hardly slept; today he will have to filch time away, sleep in the straw of the stables, snatch a few moments in the shade to be ready for the coming night.

Tonight—when it will happen.

The eighty or so slaves sleep in long wooden houses, nestled in the lea of a hill, raised on stilts against crabs and snakes. It is still dark as the men stretch, roll, emerge from their blankets and pull on their field clothes. Some get up already dressed. Benjamin shuffles the length of the room, pushing others out of his way and murmuring dark deeds as he goes. Michel calls out brightly, "Rejoice in this day, a gift from the Lord!" and gets a cuff on the head from Antoine. Gros Jean lies still, muttering that he is too tired; he wants to go to the hospital, even though it is known as a place of certain death. In his corner, Louis gets up. As one of the *commandeurs*—slave drivers—he has a proper wooden bed, not the rough palm-frond pallets of the others.

In the first pale light, the men tumble outside, some gnawing on a ball of cassava or a plantain from the night before, shivering in the thick dewy fog that rolls down from the mountains behind. They will breakfast later, but for now they must hurry to the fields and capture the precious hours when it is light, but still cool. Sans Quartier and Julien—two who still remember their old faith—kneel and face west to the vast sea. Agathe sits silently

6

behind them. She doesn't pray, but the incantations of the men remind her of her childhood in Hausaland.

At a trough filled with rainwater, Appollon splashes water on his face.

"How you doing, man?" asks Garifou, grinning. Appollon grunts. There are only a few slaves on the plantation who know what will happen tonight and Garifou—a spy for the white manager Brac—is not among them.

Garifou looks eagerly at Appollon. "So how are you?" he repeats.

"I am here," replies Appollon, not bothering to look up.

"Full moon tonight, eh? Last night too, but you didn't go out."

"Don't follow my movements, rat," says Appollon, spitting on the ground.

"I'm not following you, brother, I just want to be your friend," Garifou whines and Appollon thinks what a poor choice Garifou was to be the eyes and the ears of the whites. Better to have chosen Pa'Oreille—*No Ears*—who lost both of his after two escape attempts; he has run away many more times, but these days slaves are too scarce and valuable to be put to death for the third attempt as the law prescribes.

The women have joined the men in the clearing, washing their faces and tying their head scarves. Appollon seeks out Jeannette by the kitchens but he doesn't see her; as the cook for the big house, she is free from these morning gatherings. Brac the manager rides into the clearing on his mule, his slave *commandeur* La Fleur at his heels. La Fleur has a curious habit of singing his commands, and all the slaves hate him and call him *the singing dog*.

Appollon slips into the crowd, still rubbing the sleep from his eyes. He is in charge of the stables and livestock, a position of some responsibility that has grown since the coachman died last year. Appollon now takes on those duties, but mostly tends to the horses and mules and oversees the sadly diminished goat pen, as well as the one milking cow that remains. A coveted position, for the work is not arduous and he often serves as messenger for the whites, riding out beyond the plantation to see the comings and goings of the world.

"Tonight," whispers Pierre, sidling up.

Appollon shakes his head. "Be silent! Act like the wind can hear." Louis, Pierre and his ship-brother Capidon are the only others who know of the plan for tonight. The rest will join, or not; those who don't will be killed. Appollon moves away to the edge of the crowd of men, alone with his thoughts. Something so long anticipated and planned, now come so close he can almost touch it.

*

"All here?" snaps Brac in distaste. As manager on this plantation, he should be in an office with the account books, a constant cup of coffee and a plate of pastries. Instead he is out here at the break of dawn like a lowly overseer. After the last young man from France with a propensity for fever and homesickness quit, Madame Rose did not hire a replacement and now this ridiculous duty falls on Brac.

"On your knees!" he shouts, his eyes sweeping over the crowd; he is short-sighted and last month found his last pair of spectacles crushed to a pulvereen. Now the men and women before him meld together in a nameless black mass. La Fleur counts out the eighty-two men and women, and when all are settled—the Muslims not bothering to turn around—Brac shouts out the morning prayer. Most of the slaves ignore his words, but a few have taken a liking to Jesus and his suffering, and find some consolation for their ripped lives in his little form. This Jesus teaches them that they were born in Africa to be sold as slaves, that His Father made a fertile continent full of well-shaped, hard-working men for just that purpose.

Brac himself is decidedly irreligious but is a big believer in order, and there is nothing more orderly than religion. "Give thanks this day!" he shouts, and the slaves dutifully repeat after him. "To the Lord High Almighty who governs us, thank you for this work. We pray today there are no accidents. To your glory, Amen."

Hearing the voices raised in prayer, the four new slaves locked in the warming hut take up a shouting. On arrival last week at the plantation the four Aradas were cleaned, given a blanket and a set of clothes. Then they were locked in the warming hut with a roaring fire to help them recover from the rigors of the ocean passage and adjust to the chilly climate of the nights. They have been in there almost a week but Brac hasn't trained them yet. Only once they are past the ridiculous deadline that Madame Rose negotiated with the ship captain in Jérémie—four days to get a fortnight's worth of work done!—will Brac break them in.

"Trust in God," cries out the slave Michel to the warming hut, in a language the new captives surely don't understand. "God hears you!"

Prayers done, Brac starts issuing orders. La Fleur leads one group up to the east field, where half the coffee bushes are still unpicked and perilously close to rotting. Louis, the second driver, takes another gang to finish the south field and a group of women to bring the harvested beans to the drying racks. Brac hands out shovels, kept under lock and key alongside the machetes, to the women tasked with turning the coffee beans on the drying racks. Another group of women is dispatched to continue the endless job of sorting the dried beans, looking for grit or stones that might cripple the mill. They've got to get the mill up and running by this evening if they are to make the deadline. Saturday, thinks Brac grimly. Impossible!

Only a few slaves remain and the Aradas are still keening unhappily.

"You!" Brac looks to Laurine, who works as the laundress. "Get them to stop that unholy noise."

"Don't speak their tongue," snaps Laurine with a scowl.

"Yes, you do! They Aradas like you."

"They not," says Laurine and Brac makes a motion to kick her.

Laurine sulks away, shouting out something to the keening captives. Brac feels a small surge of defeat, as he often does when faced with the shadows of the slave's world. Laurine could be right; the captain of the ship promised they were Aradas, fine specimens from Benin, but really, how could he tell? Brac speaks Creole, the island's bastardized French that everyone, from the highest admiral to the lowest slave, learns on arrival. The other languages of the slaves—blather, all of it—are entirely alien to him.

Brac dispatches Pierre and Capidon to repair the tarpaulins

that at night cover the drying coffee, all of them found slashed last week. He turns and finds the slave Appollon watching him. Brac cannot read his expression, but he can never look at the tall Nago with his inscrutable eyes without feeling distrust, or even something like fear. Before he can shout at Appollon to stop loitering and get to the stables, the clanging of the bell from the big house rips through the clearing.

Brac frowns and sets off on his mule to investigate the unexpected interruption.

The Veranda
6 am

Brac kicks the body and declares Plunkett dead. He turns the man over and Rose gasps at the red gash across the throat, a peek of white bone shining through.

"Murdered," murmurs Brac, sounding unsurprised.

Rose stifles a completely inappropriate urge to laugh. *Murdered?* Her knees weaken and for a moment she fears she will fall down, next to the body. She looks around the garden, into the forest behind, all appearing normal but now everything tinged with terror. Evil all around, threatening to come closer. A man, *murdered* in her garden.

Brac covers the body with coffee sacking, marked with a curlicued "*BF*" for "Habitation Bayardel, Famille Fongravier"— the same stamp that brands their slaves. "We'll put him down the old well," he decides. "Keep him from rotting in the heat." The well by the washhouse gave bad water for a decade and is now mostly used to store meats and other foods. Rose nods, unable to say anything and unsure what to do next.

She flees back to the safety of the house and finds her cook waiting for her on the veranda, the woman's face as impassive as it always is, her eyes downcast. Jeannette is a beautiful woman, and in her coppery skin and high cheekbones there is a perhaps a hint of the native inhabitants of the island, the Taino; some of the earliest slaves intermarried with survivors of those people, now mostly gone from the earth.

11

Rose marvels at how calm her cook appears—if she is nervous or upset, she is hiding it well. Acting as though the death of Plunkett were of no more import than planning the day's meals! But perhaps that is what Rose should do as well: bury the horror under the mundane details of life. And they do have to eat.

"The bacon is almost finished," says Jeannette softly.

"How can that be? The last pig was almost five hundred pounds!" A massive brute that might have fetched eight hundred *livres* in town, the price of a young slave, but Rose had craved bacon and the happiness found in small luxuries.

Rose glares at her cook; sometimes she thinks Jeannette delights in bringing her bad news. Though it seems impossible now, they had once almost been friends. When Rose was a young bride, newly arrived from France and eager to take care of her husband, she had wanted, if not to actually cook, to at least help plan his meals. To her mother-in-law's disgust, Rose often spent mornings in the kitchens with Cunette, the cook at that time, and young Jeannette.

Jeanette taught Rose all about the strange foods of the island: pineapples, mangoes, wild spinach and wild boars, giant cucumbers and squashes, small hard cherries. Strange alligator pears and enormous, bready apricots with their indefinable taste. Sharks, sardines, manatee and carp; even caiman lizard on occasion. Custard apples with poisonous seeds that would paralyze if crushed open. Crabs everywhere, including the *mancenille* ones, deadly when eaten.

Rose brought a recipe book from France—a wedding present from her aunt—and some mornings she went to the kitchens and read the recipes aloud to Jeannette. Together the two young girls would plot how to substitute the ingredients of France for what was available on the island. Happy times that Rose remembers fondly, but gradually her mother-in-law's disapproval stripped away any enjoyment she found in the kitchens and she stopped going.

"Well, fine, serve the last of the bacon," Rose snaps, resisting an urge to slap her cook. Their earlier intimacy is entirely gone and time has cast a deep divide that only hardens and widens each year. "But make sure there are plenty of eggs and bread and perhaps they won't finish all the bacon."

They discuss dinner and Jeannette leaves for the kitchens, located away from the big house for fears of fire and filth. Watching her depart, Rose thinks of Plunkett's neck and that gash, clean and expert, and then of the way her cook so expertly fillets carp from the river.

Rose shivers and looks around the veranda. Her two children came out with the commotion and are now huddled together on one of the hammocks. The guest Thoreau re-appears, well-coiffed and tidied—Rose's cries had brought him out to the garden earlier but when he saw Plunkett's body, he turned greener than a lizard. As soon as Brac arrived, Thoreau beat a hasty retreat, apologizing over and again for appearing in his nightshirt.

Thoreau's sister Mathilde also appears, stuffing frizzles of hair into a large red cap. Mathilde is surely into her sixties—absurdly old to be traveling—and has hardly said a word since her arrival, preferring to creep silently around the house or sit and stare at her brother in what might be admiration.

The little group coalesces under an air of general uncertainty.

"A most worrisome business," declares Thoreau, shaking his head and starting to pace the veranda. He is a plump, self-satisfied man with hands that flutter as he speaks and a suit far too extravagant for this part of the colony. The inner heels of both his shoes are worn thin, producing an odd walk that wobbles his cheeks. "Simply outrageous, a white man murdered, the collision of savagery and order! Sadly, this event may cause a disruption in my plans of inquiry, but please, Madame, do not fret on my behalf."

Her guest's work is the least of her worries, and Rose ignores him. She tries to think what she should do next: part of her wishes she could hold her breath and be reduced down to nothing, then rise up and start again once this is all over. A man, murdered in her garden. Chaos rolling through her life, dragging her along, and always that endless, endless tiredness.

"Charles," she says, turning to her two children. "I want you to take Aimée out of the house. Go down to the beach or something." She wants them far away from the unpleasantness of death; Charles is fourteen, almost a man, but her daughter is only twelve and so much more delicate, with a dramatic imagination that often surprises her. There are men in this colony, Rose's dead husband amongst them, who believe that children should not be shielded from the harsher facts of life that surround them here. But Rose is alone now and will make her own decisions. She wants Aimée gone before what is surely to come: one of the slaves will be found guilty and punishment will be swift and cruel.

"Go," Rose repeats harshly. "You have been whining all week about being kept inside."

"Shouldn't someone ride to Dame Marie and inform Bassompierre?" asks Charles. Captain Bassompierre is in charge of the parish constabulary, responsible for order on the plantations in his district.

"No," says Brac quickly. Plunkett's body secured down the well, he has returned to the veranda and is now lounging on one of the benches and picking his teeth with a twig. Brac appears strangely calm, especially in comparison with the anxiously pacing Thoreau, but his presence on the veranda makes Rose uncomfortable. The plantation manager, with his dirty clothes and mocking servility, belongs *outside* the perimeter of the house, not up here. From the start she had disliked him, his face as coarse as a nutmeg grater, the air of swaggering arrogance he wore at all times. Their relationship has not improved since her husband's death.

"This is an internal plantation matter," Brac continues. "No need to involve the authorities just yet. We'll find out who did this and take care of him ourselves."

"I meant, to inform them of Plunkett's death," says Charles, looking at his mother. Rose guesses he is troubled by the idea of his tutor hanging down the well next to a great wheel of cheese purchased in Jérémie last month. Her son is fourteen, tentatively trying on the trappings of manhood and the dignity he feels is his due.

"I suppose we could contact the magistrate in Jérémie," murmurs Rose. "But who could we spare to make the trip? The mules are needed to bring the coffee bags to the boats."

"Later, we can deal with that later," interrupts Brac, flicking away his tooth-picking twig and standing up. "You go along now, boy, do as your mother says. We can manage this."

Rose frowns at the tone her manager takes with her son—

recently she has noticed a certain sly collusion between the two of them but she can't figure out where it comes from. Surely Charles doesn't see a father figure in this base man?

"Get some fruit from the kitchens and go, don't come back for a time," Rose says, steering her daughter towards the steps. The children leave, reluctance dragging their feet. Usually she doesn't encourage them to roam; whenever Aimée returns, exhausted and tattered from an afternoon exploring with Charles, Rose cannot help but tut and lecture her daughter about her own girlhood in France. There, life was church twice on Sundays and on other days there were no novels, cards, or music—and certainly no outdoor adventures! Just dull hours spent stitching or doing chores under the watchful eyes of her aunt. Seeing Aimée run around with the freedom she was so denied irritates Rose in a way she cannot quite define.

She sits down again and looks at Brac.

"Right. We'll get everyone back from the fields," says Brac after a pause. "Tie up the men then search the houses. If we don't find anything, then interrogation. Won't be long before it's all squared away. By this afternoon, not later," he promises.

Rose nods.

"And are we most certain it is a slave?" asks Thoreau, stopping in mid-pace and cocking his head in a delicate, inquiring manner. He is wearing a neat white wig with a queue, tied with a velvet ribbon. Rose had thought that wigs were now shunned in France, in the name of revolution and equality.

"Of course, it's a slave!" says Brac. "Plunkett probably came across one of them doing something they weren't supposed to. Or a *maroon* or a brigand," he adds but Rose shakes her head: bands of maroons—runaway slaves—might occasionally carry out raids on plantations but murder is rarely a hazard. And that quick, surgical cut—

"But—?" Thoreau frowns, looking between Rose and the plantation manager. He purses his lips and Rose fears he is about begin another oration.

"Please, Monsieur Thoreau," says Rose, with a dose of sweetness. "We must let the manager do his job; he knows the situation best." And Brac is right. It has to be a slave, thinks Rose in sudden determination. Unfortunately, that means she will lose

15

another one, when she has already lost several over the last months, not counting two of the newly purchased Aradas: they started as a group of six. Earlier she heard their cries, carrying through the moist dawn air.

"Very well, Madame," says Thoreau, bowing. He turns to the plantation manager and nods, as though giving his blessing. "And I shall assist with the corralling of the slaves—an excellent opportunity to observe the dichotomy between their natural lives and the rules imposed upon them."

Brac snorts.

Thoreau misinterprets it as a sneeze and proffers a flowered handkerchief from his jacket pocket.

"Breakfast will soon be served," says Rose quickly. "Best to join the work after breakfast, perhaps?"

"Ah, indeed," says Thoreau, his voice lighting in pleasure; he has shown himself to be easily distracted—and silenced—by food. "That bacon yesterday was superb. Will we have some today?"

"Yes, yes," says Rose.

"Bacon," murmurs Mathilde with a little sigh; she has been sitting silently, watching the men.

"Very well. Then I shall help you, Monsieur Brac, once I have taken my morning repast. Indeed, I shall be of more help when my brain is nourished."

"Right," shrugs Brac, a barely concealed look of contempt on his face. "I'll get to it, Madame, and it won't be long."

I feel as though I should be more upset, thinks Rose, watching Brac depart on his mule with the dogs trotting alongside. It's going to be another hot, loathsome day. Gathering the slaves means the loss of another day of harvest, thousands of plants still un-picked and perilously close to rotting. Not to mention they haven't finished drying or sorting the beans that need to be milled, and the ship is leaving in four days.

And Plunkett, dead.

Rose sits back down, suddenly exhausted. What a strange morning.

"It is beginning," Mathilde whispers in her dry, papery voice.

Rose frowns. "What is beginning?"

"The darkness," says Mathilde, nodding.

"Nonsense, sister," says Thoreau swiftly; he often tries to contain his sister's rather odd speech. "Such a strange thing to say when dusk is eight hours away."

But perhaps it *is* beginning, thinks Rose as a slick, helpless dread spreads through her. What if Plunkett's murder is the beginning of more disorder, or even—unbearable to think about—another slave uprising?

ROSE'S JOURNEY

NANTES TO SAINT DOMINGUE
1774-1792

It begins at a picnic on a bright summer evening. Marcel Fongravier is visiting from Saint Domingue, staying with his cousins—Rose's neighbors—a raucous family of six children who host an endless rotation of relatives from the West Indies. Like so many other families in Nantes, the Fongraviers look outward: down the bleak Atlantic to the African coast where slaves are to be had, then over to the Caribbean where fortunes are made. Marcel is twenty-five, in Nantes to help settle his grandfather's affairs and Rose suspects his cousins gave the picnic out of sympathy for her, their poor cloistered neighbor.

It is a beautiful evening, and when Rose first sees Marcel—so handsome with lively blue eyes—something inside her lights up. Then the next day, the sound of the gate as the lock is lifted, iron scraping over iron. Rose runs to the front parlor, peeks out the window and yes! it is him, his visit confirming that yesterday meant something.

"It is the young Fongravier," says her aunt, frowning, and Rose struggles to contain her smile. With obvious reluctance, her aunt allows Marcel's visit then supervises their courtship through the following weeks.

"We'll make our future together," Marcel promises her, and in the furtive pressure of his hand on her arm, just where her sleeve ends, Rose senses a chance for a different life, far away from the narrow confines of France. She is an orphan—her father dead before she was born, her mother carried off by smallpox when she was five—and now she lives in her uncle's house where thick curtains block out the sun and her aunt's disapproval drapes over everything. They are comfortable—her uncle is a successful saddle-maker, and their house on the Rue des Bordes boasts four bedrooms and an elegant salon—but suddenly Rose despises everything about her life. Adventure, something she never thought her due as a girl, now beckons from a colony so far from France one could think it lost.

"Yes!" she says when Marcel asks—quicker than is entirely appropriate but his ship is leaving and he wants her on it. Marcel grows pink with delight and only hesitates an instant before leaning in and kissing her on the cheek.

"I think you're mad," says her aunt when Rose shares the news. "Loose women and other unspeakables out there. How could you even think of such a place?"

"But there are many ladies there now!" Rose protests. They are eating their evening meal and though the table is usually reserved for silence, this conversation cannot wait. "Marcel says there are 400 French families in his district alone."

"What about Monsieur Lascoux?" demands her aunt.

"What of him?" replies Rose. Lascoux is a saddle-maker known to her uncle, an older man with dead eyes and an affected laugh. He had been courting Rose with staid intent and recently the hints from her aunt, no doubt eager to see her married and gone, have become more pointed. Before Marcel, Rose was prepared to accept that fate but now... no.

"There is no... understanding," Rose says carefully. She holds her breath and stares down at the bowl of soup in front of her. She can't move; if she lifts her spoon, everything will go wrong, and Marcel will disappear from her life forever.

"Jerome?"

Rose's uncle is silent, mindlessly eating his soup. Still Rose can't move. He must let me go, she thinks in sudden fear. He *must.*

He does, and she and Marcel are married. There are promises to write, of course, but as the ship sails and the people on the pier are lost behind the ocean spray, Rose feels no sadness. Instead she is infected by her new husband's excitement about *going home*—curiously he sees Saint Domingue as home, even though she thinks of him as entirely French.

"Pineapples every day!" Marcel promises. "Flowers as big as your head that never fade. Beautiful sea and delicious crayfish, sun to warm your face."

"Will my roses grow?" Rose asks, referring to her cuttings of yellow roses, wrapped in cloth, damped daily with precious fresh water.

"Of course," Marcel says, his arm around her waist. They are on deck, sitting beneath a makeshift awning that shields them from the sun. "Everything grows there! Your roses will bud, just as you will. Or as you did last night," he adds, his wicked smile cutting through her with shiny pleasure. The nights in their cabin, pressed together on a hammock, are a sea of endless, slowly unfurling delights; another new world to discover.

"The best coffee and cacao in the world. And indigo—I wager you'll grow sick of the color blue, so fine is our cloth." Marcel's father was born in France and purchased a concession in the 1740s when Saint Domingue's southern peninsula was opened to settlement. Up north around the glittering capital of Cap-Français, sugar booms but down in the remote Grand'Anse where Marcel lives, coffee is king and indigo, cotton and cacao its princely courtiers.

Marcel warns her that their plantation is isolated but that the town of Jérémie is but a few hours away. He paints Jérémie as a growing metropolis that offers a small but cheerful society, a meeting hall, talk of amateur theatricals and a billiards hall—"where even women sometimes play!" Rose giggles, trying to imagine what her aunt would say if she saw her niece bending over a billiard table.

"And," Marcel adds, "a life of luxury for you, my dear. You can have fourfold as many servants as you had in

France."

Rose nods, aware he means slaves. Her very own slaves. The ship they are on is an old slaver, now transporting cloth, wine and passengers. A small cupboard, roughly partitioned off from their cabin, holds a pile of chains that clink relentlessly and warn of the darker side of the colony that is soon to be her home. There is also an odd smell, which the captain dismisses as rotted rum but Rose thinks not. Though the bodies are long gone, it is the odor of human misery captured in the wood.

*

Finally, after eight weeks of ocean voyage they reach Jérémie, then take another smaller boat along the coast to Bayardel, his family's plantation.

"My dear, we have heard so much about you!" Marcel's mother embraces her and Rose feels brittle tension beneath the surface; perhaps she is not what Madame Francine had hoped for her son. Rose drops a curtsy while trying to keep the smile on her face. All the strange sights and sounds of the journey have made her tired and anxious: turquoise water, blood red earth, enormous trees, insects everywhere, people of every hue. Not to mention the sweat dribbling over her whole body, her gauze fichu sticking to her neck like a leech, the merciless sun beating through her straw bonnet.

Rose thinks his parents coarser than expected. Monsieur Marcel *père* is a rough man, portly with leathery, tanned skin, and he doesn't even wear a wig. Madame Francine has ash blonde hair, half-concealed under a trim little cap, and Rose soon comes to think of her as a white cat, purring and scratching at the same time.

Marcel's two unmarried sisters hug Rose and shriek over her stiff gowns. Isabelle and Julienne are vacuous girls, as frothy as well-whipped cream, and they furnish her with soft cottons and organdies, many of them blue as Marcel promised. Loose and flowing with the delicious liberty of just one petticoat. Rose notices Isabelle occasionally doesn't even wear stockings.

All that Marcel promised is true: the fruit, the flowers, the lushness of life. Pineapples and mangoes that explode with sweetness; the abundance of sugar, no luxury out here. Her yellow roses are planted and thrive, though if not tended daily they are quickly choked by plumeria, hibiscus and other nameless flowers that strangle everything in their path.

But there is so much Marcel never mentioned: the heat, merciless and draining; the chiggers that dig through the skin; the poisonous trees with bark that stings; the tiny ants pincing the skin all day long, their feet so light Rose never notices them until the itching starts. The smell from the indigo vats that wafts through the house—a primitive wooden structure with few windows and low ceilings—and fills every corner with the nauseating stench of a graveyard. The intermittent fevers which plunge Rose deep inside herself and make her limbs ache, and for which she gets no sympathy. "Everyone gets them when they first arrive," sniffs her mother-in-law. "You'll get used to them."

*

"Don't be nervous," whispers Marcel. They are in the carriage, pulled by mules, lurching along a rough track on their way to a dinner party hosted by Mercier, owner of the neighboring plantation. A grand affair, to celebrate Isabelle's upcoming marriage to Mercier's son as well as Rose's own arrival. Two barefoot slaves run alongside the carriage and a pair of matched boys—negrillons—ride out back in the pink livery of the Fongraviers. A carriage with livery pulled by mules! These contradictions of wealth and poverty fascinate Rose but she quickly learns not to voice her observations: any perceived dislike of the way things are done in Saint Domingue is met with steely stiffness by Marcel's family.

"I'm not nervous," Rose whispers back, squeezing Marcel's arm as the carriage jostles along. "You're with me."

The neighbor Mercier's house is much grander than the Fongravier's house at Bayardel. The salon is painted in cheery shades of green and yellow and the table is set with an extravagant dinner set from Sèvres, part of Isabelle's dowry. The food is again that delightful mixture of plainness and sophistication: chicken legs; conch served in shells alongside an exquisite cream soup; an elegant, towering cake decorated with candied fruit.

Monsieur Mercier makes a toast to the young couple and they kiss. Rose gapes in amazement. The French consider Creole women to be loose and highly sexual, and this public display is proof enough. As highly sexual as me? thinks Rose in alarm; sometimes the pleasures of the night are watched over by the imaginary form of her disapproving aunt. Rose steals a glance at Marcel, sitting down the table with the other men. He catches her eye and winks.

At dinner the conversation is dominated by the captain of a slaving vessel, a loud, garrulous man confident in his skills. Rose listens in fascination. Back in Nantes involvement in the slave trade was rarely talked about, kept hidden like a disfigured child or a birthmark, but this captain is talking of it quite openly.

It is a point of professional pride, the captain tells the assembled guests, that he never takes babies or young children; even if they were to reach the colony alive, the price for a child is far too low. "Yet despite my vigilance, one of my crew let aboard a woman with an infant clutched to her breast. *Get rid of it*, I instructed, and one of the men tossed it overboard."

The guests nod in understanding and Rose holds her breath.

"And yet," says the captain, prodding his fork at Rose, as though he knows she needs the most convincing, "the Negress cried out and flung herself into the sea after her baby, even though she could not swim. Almost as if she were affected with maternal instinct, that noble devotion I may credit my wife with, but would scarcely expect in a savage."

Rose feels the truth of his words even as the other guests twitter in polite disbelief. Savages, yes, but also human. She has seen the look of tenderness on a house slave nursing her baby or the way a slave boy responded to its mother, its face brightening as Rose hopes one day her own child's will.

The knowledge makes her uneasy; hints of their humanity only confuse her.

"But they *are* people," she whispers to Marcel that night, lying in the intimacy of his embrace and struggling to make sense of her new world. "And they must hate us." How could they not? The houseslaves are mostly silent, taking orders without blinking, and when they do talk their voices are servile and sullen.

"Not hate," Marcel scoffs, running his fingers along her nakedness then twining her hands in his—Rose loves the way the outside world recedes when they are together in bed. "They are not capable of such emotions. Think of them as animals. A dog may growl at you, but what does that matter? As long as it is chained, it is harmless."

Her husband falls asleep but Rose lies awake, listening to rain pattering down on the wooden roof. *Chained.* Before leaving for the dinner party, Madame Francine slapped one of the slaves for touching her neck with hot curling tongs. Perrine took the blow without flinching but when Madame Francine turned away, Rose saw anger in the girl's eyes and clenched fists that she knew longed to hurl the tongs at her mistress' back.

Rose thinks of the maid her aunt kept back in Nantes. Manon was a cheerful girl, often tired, but always easy to talk to. If there was resentment, it was well hidden. But here, surrounded by the house slaves that seem to ooze resentment, Rose feels such tension: snippets of hate and fleeting hostility, darting here and there like the crabs that infest the house and add to the general unease of life.

Marcel's family treat their house slaves with a strange mixture of casual cruelty and indifference but also with an intimacy Rose can scarcely comprehend. She can't imagine ever being like Madame Francine or her daughters, happy to lounge naked while their slaves pick nits out of their hair, then slapping them or poking their eyes when they displease.

*

All along the coast, the hillsides are alive with fires as forests are stripped to make way for new plantations. Roads are paved and port towns explode with commerce. Regular postal service and even a small opera house are established in Jérémie, now a bustling town of a hundred houses neatly laid out on cobbled streets, boasting a fish market, a cathedral, and a public gibbet.

Though everything around her churns with energy, Rose's world comes to feel small. The Fongravier women spend their days lounging or doing embroidery, choking on gossip and complaining about life in general. Though they dress like servants in simple skirts and blouses, their idleness is supreme. Here, the industriousness so praised by Rose's aunt is entirely missing.

Rose dreamt of keeping house for her husband but soon learns that she is expected to do nothing. She tries to help in the kitchens—Madame Francine quickly puts a stop to that—and even expresses an interest in the workings of the plantation. Marcel, surprised, takes her to the field where they are planting their first coffee bushes. Rose finds everything distasteful, especially the hordes of half-naked black men who stop and stare at her even as the overseer shouts and whips them back to work. Rose retreats, never to return, and learns to content herself with dinner parties, picnics, endless visits and long afternoons playing Faro, waiting for the men to return. Emptiness, all around.

In Saint Domingue Rose finds a society as rigid as any in France. The Fongraviers are *grands blancs,* part of the plantation class, and their social world is limited to the other white planters in their district. The *petits blancs* are mostly white tradesmen who live in the towns, treated with disdain by planters like Marcel. Special animosity is reserved for the free colored class, descended from slaves and white men.

Occasionally mulatto children are born on the plantation and soon Rose learns the ways white men have with their slaves, and the ways white women fight back to protect their dignity. Her father-in-law Monsieur Marcel *père* has a concubine he openly acknowledges, a young woman named Zo, black as pitch, who sits in a corner of their house in a rocking chair reserved just for her. Madame Francine ignores her completely and simply pretends she doesn't exist.

Madame Francine counsels Rose that colored women, slaves or free, are to be especially feared. On visits to town, Rose sometimes sees these mulatto women, flittering in the shadows between houses of ill-repute. *Butterflies of the night* and the men joke openly and lewdly about them. But Rose has no worries on that account: Where would Marcel even find the time?

Rose learns that many planter families in the district have cousins from the wrong side of the bed and the color line. Intermarriage was common in the early days of settlement when white women were scarce and everyone mixed easily. Not so any more: as Saint Domingue attracted more colonists, a raft of laws curtailed the pretensions of the free coloreds, many of whom were very wealthy: no carriages nor carrying of swords, a cherished right of any gentleman. Banned from public service. Forbidden from taking French surnames and not even allowed the dignity of being called *Sieur*—Sire—an honor accorded to even the lowliest of whites.

"Rightfully so," sniffs Madame Francine.

"Jealousy," explains Marcel. "Though I bear them no rancor personally, it is just not right that a newly-arrived Frenchman should feel inferior to a man with the blood of Africa in him."

Shortly after they arrive, they are invited to an annual strawberry party hosted by a Monsieur Azor, one of the wealthiest planters in the district and a keen horticulturalist. Rose is delighted with the invitation and pangs of homesickness ripple through her. Strawberries! Her aunt grew them, along with blueberries, blackberries and crab-apples. The tart, restrained fruits of Europe; sometimes Rose finds herself hating the bloody mangoes and perfumed guavas that are everywhere here. Does she miss France?

Monsieur Azor is also a free colored. Though the family have always attended in years past, this year Marcel and his mother fight over whether to go or not; apparently even social gatherings are now forbidden between whites and coloreds.

"Well, I hardly think the magistrate is going to be paying a special visit to La Fraternité today!" says Marcel firmly. "We have enjoyed their hospitality for many years and Azor is too old a family friend to let go lightly. I for one am going, and Rose and Julienne as well."

Madame Francine glares at him and waves her fan fretfully. Open rebellion, thinks Rose gleefully; Marcel is far too under his mother's thumb and the women here, used to commanding slaves, can be very imperious. In the end they do attend the strawberry party but just as Madame Francine predicted, they are the only whites there; not even the Gaultiers, the white cousins of the Azors, deign to attend.

Rose thinks Monsieur Azor kind and friendly, and the ten strawberry varieties delicious. Marcel feeds her a pale white one that explodes in her mouth with taste and life, so unexpected she laughs out loud. A delightful day, until her sister-in-law Julienne takes it upon herself to taunt Madame Azor about the satin dress she is wearing—coloreds are also prohibited from satin and silk.

The next year, the Fongraviers receive no invitation.

*

Through the years Bayardel prospers in tandem with the colony. After a great *ouragan* storm uprooted the last of the indigo plants, the plantation is given over entirely to coffee. This crop affords them the home Marcel always promised, and Rose delights in her new house with its separate dining room, sturdy stone cellars, large windows and wrap-around veranda. When she holds still and ignores the heat and overall dampness, she might imagine herself in France, just barely.   But when Rose opens her eyes, she is in Saint Domingue.

Monsieur Marcel *père* died the year before the house was built, Madame Francine following shortly after. Julienne married and moved up north, and her other sister-in-law Isabelle died in childbirth. Now it is just their little family:

Marcel, Rose, their son Charles, daughter Aimée and the baby Aurore.

Rose no longer finds her world so strange; it is just her own. After fifteen years here—almost half her life, she sometimes thinks in amazement—she finally feels at home. She is content with the joys of motherhood and the love of her husband, and she cannot stop thanking her lucky stars— and matchmaking neighbors—that led her to Marcel on that May evening so many years ago.

But she has become, Rose realizes in equal parts despair and amazement, what she always dreaded: a woman succumbed to the apathy of colonial life. The heat is so merciless and thorough, and the comfort of cool spaces and the delights of inertia have quite taken over her life. Some days she hardly even bothers to oversee the garden she long planned for. Rose also distances herself from the questions about the slaves that troubled her on first arrival; now she knows it's better just to pretend they don't exist.

Still, there are little tears in the protective fabric of her ignorance: the look of excitement on Marcel's face when one of the female slaves must be whipped. The slaves branded and burnt for running away. The day Monsieur Marcel *père's* slave concubine Zo went mad and ran through the gardens, ripping up her roses, shouting about worms and death.

The nights when Marcel comes late to her bed, or not at all.

1790 is a seminal year as the colony is buffeted by the extraordinary news from France: the storming of the Bastille, the removal of the king from Versailles to Paris, the creation of a new 'revolutionary' government. The *Declaration of the Rights of Man* that declared all men are born free and equal.

But what Rose remembers the most about that year is a Sunday in April. They return from the church in Dame Marie and Perrine greets them with the baby. Usually Aurore is such a cheerful child but now her face is puckered and red.

"She not happy," says Perrine in her dull voice, stroking the girl's downy head.

"Give her to me." Rose takes her baby and looks down at the sweet face, into eyes that roll away. She will often think back to that moment: the moment before, then the moment after when dreadful understanding dawned. Within a week Aurore, just eight months old, is dead. How did Rose ever take happiness for granted? Grief wraps itself around her and threatens to snuff her own life away. She sobs endlessly, refusing to believe her little Aurore, so pale and so perfect, is gone and buried beneath the earth.

"We'll have others," promises Marcel. He hugs her; they are both shorn in their grief. "And Charles and Aimée are so healthy."

"But I don't want others," cries Rose. "I want my Aurore."

Then not a few months later, Marcel kisses her goodbye.

"I'll be back Monday, at the latest Tuesday," he says as he mounts his horse. He is going to Jérémie to meet the agent responsible for buying and selling their coffee—a monthly outing that will last a few days and will end with his return and small presents for Rose and the children.

"Brac will take care of everything," Marcel continues. He leans down and kisses her again, just the top of her head this time, and for some reason Rose can't let go of the bridle.

They fought bitterly last month. Rose is largely indifferent to politics but Marcel is enlivened by all the changes in Europe. Like most whites, born here or not, he wants Saint Domingue to be independent from France, just as the Americans up north freed themselves from the British. When a group of Saint Domingue planters decided to send a delegation to Paris to lobby for colonial rights, Marcel wanted to go with them. Rose wept and pleaded and cried: How could he leave her alone? Eventually Marcel relinquished his dream. Rose won but it was a hollow victory that left them strained and cautious with each other.

"Ride carefully," Rose says, squeezing the reins and hating the flicker of foreboding in her stomach. "And don't drink too much at the Vauxhall."

Marcel laughs. "No, I'll just have to remember my headache from last time."

A few days later a messenger comes thundering into

Bayardel with the news: Marcel, struck down with one of those nightmare tropical fevers that hits a man midday and has him felled by night. Rose rushes to town just in time to see his face, swollen in the heat, one last time before they close the coffin and bury her happiness.

Every wave that rises in the sea must crest before it begins its inevitable descent to end in a crash of dirty sea foam on the shore. Now, when Rose looks back, she sees with clarity exactly when her happiness was at its height, and how ignorant she was then that all her best days were behind her.

The Dining Room
7 am

Pomponne, the cook's little daughter, comes up the path from the kitchens carrying the coffee urn. Rose follows her into the dining room and watches as Pomponne sets the urn down on an iron trivet and lights the warming candle underneath.

Rose's heart curdled the first time she saw Pomponne. Jeannette's daughter was born just a month after Aimée, with pale milk coffee skin and eyes as blue as Marcel's. Sex, thought Rose bleakly. Men and their urges, creating these half-castes. The sad lessons of Madame Francine came back to haunt her but she could tell herself—and she often did—that Marcel was not the only white man at Bayardel. At that time, there was the manager and two overseers, as well as visiting doctors and notaries and of course the neighboring white planters who seem to rotate through the plantations' women with tacit understanding. Pomponne's father was probably Brac, who arrived the year before her birth, and who was always pestering the slave women.

By unspoken agreement Pomponne—a delightful child, Rose has to admit—was raised in the big house and now she and Aimée are inseparable. Rose is fond of the girl, though on occasion unsettled by her all-seeing blue eyes and intelligence. Whenever she asked Plunkett for a progress report on his pupils, he was generally lukewarm about Charles and Aimée but never ceased to gush over Pomponne.

"Madame, don't forget this," says Pomponne, holding out

a note from the sideboard. Rose takes it and another millstone falls from the sky and lands in her lap. Oh God—the note that arrived yesterday. From Noel Azor, requesting an interview for this very afternoon. Monsieur Azor indicated no reason for his visit, just expressed a hope that Madame Widow Fongravier would be at home to receive him.

Noel Azor—one of the wealthiest free colored planters in the Grand'Anse and erstwhile host of that strawberry party so many years ago.

Since then, no contact. Social, at least.

Rose stares at the note, aware her hands are shaking. The impending visit had weighed heavily on her yesterday and remembering it now plunges her back to the bottom of her despair. Oh God, what if Azor is calling in the loan? She took it out last year, 5,000 *livres* to re-lime the drying platforms, arranged by Azor's factor in Jérémie. There is no way she can pay it back already.

Or perhaps—hopefully—he is coming on behalf of a returning slave? How wonderful if Mercure and Claudine, her house slaves and both runaways since last year, have decided to come home. Asking a neighbor to intercede and mediate a return is quite common. But no, that can't be it: no one is coming back these days.

Rose pauses in indecision. Given the events of the morning perhaps she should send quick word to Azor that she is unavailable. But she does not wish to appear unfriendly; while all the unrest in the colony has complicated everyday interactions between the whites and the coloreds, as it has complicated everything, he is still her neighbor. And holder of that loan. No, let him come with whatever he brings.

Pomponne leaves and Rose is startled by the appearance of a pale brown boy in the dining room doorway. Gangly and freckled, with the unmistakable print of Negro blood. Of course: Plunkett's son. The boy accompanies his father most months and sleeps down on the beach by Brac's house. Rose hadn't known that until Brac told her, but the list of things she doesn't know about her own plantation is something that no longer worries her.

Rose fights down her annoyance at the boy being inside her house—she must remember he just lost his father. "We are most sorry for your loss."

The boy says nothing but stares at her with green eyes, strange in his dark face. The hints of Plunkett are there but faint, features reflected through the ripples of a pond.

"Of your father," Rose clarifies. Oh goodness, has no one told him?

The boy doesn't flinch, just nods.

"We have sent for the authorities," Rose continues, lying easily. "They should be here soon."

The boy continues to stare at her with what, improbably, looks like a smirk. He is wearing a dirty white shirt and breeches and is barefoot. He's younger than he looks; his height makes him seem older but really, he is young. Charles' age perhaps.

"I want my father's things," the boy finally says, in passable French.

"What things?"

"His things he came with."

"Yes, of course." Rose looks around the dining room; this is where Plunkett was sleeping and there is his nightshirt, draped distastefully over one of the chairs. "Yes, of course, we will make sure that he is buried in his chemise, you may take his jacket and, ah, breeches, books and—" Rose takes a deep breath. Too much to consider. "For now, go to the kitchens and Jeannette will give you something to eat."

"I want to eat here."

"What?"

"I want to eat here. I can—I'm free. Pa said I would be when he died—I am now *a free man*." The boy puffs slightly on the last words, long rehearsed and now finally aired.

"Well, yes, but—" The absurdity of the moment is not lost on Rose. "No!" she says firmly. "Even your father did not eat in the house."

"He did last night."

"That was not a usual occurrence," Rose stammers. Why am I even having this conversation, she thinks in exasperation, her sympathy quickly dying. "Get out!"

"I'm a free man," the boy repeats, still staring at her with those unsettling green eyes.

"Go before I set the dogs on you," Rose says as sternly as

she can. *Dogs and blacks—never let them know your fear*, her husband always counseled.

Thoreau comes in from the veranda. "Madame, I overhead, permit me—what an exhilarating moment! Liberty, the shackles thrust off, one moment a slave, the next not, the boy become a man, and a free one at that! I must speak with him, be witness to this seminal occasion, the dream of darkness exploding into light—"

"Please, Monsieur Thoreau, I just need this boy out of my house!"

"I will remove him," says Thoreau, "then avail myself of the opportunity to understand more of this fascinating situation. We might ask: Do the young feel their chains as heavily as the grown?" Thoreau makes a—completely inappropriate, thinks Rose in despair—half-bow to the boy. "Now, what is your name?"

"Yorick."

"Yorick? Ah, but of course! Your father was learned and an Englishman to boot—no doubt a devotee of the *Great Bard*, as he is known. From *Hamlet*, is it not? 'Alas, poor Yorick,' and in this case that pithy line—"

"Monsieur Thoreau!" pleads Rose, then shouts again at the boy to get out. Yorick backs away, though whether at her words or the increasing encroachment of Thoreau—his hand now creeping on the boy's arm—it is hard to tell.

"Go!" shouts Rose, and to her relief Yorick casts a last venomous look then heads down the veranda steps.

"Ah, Madame! Then perhaps I might hope for a conversation with him later? This momentous occasion, the transfer from slavery to freedom, the—"

"He's hardly a slave," snaps Rose, putting her hand to her brow in what she hopes is the universal sign for *be quiet*. Though technically he is (was?): Plunkett's wife was, and by the laws of the colony children born of a slave mother are slaves themselves.

"Perhaps not anymore," agrees Thoreau, "if indeed it is true the death of his father freed him. Ah, what price liberty, Madame?"

"Oh, it has a price," Rose retorts. "It's now 800 *livres* for the notarized manumission papers. And that's just for him—he's got siblings, too? Poor boy. He won't enjoy his freedom so much when the debt collectors come looking for him; I heard his father had quite the bill down at the gambling house in Apricots."

"But if the son becomes free on the death of his father…" muses Thoreau, "does that anticipation not perhaps form the basis for patricide?"

Rose looks at him with some respect. "Yes—the government attempted to ban such manumissions for precisely that reason. But I can hardly credit that ungainly boy with killing his father, and in such a vicious way."

"Interesting," murmurs Thoreau.

The Swamp
8 am

"Come on," says Charles to his sister. He is fourteen and taller than Brac and part of him feels that he should be one of the men making the important decisions this morning. But instead I'm a *babysitter*, he thinks in disgust.

"Don't be mad, Charles. We might see the turtle!" says Aimée.

Last week, before Plunkett's week of lessons sequestered them inside, they found a large turtle floating in the swamp where they sometimes boat. They greeted it every morning, fretted when it wasn't there one day, overjoyed at seeing it the next. When they rowed close it stayed motionless, its eyes filled with unblinking sadness. In all the years that they have been exploring the coast and countryside, they never saw such an enormous turtle.

But even the possibility of seeing it again does not mollify Charles. He stalks ahead angrily, Aimée trotting behind. Before them the Bay d'Airdelles that gives their plantation its name stretches in a gentle curve for three miles, a swamp lying between a strip of white sandy beach and the hills that rise behind. Picking through creepers and vines, they work their way down a path to the beach. Aimée calls out a cheery greeting to Ernestine, Brac's slave and housekeeper who lives with him in a house set in the lea of the bay. She receives a grunt in return.

Out in the bay a small *pinnace* floats lazily, its wide-bottomed berth waiting to transport their coffee to Jérémie.

Anchored further out in the bay there is another boat that Charles doesn't remember seeing yesterday; he squints at it but it remains undefined.

A way along the beach they come to the mouth of the river that starts high in the hills behind them and reaches the sea through the swamp. Charles unties their canoe, made from the trunk of a single mango tree, and helps his sister in. They row into the swamp, hemmed in by frayed remains of dead trees and clusters of mangroves with white, arm-like roots that reach deep into the water. The water is dark and muddy from the night rains, and a cluster of parrots shriek, terrible and loud, and fly out of their hiding place.

"He's gone!" sighs Aimée after they have circled several times.

"I knew a week was too long!" says Charles in annoyance.

"Do you think he's dead? The turtle?"

"We'll wait, maybe it'll come," says Charles, feeling a sudden misplaced anger at Plunkett—had their tutor come *next* week, as he was supposed to, they might not have missed the turtle's departure. Serves him right if he's dead, Charles thinks, then immediately regrets his logic. He must remember that despite his bad breath and suspected stupidity, Plunkett was still a man and probably wanted to live just as much as he, Charles, did.

Giving up on the turtle, he stows the oars and the small boat floats lazily through the swamp. He lies back and stares up at the sky, already deep blue though the hour is early. A bead of sweat runs down his chest and he scratches his arm. It rained last night and he half-remembers a dream that fled with the morning: a rocking boat and a cabin too small for even sleeping.

He is leaving soon for France to finish his education. They have it on good authority from family in Nantes that the political upheavals in France are over and done with. The king—though he is, confusingly, no longer the king—has accepted a new constitution and peace is imminent. Charles's passage is booked on the *Esprit*, leaving next month.

Thinking about his departure fills him with a mix of emotions. While he hearkens for the adventure that France will surely bring, he worries about leaving his mother and sister and even his mad Aunt Julienne. Especially now with all the unrest in the colony. That dreadful slave insurrection last year... even though Cap-Français is far, it sometimes feels too close. And just south of them in the area around Les Cayes slave rebels have taken over the countryside, all the whites fled to the city and hundreds of plantations burnt, cotton and sugar reduced to ashes.

Though his mother keeps a pistol, loaded, under her pillow—every plantation is required to have firearms at the ready—she doesn't seem overly concerned. Then again, she doesn't seem to care about much these days. Whenever Charles asks her about politics or the troubles, she just scowls and claims her head aches at the thought of it.

And big things await him in France, a real education of the sort that Plunkett's half-hearted lessons could never provide. Sophistication, great cities and a world of learning. Snow and fog; summer evenings that stay light until almost midnight. He will meet his father's relatives and when he returns to Saint Domingue, he will be ready to take a position of importance amongst the men of the colony.

Charles is Creole and he sometimes wonders if he is French, or not? Regardless, his mother tells him that in Europe he will be seen as a colonist first and as French only second. It is understood that *colonist* is a pejorative word. In France there will be many who will attack him and his way of life, and Charles must be ready to defend his culture. Especially these days when everyone is talking about the *Declaration of the Rights of Man* and the abolition of slavery, a move that would be disastrous for Saint Domingue.

"It's so quiet today," observes Aimée, breaking his reverie. She runs her hand through the water and pulls up a slick weed. "Even the birds are quiet. Perhaps the swamp is mourning the turtle."

"Flore would say a storm is coming," says Charles. The old slave Flore knows everything about the weather, or at least pretends she does. A gift highly prized on a coffee plantation where rain is the enemy of the drying process.

"I can't believe it's gone," says Aimée sadly. "I couldn't bear it if he were dead!"

"Perhaps it just swam away for somewhere else. Thoreau might know where it has gone," suggests Charles. He grins, imagining the hour-long discourse that would follow an innocent question about turtle habitats. "Perhaps not."

Last night at dinner Thoreau talked at length while the other guests sat in resigned silence. Plunkett didn't normally eat with them but Thoreau was intrigued by the idea of an Englishman in Saint Domingue, and had requested his presence. Plunkett choked on his crab soup, ate greedily of the tender goat and disagreed with Thoreau about the position of the colored man in society. He was the only one who dared, or bothered, to interrupt their guest. Mama drank almost an entire bottle of wine and Miss Mathilde, Thoreau's silent sister, sat with her eyes downcast. After dinner the two men continued to argue long into the night. Charles wanted to stay and debate with them, but sleepiness and boredom soon overcame him. And now Plunkett is dead. Murdered. It doesn't seem possible, somehow.

"A murderer loose on the plantation," intones Charles, looking to scare his little sister. "Perhaps it was not a slave— perhaps it was Thoreau!" A sudden image of Thoreau leering over their dead tutor flashes through his mind. But no, it must have been a slave, perhaps one inspired by the unrest in the colony. But why Plunkett? No one would much care about his death. Well, perhaps his wife and children might. Charles remembers how he felt when his own father died two years ago, and frowns.

"It's true," Aimée says. "Thoreau is a stranger and they were fighting last night. What do you think Plunkett was doing outside, in the middle of the night?"

Charles is silent. He knows what Plunkett was doing, or suspects as much. He himself did it for the first time just last week. The laundress Laurine is privy to all sorts of embarrassing details and from his sheets she knew (smelled?) that he was becoming a man. Probably trumpeted as much to the whole plantation, because last week Brac whispered to meet him out back when the moon was high. Charles wanted to say no but he also wanted, just as urgently, to say yes.

That night Charles hurried out to find Brac waiting for him in the velvety darkness. Together they passed through the clearing between the long slave houses, guarded by an enormous apricot tree with silky white flowers that seemed to glow in the half-light of the moon. Charles saw a slave sitting on the steps of one of the houses, watching them.

Brac led him to the old pigpen behind the kitchens, empty now.

"Go," said Brac, pushing him in. The rustle of a rat and the stench of piss. Through the shadows Charles saw a waiting, dark figure. He was disappointed, for he had hoped for the slave Zabeth who had such a pretty smile and who had, in fact, figured in his dream. But there was no room for protest—Brac just laughed and closed the gate behind him.

This past week has been one of exquisite torment. Charles is choked with nervousness that his mother will find out and now Brac has started looking at him with mocking eyes. Though the memory is hot and shameful, Charles cannot stop thinking about it or wanting to do it again. And the women in France—do white women do *that*?

"What was Plunkett doing in the garden?" repeats Aimée. "If he was going to the women's house or the pigpen, then why was he at the *front* of the house? There's nothing there but the flowers. The tombs, but further along. And he wouldn't go there at night, surely?"

Charles is glad he is still staring up at the sky. How does his little sister, just turned twelve, know about the pigpen? He swallows nervously and repeats: "A mysterious murderer, prowling the plantation!"

"Don't, Charles!" squeals Aimée.

"Don't be scared, Aimée," he says as authoritatively as he can, to put things back in their proper place. "It was just a slave and Brac will find out which one and then they'll whip him dead and bury him."

Alive, perhaps?

Aimée stares into the water and pulls another black weed out. Mr. Plunkett dead, like the slave Zola last month. And what a funny place to die, at the edge of the flower garden beyond the statue of Venus. She would die, too, if she slipped over the side of the boat and disappeared into the green depths of the swamp.

"Pomponne said his throat was slit. Like this." Aimée runs an exploratory finger across her own throat and imagines a knife plunging in and cutting. What would it feel like to have your flesh sliced, blood running out of you and unable to breathe? "It couldn't have been one of the slaves—where would they get such a knife? You can't slit a throat with a pruning saw."

A faint rustling at the side of the river, coming from a thicket of mangrove roots. They both look eagerly over but see nothing.

"Probably just a caiman," says Charles, sitting up.

"I wish we could find the turtle," says Aimée in a sad, dreamy voice. "Then everything would be right."

"Don't be silly," scoffs Charles.

Aimée ignores him; her brother thinks he knows everything but he doesn't. The last few weeks have been dreadful. There are drums at night, relentless and eerie, that no one else seems to hear. Well, not her mother or brother at least. She has stopped talking about them for fear of being called fanciful or hysterical; Charles in particular seems to delight in those words as he grows older and threatens to disappear into the world of adults.

But still, she has heard the drums.

Aimée continues to scan the riverbank. How dark the swamp is today. If they could only find the—

"Oh!" she gasps. Through a tangle of roots, she sees a glint, something like eyes but not the amber eyes of the turtle. She looks again but they have disappeared and the water barely ripples.

"What?"

"I saw something… over there!" She points. "Eyes. Human ones, I think."

Charles looks over. "Stop making things up."

"I'm not! I saw them. Charles, let's go back!" Aimée pleads, suddenly urgent.

"Let's go look," says Charles, picking up the oars.

"No, don't!" says Aimée, grabbing an oar. "I want to go. Now."

"You heard what Mama said," says Charles. "It's going to be unpleasant."

Aimée kicks his leg and the little boat wobbles. "Let's go!" She looks back at the white gnarled roots and the swaying weeds. Something is wrong, terribly wrong. The drums last night, so loud…

"All right, but you know Mama is going to be upset."

"Please, Charles, I'm frightened."

"I'll tell her it was your idea."

After one last reluctant look around, Charles rows back towards the mouth of the river and the beach. Aimée stares at the roots until they are a safe distance then turns away. She saw something, she is sure of it, and she doesn't care if no one believes her.

"I saw eyes," Aimée whispers, and hugs herself.

The Clearing
8 am

Brac and the *commandeur* La Fleur gather the men and women in the clearing between the slave houses, watched over by a giant apricot tree that towers sixty feet above. The gangs from the fields, the women from the drying platforms and the men who have been repairing the washed-out paths to the fields or the warehouse roofs. Samedi and Dimanche, both twelve, drop their bundles of forage and join the adults. Apart from Pomponne, they are the only slave children now left on the plantation. Chereze, a great breeder but feeble-minded, is called back from the kitchen gardens where she is in charge of the vegetables destined for the whites' table; under her fuddled care weeds have overtaken the cabbages and carrots but have left the artichokes curiously unscathed.

La Fleur herds the men under the tree, instructing them to tie each other neck to neck with lengths of rope normally used for securing sacks of coffee to the mules. The women sit silently to one side, cautious and untethered. Many of them ignore the coming danger and close their eyes, glad of the unexpected reprieve. This week has been busy with Brac shouting at them about a ship and Saturday, overworking them and canceling rests.

Only a few slaves are not gathered in the clearing. Those in the hospital, a pretentious name for another dark hut, are left alone. A plantation the size of Bayardel should warrant a full-time doctor who would also double as a veterinarian, but the money simply isn't there. Inside lies Chevalier, both his legs covered by yaws,

43

and Charlotte, most of her jaw destroyed by an incorrect dose of mercury for a toothache. Victor, known as an incurable malingerer, lies beside them awaiting death. A slave is only useful when able to work so there is no house so feared as this hospital; masters generally welcome death when it comes for those too weak to work yet who must still be fed. On some plantations sick slaves, or those too old to work, are quickly starved to death.

Lubin, insane since the previous year, is left tethered by the slave cemetery gates. He is fed once a day and it is a surprise he has lasted so long. Also absent are the four shivering Aradas purchased last week; faint cries of anger can still be heard from their locked hut.

Since the disappearance last year of the manservant Mercure and the housekeeper Claudine, the only house slaves are the cook Jeannette and her daughter Pomponne. There is also old blind Flore who sits in the kitchen and helps shell the peas and pluck the chickens. They are not gathered with the others; food still has to be made for the whites.

La Fleur sits on a log and surveys the group while Louis, the second *commandeur,* stands off to one side. Brac leaves for the big house and everyone is quiet, waiting and watching; the inactivity of the plantation, usually thrumming with life and disorder, hangs awkwardly over the clearing. La Fleur flicks his whip lazily back and forth and wonders if he should move the men out of the shade of the tree.

"More work tomorrow," La Fleur sings. "Work all day and through the night. Bad times coming," he adds with a chuckle, thinking that white men should get their throats slit more often. Life here is too dull; he misses the viciousness of the sugar plantation where he and Brac worked before.

He is like my arm, Brac once said of La Fleur, and the compliment puffed up his pride. In the eyes of the law, Madame Rose may own him but La Fleur knows he is Brac's man. He sleeps behind the manager's house and eats the meals Brac's slave woman prepares, though he doesn't sit at the table. Sometimes when Brac is feeling generous, or lonely, he gives La Fleur some rum or lets him have his way with his housekeeper Ernestine—a welcome gift, for despite his position of authority, none of the other women will have him without a fight.

La Fleur looks over to the kitchen house where Jeannette is preparing the whites' breakfast, then over to Zabeth. He tried several times with her but was always beaten back by Jean Louis who quickly claimed her as his own. Not how it should be, La Fleur thinks sourly, and flicks his whip at the nearest slave. Everyone should be in awe of him and of the power that rests in his hands.

He seeks out Appollon, roped amongst the rest. La Fleur stares until Appollon raises his head and they lock eyes. *Cur*, thinks La Fleur and spits; he suspects the man was behind the death of the spy Paris earlier this year. After the slaves complained of brackish water, Paris was found stuffed down one of the cisterns. The whip ran wild for several days. No one talked and finally Madame Rose—Brac calls her a *batty bitch*—put a stop to the games and demanded they take up work again.

Now they are reduced to Garifou as their spy, when all the world knows he is an idiot.

La Fleur growls in annoyance, his eyes still on Appollon. He knows something is afoot and not only for the sound of drums that rides through the hills most nights, the noise eerie enough to raise the dead. There are other signs that La Fleur recognizes but that Brac refuses to acknowledge: the constant squawking of carrion crows, and the appearance of a wild albino pig. The giant turtle Pierre caught Sunday at the edge of the swamp, the size of which has never been seen before. So many strange occurrences, as though the gods are playing with them.

And those damn drums.

La Fleur pleaded with Brac to lock the slave houses at night but Brac refused, saying that the men need their midnight rutting. Brac cannot see the evil around them, coming closer. Every evening La Fleur interrogates the spy Garifou but the man can only giggle and laugh. To stop the cuffings and to ensure his ration of rum, the idiot invents stories about the presence of a *Vaudun* priest, high in the hills on an abandoned plantation, a fearsome man who led the slave rebels around Les Cayes to the south. But the constabulary from Dame Marie has searched that plantation many times and concluded there was no truth to the rumors.

Now La Fleur is as scared as he thinks the whites should be; if trouble is coming for the whites, then it is coming for him as well.

"White man murdered," sings La Fleur. "Much play today, much play today," he croons, enjoying the sound of his voice through the stillness of the clearing. It's oddly quiet this morning, the only sound the bleating of the nanny goat looking for her kid that was served to the whites last night.

He glares at Appollon, but the tall Nago refuses to look down. We'll get you, thinks La Fleur. You think you are safe but you are not, and the whites always win.

*

From the kitchen house set next to the clearing, Jeannette glances over to where the men are roped. She seeks out Appollon but he does not look her way, the twenty feet between them an uncrossable chasm. Last night she waited for him but the hours passed without the scratch of his fingers on the wall beside her bed.

She can't think about it—best to concentrate on more immediate matters. Jeannette drains the bacon sizzling over the fire and lays out the eggs, bread and fruit for the big house. She opens up the flour barrel and scoops out enough to start on tomorrow's loaves. Brown flour—they haven't had white for years but even this barrel is running perilously low. Lunch will be light pickings, bread and cheese as is the custom, but with all the visitors there is still a lot to do. One less visitor, Jeannette thinks, remembering the dead white in the garden. The *murdered* white. She crushes a weevil worming its way out of the flour and her stomach tightens.

Jeannette has been in a state of nervous tension for too long; something is happening and Appollon is at the center of it. He tells her nothing and she asks nothing, but she knows that he has been going to the abandoned Pellegrin plantation on Saturday nights. He returns from those midnight meetings fired up, tension coiled tight inside him. *It* is coming closer, drums in the night foretelling its arrival: chaos, revolt, an uprising? Trouble is all around them and though Jeannette tries to ignore it, she can't.

Every time Jeannette wakes to Appollon's tapping, or sees him in the clearing in the dawn light, she breathes and thinks: One more day. One more night. Before whatever is coming comes and snatches a good portion of her happiness away.

And now a white man murdered in the flower garden.

Roughly she kneads the dough.

"Too much," warns Flore in her rasping voice from the corner. The old woman is blind but her nose tells her everything, including when the dough is near to tearing.

"Never enough," retorts Jeannette, slapping the dough against the wooden table. Her relief that Appollon is still here is tempered by an immense fear that the death of that white man is connected to him. Jeannette wants to believe Appollon had nothing to do with it, but she knows not much happens at Bayardel without his knowledge. And though they might twine to each other like one soul, there is still a part of him that remains hidden and closed off. He never talks of his past—of his life in Africa or the one on the sugar plantation near Les Cayes where he worked before Bayardel. Now Les Cayes is fallen under anarchy, rebel slaves controlling the plains and the mountains around. Was he involved with what is happening there? Is that what is coming here?

Jeannette hears La Fleur singing that the white's throat was cut with a knife. Not a machete or a pruning saw. A kitchen knife. Jeannette wants to bury her face in the dough, suffocate in its soft embrace. She gave Appollon a knife last week. During the weekly inventory of knives and tools its absence was quickly noted; to much tired interrogation by Madame, and then by Brac, Jeannette claimed it fell into the well when she was drawing water.

But surely Appollon is too smart to slit a white's throat as though he were a goat? There are other, more subtle ways to kill—accidents or poison. Jeannette glances briefly at the dried cassava leaves hanging innocently from the ceiling amid bunches of wild spinach and parsley.

JEANNETTE'S JOURNEY

BAYARDEL PLANTATION
1758-1792

"I'm hungry," whines Marcel.

"Silence, son!" raps Madame Francine. "Some things cannot be hurried."

All eyes turn to Jeannette, seated beside Monsieur Marcel *père* at the head of the table. A charming child. As soon as she could hold the weight, she was brought to the house to spend the hot afternoons waving a peacock-feathered fan over the old mistress, not really old then but wrinkled in the way that white women always become under the sun. Often Madame Francine would fall asleep and then Jeannette would curl up on the floor and play with one of the kittens, or sneak onto a chair covered with soft velvet or scratchy tapestry. Once she even fell asleep herself, stretched out in the daytime like a white woman, privy to all the luxury in the world.

And now she is seated at their table!

Jeannette is only five but she understands what is happening: a one-armed slave named Macandal, a runaway who lives in the mountains up north, is spurring slaves to poison their masters. Hundreds—some say thousands—of whites perish and many more who die of other causes are still considered victims; hysteria runs deep against this invisible enemy. No white considers themselves safe, and at Bayardel, alongside a new regime of vigilance over Cunette the cook, little Jeannette is installed as a taster for the family.

"Don't worry," Cunette whispers every evening. Cunette is a tiny Fon woman with deft hands and a scarred face who raised Jeannette after her own mother died. "There is nothing to fear."

Jeannette knows Cunette would never poison her and so she relishes every morsel she must taste, any fear dying under a deluge of delicious food: beefsteaks and boar cooked in cider; wobbling jellies full of sweetness and delight; milk pudding; chicken stuffed with mushrooms. Artichokes dripping in butter. All belonging to a world so different from the bland fare of cassava, beans and plantains that makes up the diet of the slaves.

"You may begin," directs Madame Francine. Jeannette smiles and takes a small bite of the bread while Monsieur Marcel *père*, his wife and the children Marcel and Isabelle sit in tense expectation. Then a spoonful of soup. Delicious. Carp fried in garlic and butter. Even better. Finally she tastes the mango pudding and sighs in delight; last week they had a chocolate cake for Isabelle's birthday. How she loves her job!

"It is all very good, Madame," says Jeannette, finished with the dishes but still eyeing the pudding, wishing she could take another bite. Or have a whole bowl to herself.

"Come on, Mama," whines Marcel. "The soup will be cold." He is a few years older than Jeannette and she doesn't like him very much; he is so spoiled and likes ordering her around.

"Son, the temperature of the soup is not important when lives are at stake," replies his father.

"We must wait the full five minutes," says little Isabelle primly. Silence in the room. Outside they can hear the overseers shouting at the slaves; this house was built, like so many in the early days, close to the fields and indigo vats. The clock ticks loudly on as Mercure, their manservant, waits in the shadows. In another corner old Sylvie snores, her arms around a bowl of sticky molasses that draws the flies away from the table; when Madame Francine snaps her fingers, Sylvie lumbers around the room, trying to catch more flies.

Jeannette is a bright, cheerful child and sometimes

during the waiting she has the overwhelming urge to grasp her neck and fall to the floor in spasms, then jump up again and smile! and declare she was only joking. Cunette catches wind of her whimsies and beats the urge out of her, saying they will both surely die if she attempts such a silly trick.

After several minutes when he is confident the danger is past, Monsieur Marcel *père* nods and Mercure starts to serve the family. Madame Francine flicks her hand and Jeannette slides off her stool and drags it back to the wall. How she would like to stay and eat more! Madame Francine is pregnant again and rarely has an appetite, so there might be food left over. Hopefully some mango pudding, Jeannette thinks wistfully as she heads back through the twilight to the kitchens, away from the glorious food of the white world.

Then the slave Macandal is caught and burnt alive, along with his accomplices. The slaves who were forced to watch swear that out of his ashes a mosquito rose and flew away: the spirit of Macandal, forever free. Gradually the panic subsides and while some of the more pretentious plantations still employ full-time tasters, Bayardel had no such affectations and so ends the happiest period of Jeannette's life.

She stays on in the big house, waving her fan, dressing her mistress, combing the hair of the children and caring for them until she hovers at the edge of puberty—an age when the white men of the colony, so used to indulging their basest desires without restraint, might feel free to follow their eyes with their hands or worse.

"Mama doesn't like you anymore," taunts Isabelle as her little sister Julienne giggles. "Because Papa likes you too much!"

Jeannette is only twelve when she is banished to the kitchens but her exile does little to stop the parade of white men—Marcel *père*, his son, the managers and overseers—that come through her across the years.

In the kitchens Cunette teaches her everything she knows. Jeannette learns quickly and loves cooking. She is delighted by the interplay of flavors and textures, the magic of starting with one thing then ending with something else entirely. Heat transforming foods, spices changing taste, two ingredients that apart are tired but together sing a song. I am an artist, Jeannette thinks, creating something out of nothing, like the tapestry frame in the big house stretched with pieces of stiff cambric that Madame Francine transforms with needle and thread.

*

"Oh!" Jeannette stands up, the peas she was shelling scattering to the floor. Cunette turns vaguely; these days her eyesight is failing and it is she who helps Jeannette and not the other way around.

"I'm sorry," says the girl, framed in the kitchen doorway—young Monsieur Marcel's new bride from France. At the sound of the voice, Cunette stiffens and Jeannette feels the familiar breathlessness that comes over her when she talks to whites.

"Madame, please don't apologize," says Jeannette then remains silent as the girl—Madame Rose, they call her—looks around the kitchen. The girl has an open, cheerful face and is very pretty. What does she want?

"Please Madame, how can we help you?" asks Jeannette softly.

"I just—" Rose looks around. "I just wanted to come and..." Jeannette is aware the girl is nervous. A white, nervous? The knowledge makes her giggle and Rose laughs apologetically alongside her, then rushes in with a garbled explanation: "It's my husband's birthday today and I thought to make him something... I have here a recipe book, from France..."

Jeannette understands what the girl wants. "Madame, we will prepare anything you wish."

"No, well, here is a fruit cake recipe," Rose says, proffering the open book. Jeannette takes it and nods carefully over the black marks on the page, the paper moist and curling at the edges. "My aunt made it for him—for Marcel—in France and he loved it and I want to make it. Oh, I'm sorry!—you probably don't read."

"Oh, Madame, please no apologize," stutters Cunette, hovering nervously behind.

"I can read the ingredients and you can tell me if we have them," says the young woman, putting the book on the table and reaching down to pet one of the kittens. "We can make it together." Rose smiles, warm and friendly, so different from tight-lipped Madame Francine or her blank, giggling daughters.

Jeannette smiles back, breathing again. "Yes, Madame Rose, we can do that."

"Oh, call me Rose! Now look, we need dates, and figs and currants..." Rose reads the recipe and describes the ingredients required. Many substitutions are needed and they decide—*Very creatively!* Rose declares—which fruits to use. In the heat of the afternoon Cunette falls asleep, leaving the two girls outside under the awning, chopping and mixing.

"Is she all right?" asks Rose.

"She's getting old," says Jeannette sadly. She can't bear to think of Cunette dying and leaving her all alone.

"Is she your mother?"

"My mother is dead but Cunette is like one to me."

"Oh! My mother also died when I was young. Were you born here?"

Jeannette nods. "Yes. I am one of the few," she says proudly.

Rose giggles. "So you knew Marcel when he was a boy?"

"Of course." Jeannette is chopping cherimoyas while Rose is de-pitting the hard cherries that are to substitute for the currants.

"What was he like?"

Jeannette laughs before she can help herself. "So spoiled!" She pauses, wondering if she should be more careful but Rose seems open and encouraging. "And always fighting with his mother..." Jeannette trails off but still Rose smiles. "He liked chasing the chickens and oh! so spoiled. I remember once he asked for an egg but there were none. So he said: Then give me two!"

Despite their efforts, the tropical fruits don't work well: the apricots and cherries so different and the mangoes a poor substitute for dates, no figs or hard currants to be found. Even the flour is different and the molasses too strong and nothing sets right. The mixture slops all over the pan, refusing to form a neat loaf no matter how much they bake it.

"It's the oven," grumbles Cunette, having woken up. "Too many cracks."

"No, that's not it," sighs Rose, sticking a probing finger into the dribbling mess. Jeannette is tense and alert, ready for blame. Though the girl appears friendly, the moods of the whites can turn as quickly as wind in a hurricane.

But Rose only chuckles: "It's more like a pudding than a cake. A soup!"

"Fruit soup!"

"It's good," says Rose, licking her finger. Jeannette takes a spoonful and agrees; the molasses and fruit combine in delicious stickiness.

"What is going on here?" Madame Francine casts a shadow from the kitchen doorway. Cunette shrinks away and Jeannette steps back.

"Making a special dessert for Marcel's birthday, Mama," says Rose gaily.

"I think," says Madame Francine, casting a glare at Jeannette that will leave her trembling the rest of the day, "that it would be best if you came back to the house."

That night Jeannette hears that Rose, despite her mother-in-law's protests, served the sloppy mess to Marcel. He finished his portion and requested more, then declared it the best dessert he had ever tasted and even christened it: *Tropical Rose Soup*.

Rose comes to the kitchens a few more times but eventually, no doubt under pressure from Madame Francine, her visits stop and soon she takes on the familiar distance that all whites take from the slaves who work outside their houses.

*

Bayardel is the only home Jeannette has ever known; she has no dreams of homelands lost to wrench at her and grow discontent. The old cook Cunette dies but Flore is still with her, a mother of sorts and a holder, alongside Jeannette, of the history of the plantation.

This is my home, Jeannette often thinks as she looks around the kitchen. My world: the long, warped tables, the pans on the wall, the braziers over the bricks, dried spices and herbs, the barrels of flour and salt, sacks of rice. Out back a well, the bread oven, the poultry pen, the little smokehouse where sometimes sausages are made. The kitchen garden, full of vegetables and herbs.

The years pass and Jeannette learns to seek out small joys in a well-constructed pie, a delicious sauce, a loaf of perfect bread. She focuses on her beloved daughter Pomponne and on the bag of silver coins buried under an ancient cacao tree—money from selling herbs and vegetables at the market in the nearby town of Dame Marie. Jeannette doesn't have dreams of buying her freedom—a rare event—but the coins give her a sense of security against an uncertain future.

She keeps herself apart from the other slaves, not because she feels herself better than them but because she does not wish to involve herself in the gossip, intrigue and cruelty of life on a plantation where eighty miserable souls are crushed together. Only when it is almost too late does she realize that the most bitter loneliness is the one born from the blankness of a closed-off heart.

She knows that Madame Rose is not the worst of mistresses and Jeannette still keeps some fond memories of the young bride who once came cautiously into the kitchens. In later years Jeannette often wonders if she even remembers those early times correctly, the possibility of them now withered away beneath the weight of years and the pale face of her daughter Pomponne. Sometimes Jeannette wants to tell her mistress the father was most likely Brac—she has no desire to torment her—but something holds her back. Perhaps she does want to cause her pain?

And now her daughter serves in the big house and

shares the education of the children and is treated almost like a daughter. Almost, but not quite: Madame Rose might appear benevolent but she can be scornful and cruel and Jeannette occasionally sees something like madness lurking behind the pale, tired eyes.

*

Life is passing in a small arc of contentment when Appollon arrives at the plantation in the month following Monsieur Marcel's death.

When Jeannette first sees him, something inside her awakens. She had never looked at a *bossale* before—as slaves born in Africa are known—with their frightened eyes and refusal to accept their fate but nothing can stop the lure of Appollon. It isn't just that he is handsome; no, something in his face and in the way he moves calls to her with a song that is at once both unexpected and familiar.

Against her will, Jeannette finds herself seeking him out at morning prayers, looking for him anxiously in the evenings. When he returns her gaze she looks away, only to glance back later and find him watching her as though they are linked by an invisible thread. A maddening circle she doesn't know how to break.

Instead she begins bringing Appollon his washing water in the morning, silent and with a slight scowl on her face. She pays special attention to his bed when she and Claudine clean the slave houses on Thursdays and at night she brings him morsels from the kitchens to eat. She refuses to blush when the others whistle and mock her but she lets Appollon know by her actions that she is starting to care for him.

He always thanks her and Jeannette always nods; there is so much she longs to tell him, but she can't find the words.

March—a month of too much rain and heightened nerves as one coffee bush after another yields only fermented cherries. Madame Rose emerges from the fog that has enveloped her in the months since her husband's death and orders a memorial feast. A goat is needed for the whites' table and Jeannette goes to the stables. It is a hot day, the sky above them wide and high and casting everything in brilliant whiteness.

"I need a kid," Jeannette says. Her voice is harsh, one of the bricks in the wall she has built around herself.

Appollon is sitting on a log, oiling a bridle. He listens to her request but doesn't move. Jeannette is acutely aware of the distance between them—no more than ten feet—and that they are alone for the first time.

"A kid," she repeats. "What, are you deaf?"

Appollon contemplates her silently. Jeannette can't tear her eyes away and she wants nothing more than to throw herself into his arms and feel the heat of his body around her. As though he knows what she is thinking, a look of amusement flickers across Appollon's face.

"Fine, I'll get it myself," Jeannette snaps and starts towards the pen where the goats are kept, fenced in by artful plantings of bamboo. One quick step and Appollon is beside her and has her arm. She inhales his smell, sweat mixed with the cocoa butter he oils the leather with.

"Why are you always so angry?" he whispers, bending his head close to hers, his hand firm on her arm. She stands still, staring at the ground between them. "I'm not the enemy," he says and squeezes her arm tighter.

"I'm not angry," Jeannette finally says. "I'm... I'm sad."

He lets her go and her breath returns.

"Walk with me tonight?" Appollon takes her chin and lifts her face. She looks into his eyes; since then she has never stopped looking. "I'll get you a kid, but I need you to walk with me tonight."

She nods and that night in the magical tropical hour between daylight and dark they walk along the path to the old indigo vats, lined with pink flowers. They talk as though they have known each other all their lives and when they lie down together, he holds her and a voice whispers: *Safe. Safe at last.*

Their connection is strong and instant and in his arms

Jeannette finds a peace she didn't know she was craving. Appollon holds her tighter than anyone has ever held her and she learns the difference between letting a man inside her—which she had done so many times—and letting one into your heart. So strong is their bond that she sometimes wonders if they were connected in another life or even if they shared ancestors, though he is a Nago and Jeannette's mother was from the dryness of Bambara-land, regions at different ends of the world.

Jeannette finds her happiness but from the beginning, Appollon makes no secret that he yearns for the dense mountains behind them that hold freedom and communities of runaway slaves. He pleads with Jeannette to join him in his plans for escape but she resists. Here she is a skilled cook and has an easy life, more comfortable than the one a life with the maroons could give her. And those mountains hold rebels as well; a runaway slave may be punished but an insurgent one? There are no words to describe the cruelness of that death.

At night when they lie together, he whispers: "You must come with me."

"I cannot," Jeannette whispers back.

"Why do you stay?"

"For my children—Pomponne and the ones we will have together. And if you are caught?" she demands. They have the same conversation again and again, circling endlessly like vultures over prey, picking at the same objections and same answers.

"I—we—won't be caught," scoffs Appollon. "They never catch anyone these days. And you're not even branded," he adds, cupping her breast in his large, calloused hand and squeezing gently; most Creole slaves aren't. They are in Jeannette's corner of the women's house, sheltered by swaying yellow sheets that partition her space, Pomponne asleep beside them. On some plantations slaves are encouraged to make homes but at Bayardel the men and women sleep apart and no one is married; Marcel *père* and his son never believed in it. No matter; Jeannette knows her bond with Appollon is deeper and stronger than anything the whites could give.

"Here, when I was young," she says softly, for she had never spoken about it before, "they caught a woman and a man, like us. They tied them up and burned their flesh off. Just some, so that they could still work. But the burns got infected and they died. And more recently—look at Pa' Oreille."

Appollon shakes his head. "It's all changing. You know Madame Rose has no time for that sort of cruelty. And Pierre and Capidon, coming and going so often it should make them dizzy! A few lashes but you know Brac is relieved when they return."

"But we have a good life here," Jeannette pleads, taking his head in her hands and forcing him to look at her. Why could he not see?

Appollon shakes his head: "This is not my destiny," he repeats stubbornly and she grows to hate the idea of his destiny that he clings to with such force.

"Your dreams are foolish," Jeannette says. "And dangerous."

"Your dreams are too small," Appollon replies.

"Madame Rose needs me."

"Don't talk like that. You cannot care for her."

"I don't," Jeannette replies, unsure of the truth.

"Change is coming and you will be glad when it does," says Appollon. "We need to be out there, fighting for this new world."

No! Jeannette wants to scream with every fiber of her body. She wants nothing to do with the talk of rebellions and freedom that swirl around them like ominous clouds before a great storm. She knows the whites and the other slave owners—some of them mulatto like her daughter—will never be vanquished. Never. Over her lifetime she has seen them master the land, clearing it and taming it, subduing it like they subdue their slaves, all the while their riches and numbers growing. She knows of their cruelties, their wiles, their two-faced deceptions.

There is a dreaming quality to *bossales* like Appollon who had once known freedom and they cannot accept its loss. But for Jeannette, freedom is just a fantasy saved for intimate hours in the night, an idea that vanishes with the light. *This stupid freedom,* she often thinks when she finds herself caught between the small pleasures of her life and the looming events of the outside world. This stupid freedom, coming to take her Appollon away.

The Dining Room
9 am

Jeannette sends her daughter back to the house with the last of the breakfast food. "Then come and tell me what you heard," she whispers, knowing her daughter will understand.

Pomponne nods and takes the dishes up the well-worn path to the big house. Such a strange morning, she thinks in consternation. The murder is a mystery that Pomponne wants solved. Her blue eyes see everything and her alert ears hear everything, and sometimes her head hurts from all the vastness of the world she has to make sense of. Her mind never stops for one moment and even her dreams don't let her rest at night. Most things, Pomponne knows, are simple but this murder, not of a slave but of a white man, threatens the natural order of her life with its unanswered questions and messy suggestions.

And she saw him—Plunkett—two weeks ago when she went with her mother to La Fraternité, the Azor's plantation. What was their tutor doing there? Matter out of place, like a bear she once saw in Jérémie, wearing a pink dancing skirt and looking so odd. Matter out of place, for a low man like Plunkett to be dealing with wealthy and refined Monsieur Azor. Who is coming here today, Pomponne remembers, thinking of the note that earlier had so distressed Madame Rose.

Pomponne pauses at the bottom of the steps to eat a piece of bacon and listen to the murmur of voices from the dining room. The Frenchman, talking as usual. Will their lessons stop now that

Plunkett is dead? Of course, Charles is leaving next month and she and Aimée already know so much...

But why was Plunkett murdered?

Pomponne finishes her bacon, smooths her skirts and carries the plates up to the house.

"Ah, wonderful!" purrs the Frenchman.

"Thank you, Pomponne," murmurs Madame Rose, and Pomponne smiles. She likes Madame Rose and hates to see how pale and sad her mistress is these days. She often suggests to Aimée that they do something nice for her mother, perhaps put on a little play or an afternoon of singing but Aimée scoffs at her ideas. She is always butting heads with her mother—like two rams, Jeannette says.

*

Thoreau smiles in appreciation as Pomponne places the platters of bacon and eggs on the table. What a fresh, lovely girl! A male slave would be more proper for serving at table but there have been hints from Madame Rose about financial troubles and two house slaves who disappeared last year.

Thoreau takes a sip of coffee and thinks how fantastical it is that he, his sister and his hostess are sitting around the table and calmly eating their breakfast as though a man had not just been discovered dead at the bottom of the garden. A murdered man, now cooling down a disused well! But perhaps not so fantastical—violence seems to be the normal state of affairs in Saint Domingue.

Such a savage place, the heat rendering the Negroes violent as expected but even the whites surely more brutal than God intended! There is an ugliness to Saint Domingue that Thoreau was ill-prepared for and though in public he might compare this colony to civilization, in truth and in private he thinks it as wild as Africa. That dreadful massacre up north last year; the atrocities inflicted by the rebel slaves on their erstwhile masters; the terrible penchant mobs—white mobs!—seem to have for decapitating anyone who dares speak in favor of more rights for the slaves or mulattoes. The arrogance of the colonists and their sheer disregard for all decrees and laws coming from France.

Thoreau spears a piece of bacon and eats with gusto, then

clears his throat to start sharing his views on the events of the morning. "It is well known that the Negro has a greater propensity for violence than the civilized races," he begins, dabbling at his egg with a piece of dry brown bread. In Cap-Français, the glittering capital set amongst the sugar plains of the north, they had decent white bread. But because of the slave revolt there last year, Thoreau has been forced to spend the bulk of his mission in the southern backwater of the colony. Far removed from the violence but also far removed from the niceties of life. Here, the bread situation is almost untenable.

In his year in the colony, Thoreau has developed a constant and almost overwhelming hunger for the soft white bread of France, for that delightful outer crispness and inner lightness that is so terribly missing here. Somehow proper bread has become equated with civilization and all that is good in this world. He confides his cravings to no one, not even to his sister, feeling them rather foolish and soft. Womanly. But ah, what he wouldn't give for a crust of just-baked white bread, salted butter melting on its pillowy insides! He pushes his hard brown crust into a pool of leaking yolk: soften, damn ye, soften.

He chews, then continues: "Yes, the propensity for violence is much stronger in the lower races, due perhaps to their undeveloped psyches, giving rise to animalistic behaviors, a tendency to lash out without thinking of the consequences as a rational man might." He takes another bite of bread, attempting to soften it this time with some tart cherry jam. That stuff from yesterday—apricot—tasted of nothing more than sugar. And the apricots here are nothing like the delicate fruit one finds in France but are instead hardy big things, coated in a brown shell, with a taste Thoreau can't quite define.

"Though we must always remember it is not their fault for they are like children—as the great Montesquieu said, it is only through *pity* that slavery came into being." Thoreau pauses to snip a lump from the cone of sugar in the middle of the table. He drops the piece into his coffee and stirs, aware that his audience is awaiting his further thoughts.

Ah, sugar—though necessary for drinking coffee, the taste of it can still turn his stomach.

As the most commercial crop in the colony, far

outweighing coffee and indigo, Thoreau's initial focus was on sugar plantations. Though the northern plains are—were—the center of sugar production many other regions grow sugarcane, ever more so as they fill the void left by the economic desecration of the north. And sugar plantations, with their large workforces and high mortality rates, would also benefit the most from his inquiry and recommendations.

But then, a horrible happening.

In his quest to understand all the parameters of the slaves' existence—his evolving hypothesis posits that successful breeding is an outcome of *every* condition of their lives—Thoreau was taken to observe the refining process at a truly industrial sugar factory on a plantation near Leogane. As one slave fed the sugar cane into the gaping maw of the crusher—a most impressive piece of machinery—another slave stood by with a machete, ready to chop off the arm of the cane feeder in case it got stuck in the machine.

And oh! unlucky day, Thoreau was witness to that dreadful event—the cries of the slave, being pulled into the gears of the crusher; the dreadful chop, blood spurting everywhere, even into the cane juice; the wild, feral look of the slave forced immediately to take the feeder's place, and then the slave who had cut the arm casually cleaning his machete. Worst of all, the arm, disappearing into the crush alongside the cane. And through it all, the sound of the crunching jaws of the machine drowning out the hullabaloo.

"Ah, Monsieur Thoreau, you are indeed lucky to witness this event! But be assured this is a rare, unfortunate occurrence. The balance is ever delicate—that slave is now as good as dead but it is more profitable to keep the crusher running," the foreman said, a gleam of spite in his eyes, happy perhaps to have shocked his visitor. He then informed Thoreau that many Africans believed they would never go home after death if their body were not intact; for the slave who lay screaming on the factory floor, it was 'quite the worst death, really.'

Thoreau excused himself, ran outside and threw up. The Beast of Commerce, thought Thoreau, retching. He could not help but think that the worst sound was not the screeching that men surely make from the depths of Hell but rather the sounds of industry that were now everywhere in Europe and even on this island.

Thoreau is of course a supporter of slavery, as any economist or scientist in their right mind is, and he considers himself a progressive—he has never struck a servant. But that sort of cruelty, despite the economic justification, was more than he could bear. *What price sugar,* he doodled in his little notebook even as his hands shook. The incident supported his growing conviction that there had to be a more humane way. He tells himself that what defines the man of the enlightenment and modern times is *moderation* and the slavery here in Saint Domingue is of such immodest proportions.

After that horrible incident, Thoreau decided to focus on coffee and indigo plantations, where life is generally considered gentler. By happy coincidence, those crops abound in the west and south parts of the island, far from the troubles of the north, and it was with a clear conscience that he wrote to Bordeaux to inform them of his change of plans.

"Yes, indeed, the propensity of the Negro to violence is one argument that even those fanatics of *Les Amis des Noires* cannot deny," continues Thoreau, referring to a society in France lobbying for the abolition of slavery. "As our 'vitalist' friends remind us, each race is comprised of two vital forces—the physical and the moral—and in the Negro the latter is almost entirely absent and—"

"That mulatto boy looked so violent," his sister Mathilde suddenly interrupts, holding up a fork with nothing on it.

"Yes, sister. Though mulattoes are generally considered weak and feminine, no doubt in certain individuals the violence in their blood is not as diluted as in others. Now," Thoreau continues, nodding, "tantrums ensue if a child is left too long in the sun. Imagine the Negro, raised under the merciless sun of Africa: How can we expect his disposition be even-tempered? I have in mind an experiment—"

"I saw him last night," says Mathilde. "And the white horse. Outside in the blackness."

"Yes, of course, sister, the night is certainly full of blackness," Thoreau agrees, allowing some annoyance to creep into his voice: two interruptions! Lately, his sister has been saying some rather odd things. No doubt the effect of the sun, addling her brain as it addles everything here. Thoreau has decided the best strategy is to simply ignore most of what she says. More troubling, he has observed that the tales of violence and cruelty that so disgust him almost seem to *enliven* his sister. "But I am sure you were not outside, sister, last night. Ha!"

Thoreau smiles apologetically at Madame Rose, now looking at Mathilde with a strange expression. "Right, well," he fumbles on: "So, as I was saying, an experiment, the progressive heating of room to measure the effect on the psyche and violent tendencies of the slave inside. Perhaps, Madame, the abandoned dovecote—"

The Kitchens
10 am

Through the door Jeannette risks another glance at Appollon and their eyes lock briefly. Her head throbs violently—what happened last night? I'm going to vomit, she thinks, or break apart into a thousand pieces. Whether or not connected to Appollon, the murder of this white is only bad news. Someone needs to get to town and inform the authorities before rough plantation justice is carried out. There are rules in the *Code Noire* that govern the punishment of slaves and Jeannette wants to believe the occasional story of a plantation master punished for mistreatment, or even the murder, of his slaves.

Yorick, she thinks suddenly. The dead man's colored son with the strange name. He could take his father's mule to Dame Marie.

"What's the trouble, child?" asks Flore, sitting in her corner with a basket of peas to shell. Flore is so old she can hardly remember if she was even born on this island, so old she can remember the days of indigo before coffee, when everything was blue. After she lost her sight, they let her sit in this corner; not everyone is allowed such an easy death.

"No talking," snaps Jeannette, though she suspects the old woman already knows.

Pomponne arrives from the big house with the empty coffee urn.

"Why are the slaves gathered?" whispers Jeannette.

"Brac will search the houses." Pomponne pours Flore a cup of the remaining coffee.

The knife, Jeanette thinks in panic. The knife—where did Appollon hide it?

"When?"

"I don't know, Mama. What are they going to do to Appollon?"

"What?"

"What are they—?"

"Shh! Be quiet. Why did you say Appollon?"

Pomponne makes a face. "First you say be quiet, then you tell me to talk."

Jeannette shakes her head. "Go," she says, refilling the urn from the pot on the stove. "Take the coffee and go back to the house."

"What about the dishes?"

"I'll do them," Jeannette says. Even on an ordinary day she doesn't like Pomponne washing the dishes. They need more house slaves; Jeannette is practically running the entire house alone since the disappearance of Mercure and Claudine. When it is only Madame and the two children, as well as the mad woman in the bed, things are manageable but now with those two visitors appearing out of nowhere, well, it is all too much. And Madame spending ten thousand *livres* on six new Arada field slaves, two of whom promptly died, while Jeannette's daughter is reduced to washing dishes and emptying the slop pots of the whites!

"All right. Oh, and Madame Rose told me that Monsieur Azor will visit this afternoon," Pomponne says innocently.

"What?" gasps Jeannette, forgetting her earlier warning to whisper. "Monsieur Azor coming here? Why?"

"How would I know, Mama?" says Pomponne with a pleased smile. She picks up the urn and leaves for the big house.

Jeannette stares after her in disbelief, a smile forming. Appollon may have his dreams of freedom and fighting but she too has dreams, and they are for her daughter. Pomponne is only twelve but already so beautiful, and in this place beauty is raw meat that draws dangerous predators. Monsieur Marcel had been a good man, mostly, and with him there was never the debauchery from the time of his father. But the white boy Charles has started going to the pigpen at night and though he and Pomponne may play together now, Jeannette knows how quickly that can change. And Brac is a cruel man and even if he is Pomponne's father that might not stop... Jeannette shudders and turns away from the idea.

Jeannette needs her daughter safe and away from Bayardel. She wants one of the wealthy colored families of the district—the Azors, or the Rigauds, the Dumas'—to see Pomponne and make so handsome an offer for her that Madame Rose will surely comply over Aimée's protests. And why not? Madame Rose is always pining for money and those colored planters are rich enough with their gilded carriages and wig-makers imported from France. And often they dislike seeing one of their own enslaved, reminding them as it does of their own roots.

Two weeks ago Jeannette took her daughter to the Azor's plantation and sent her to walk the grounds while she helped in the kitchens. Pomponne did as instructed and apparently there had been a conversation with one of the sons. Her daughter was modest about the scene but surely she made an impression. And now Monsieur Azor is coming here!

Jeannette knows she is gambling with her daughter's innocence but they are running out of time. She doesn't know what the coming changes mean for a girl like Pomponne—last week she heard Capidon boast that among ten thousand rebels in the mountains at Les Platons, not a single colored face is to be found. Jeannette needs her daughter safe and settled and only then might she follow Appollon to wherever their new world might take them.

The Road to Bayardel
10 am

Noel Azor pulls on his gloves, dons his tricorn hat and smiles at his wife. Suzette shakes her head; she is not in favor of today's excursion. Not in favor of any excursion, really, but she knows her husband can't be cooped up like a cock in a hen house. These days they mostly keep to themselves, though two weeks ago they hosted a party to honor their sons' return from France. That event was an oddity in their ever smaller and ever cautious world. After two years of a simmering civil war with the whites, their fight pre-dating the slave revolt up north, the free coloreds now have the vote and supposed equality. Nonetheless tensions remain high and travel anywhere—even in the Grand'Anse, so far free of the troubles—is fraught.

"You're worrying," says Azor, leaning in to kiss her cheek. "Fret not." Azor is an older man in his fifth decade, lightly colored with silver hair and eyes that have grown heavy and cheerless in recent years.

"How can I not worry?" demands Suzette. "I told you what Euphrasine wrote last week!"

"An exaggeration, no doubt," replies Azor easily. His wife is one of six sisters who married all over Saint Domingue and their constant flow of letters back and forth keeps him well informed about events beyond the Grand'Anse. More efficient than a network of homing pigeons, he sometimes thinks, and often there is useful information hidden beneath the gossip and fashion woes and triumphs. Through his wife, Azor is allied by marriage to many of the leading colored families of the colony and the connections her relatives bring are all the more important in these times when family can be counted on, but the law cannot.

"You'll be back by nightfall?"

"Yes," Azor nods, checking his pockets. A slave arrives with a hamper of food and places it in the carriage.

"I don't know why you have to go! I wish you'd tell me."

Azor shakes his head and smiles sadly. He never discusses politics with his wife but he suspects that she understands more than she should. She might even know of the reason for his trip to Bayardel and of his business with the Englishman Plunkett.

"Fine," she mutters when he doesn't answer, running the toe of her silk slipper over some moss wedged between two flagstones. "Stubborn."

He chuckles; it is a woman's place to worry about the home, and his to go out. "All will be fine, wife. You concern yourself with that," he says, gesturing down at the offending moss.

"Henri wants to go with you," Suzette says suddenly, as though just remembering. "I'm not sure about Lucas."

Their youngest sons—twins—have been back in Saint Domingue a month but Azor is beginning to see that their fine education in France, first at the College Sorrèze and then with a series of expensive tutors, has only produced two feckless, lazy and, yes, rather stupid young men who further dismay him with each passing day.

"Let Henri come, then," Azor says. "The drive out might do him good."

"Keep him out of trouble?"

"Of course, wife," he says mildly. He hasn't complained yet to Suzette about their sons but doubtless she shares his concerns.

"There was a little miss from Bayardel slinking around here the day of the party," Suzette says. "I heard Henri had quite the flirtation with her."

"Oh?" Azor raises an uninterested eyebrow and inspects the hamper—hard-boiled eggs, some chicken and fruit. His son's escapades are not of his concern. There are ninety female field slaves on this plantation—no, eighty-nine, Sanité died last week—

as well as twelve clean females of varying hues working in the house and gardens. What his sons do or don't do with them is not his concern. And a little miss from another plantation? Hardly an issue.

"Just keep him out of trouble," Suzette repeats.

"Of course."

"He wrote to Antoinette Rigaud," Suzette continues, referring to one of the guests at the party. "I was hoping for her for Jonas, of course," she adds, speaking of another son, still unmarried at twenty-five, "but I can't seem to move his heart."

"Excellent." Azor plants a kiss on her brow. Dalliances are personal but alliances—marriages—are the domain of his wife and something she excels at, with the stubborn exception of Jonas. All his elder children are well settled, one daughter even with a white man. He was against that match from the start: many newly-arrived Europeans are beguiled by the beauty and wealth of the free colored women and marry them without fully appreciating the burden it may put on their future careers.

Henri comes loping into the courtyard, wearing a pair of absurdly cut breeches that he insists are the latest style from Paris. Long—almost like *trousers*. "I don't care if they are fashionable in Paris!" Azor roared the day of the party, "They make you look like a worker. A *sans-culotte*. Go and change!"

And now here he is wearing them again.

"You wish to accompany me?" Azor says coldly. "And your brother?"

"Lucas is still sleeping," says Henri. He grabs his mother around the waist and kisses her soundly. "Farewell, dear Mater, I shan't be gone long and will be back to kiss you before you sleep in fair slumber."

"Oh, get in," grumbles his father, patting his pockets to make sure the letter and the money are where they should be.

The carriage rolls out of the courtyard and Azor takes an orange from the hamper and peels it. He settles back; the journey will take at least two hours. The rains and the lack of maintenance—the usual system has broken down in the last two years—have made this coastal road almost impassable. Carriages fall off cliffs with disturbing regularity and it would almost be quicker to walk.

Azor regards his son from under half-drooped eyes. They are on a rare good portion of the road, coming through the flat bay around Islet Pierre Joseph and the rhythm of the carriage is making him sleepy. Henri is playing with his watch fob, gazing out towards the sea and tapping his foot in impatience. Azor looks again at his ridiculous white trousers and grimaces.

There is a puppy-like quality to Henri that endears, even as it frightens. With events in France taking a radical turn and the uneasy truce between the whites and the coloreds here in Saint Domingue, Azor thought the time right for his sons to return and take on the mantle of their class and interests. But even taking into account their youth, Azor is beginning to see that his twins have no desire to participate in the birth of a new Saint Domingue.

So naïve and pampered! They finished their formal schooling two years ago and since then spent time under the guidance of a tutor in Bordeaux. The twins complained he ran them ragged but despite their grumblings, Azor has no doubt it was an easy time, replete with girls, drink and gambling. He tried to arrange a meeting for them with Julien Raimond—the boys' great uncle and a leader of the colored cause in Paris—but they always claimed some excuse. And though the twins expressed the right amount of sadness at what happened to their eldest brother Simon, Azor is fairly certain neither of them cares very deeply.

They are quite the opposite of Simon, thinks Azor sadly, watching Henri chomp on an egg and stare out of the window. Entirely lacking in the passion and intensity of his eldest son. But perhaps that was something to be celebrated; it was those very traits that had led Simon down a dark path that ultimately ended in tragedy.

Azor stares at his son, trying to quell the emotions he suddenly feels. The past is a house locked up and shuttered, never to be re-opened. Simon is dead but his other sons live.

"What?" Henri asked him a question.

"I said, why are you going to Bayardel, Pater?" his son repeats. "A sorry plantation, I hear. Are you calling in a debt? They are indebted?"

"Certainly, yes, but that is not my intention. One's neighbors are one's neighbors and it is always advisable to keep good relations," Azor answers. He would like a confidante but this feckless son is not a contender. He sees, by the large pile of shells on the handkerchief next to him, that Henri has eaten all the eggs.

"I would think the Widow Fongravier the least of your worries, Father. An inconsequential woman."

"She has her struggles," agrees Azor. The cycle of debt and downward mobility is a hard one: no money to keep infrastructure repaired or aging fields replaced, leading to lower production and less income and then again, nothing for investment. Once the cycle starts it is difficult to stop and too many plantation owners hold on long after they should have quit. "I remember her husband and father-in-law: both good men. A partnership with the father importing pitch in the early sixties. And we socialized with them, back in the day."

Almost twenty years ago; hard to imagine that there was ever a time when relations were easy and families attended marriages and christenings across the color line. Before our success wrought our constraints, thinks Azor ruefully, before all those stupid laws to preserve the interests and superiority of the whites.

Now they are starting the descent from the Anse de Clerc, the generous sweep of the Bay d'Airdelles stretching before them. Only a few miles now. Azor spies a boat anchored in the distance at the north end of the bay where the Fongravier plantation lies. Two boats. He squints. Which is the boat that is waiting for him?

He turns back to Henri and casts about for some distraction. "So, your mother informs me you wrote to the Rigaud girl?" The Rigauds are another wealthy colored family from the district who took the risk to travel to their house party. Their twenty-four-year-old daughter is lively and well-formed, with a certain talent at the piano. A trifle old, but such things could be forgiven in these turbulent times.

Henri grins. "I have, Father. Your household spies are well informed."

Azor laughs, almost relieved at his son's wit. Perhaps he does have a sharp mind, hidden beneath his annoying air of insouciance.

"A fine girl," agrees Azor, remembering her smile and pretty green dress. Very pale—her father a mulatto, her mother a *quateronne*, as those with three white grandparents are known. The gathering two weeks ago had revived the whole plantation. Like old times: twenty guests, all of whom stayed the night; several pigs roasting in the courtyard and mountains of delicacies. Dancing and music, laughter and fine claret from the cellars. It all created a general feeling of optimism: the coloreds have the vote, won at great cost, and now are allied with the whites. A feeling that perhaps, just perhaps, the troubles were behind them. But it was a hollow optimism that withered with the light of the next day, and Azor's current mission is a hedge against such feelings of premature satisfaction.

"Witty, yes," says Henri. "And she is very well read."

"A fine attribute in a future wife. Nights of intimate conversation are a thing to be savored."

Henri shrugs. "I know you would like to be allied with the great Rigaud," he says.

"Do not have me lecture you on the importance of family. Besides, love and utility often intersect," Azor replies in a smooth, tired voice. The follies of youth—does he even have time for them? "Your mother is looking out for your heart, and I for your future."

Silence for a few jolts as the carriage navigates a tricky downturn, the coachman calling out to the horses and cursing as wheels slip on loose rocks.

"And what," Azor says when the danger is passed, "are your plans, now that you are back?"

Henri shrugs again. "I am awaiting your pleasure."

"Good. I am glad you are amenable to work." Azor watches with amusement as his son struggles to avoid rolling his eyes. "Annatto—I think it would be good for you to start there, working with Bouchard," he says, referring to his overseer for the new annatto fields, optimistically planted four years ago. The berries of that small tree produce a rich red dye, and having heard reports of its success in the colony of Cayenne, Azor had sowed an acre with five hundred seedlings and now the first harvest is approaching.

Recently Azor has heard troubling reports from India: the British are expanding their indigo production and can hire laborers at a penny a day. Azor felt a pang of envy when he heard of the wage; he spends far more on his slaves. And the Indians there, unlike the Indians of these islands, are reputed to be decent workers. Labor at a penny a day! What might that foretell for their future?

"A few years learning the ropes and it might be the time to loan you the money to buy your first land and slaves." Azor enjoys the look of consternation on Henri's face; doubtless his son's vision and timeline are somewhat different.

"Or sooner," Azor adds kindly. "Perhaps we should profit while we are here and look at the Pellegrin place. Buildings doubtless in poor shape, but the land is good."

"I don't like this area," says Henri sullenly. "Surely there is something to be brought around Les Cayes? I have a fancy for sugar—I'm not sure about *annatto*."

"Les Cayes," Azor repeats. The area to the south of the them, currently besieged by slave rebels, headquartered in the mountains at Les Platons. "Times of unrest can be times of opportunity but I am not sure they are coming back from the troubles. The situation is quite dire. I had my man look at the Collet plantation, ideally situated, but even at 10,000 *livres* for all that land—"

"Poof, a few thousand badly armed slaves!" scoffs Henri. "They cannot hold out forever."

"More like eight thousand, possibly ten," Azor says quietly, thinking of the latest reports. Ten thousand escaped slaves, their numbers growing daily, wreaking havoc on the plains below the mountains. "The Grand'Anse is a far safer bet."

Henri shrugs. "Whatever. You wish."

Azor wants to shake him—is this affected disdain all that the finest education in France could produce? That all young idiots are equal, with equal disdain for all things?

They pass the gates of the Fondin place and then one of Antoine Mercier's plantations. Mercier is the leader of the Security Council of the Grand'Anse, a spurious body set up by the *grands blancs* to guard against unrest in their district. He was also one of the ringleaders of a diabolical plan to exterminate all the coloreds in the Grand'Anse. And how closely they almost succeeded. Azor flinches, but no—he must steer clear of those memories.

"You might even consider Bayardel while we are there. I believe Madame Fongravier's son is off to France soon"—to the same school that Henri attended—"and she might do well to follow. I always thought the swamp here could be effectively drained, perhaps put to rice cultivation."

Henri shows some interest, finally.

"Rare that one on the coastal road is available and I am sure we can get a good price. Or call in the loan," Azor adds casually.

Henri smiles. "A consideration."

Azor takes another orange from the hamper and eats it thoughtfully. Almost there. Again he touches his pockets, feels the slight crunch of paper. A letter in one pocket, Plunkett's payment in the other.

NOEL AZOR'S JOURNEY

SAINT DOMINGUE
1775-1792

Azor's grandmother was a slave woman from the delta of Calabar, loved by a Frenchman from Le Havre—Azor's grandfather. Freed on his death, she lingered for many decades in shadowy limbo. Some joke, cruelly, that men of mixed blood such as Azor have no parents: they do not acknowledge their mothers, just as their fathers do not acknowledge them. But certainly not all: Azor's French grandfather educated his sons, freed them on his death and having no legitimate children left them his considerable fortune.

"Do me proud," his own father rasped on his deathbed, and Azor did. He took his portion of the inheritance and multiplied it tenfold. While petty white officials were dictating the type of cloth his wife might wear, limiting their participation in public life and dreaming up new humiliations and insults, the free colored community was busy doing what they were allowed: producing the commodities so eagerly demanded by the world. Azor improved his father's cotton and indigo plantations; diversified into coffee; developed a side business in livestock, as well as a reputable stud farm and a network of property rentals in the towns of Jérémie and Les Irois. Another side business was lending money: though publicly the whites wanted nothing to do with the coloreds, they were not too proud to take their money.

Azor also invested in a cotton plantation in Jamaica. With the political climate changing, he is not convinced that his future lies on the island of his birth but perhaps elsewhere in the West Indies? Like many of mixed blood born in Saint Domingue, Azor believes himself to be a true son of the Americas, a new species, created for a new world: a true *American.*

As the years pass and the restrictions on the free coloreds become more rigid, Azor watches cautiously from the sidelines. He keeps his head down, far from the dangerous purl of politics, and focuses on building alliances and stockpiling for the future. He prides himself on his *unflappability*; a convoluted word, but one that captures the essence of how he tries to approach life.

Still, he can't always remain invisible and sometimes the law reaches down to shake his complacency.

"Your papers," demands the official. They are in the central square at Jérémie. Azor is in town to discuss a business venture with a flour importer, check on the status of his warehoused indigo and evict a white tenant who has not paid rent in over a year. That last situation is possibly connected to the scene that is playing out right now, or possibly not: this might simply be a bureaucratic nightmare.

"Your papers!" repeats the officer.

"What papers?" asks Azor, stalling. He is aware of a small crowd gathering, ready to enjoy the coming spectacle. Dignity in the face of indignant situations, he reminds himself, but he can feel himself growing hot and his lips starting to tremble, just slightly, at the absurdity of what is happening.

"Your freedom papers," replies the officer. "As per Section 8.2 of Law 744 it is required for any man of color, which you obviously are, to show their manumission papers on demand from an officer of the law."

Who is this man? Perhaps the new sub-intendant he had heard about. From up north somewhere—immune to the nuances of Grand'Anse society but surely the man had been in the colonies long enough to know that not every law was rigidly applied?

"I see." Such idiocy—of course he doesn't carry his grandmother's emancipation papers with him—his family has been free for nigh on sixty years! They are kept in the cellars at La Fraternité in a strongbox wrapped with hammered iron to guard against fire.

"You *see*?" says the officer with a curled lip, playing to his audience which is growing by the minute. "If you *see*, then where are they? You will also *see* immediate imprisonment if you don't produce them."

Azor nods at the officer then glances at Plato standing by his carriage and briefly inclines his head. His trusted slave will know what to do. Plato slips away and Azor raises his hands in a supplicating gesture.

"I do not believe I have them with me," he says softly. Jouville, yes, that is the name of the new sub-intendant. "Monsieur Jouville," he adds.

"Then it's trouble for you!" exclaims Officer Jouville in satisfaction and someone in the crowd whistles.

"I am well known to Monsieur L'Intendant Desombrages," says Azor. "He would be happy to vouch for me."

"I'll not bother the Intendant over this!" scorns the man on horseback. "Uppity colored! I know all about you people and your arrogance."

"It would be no trouble to Captain Desombrages," protests Azor as politely as he can.

"Boy! You have had enough time. I see you speak the truth when you say you do not have them. Now I must follow the law!" Jouville gestures to a black militiaman standing beside him. With a sinking heart, Azor sees him approach with a set of manacles. He feels faint and looks up at the high blue sky. What is happening to his country? We are become the whipping boys for the small whites and their venal jealousies. Envy without respect, a perilous combination.

"There!" cries a woman from the crowd. "After what you did to Roget this morning, this is justice! Throwing him out on the street like you were better than him!"

The crowd laughs in approval. Jérémie is full of *petits*

blancs—tradesmen, surgeons, bakers and butchers, warehouse managers and petty officials. In a society built around plantations, these men feel their low position keenly and many must compete with coloreds in the same professions. Out in the countryside the planters may rule but here in town this rough element reigns.

Azor holds out his hands, still looking up at the sky. The clink of chains and an iron fastens around one wrist.

"What is going on here?" demands Intendant Desombrages, cantering up on his horse. The policeman quickly unsnaps the manacles and retreats.

Thank god for Plato, thinks Azor. And for justice.

"Monsieur Desombrages," gasps Jouville, his face a pleasing rose color.

"Jouville, are you mad? This is Noel Azor, an upstanding citizen. What are you doing?"

"His freedom papers, sir," stutters Jouville. "He could not produce them as per the law!"

"Don't be a fool, Jouville. His family has been free for generations."

"Three," clarifies Azor, regaining his breath and trying to quell the shaking of his legs.

"French poof, protecting the colored bastards," hisses someone from the crowd; high officers are regarded as instruments of Versailles and generally hated by the Creoles. Desombrages wheels around and searches the crowd but the men and women are now intently studying the cobblestones.

"That's enough," Desombrages shouts. "All of you disperse! Back to work." He turns to Azor and Jouville. "Noel, I am deeply saddened," he says but Azor notes he does not dismount. "Officer Jouville is new and we must forgive him. Jouville, apologize to Monsieur Azor."

Jouville's eyes bug out. "Apologize to that man?!"

"Now!"

"I apologize," mutters Jouville, looking as though he has just swallowed dog shit. Azor catches a flash of pure hate in the man's eyes.

"Thank you," says Azor to Desombrages, unsure if he should use his Christian name or his title; these days even a simple greeting is fraught.

"But perhaps in the future, just bring them along, why not?" suggests Desombrages, looking slightly uncomfortable. "Have a few copies made and keep them on you?"

"Of course," says Azor. Desombrages half-bows from his saddle and rides off, perhaps as embarrassed as he is.

*

His eldest son Simon is a passionate young man, inspired by politics and injustice—which often, Azor reflects, amount to the same thing. When Simon completed his education in France and returned in Saint Domingue, he served in the militia as all young free coloreds were compelled to—the whites had managed to weasel out of that duty by passing it off to them. Then in 1775 the American Revolutionary War broke out and, inspired, Simon signed up for the *Chasseurs Royales de Saint Domingue*, a colored company led by the great French military leader d'Estaing. Simon fought alongside the Americans at the invasion of Savannah and helped to liberate that city from the British.

Simon returns to Saint Domingue as a young and idealistic man of twenty, ready to chafe ever more under the weight of inequality suffered by his people. He compares it unfavorably to the status of free men in America—there, to be free is to be free, and there is no indeterminate 'half-equality.' The events in France of 1789, particularly the *Declaration of the Rights of Man* which proclaim all men equal, further inspire him.

"We must fight for our position in society!" Simon declares. "They can no longer treat us as mongrels—we must claim our rights, by force if necessary!"

Azor counsels prudence; there are several influential colored lawyers pressing their cause in front of the new Legislative Assembly in Paris and he is confident their efforts will pay off.

"Meetings!" scorns Simon. "That's all they are doing. And the French are worse than the British. We will never achieve anything while we remain under the dominion of

France! The most backward country in Europe," he finishes in disgust, "no matter how elegant they suppose themselves to be."

"I believe the French in Europe are more open to rational, economic arguments than the whites here," replies Azor. "They are not so blinded by hate and can appreciate our civic contributions and economic importance, the taxes we pay."

"Taxation without representation," mutters Simon. "That was the rub of it in America! But I disagree, Father—we will get no help from Paris. They are too scared of what happened to the British in America and will not risk alienating the whites here by improving our situation."

Others are as impatient as Simon: in 1790 a colored man by the name of Vincent Ogé, fed up with the pace of change in Paris, returns to Saint Domingue determined to fight for the colored cause. His insurrection is quickly put down and he is put to death—in a most gruesome manner, broken on the wheel with the colored community forced to watch—but his actions inspire other sporadic outbreaks of resistance around the colony. And even, say the whites, ever ready to blame the coloreds for all the ills in the Saint Domingue, Ogé inspired the great Northern slave revolt of August 1791.

News of that revolt rips swiftly through the delicate fabric of their lives. When Azor hears of it, his first thought is: *Nothing will ever be the same.*

The news inflames and excites his son.

"It is beginning!" declares Simon, delighted at the scale of the insurrection and ignoring the colored planters who were also victims of the violence.

"The only thing that is beginning is a regime of more vigilance over our own slaves," retorts Azor. Practical and cautious, Azor knows that the slaves have *Vaudun* and a universe separate from their masters and that they are not as stupid as most like to believe. Instead they are well-trained in the art of subservience and hiding their true emotions; his son not so much, he thinks, looking at Simon's flushed and excited face.

"This will finally force those buffoons in France to make common cause with us, to defeat the slaves!"

"I hardly see how the slave insurrection helps our cause," replies Azor with a sigh. "And I imagine slave prices will rise because of this—think of the demand when order is restored and the rebels doubtless put to death." Ten thousand of them, he thinks in amazement. Twenty thousand even— that is the latest number circulating. And far better organized than anyone could have imagined or conceded. Unlike their counterparts in Martinique or Jamaica, and the Macandal poisoning scare aside, the history of Saint Domingue has been relatively free of slave unrest. Complacency, now shattered.

Simon looks at his father with impatience. He is a racehorse, chomping at the bit. "Now is the time! Armed struggle is how we will win and the slaves are proving the whites are not infallible."

"You had better hope they are infallible," snaps his father. "Or it's an end to Saint Domingue and to everything we have. Promise me you won't do anything foolish."

"You think anything that doesn't make you money is foolish!"

"Promise me!"

Simon refuses and the next day he is gone, leaving only a note saying he is traveling to Jérémie to meet a friend.

Meet a friend—Azor crumples the note, anger coursing through him. What is his passionate, foolhardy son doing?

*

Similar to much of the colored resistance on the island, the attack is carelessly planned and unfurls with spontaneous folly.

On Page's plantation a league outside Jérémie, a group of young colored men gathers: some of decent family, some from the town, and one stranger from Port-au-Prince who arrived the week before. They have with them a smattering of their own slaves, who promise their masters that once they rise up against the whites, they will have the support of the substantial slave population in Jérémie and the surrounding areas.

There are some speeches, a lot of rum, and a night of grievance that gives way to vengeful plotting. When noon approaches, the men leave their den and descend from the hills. At the edge of town they come to the house of Monsieur Sejourne, the Receiver of Posts.

Like the attack, their choice of target is not well thought out. They enter the house and first bayonet an old woman. When Sejourne comes to investigate the commotion in his front room he finds his mother dead and offers only a brief, surprised resistance—"But I—!"—before he too is struck down.

They find his pregnant wife in the courtyard. By that time the small colored mob, fired on rum and hate, has ceased to think of their prey as human; it is as if the murder of one white lets loose some instinct they no longer control. They kill young Madame Sejourne and then, perhaps in a thirst for another victim, cut open her pregnant belly. They dash the quasi-infant on the floor and feed the remains to the pigs while the few household slaves cower in the corner. They cut off Monsieur Sejourne's head and affix it to a bayonet and burst back onto the street, calling on all the free coloreds and slaves to rise up with them.

Not one does and the town's militia quickly captures the group and flays them alive. Fearing for their lives, the many law-abiding colored citizens of Jérémie flee to the authorities; others head for the hills before the Security Council of the Grand'Anse brings them back and herds four hundred colored men onto two ships, commandeered from two surprised American sea captains. *For your safety,* they are informed.

Azor's son Simon is among them.

Azor is not—perhaps his old friendship with Desombrages has spared him? When he hears the news his first thought is relief: his son was not among the idiots that murdered the Sejourne family. Azor hurries to Jérémie with his daughter-in-law and a male cousin who also escaped the general round-up. There they are joined by the wives and mothers of the captured men.

"Don't worry, we are keeping them safe from further harm," smirks Intendant Desombrages at the town hall where the families go to petition for the release of their menfolk. Beside him stands the planter Mercier, the head of the Security Council and a known hardliner. A man who fills Azor with dread and disgust.

Mercier nods: "We will hold them while the Security Council fully investigates the rebels and their accomplices." He then motions to the black soldier beside him and the man strikes a decisive note on a drum stretched with pale leather. Later they find out it is made from the skin of Boury, one of the rebels. What was left of it; there are rumors that the others were forced to eat some of the skin before being flayed themselves.

"The men will be released from the ships once we have satisfied ourselves that we have caught *all* the perpetrators of this heinous plot," continues Mercier, regarding the gathered group with disdain. "For now, your men are being kept in comfort. They might even feel at home there, eh?" he jeers. "Were not your ancestors also held on boats?"

When Desombrages turns to leave, Azor hurries after him.

"Joseph—" he checks himself. "Monsieur, my son Simon is newly married and his wife is pregnant," he pleads. "I can vouch for him, or let me take his place, offer a financial surety—?"

Desombrages laughs, spits in his face and strides away.

Azor wipes his face as despair sweeps through him. There is no cure for that kind of hatred; all Desombrages sees now when he looks at Azor is a hated colored, not a living, breathing man that he once called friend.

Azor's townhouse becomes a gathering place for the families of the captive men, among them a few white men with sons or relatives on the boats. He comforts the women as best he can and seeks to diffuse tensions between the womenfolk of the instigators and those who were not involved, rightly angered that innocent men are paying for the folly of others. Azor mediates between those who argue for negotiation and patience, and those who want to raise an army and storm the boats. Daily he presents petitions to the authorities and even sends two emissaries to Port-au-Prince to see what can be done.

Nothing.

The weeks pass.

From the second floor of his townhouse, Azor watches the harbor as a hopeless, impotent rage consumes him. They learn of the squalid conditions aboard the ships: the men near starvation, locked in the hold and never allowed into sunlight; scarce rations of water and beans thrown down occasionally. Daily, crowds of whites—and some slaves—gather to shout obscenities at the boats. Azor has his own slaves standing guard around the house; all he can hope is that the strength of his reputation and the force of their arms will be sufficient if the mob turns on him and his brood of distraught females.

The Security Council—established, boasts its members, for just this type of emergency!—debate what to do with the men on the boats. Some argue for a mass drowning by holes drilled in the hold and the ships sunk, but this plan is vigorously resisted by the two enraged American sea captains.

"So starve them," suggests one planter.

"Throw them all overboard."

"Exile them to Ile Navasse," another suggests, referring to a rocky island off the western coast. "They can be joined by the rest of their families! Get rid of all of them, forever."

"Poison."

As the starved men on the ships weaken and start to die off, Monsieur Mercier comes up with what he contends is the perfect plan: they will deliberately infect the remainder with smallpox and in this way, nature can be seen to finish the job they started. The doctor Doucet obtains pustules and crusts from the local traveling inoculator—a man with a brisk business offering his services to plantations—then rubs them on meat they throw into the hold.

Eventually Blanchelande, the island's unpopular royal governor, sends his troops to negotiate for release, arguing that the whites and coloreds should set aside their hatred and allow government troops to concentrate on the slave rebellions, still going strong in the north and quickly spreading over the island. But by then it is too late—more than half the men on the ships are already dead.

Finally, the survivors are released and limp ashore over planks, those who can walk helping their brothers in distress. The smell of rot and death follows them, as do jeers and stones from the crowds.

Azor's son Simon is not among the men who stumble onto land.

"Late December, only a day after the pox first appeared," Azor's friend Durocher whispers. "I wish it had taken me, an old man of almost seventy! I survived but so many did not. And Simon..." Durocher's voice cracks and tears swell in his watery gray eyes.

Azor does not trust his voice; he feels the same. Why had old Durocher survived, Azor thinks with a bitterness he does not know he possessed, while his son Simon, the pride of his life, did not?

The authorities throw the bodies of the dead men overboard and so there is nothing even to bury. Sometimes it gives Azor comfort to look at the sea and imagine his child held in its blue embrace. Then his daughter-in-law loses the child and now there is nothing in this world that remains of his Simon.

A few months later the French government grants full legal equality to the coloreds. Perhaps Simon's sacrifice was not in vain but the changes mean nothing to Azor, who only sees in them the specter of the abolition of slavery, inching closer.

I'd rather be rich than free, Azor thinks sadly, ashamed of himself. In some ways he envied his Simon. Had he ever been that passionate? Had he ever once looked for meaning in something that did not involve making money? He settles for lying to himself that had he been his Simon's age, he too would have been as passionate. But Azor is now past fifty and he is able to tell himself that it is his age, and not some fundamental flaw, that explains his apathy.

The Dining Room
10 am

"Yes, the stone pigeon coop heated, to different temperatures, then the means developed to tabulate control," continues Thoreau, spearing the last piece of bacon from the platter. He burps delicately. "A *scientific* way of measuring control, determine certain heating points—"

Would the man never shut up? And he has eaten four slices of bacon and now it is all gone! Rose nods politely at her guest and fights the urge to close her eyes. The only way to survive, she decides, is to let his words flow over her, paying him no more heed than a buzzing fly. As if on cue, a fly drops into the jam bowl. Pomponne jumps over from her perch in the corner, pinches it up and dutifully takes it out of the room. She comes back in, licking her fingers.

Then the sound of a horse racing up the front path, hooves mucking over the gravel. Rose rises and relief floods her when she sees it is her neighbor Mercier. Brac must have sent word.

"Monsieur Mercier," says Rose, greeting him at the top of the steps. Mercier pats Sheba, barking happily, and bows to Rose. He is wearing a rough brown coat streaked with mud and smelling, improbably, of rotten crab.

"Thank you for coming and so fast," says Rose, ushering Mercier through to the dining room. She fights the impulse to take and hold on to his arm. Normally Rose has little time for her arrogant neighbor but right now it is a relief to have him here. He isn't a clueless outsider like Thoreau or a shifty manager like Brac.

Antoine Mercier first came to Saint Domingue a few decades ago as a surgeon—a profession always in demand in plantation society—seeking his fortune away from a France that continued to groan under relentless stratification even as the rest of Europe tried on the trappings of social mobility. In Saint Domingue in the early days, success stories were common and until the 1760s, here on the southwestern tip of the island any man who could clear trees from a hillside could easily claim a concession.

Gradually, through thrift and risk and bullish zeal, as well as marriage to the only daughter of a prosperous early settler of the Grand'Anse, Mercier acquired his first plantation and made the transition from the ranks of the *petit blancs* to the ranks of the plantation class.

Now he is the leader of the Security Council of the Grand'Anse and has a reputation for being a ruthless hardliner. Rose winces as she remembers the plans he proposed, immediately in the aftermath of the August '91 slave rebellion, to exterminate all existing slaves in the Grand'Anse. Mercier contended that news of the rebellion up north had, or soon would, infect all their slaves with ideas of revolt and freedom. "In order to survive, we must start over! Like a coffee field, infected by wilt," Mercier argued. "When disease strikes, one doesn't just trim the offending bush; accepted agricultural wisdom is that the entire field must be replanted!"

His plan never caught traction but then he was involved in the dreadful smallpox infamy in Jérémie, against the colored men on the ships… Rose shudders and thinks again of Monsieur Azor, probably heading towards their plantation right now.

In the dining room Mercier wipes his sweating brow with his sleeve and looks around in some puzzlement at Rose's guests.

"May I present Monsieur Antoine Mercier, our neighbor to the south," says Rose. "And Monsieur Mercier, I am delighted to introduce our guest Monsieur Thoreau, of the Royal Agricultural Society of Bordeaux, and his sister Demoiselle Mathilde. They have been with us for five days now."

Thoreau inclines his head and his sister Mathilde twitters with inappropriate coyness. She simpers, "We are so glad you came, Monsieur, how wonderful to have another man with us at such a time." On the last word she stretches out her hand as though expecting Mercier to take it, and it hangs like a little hummingbird, alone in the air.

Mercier ignores the hand, looks around, then settles on Rose as his audience.

"Two of them!" he says, his chest heaving and his black eyes darting in anger. "You permit me, Madame?" and without waiting for a response he takes off his jacket and throws it on the chair. Still breathing heavily, he takes a piece of the bread from the table and dips it in the jam bowl. "I want a quick word with Brac, then I'll continue the search myself. They've come this way—I know it. My wife always says I have a second sense when it comes to the hunt." He chews on, seemingly unaware of the confusion in the room. "They're well stamped and won't get far. I'll have the Fouache brothers from Jérémie on them if I don't find them today," Mercier says, referring to a pair of bounty hunters known for their success in capturing slaves alive. "They're too valuable to go lightly..."

He trails off, the tension in the room finally reaching him. He licks the corner of his mouth.

"What are you talking about?" asks Rose in confusion.

"Two runaways. Samson and Dieudonné—you leased them last year for the harvest. Good workers and I'll not let them go without a fight! What are... what is going on here?"

Oh. Mercier is just on one of his interminable slave-hunting expeditions, though as far as Rose knows he has never once been successful. Men and the chase, she thinks dryly, offering him a chair. But odd that he should think they had come this way, instead of heading for the mountains behind. Bayardel on the royal coast road is not a usual destination for runaway slaves.

"Please, Monsieur Mercier, you must sit down," says Rose. "It's, it's..." How awful to have to say the words aloud.

Thoreau steps into her confusion, eager to take back attention from the ill-dressed interloper who smells strongly of horse manure and coffee. And crab. Thoreau rises and bows, then announces with some importance: "Mr. Elijah Plunkett is dead."

"Plunkett—the English fellow who tutors your children? Lives down in Apricots?"

"Yes, Plunkett the Englishman," confirms Thoreau.

The two men regard each other, the contrast between them strong and stark: Mercier every bit the rough colonist with his dirty chemise and sweat-stained neckcloth, Thoreau the quintessential French academic with his lace cuffs, a monocle poised neatly on his breast, a pale blue jacket.

"Well, that is shocking, yes indeed," says Mercier, raising an eyebrow. He pauses, as though thinking of something. "I saw him last month in Apricots and noticed he looked very flushed. An attack of apoplexy, no doubt? Such a pity for you, Madame, that it should happen here."

Rose stares at her neighbor, not sure how to say the word. *Murder.* Mercier misinterprets her hesitation and holds up a hand: "Say no more, my dear woman. Found dead with one of the women, no doubt."

"No, it was murder," says Mathilde from her corner of the table, her eyes bright. "His throat slit."

"Hush, sister!" says Thoreau.

"Murdered?" Mercier's voice is quizzical but there is an undercurrent of something Rose can't quite place. Excitement?

"Yes. I found his body early this morning. At the bottom of the garden," Rose says. "His throat slit. It was terrible, terrible." Saying the words aloud makes them real, and to her dismay she starts crying. To her even greater dismay Mathilde is suddenly beside her, patting her sleeve.

"But my dear woman, this is dreadful!" Mercier exclaims. "Get some rum, rum," he roars to no one in particular. Thoreau leaps into action and dispatches to fetch the rum from the salon. Through her tears Rose sees Mercier's curled lip and knows what he is thinking: only a Frenchman would be proud of such service and not wait for a slave.

Mercier turns to her: "We must act at once, Madame. Gather the slaves, inventory the knives."

"Yes, Brac is already doing that," says Rose, hiccupping and trying to stop her tears. She stares down into her coffee cup, aware of an enormous lethargy looming on the horizon. Why did the man have to be killed *here*?

"And do we trust Brac, Madame?" asks Thoreau, returning with the rum. He holds the bottle partially behind him, to hide the level of the liquid that has gone down significantly from the previous night. He pours Rose a splash before realizing she still has coffee in her cup.

"What?" says Rose, annoyed that Thoreau is again questioning the course of action. Of course she doesn't trust Brac—the man is a sly drunk—but he is white and French and knows how to work the slaves. And who else could it be but one of them?

"It would seem to me that cut on the neck, quite clean and surgeon-like, suggests an educated—"

"Nonsense!" roars Mercier from across the table, his face suddenly and violently red. "You, sir, must be very recently arrived to accuse another white man! Crimes of this nature are unknown in our little society; it is only the savages that commit such acts. When they are not properly managed," he adds, and Rose grimaces at the jab. Mercier's words are not entirely true; there are certainly murders committed by whites against other whites. A recent case that shocked the island was the patricide of a man whose sons who did not approve of his proposed second wife.

Thoreau glares at Mercier. "Sir, nature has not refused me the gift of memory. There was the case of Maginot I heard about last month. A heinous example—"

"A domestic affair, nothing more," retorts Mercier. "It is treasonous what you say! To accuse a white man of murder!"

"I am not accusing anyone, my dear man," says Thoreau, allowing just a slight note of protest to slip in.

"And doubtless Plunkett's body was marked with some signs of magic, some *Vaudun*?" demands Mercier. "Further proof it was a slave."

"No, I don't think…" says Rose, trying to recall then wishing she hadn't; she would be quite glad never to see Plunkett's neck again.

"And so what about you?" demands Mercier, glaring at Thoreau. "You arrive a few nights ago and now a man turns up dead?" Thoreau splutters like a fish on land and the two men stare at each other with a thick, mutual hatred.

"Gentlemen, gentlemen. Please! This is a shock, certainly, but there is no need to get so—excited." Rose stands up. Men could be so tiresome with their peacocking and inappropriate sparring. Despite the early hour it is already hot inside and the rum is making her cheeks tight and heavy. Quite amazing, really, the way just a tiny bit can make one feel so much better. Rum in coffee? But why not? And I was crying, Rose thinks in amazement, something she has scarcely done since the weeping months that followed the death of her husband.

"Clear the dishes, Pomponne," Rose says, "and tell your mother we have another guest for the day. You will stay, won't you?" she asks, turning to Mercier.

"Of course, Madame."

Out the back window she sees her two children working their way up towards the house. Thank goodness. Perhaps it was foolish to have sent them away; they should be inside and close, away from the horror. But who knows where the horror comes from? And what if Plunkett's killer isn't one of the slaves, as Thoreau keeps suggesting?

Rose, Mercier, Thoreau and his sister make their way to the salon at the center of the house, a large room with doors and windows that open to both the front and back verandas, welcoming the sea breezes that occasionally roll through. It is here that Rose spends the long, hot afternoons, sometimes with Pomponne waving a fan over her, sometimes with just a glass of rum to ensure the sweetness of sleep and forgetting.

"Mama!" Aimée flings herself in her mother's arms.

"Darling," murmurs Rose.

"I'm sorry, Mama, I wanted to come back."

"It is better you are here with us. You look frightened, my dear." Rose hugs her daughter and feels her delicious need; soon she will become a young woman resistant to her mother's embrace.

"Master Charles," says Mercier, coming forward and putting his hand on the boy's shoulder. "You are the man of the house now and must take care of your mother and sister."

"Of course, sir," says Charles, bowing slightly. "Thank you for coming."

"A happy coincidence—I was on the hunt and happened up here. Two escaped slaves, one of them my best worker."

"Oh!" squeals Aimée, looking at Charles. Rose hears her whisper: "The eyes."

The Salon
11 am

Thoreau settles in a corner, fuming at the intruder Mercier now seated in the grandest chair in the salon. How that man had roared at him! Thoreau has seen many such as Mercier on his travels through this island: rough men who in France are nobodies but who out here assume importance, and riches, completely out of keeping with their predestined place in the world. Pretending to be gentlemen when all the world knows—current vogue notwithstanding!—that that is a prerogative of birth.

Here, the fine distinctions that make a just and godly society are lost beneath the broad brushstrokes that place all white men above anyone with black blood. Natural, of course, but also bothersome in a way Thoreau hasn't quite yet defined. Since his arrival in Saint Domingue, Thoreau has felt keenly the lack of servility that he was accustomed to both giving and receiving in France. Here, even barbers and butchers, if blessed with white skin, jealously guard their right to the honorific *Sieur*, whereas in France that title is reserved for the gentry and higher—or at least was, until that silly vogue for calling everyone *citizen* came about.

Thoreau glares at Mercier lounging in his chair, then sits up straighter. He will show by his even, calm manner that he is not subject to the overheated emotions of these Creoles. He casts another venomous glance at Mercier but the other man ignores him.

What a bullheaded man! Villainous, crouching ape!

The single-minded insistence that it is a slave they seek confuses Thoreau, though he has heard that slaves prefer underhanded, more subtle ways of wreaking revenge on their masters. Poison in particular: near Petit Goave he stayed with a family convinced that their elderly mother had been poisoned by her nursemaid. Remembering the family's description of the agonized death throes of their mother—and the subsequent horrors visited upon the nursemaid—Thoreau shudders.

He considers voicing his concerns again but decides not to risk another roar like the one Mercier produced earlier. It is possible, perhaps even probable, that the colonist is mentally unstable, and while Thoreau's opinion of his abilities is generally high, he is realistic about his physical prowess. Thoreau decides he will follow that line of inquiry independently; these colonists are too blinded by their prejudices and fear of their slaves to imagine it could be anyone but them.

Heavy boots on the veranda and Brac enters, carrying a whip and bringing some of the horror inside the house. Mathilde leans forward and Thoreau sees her face is bright and alive.

"Brac, my man," says Mercier.

"Monsieur Mercier. Glad you could come, sir, and so quickly," says Brac, nodding and running a hand through his sweating hair. "A right frightful business."

"I was on the hunt, perhaps guided this way by a dose of luck."

Luck—the only ambition of fools, thinks Thoreau in contempt and considers making his observation out loud. Instead he stands up and thrusts himself forward, determined to take his rightful place as the senior male in attendance: "Now, Brac, tell us how you have progressed and what you propose next."

Brac winces and turns back to Mercier: "We've got the men tied. The women there as well and I propose we start the search in the men's houses."

"Good," says Mercier. "And you haven't involved the authorities?"

Brac nods.

"Excellent," says Mercier. "They have more pressing matters in these times, I can assure you."

"Yes, we can take care of justice ourselves," agrees the

manager. He goes to sit down on one of the sofas but catches the look on Rose's face and straightens up instead.

"Better we find the culprit before a damn bureaucrat does and wastes time and money on *justice*," continues Mercier, placing mocking scorn on the last word—the French courts, still functioning, are widely despised by the colonists. "As for Plunkett, no need to worry the magistrate just yet—perhaps we even say he died a natural death and avoid any bother."

Thoreau does not approve of what Mercier is proposing— to pretend a white man's murder did not happen!—but decides against engaging with the volatile colonist; he is more interested in allying himself with the plantation manager. "Very well, my man," he says to Brac. "A search of the slave quarters is the appropriate course of action and now, having breakfasted, I shall accompany you."

"No, stay here. You'd be no help," says Brac brusquely.

Thoreau gapes, aware of a red tide inching up his neck. To be dismissed by the manager as if... as if... he motions to his sister and she dutifully produces his notebook. He shakes his head in annoyance and she quickly proffers a handkerchief. He nods and mops his face. What a world, where hired men speak to their betters in such a way!

Rather than trust his voice, Thoreau bows stiffly and returns to the dining room, now cleared of the breakfast remains except for the cone of brown sugar sitting like a reproach in the middle of the table. He helps himself to a boiled sweet from a dish on the sideboard and then, with mildly shaking hands, serves himself another cup of coffee from the urn.

There is a mirror over the mantel—the fireplace just a European conceit, though the mornings can be chilly—and Thoreau stares at his reflection. He sees not what his face has become, soft and drooping, but what it had been in his prime, with its fine nose and high color, the determination in his eyes and chin. A noble face, he thinks in satisfaction, and indeed he is connected (albeit distantly, by marriage through an aunt) to the grand family of Dufort!

They—Mercier and Brac—should be considered the prime suspects, thinks Thoreau, nodding to himself in the mirror. Phrenology is another of his pursuits and there is no doubt that the perfidious physiognomy and obvious physical defects of the two men—the small, piggish eyes of Mercier and the overly heavy brow of Brac—proclaim their criminal destiny. He has noted that Madame Rose does not think highly of her manager and Mercier's sudden arrival—he certainly didn't look like he had been riding all morning.

And there is something else Thoreau hasn't yet shared with his hostess, something that perhaps points beyond the killing of Plunkett by a slave. A curious incident last Sunday after church. Madame Rose was sleeping and the whole household—nay, the whole plantation—had descended into tropical torpor. Thoreau was swaying in a hammock on the veranda and thinking interesting thoughts about a Negro albino, seen that morning outside the church in Dame Marie.

Thoreau had heard of these creatures, and his host back in La Leogane had even promised to show him a specimen, an offer that sadly never materialized. But the girl that morning! Thoreau was immensely intrigued by the whiteness of her skin, juxtaposed against obviously Negroid features. What a bizarre and surprising effect of nature but how troubling to the scientific order of things! If skin color is the defining trait of the different species, as Thoreau firmly believes, then how does a white Negro girl fit into the established order?

In 1755 the great scientist Buffon cut open both black and white bodies and claimed that the blackness of the Negroid race, caused no doubt by a superabundance of black bile, extended to its internal organs. Buffon contended this fact was irrevocable proof that the Negroes were a different species from the whites. But what would the inside of an albino look like? Would this prove once and for all the scientific rationale of Buffon? Could he buy that little albino girl? Cut open a finger? What an exciting proposition and why had no one thought to do this before?

Hammocks are so comfortable once in, and so damnably difficult to get out of, that Thoreau suspects they must be partially responsible for the sloth he has observed in the colony. But he did want to capture his thoughts in his notebook and so with some difficulty he sat up, then saw Plunkett through the dining room window.

The tutor's presence in that room was to be expected; he

gave his lessons there and was apparently sleeping on the table. Plunkett was standing before a glass-fronted cabinet that held the china service. As Thoreau watched, Plunkett bent over and he heard him open one of the drawers that made up the bottom of that piece of furniture. After some time, Plunkett straightened up bearing a sheaf of papers, then disappeared from view.

Thoreau had thought about rising from the hammock—no easy feat—and inquiring what the man was up to, rifling through the Fongravier family papers! But instead he reached for his notebook, then lay back in the hammock and had a very satisfying nap.

Now alone in the dining room, Thoreau inspects the cabinet. He tugs gently but the drawers at the bottom are locked. How had Plunkett a key? Thoreau peers through into the salon but Brac is gone and Mercier is entertaining Madame Rose—who appears to be sleeping, albeit with her eyes open—with stories of his hunting exploits. Charles and Aimée are sitting quietly, talking on one of the sofas. A dog looks up at him from its spot on the floor, then closes its eyes and settles its head back between outstretched paws. Outside it is a brilliant, silent blue morning.

Thoreau looks around the dining room and fixes on a chest in the corner. Unlocked, and sure enough, it contains a few instruction books, a white shirt and a heavy leather satchel. Plunkett's things. Thoreau reaches for the satchel, his breath quickening as he imagines excuses were someone to come in and see him meddling with Plunkett's affairs: *Preparing them for his boy! Left my notes here yesterday!*

Would he find in the satchel the papers Plunkett had taken so mysteriously from the cabinet? What secrets did that man have, Thoreau wonders, aware that he too has his secrets. Perhaps everyone does?

THOREAU'S JOURNEY

FRANCE TO SAINT DOMINGUE
1788-1792

As a learned and enlightened man, Thoreau is excited by the rumors of political reform that infuse French society. All agree France is a mess: a queen acting like a harlot; a king who seemingly does not want to be king; worsening famines and general social unrest. The thorny problems of equitable taxation and each man's role in society on everyone's mind with no clear solution. A government plagued by debts from too many wars and a hidebound political system yet to catch up with the rest of Europe; Britain, though rightfully despised, is nonetheless a model of political enlightenment.

Change is in the air and it is as though the seeds of liberty, sown by the American Revolution, suddenly spring up that fatal year of 1788. The momentous news breaks that the king is to convene an Estates General, a meeting of all three classes, or "Estates," of French society. Not just the First Estate—the clergy, who traditionally pray for the king— or the Second Estate, the nobles who traditionally fight for the king—but also the *Third* Estate—everyone else, but generally understood to be the bourgeoisie, men of substance and education but no nobility. Last invoked well over a century ago, convening the Estates General was an improbable and rare decision, now with the goal of reforming the taxation system and getting France's financial affairs in order.

Most exciting of all, directive comes that the town of Bordeaux is to elect three representatives of the Third Estate to attend the meeting at Versailles!

"I am the ideal candidate!" Thoreau enthuses to his sister Mathilde. He scarcely slept all night, imagining himself part of that august body, lecturing a group of impressed aristocrats. Perhaps even the king! The praise that would surely flow in response to his oratorial style—flowery, yes, but with just the right amount of gravitas and humility. "I must be a part of this historic occasion! Next week we meet to begin the selection process. I believe de Sèze, the rector of the *Académie Royale*, will be one of the delegates but there are two other seats and I fancy my chances are strong. Berquier the lawyer is also angling but one cannot overlook the fact that his mother started life as a scullery maid!"

Thoreau and Mathilde are in the breakfast room at the front of their house overlooking the Atlantic Ocean, their mother and father watching them solemnly from portraits on the wall. There had been other siblings, a brother who died of consumption at twenty and two sisters who married, and now only he and Mathilde remain.

They share this modest but comfortable house as well as their lives, an arrangement that Thoreau thinks quite suitable; their needs are few and Mathilde runs the house well and is a companionable listener on nights when fatigue or the weather prevent him from venturing out to his club. Thoreau imagines that Mathilde must be content as well: this is her childhood home and is surely preferable to a convent, the traditional refuge of unwanted women, or to the house of one of their sisters with their many noisy children.

"So yes, I am well placed," Thoreau concludes in satisfaction. "The king specifically called for 'the most notable persons' from each town and that is a position I doubtless occupy in Bordeaux."

"Yes, brother," says Mathilde dutifully, scraping a thin drizzle of butter over her toast. "But what about Saint Domingue?"

Thoreau shakes his head and sips his chocolate, almost burning his tongue. Infernal newfangled pot resting over an open flame, keeping drinks hot long after they should have warmed! "Saint Domingue be dashed! I would rather stay here and participate in the future of France."

The proposed mission to Saint Domingue was certainly an interesting opportunity and Thoreau had been somewhat flattered (and surprised) to be asked. A decade ago, he had accepted a mission from the *Académie Royale des Arts et des Sciences de Bordeaux*, ever preoccupied with maritime commerce, to visit Guadeloupe and study the possibility for ginger cultivation there. He had spent almost a year on that island at the tip of the West Indies but the trip had not been a success. Professionally, yes; his conclusions were well received and many were appreciative of the report that he presented over the course of several nights of dwindling attendance in front of the *Académie*. Some complained of its length but seven hundred pages was scarce time to unravel all the intricacies of that humble plant!

But there had also been... an incident.

Guadeloupe, 1775. Over a decade ago but the shame still stinks fresh. His scientific mind had run away with him, dragging him to places he never thought to go. Strange things happen in strange places, Thoreau often tells himself; he cannot be held responsible for what happened!

He purchased a slave boy—well, if he were being honest, not so much a boy as a youth, a strapping fellow that Thoreau developed a certain fondness for. Finally giving in to an urge that followed him all around that cursed island, he made the purchase and allowed himself certain liberties with the boy. All in the interests of science, of course; Thoreau had noted that while there was much literature on the sexual nature of the African woman, there was scant work out there on the sexual potency of the African man. Perhaps due to the disinterest of most writers in that subject.

Thoreau was determined to rectify that lack and, alongside his investigation into ginger, he pursued his side passion. Though passion was the wrong word—a hobby more like, a scientific hobby... an *interest*. Well, suffice to say he was lulled into a false sense of security by the laxness and lascivious nature of Guadeloupean society and had allowed himself to believe there were no bounds. Alas, when the youth had turned up dead after an excess of... well, there were raised eyebrows and some public opprobrium which had followed him back to Bordeaux.

The opportunity to visit Saint Domingue had surprised Thoreau but perhaps the cloud of disgrace that he fancied hung over him since Guadeloupe was only in his imagination. He was about to accept when this new and far more exciting opportunity arose.

"To be a part of the Estates General! Think—I may meet the king! And I might even see the queen," Thoreau adds, seeking words to interest Mathilde but his sister only wrinkles her nose. Like most French she is not an admirer of their Austrian queen, even now that Marie Antoinette, after an awkward and scandalous decade involving rumors about the king's potency and her own whoredom, has done her duty and produced two heirs. Thoreau is mildly troubled by the disrespect shown to the Queen, not just by Mathilde but by society at large. But such is modern life, he decides.

In anticipation of the Estates General selection, Thoreau practices his speech throughout the week, pacing in excitement: *Law studied under du Mont... vouched for by leading men of the* Académie... *experience with scientific methodology... the respectable lineage of both parents, his mother's connection to the Duforts.*

"Too long?" he asks. Mathilde is sitting patiently and the clock shows almost an hour has passed.

"Not at all," she replies, a trifle doubtfully.

At the selection meeting he sees just the right amount of interest and even some polite applause at the conclusion of his speech. As he makes his way back to his seat, he receives modest congratulations, though he does notice that several men appear to be asleep.

"And how does your experience in Guadeloupe pertain to the issue at hand?" calls the lawyer Berquier from the crowd. There is an undercurrent of challenge to the vile man's words.

Thoreau stops and splutters. "Guadeloupe! But that... a *scientific* investigation and as I explained, the precepts of science can be applied to all manner of investigations... ginger! Deductive *theory*..." Thoreau trails off to silence in the hall. They know, he thinks in panic. He mops his cheeks, sweaty despite the chill in the hall, and settles in his seat.

"What does your wife think of it?" comes a low whisper. Thoreau stares straight ahead. Berquier takes the podium next but Thoreau can't listen through the thundering in his ears and the vigorous thumping of his heart. He must think of something, a witty retort, a quip to wound just as Berquier had wounded him. His mother a scullery maid! *Crawl on your knees*, Thoreau thinks in a panic, but he hasn't the time to develop his slur properly because too soon—less than five minutes!—Berquier finishes to much applause. Thoreau exits swiftly through a side door.

"A scullery maid!" Thoreau shrieks later to Mathilde. "What does a man like that have to contribute to government? Berquier risks sullying the name of the entire Third Estate! That would be like a... a *baker* participating!"

"I thought the Third Estate included *all* men who are not nobles or clergy?" asks Mathilde. In her hands knitting needles and fuzzy wool, soon to be a house cap for their maid. Thoreau stares at her: Is that sarcasm under her voice? But no, surely not. It is just his agitation, making him see insults and barbs where none exist. That voice from the back of the hall. *What does your wife think of it?* He has no wife, in fact never married, and that allusion...

"Yes, certainly," Thoreau snaps, "but it is understood that such men... decision-making is... education required... Oh, never mind!"

The wind rattles through the shutters. Soon it will be November, bringing winter and all that is bleak in the world. The next week de Sèze, Duforge and Berquier are elected as the representatives for Bordeaux and Thoreau is filled with a ferocious disappointment that he is to be denied his place in history. At night he lets doubts creep in and a tear dribbles down his face. When was the last time he wept?

"I have decided I shall accept the Society's commission," Thoreau announces bitterly the next day, still trying to come to terms with his defeat. "If they wish to sideline me, then so be it. I shall remove myself to Saint Domingue, to the very periphery of the world!"

*

Preparations are underway while Thoreau follows the events in Paris as best he can from Bordeaux and his perch of wounded pride. Initially, Thoreau supported what they are now calling the Revolution: the need for a more equitable taxation system and the representation of learned and propertied men in the country's government were admirable goals. It was—should have been—a movement of the bourgeoisie, for the bourgeoisie. He was as euphoric as the next man when the Third Estate banded together at Versailles and declared they would not leave until a constitution was created and approved.

Soon, however, events in Paris start to distress him. Within four months of the convening of the Estates General come the storming of the Bastille, the abolition of the nobility and of feudal rights, and the Great Terror where chateaux were attacked and papers burned. The establishment of a new government known as the National Assembly and yet more mobs, marching on Versailles and forcing the removal of the royal family to Paris.

Then the *Declaration of the Rights of Man*, a document Thoreau initially lauded as progressive and long overdue. Alas, it had never occurred to him that men of the lower orders would also take on that document as their own and would then indeed take over the entire movement!

All these events, coming fast and furious, seem to hint at something darker that he can only dimly discern; something that threatens the very basis of a good and just society. Thoreau cannot help but think that if *he* were at Versailles, instead of the scurrilous Berquier, things might have turned out differently! He might have used his powers of oration and perfect logic to quickly establish a constitution and preserve peace and order.

As 1790 gives way to a blustery and cold 1791, Thoreau's departure nears. He does not pay much heed to news from Saint Domingue of the colored uprising and the gruesome execution of the mulatto Vincent Ogé. Paris, indeed, dismisses the brief revolt as a failed royalist plot, claiming those loyal to the king and not to the National Assembly had funded the coloreds to rise up and spread destruction in their most prosperous colony.

Regardless, it isn't a matter of professional interest to Thoreau: his mission centers on the slaves of the colony, not on the half-caste coloreds with their pretensions of whiteness and designs on French citizenship. Thoreau's mission is to study ways to improve the appallingly low birth rates and high death rates of slaves in Saint Domingue. Above all the other colonies of the Caribbean—French, English, Dutch and other—the slaves in Saint Domingue perish quickly. It is well established wisdom that working the slaves to death, extracting their souls from them as crushers might extract juice from sugarcane, is the only path to real profit: *rational extraction*, the planters smugly contend.

Thoreau is shocked to learn the statistics: half of new arrivals dead within five years, less than a quarter of live births attaining adolescence. The more he considers his mission, the more appealing it becomes. Though very few—just a smattering of voices from England and the radical *Les Amis des Noires* in France—are calling for the abolition of slavery, there is growing consensus that better conditions for slaves is generally desirable and in step with the emerging humanitarianism that is starting to rustle the ground in Europe.

Some more fanatical French—mostly lower folk, Thoreau believes—are even calling on their fellow man to stop using sugar or drinking coffee that comes from Saint Domingue, claiming it is drenched with blood. Absurd, of course—one cannot forgo one's own luxuries for something that one is not responsible for—but it does perhaps point to a changing mindset.

As radical factions with more interest in the ideology of the *Declaration of the Rights of Man* take over the French government, the issue of slavery comes to the forefront. If the unthinkable were to happen and the slave *trade* be abolished, as a growing chorus is demanding, then that would make the issue of the natural increase of the slave population ever more critical. It occurs to Thoreau that his mission of improved breeding fits neatly at the intersection of morality and economics, a place that is often troubling to find but very pleasing on arrival.

Thoreau even catches himself secretly wishing that the slave trade be abolished! Private thoughts only, of course; after a few too many debates with his fellow Bordelais turn ugly, he knows to keep his scandalous thoughts to himself.

"There can be no agriculture in Saint Domingue without slavery—we did not fetch half a million savages off the coast of Africa to bring them to the colony as French citizens!" snaps one of his friends, owner of five slave ships. "Though these are volatile times, we can trust the National Assembly would never be so foolish as to abolish the trade that is so vital for France's economy!"

But, reflects Thoreau in private, Paris has been doing a lot of foolish things recently, including granting Protestants and comedians the right to vote. And Denmark, though a small and unimportant country with just two little colonies in the West Indies, recently announced they would abolish the slave trade. So perhaps...

Finally, everything is ready: letters of introduction written (on new letterhead—the *Académie Royale* is now the *Académie Nationale*); medicines stockpiled; an itinerary developed and passage booked, and all the paper and ink he might need in case such luxuries are hard to find out there.

Time to move forward and embrace his work!

Surprisingly, his sister Mathilde insists on accompanying him. Thoreau agrees with some reluctance—his dear sister does not understand the exigencies of travel and her motivation is somewhat of a mystery. But then again, his sister has always been a bit of a mystery to him, and perhaps her company will be welcome.

Their ship departs Bordeaux in July of 1791 for six weeks of brisk ocean travel. Amongst the fellow passengers are a number of émigrés from the upheavals in France, traveling to Saint Domingue to see the plantations that once allowed their elegant life at Versailles.

Around the end of August their ship approaches Cap-Français, known as *The Paris of the Antilles*, though some joke that that sobriquet is unfair to Cap-Français, Paris now being in such a degraded state. Those returning to Saint Domingue boast of the elegant city with its theaters, libraries, taverns, billiard rooms and chocolate shops, all supporting a general ease of life and sophistication. Two scientific societies, including the Chamber of Agriculture which is funding Thoreau's mission in collaboration with Bordeaux; a gracious cathedral that spans two blocks and holds the highest bell tower in all the West Indies; a printing press and two weekly newspapers. Rich sugar plantations surround the city and one passenger proudly lists all the planters who own four-horse carriages, and describes the Marquis de Lafitte's house with indoor plumbing!

Their ship draws closer and the passengers gather on deck to celebrate their arrival. The captain promises a bottle of fine claret to the passenger first credited with spying the broad mountains that rise behind the plains around Cap-Français. But instead of such views, all they see is a thick cloud blackening the horizon. Gradually the rambunctious passengers, half-drunk on champagne and excitement, fall silent. No cannon shots fire out, the traditional greeting when a French ship is spotted.

"An inferno on earth," someone whispers as the ship sails closer. They realize they are looking at enormous fires covering the hills and all the land in between, the smell and the smoke stinging their eyes even as they hover off shore.

"An earthquake?"

"God's wrath!"

"The whole plain is aflame!" Some of the women begin to weep in fear and confusion. Mathilde clutches his arm as Thoreau looks on in befuddlement. What is happening?

Then one passenger voices the vile reality, clamoring to be let in: "Insurrection," he murmurs. "The slaves."

His words hang in the air as an explosion—a rum refinery perhaps—roars through the dense smoky skies, a sound greater than anything Thoreau has ever heard.

Originally Thoreau's intent had been to lodge in the civilization of Cap-Français and confine his study to the sugar plantations surrounding the city but with the plains of the north now transformed into an enormous charnel house, that is patently impossible. The city is safe but the black hordes outside are threatening to overrun the barricades and when all able-bodied white men are pressed into military service, Thoreau and Mathilde quickly depart for the West Province, as yet unaffected by any troubles.

*

In their year on the island there has been the usual indignities and little miseries associated with travel, as well as several changes in itinerary occasioned by smaller revolts or plantation-level skirmishes, giving a hopscotch pattern to their journey. But all in all, things go smoothly; their greatest travails to date are a severe toothache of Mathilde's, only alleviated by pulling two of her remaining teeth, and the occasional hysteria (from both of them, Thoreau must admit) over the enormous spiders known as *tarantulas* that keep turning up in inopportune places, and once in his wig chest.

And ah! how much he is learning! Such an interesting society, full of provocative contradictions that simply beg for a scientific mind to impose order on it. Saint Domingue has no comparison amongst the other colonies of the Caribbean—French, English or Spanish: it is by far the largest and richest, ten times the size of Guadeloupe and Martinique combined. This is no small sugar island but a large, commerce-oriented economy that reminds Thoreau of the industrial centers of Bordeaux or Nantes. The rum refineries; the lime kilns and brickworks; the thriving wharfs where millions of pounds of sugar, coffee, indigo and cotton depart for Europe. Saint Domingue is—or was—a literal market for the world. The year before their arrival, two thousand ships of all nations docked in her harbors and she exported even more than the new and robust United States of America.

The further they travel from Cap-Français the less their hosts seem to care about the northern slave rebellion. All are shocked, certainly, but there exists a common understanding that it was simply an unfortunate incident that will not be repeated: mere banditry, is the message. Each plantation owner believes himself too benevolent, his slaves too happy and too bound by feelings of loyalty to ever turn against him.

"We feed them, we clothe them!" are common refrains that Thoreau hears. "We protect them, tutor them as we might young children. Can you imagine my horse turning on me suddenly? My pig chomping the hand that feeds? Impossible!"

And besides, the blacks are scarcely capable of organizing themselves! There are many possible culprits behind the rebellion: the Spanish, the British, the coloreds, the Royalists, the Jacobins (as those supporting the Revolution in France are beginning to be called). A range of suspects but all are in agreement that the revolt is a plot funded by someone or something determined to ruin Saint Domingue. Behind the slaves is some larger, more sophisticated body; alone the slaves are not capable of destroying the richest colony in the world! Surely not?

As they travel, Thoreau ponders what he comes to consider the fundamental question about the northern rebellion: Is it a mere revolt, or is it the beginning of something larger and more terrifying? He remembers the declaration by the Third Estate at Versailles that they would not disband until they had a constitution. A simple act of protest that at the time was noted, but not overly so, yet which turned out to be the starting point for sweeping, historic changes. Is the same thing happening here? Does the northern rebellion represent a fundamental shift, cracking open a rotten society that has been breaking apart for quite some time?

Daily news comes of more unrest, mostly plantation-level but also some infiltrating the towns, the mulattoes now with the slaves, the slaves against the mulattoes, the mulattoes for themselves, a third of the north still in rebel hands. Still his hosts insist the revolts are mere hiccups and everything will return to normal once more troops arrive from France. Most whites continue to consider the mulattoes and their quest for political equality to be a far greater threat to the future of the colony than the slaves are.

Thoreau finds this attitude most stark as he makes his way to the remote Grand'Anse region on the southern peninsula. This area has remained largely free of unrest and, with just one barbaric exception in the town of Jérémie, remains a haven of relative peace. Bound on two sides by the sea and on two others by high mountain ranges, the Grand'Anse is called *The Desert* by other colonists, its inhabitants considered poor country cousins. Here, it almost feels as though the rest of the colony is not on fire.

The planters of the Grand'Anse seem to Thoreau to be most self-interested and determined to keep commerce going at all costs. They are well organized and while heavily anti-royalist (a catch-all for anti-French), they are not patriots, as those supporting the revolution in France are called. In truth, Thoreau does not know what they stand for, apart from their own self-preservation.

The Clearing
11 am

Brac rides to the sunbaked clearing where the slaves are still gathered under the apricot tree. This trouble means another day of work lost and God knows money is tight around here. Not that he should care; Madame Rose never gives him a share of the profits when times are good, so it matters not to him if times are bad. If they don't make the ship in Jérémie they will have to warehouse the sacks or send them further afield to Port-au-Prince. The additional cost is not his concern.

After Monsieur Marcel's death, Brac aspired to marry the attractive young widow—and her plantation—but the stingy bitch was having none of it. Madame Rose was infused with the casual snobbery of the plantation class, though Brac knows her uncle was a saddle-maker in Nantes. A saddle-maker!

From his mule, Brac considers the scene before him, noticing with disapproval that the men are mostly in the shade of the tree. Three slave houses ring the clearing, as well as the warming hut where the four shivering Aradas are still confined. Highly unlikely the culprit is among them. Brac knew immediately they were low quality but despite his advice Madame Rose went ahead and bought them. And what a disaster, Brac thinks with some satisfaction. Two dead immediately, almost 4,000 *livres* gone as smoke in the air! The four remaining ones keening constantly and he noticed one of them has six toes.

In Brac's eyes, Madame Rose has no business running a

plantation. Not that her sex makes her ineffective; widows are common here and they often run their plantations well, the satin glove hiding the chain mail fist. Up near Limonade, a female planter was notorious for making her slaves eat their own ears as punishment for running away and once tossed her cook into the fire for burning a cake. Her savagery was so legendary that the authorities had to intervene and ship her discretely back to France, an honor previously reserved for men.

But Madame Rose—she is far too generous and abhors violence of any kind. It is common practice in the Grand'Anse for slaves to feed themselves from their own provision plots and Madame Rose allows, even encourages them, to sell any surplus at market. A practice that can only engender dangerous feelings of independence! And incentives are not aligned—if no threat of starvation follows them, why should slaves care for their masters' profit? On the sugar plantation where Brac worked before, they had a famine every few years when the price of provisions for the slaves—imported rice or flour—rose too high. Brac believes that once slaves have suffered true hunger and survived, they are better workers for it.

Brac suspects Madame Rose's benevolence is not from infection with new ideas of equality or enlightenment, but rather from simple apathy. Monsieur Marcel, who hired him and La Fleur over a decade ago, better understood how things should be but since his death Bayardel has been slowly sliding into chaos. Madame Rose's list of negligence is long: refusing to repair the mill, resulting in a poor grade of hulled beans. Putting off replanting the east field where the aged coffee bushes give less fruit than a barren oak. Keeping no proper doctor on staff, despite the endless eye infections and half the field workers infected with yaws; Brac has even seen them suppurating into the coffee beans. And those six—four—Aradas: to not care about the mix of slaves! Prudence mandates avoiding too many of the same tribe or language group, for fear of collusion or worse. Buying six from one tribe, even possibly from one village!

Brac snorts and dismounts his mule. He is in a foul mood— not because of the murder of Plunkett and the loss of a day's work—but due to something more indefinable, an angry unease that has been digging at him the last few months. Everything about his life combines in general dissatisfaction; he is approaching fifty and God knows men who work as hard as he rarely live long in the tropics. Over a decade ago Brac was glad of the move to Bayardel and the promotion to manager. But now he's reduced to the work of an overseer and not welcome to dine in the big house! Somehow, that last demotion seems most reflective of his life so far.

Brac is a man who has been successful in none of his pursuits. Thirty years in Saint Domingue and he has only one slave—his housekeeping mistress Ernestine, whose enormous girth makes her unsuitable for hard work. He has no progeny, no talents and little of movable furniture or other assets, eking out a living on 800 *livres* a year, too much of which he spends in the gambling houses in Dame Marie or Apricots. Brac feels his failure keenly, especially when men from similar backgrounds have risen to prosperity. Though these days it is hard to profit like men of previous generations did, what with the coloreds taking everything for themselves and too many fortune seekers from Europe, all looking for riches on too small an island.

Like many of his class, Brac is hoping that the revolution in France will make things better, even though the mechanics of just how that will happen remain hazy. Certainly, the *petits blancs* have taken control in some towns and banished the Royalist governors, even before France sent out two new Jacobin replacements. But those new governors seem mostly to care about the coloreds and the slaves, two groups hated by the *petits blancs*.

But more positive changes are bound to come.

"I'll search that one first," Brac says to La Fleur and spits towards the larger men's house. He takes off his jacket and flings it over to his *commandeur*, feeling immensely annoyed and sour. Despite what he said to Madame Rose, Brac thinks it doubtful Plunkett was killed by a slave. Brac knows some of what Plunkett was involved in—his dealings with the British and the blackmail of that notary last year—but an ill-placed solidarity with the dead man keeps him from voicing his opinion. Let's just have some fun, thinks Brac spitefully, and Madame can suffer the loss of another slave.

The men on the ground start a low, eerie humming.

"Shut up!" Brac cries and La Fleur flicks his whip blindly,

catching Michel on the side of his face. The murmuring continues—it seems to be coming from the women now—and Brac feels a frisson of fear as he often does when the slaves make any unified movement.

"Get them to shut up," Brac shouts, shaking off his fear and striding towards the house.

*

Appollon watches Brac mount the steps to the house where he and thirty others sleep. He closes his eyes and leans back against the trunk of the apricot tree, a chance for some moments of rest after his sleepless night. The low humming around him is soothing but not enough.

To be so close... and then that white man turns up dead. Appollon saw him yesterday at the stables where his son had been loitering all week. Plunkett talked to his boy then washed his face in the mules' trough before setting off for dinner at the big house. *Goat,* Appollon heard him say and he had disliked the idea of Jeannette cooking for the man.

Now Plunkett is dead and his death is causing this disastrous search. A small leak can sink the greatest of ships and the murder of a white man is a great gash in the hull. Appollon's throat tightens. He closes his eyes, opens them again, watches a silky white blossom float down from the branches above. There will be a full moon tonight, the silvery light guiding the way for what is to come.

Appollon was working on a sugar plantation near Les Cayes when, two years ago, the world around him started to change. Rumors reached the slaves of unrest in far-off France, the news coming from gossip on market days or from visiting slaves, hired for work from other plantations or accompanying their masters. Magazines and illegal pamphlets from the *Les Amis des Noires* found their way to the island and out to the slave cabins where some can read. Black domestics went to France and brought back new ideas. House slaves listened at the tables of their masters as they discussed the changes in France, oblivious to the eager, hostile ears that surrounded them.

The slaves knew that in France there were white men who

support freedom for slaves. They knew about the document called the *Declaration of the Rights of Man*, which said all men are equal, and should that not include them? They heard persistent rumors that the fat white king—a downtrodden man, they say—has decreed that slaves must only work three days for their masters, four for themselves.

All this knowledge was thrown like wood chips into flames, causing the fire to crackle ever higher. Perhaps the time was coming to cast off the shackles that kept them enslaved; a piece of iron is just a piece of iron and cannot hold them forever.

Then news broke of the great slave revolt up north. Inspired, visions from priests and shamans were passed from plantation to plantation: all the whites in the sea, drowning as they deserve; earthquakes and a great inferno that would burn for twenty nights. Unrest spread to the plains of Les Cayes where a band of rebel slaves waged war on the countryside from their mountain stronghold at Les Platons. Appollon dreamt of joining them but before he could his plantation was pillaged and all remaining slaves sold. He was brought to Bayardel but from here he can still see the same mountains that hold his dreams. And a few months ago, men from those mountains came with a plan for the Grand'Anse.

A plan Appollon eagerly embraced.

But now—Brac can hardly miss what he is going to find under Appollon's bed and then it is the end for him.

Why was he so stupid? Jeannette gave him the knife last week—a gesture that told him that though she hated what he might be involved with, she still supported him. Appollon hid the knife under his pallet. The local constabulary from Dame Marie, staffed by surly coloreds and captained by the white Bassompierre, had been at Bayardel just the week before. While the coloreds performed a desultory search of the houses, Bassompierre enjoyed a drink with Madame in the big house. Their visit had given Appollon confidence: chances were low they would come again so soon. How was he to know that a white man would be *murdered* here?

Appollon wills himself to breathe in, out, squarely and surely. He stares at the warped wood walls of his house, Brac now inside. Acceptance. We have failed, but only on this plantation.

The rest may continue as planned.

And we were so close, thinks Appollon sadly. He decides he will fight. He will slay Brac before the man ever sets another hand on him and though it will hasten his own death, it is but a death foretold by what lies beneath his mattress.

*

Inside the men's house, the smell of manure, mixed with something darker, greets Brac. Animals, he thinks, and the pigpen slides into his mind. He walks the length of the room, lined with some thirty makeshift hurdle beds lined with palm leaves, a couple of hammocks and a few baskets of personal possessions. Shards of weak sunlight come through the uneven slats. A cat meows and tries to rub against him, but he kicks it away. Too many on this plantation. Not like where Brac worked before, where both slaves and cats were in constant competition for rats and lizards to eat.

Brac pushes a pallet with his foot and dust swirls up. There are no windows and the open door doesn't give enough light to see much. He goes to the door and tells La Fleur to bring a lantern from the kitchen. The slaves are still humming softly and at his words seem to sway towards him.

We'll see how you sway this afternoon, Brac thinks grimly. It will be like the old times on the sugar plantation: there the vast slave gangs were controlled by cruelty and oh, the magic and talent of it all! Men tied to ant hills, tossed bound into swamps at the mercy of mosquitos and caimans, or thrown in boiling cauldrons of cane syrup. Dogs trained to eat men. Runaways nailed by their ears to the carts that brought them home.

And there can be no limits imposed when dealing with a slave who murdered a white man.

Jeannette emerges from the kitchens with a lantern. The low humming of the slaves ceases and they all watch her as she sashays across the clearing. Brac has the odd impression that the world has stopped and just for her. How still and silent everything is today; even the sea's lapping, usually the background of their lives, is oddly absent. Brac backs into the house as Jeannette comes up the steps, holding the lantern high and looking him in the eye.

Once inside, she stares at him. *She knows*, Brac thinks in alarm, *she knows*, but he grabs the lantern and pushes away his unease. He strides the length of the cabin and when he turns, she is still standing at the door, the white light of the morning behind her silhouette. Bitch. Nothing but a helpless slave woman, even if they sing of her beauty for miles. And he is the manager here—not her owner, but good enough.

"You," Brac says, as though he doesn't know her name, as though he hasn't had her in his house or in the pigpen so many nights. "You—help me check the pallets."

Jeannette closes the door and the lantern's flickering orange flames spread through the room. She goes to the first bed and bends over, slowly, deliberately, still watching him. She pushes the pallet over and he sees right down her blouse to her breasts. She wears an old skirt of Madame's but with no petticoats or stockings; the thin material floats around her thighs and half reveals the promise beneath. Jeannette straightens up, then leans down again. She looks at Brac over her shoulder with what he could swear is a smile.

Brac knows what she is doing but still his crotch throbs in anticipation. Usually Jeannette is scared of him or at least pretends to be. She does all she can to avoid him and always suffers his rough riding without a word. But now Brac feels a milky desire coming off her, pulling him towards her. He stares at her, breathing carefully, and she rises and turns to him, her eyes limpid and large—and yes, she is smiling!—and Brac knows then that she wants him.

"I know what you're doing," he says, striding towards her, his mouth dry. "You think I'll jump you like a goat and not wonder what you're hiding?"

Jeannette smiles.

"I know what you're doing," Brac repeats and realizes he is whispering. Good mother of God, she is beautiful—dark and smooth, with large eyes and full lips and curves to make a man weak. All that a woman should be and now she is looking at him with what can only be desire.

"Yes," she whispers back. She speaks in an old slave dialect he doesn't understand but her voice is molasses, warm and inviting. "Of course, you know what I am doing. You know."

He has never seen Jeannette smile like this. He always thought her magnificent in her sulkiness but now it occurs to him that he was missing something. He turns her around and pushes her down, fumbling with his breeches. She wants it, she really wants it, he'll get it over with and back to work. Not that there should be anything to find but she doesn't know that. Brac enters her and gasps in pleasure.

"I'm not going to miss anything because of this, you bitch, you think you can fool me," he says over and again as he thrusts into her. "Fool me." Jeannette starts to move as well, pushing against him in a strange motion that makes Brac want to prolong the push rather than head straight for the delicious end. God, but it feels good.

"Not miss anything," he pants, burying his head in her neck and smelling yeast and sweat. "Oh God, I love you. I know what you're doing."

Sated, Brac pulls Jeannette down next to him and revels in the glow of her body. His mind is blank and empty, completely at peace. What he wouldn't give for a drink right now and he imagines the sweet scorch of rum down his throat. He could order her to fetch some but he doesn't want to let her, or this moment, go.

"I know," Jeannette says, though he hasn't said anything. "I know."

She strokes his head and Brac feels like weeping under her touch. It pulls forth a memory from the faintest edge of his mind: his childhood and a hand stroking him, warm cuddles and more. His mother, probably, before she died. And now here it is again, so sudden and unexpected. He wants to lie like this forever, even though the smell of piss is overpowering and something is biting his arm. Now Jeannette is whispering to him tenderly that he is a strong man, a stallion, and that he carried her to joy when he rode her. "And I know," she says again, still stroking his head and looking at him with such tenderness that for a moment he thinks he could go again.

"You're a fool," Brac whispers back. "We could have had this all along."

Jeannette doesn't answer, just holds him and continues to murmur until he falls asleep.

They stay like this for some time.

*

Appollon saw Jeannette walk through the clearing, holding her head and lantern high. He knows what she is going to do and he knows that he is saved. Relief overcomes him and he exhales, bows his head, breathes again.

Saved, but only in the cruelest of ways. Now he is in that special hell, robbed of the one thing a man should know beyond doubt: that his woman is his. That certainty never exists on this cursed island, an insupportable truth Appollon refuses to confront—like glancing at the sun, he can only look at it for a second before turning away.

I'll cut off his cock, Appollon thinks suddenly. Every man on this plantation has his dreams of how they would kill the whites and Appollon has many times pictured Brac impaled by a stake through his stomach, watching the mayhem around him as he slowly expires. But no, Appollon decides, squeezing his eyes shut: I'll cut off Brac's dick, stuff it in his mouth and let him bleed to death that way.

He picks up a white apricot flower, and pulls off one waxy petal. Saved, perhaps, but how can they do what is planned for tonight if they are kept tethered here like goats in a pen, awaiting their own slaughter? La Fleur goes for a piss behind the women's house and Appollon seeks out the other men who know about tonight: Capidon and Pierre, and the other *commandeur* Louis. Appollon keeps his face blank and nods ever so slightly, trying to reassure them across the space. *We are fine. The plan is fine.*

"Oh, what is happening?" giggles the spy Garifou, hoping for some nugget he can share with his masters. The man sitting behind him yanks on his neck rope and he is silenced with a yowl of protest.

How can they make the night come faster? The day stretches before Appollon, a void to be filled with everything that could go wrong. The sun climbs higher as the morning approaches noon. All is quiet, the eerie silence only broken by a bird trilling a three-point song high above in the branches of the apricot tree. A brief patter of wind blows across the clearing and rustles the branches; more of the white flowers float lazily down.

La Fleur comes back and sings that Brac and Jeannette are searching *hard* inside the house. He laughs. Appollon stares at him and when the dog looks away, quickly, Appollon knows the slave driver is afraid. La Fleur might be stupid but he knows the hatred the other slaves have for him, and must surely sense some of what is coming. That fool and his master Brac, stupid dogs, drunk every night on rum and sharing that foul, fat woman. They will get what they deserve.

Jeannette also doesn't know—doesn't want to know—what is planned for tonight and Appollon thinks he understands her reluctance to get involved. Bayardel is the only home she has ever known and she is nearing that age when a woman's adventurous spirit, always so much paler than a man's, disappears completely. Like many women, she is chained to this plantation by the safety it offers and the children she loves. Men are free of those invisible chains, so they are the ones who must fight.

Though it kills him, Appollon must be thankful for what Jeannette is doing inside the dark house. She is doing it for him, he reminds himself, and she will consider it no more than a passing nuisance. That was something Appollon saw in Jeannette from the beginning, how her beauty and steady heart remained untouched by the squalor around her. Like a palm tree growing from the muck of a swamp, always tall and elegant; she may sway in the wind but nothing breaks her. No matter what life throws at her, she accepts everything without complaint. Was it because she was born here, in captivity? Appollon sometimes tries to understand how she sees her world but it remains mostly a mysterious place.

Appollon never tells Jeannette about his own past, the one that is buried deep down inside him. Sometimes he wonders how she might react if knew. With understanding and respect? Or, if there are limits to her tolerance, with repugnance?

AKANDE'S JOURNEY

THE SLAVE COAST OF AFRICA TO
SAINT DOMINGUE
1784-1792

Akande's mother was the laundress and occasional whore of a French official stationed at the Fort of Whydah, flush by the Bight of Benin. As a young woman, pregnant with her son, she was captured in one of the endless wars that cursed her homeland and brought to Whydah, a dusty coastal town of ten thousand souls, peopled by soldiers, traders and half-caste merchants, dominated by a central marketplace for food and humans.

Flanking the town were several stone forts, some of them two hundred years old, all of them protecting European interests in the area. Akande's mother was sold to a petty official at the French fort, waiting out his days in heat and boredom until he could be recalled to life and Europe. Though the slave trade was mostly in the hands of private merchants who worked concessions in the interior then sold their cargo to French ships, they operated under the protection of the French crown.

The French fort was on a spit of land to the west of town, rising against a backdrop of English, French, Dutch and Portuguese slave ships that docked out in the wide bay, sometimes waiting there for weeks or even months for enough black gold to fill their holds. Akande grew up playing and fighting and running through the crannies of the fort, learning life and languages from the captives held in the barracoons—as the slave pits were known—as well as the languages of the traders and other Europeans. Akande called himself a Nago, because that was what the whites called people from the lands where his mother came from. A multitude of ethnicities passed through the forts at Whydah but the slavers didn't care much for nuances and grouped them mostly as Ibos or Aradas.

When Akande was fourteen his mother hugged him but he pulled away—he felt himself too old to be petted like a child and he was also jealous of her new baby, a small white grub born the week before. They were in their shack in one of the courtyards, beside the wells; outside wet sheets flapped in the wind, bringing in their odor of lemon and lye.

Akande knows his mother is dying. A witch doctor prescribes her a soup of snake and spices that the Frenchman Chalumette agreed to pay for. The soup rallies his mother some, the lull before the storm, but still she is dying. And the pale baby too. Just as well; those mongrel babies are cursed.

All day, feeling her mortality coming closer, his mother tells Akande stories about his father, killed in a dispute before his birth, and about her own father who lived for more than eighty moons in a village a day's walk from the great city of Ketu. Akande half-listens; his mother's past has nothing to interest him. He doesn't want a dull country life of farming, instead preferring the energy of the ocean and the excitement, revolts, cruelty and strange moments of fun in Whydah. Life in the villages just sounds boring.

"Chalumette," his mother whispers and he sees her eyes growing white, her strength eaten away. "Chalumette has great plans for you. Tomorrow you will become a man."

In the morning he is bought up to Chalumette's office, a room previously only seen peeking through the keyhole while playing with the other children.

"My boy," says Chalumette, though Akande knows he is not his father. He has never been this close to the great man before; his mother always attended to him in his private quarters on the third floor of the fort, a place so far away from Akande's life it could have been on the moon. There is something in the man's pale gray eyes that makes Akande shiver and he thinks of the stories he had heard of water turning hard when cold enough.

"My son, it is time to stop playing and start working."

Akande nods, suddenly tongue-tied.

"You're a fine lad. What age?"

"Fourteen years, sir," he manages to croak, standing taller.

"Passable French," chuckles Chalumette. The gossip in the fort is that he is a cruel man—cries are often heard from the women he keeps for his pleasure, Akande's mother among them. "Your mother tells me you are good with languages?"

"Yes sir; I can speak many languages." Chalumette has an ugly scar running across his cheek and his coat is fine white linen. Well washed, thinks Akande with pride then remembers his mother is dying.

"Good, good." Chalumette plays with the lace of his cuffs as he contemplates the boy before him. "You'll be a strapping buck soon. I'd get top dollar for you, now, wouldn't I?"

Chalumette chuckles and Akande doesn't know whether to laugh or run. By tradition, none of the Africans who work in the forts are enslaved but this man is still his master.

"Yes, time to work. I'll start you in the barracoons and helping the men with the rowing."

Akande swallows nervously and nods; he knew this day was coming and much as his mother had tried to hide him, Chalumette had remembered.

"You'll be a man," says Chalumette, rising and slapping him on the back. Akande beams even as he knows his carefree days of play and fun are over.

And so his new life begins: helping to herd convoys of captives into the barracoons where they are guarded until it is time to parade them for sale. Once sold, the slavers prefer their cargo to be held aboard ship, sometimes for months; revolts in the barracoons are even more common than on the ships. Akande helps load the prisoners onto small boats that are rowed out through the lagoons and crashing surf to the ships anchored offshore. Young and agile, Akande's job is to spear the ravenous sharks that lurk in the waters and ensure that their shackled cargo does not throw themselves overboard.

"Like this!" says Inch, another boy not much older than Akande. He gives Akande an iron shovel. "Smash at them, they'll get the message."

Akande nods nervously and tries to stand at attention in the rocking boat. That first day they don't see any sharks and the passage is smooth. They breach the surf and row past a ship flying the colors of the Danish flag—a small nothing country, Inch tells him, pointing to a red and white flag—then approach the hulk of the *Felicité*.

Everyone in the canoe falls silent as they near the giant ship, rising out of the sea like a mountain, so much bigger up close than it appeared from shore. Like a floating fort, thinks Akande, wondering at the witchcraft of the whites that could make this heavy thing stay afloat. As they near, the stench hits him with force—it has been anchored out here for months, filling its hungry belly. But what Akande thinks more dreadful than the smell is the sound the ship makes, creaking and straining at its anchor across a chain thicker than his leg.

"*Hup hup!*" cries Inch, whipping the first captive up a rope ladder. Akande sees white faces above him holding on to the rope. He shivers; thank the gods he does not have to make that fatal climb. One captive struggles so hard he gets tangled in the ropes and has to be cut free, then is bound and passed up like a trussed pig.

Akande holds his mother in his arms as she passes away, the baby grub dying a few days later. His youth and childhood are firmly behind him and soon he is wearing the white pants and shirts that mark him as a man and a worker, a small cog in the system that turns captives into fodder for the whites of the new world and their endless appetite for the strong men and women they find in Africa.

Gradually Akande finds his footing with the sharks

and learns to thwack them with excellent precision; he is proud to have only lost two women to their jaws. At first the captives in the barracoons, sensing a new and innocent heart, beg him to help them, to kill them, to tell their families where they were going and that soon they would return. When Inch sees how Akande is troubled by those pleas, he takes him under his wing and talks away his fears. "They are not people," spits Inch. "They are war criminals! And we know those who come from the west are scarcely human and eat their own babies; do not lose sleep over their fate. They deserve it."

Akande nods, uncertain. Though he knows that some of what Inch is saying is true, some of it is not. The prisoners are not all war captives or adulterers and thieves. Most are just village folk, captured in wars that aren't really wars but just excuses to plunder more black gold.

"Don't be fooled just because their skin is like ours," Inch would say. "They are not our people—we are no more brothers with them than we are with the whites. The whites are all the same ugly color but do you think they love each other?" Akande nods—last month the Dutch tried to burn the British fort down and he has certainly seen white men kill other white men.

Gradually Akande becomes inured to the cries and the suffering of the captives and learns to close his ears when he hears his mother's tongue. Not my people, he thinks, not my people. Sometimes he shouts at the captives not to worry, that they are just going to work for a few years before being brought home and that the white man will give them clothes finer than anything they have ever worn. Other times he cries that they should shut up, that they are doomed and the whites are bringing them across the seas to eat them.

Despite his hardening shell, once a captive pierces his carefully constructed shield and makes Akande feel what he thought he had lost: pity. And humanity.

"I am Sola!" The young man is about twenty, Akande's age, and has been shouting all night. He struggles against the piked walls of the pit when he sees Inch coming to unlock the gates. Akande makes the mistake of looking in his eyes and something in the man's face reminds him of his mother. "I am Sola! Send word to my father!"

The boy is speaking the tongue of Akande's people with the same intonation as his mother and even though Akande doesn't say anything, just hits him and throws him on the ground to bind him, this man Sola sees him.

"You are my people, my brother!" Sola pleads. "Help me, you must help me. Send word to my father!"

"Shut up!" cries Akande, even as he knows his voice will betray their common bond.

"I have a wife and son who need me. Without me they will starve!"

Sola has a crazed look on his face, the whites of his eyes bulging and contorted. There are five men to be loaded on to the boat this afternoon. It is a thick and humid day, and now Akande is in a bad mood; Sola's eyes have shown him something he does not want to see.

He thwacks the man with a shovel and cries out that if he doesn't shut up, he will toss him overboard to the sea monsters. There is one trailing the canoe; last week a young boy freed himself from the loose ropes and threw himself in.

Still Sola does not stop.

"My brother, please, for the love of our people, save me. I am Sola, from Ketu, my father's name is Taiwo, you are my brother. Please, please! Why are you doing this?"

Inch steadies the boat beside the black hulk of the ship and he and another worker start whipping the captives up the rope ladder.

"Don't be scared," says Akande, finally looking at the man. "Don't worry." I did it, he thinks in something almost like terror, I looked *it* straight on. He hears himself continuing: "You are just going to work for a few years on a farm. The whites will clothe you and give you food. Then you will come back."

The man falls silent and Akande sees tears in his eyes. "Please, my brother, please," Sola says, softer this time. "I don't want to go."

"I can't help you," says Akande and he doesn't hide the pity in his voice.

Now they are whipping a third man up the rope ladder. The ship creaks above them, waiting.

"Please—send word to my father! My wife, my son..."

Inch reaches over to grab Sola. "Get up!" he commands, then calls to the white faces above him. "A fine one coming."

"My name is Sola," cries the man one more time, shouting his soul to the wind, his words drowned now by the creaking of the boat. "I am Sola!" The whip lashes him up the ladder and soon he disappears into a sea of white hands, pulling him over the edge.

"Stupid man," says Inch.

That night Akande can't sleep. He gets up and looks in the cracked mirror that sits on a chest in his room, his face illuminated by moonlight. "I am Sola," he says softly, starting to cry at his reflection. "I am Sola."

*

When Akande was younger and his mother still alive, she would calm him when he complained about some small indignity or trouble. "Remember, my son," she would say. "Remember that your destiny is a ship that has already sailed. You cannot change what has happened or what will." She would comfort him thus when he railed against whatever turn of fate had ill-used him.

Later Akande thinks of the small trials she urged him to accept: the indignity of being beaten in a courtyard fight or the death of a pair of goats he had been set on raising to adulthood and riches. Such things seemed so unfair at the time. Little did he know then that his life's greatest injustice was waiting for him, just around the corner.

At the slave fort in Whydah, Akande works closely with French officials and traders from other European nations. He thinks he knows what a white man is, with their mottled skins that show emotion so easily, their pale eyes that reflect light like dirty water. But he doesn't know them as well as he thinks, and he doesn't see the betrayal coming. He is twenty-four, tall and muscular with quick eyes and strong arms when the French official who bought his mother is recalled to France.

"Thank you," smirks Chalumette. He is a bored man with a nose reddened from too much brandy and sun, disappointed by life. "Thank you. My intended has been my intended for so many years but now I can return to France with confidence and money to furnish the house that she set as a condition of her acceptance of my suit."

"You are blessed," murmurs Akande, struggling to understand the man's florid words. He is standing in Chalumette's office, one window open to the brilliant sea beyond, two of the fort's henchman alert behind him. "May you be blessed with a fruitful marriage."

"Ah, I will be, I will be, and some thanks is due to you."

One of the henchman steps forward and gives Akande a great blow across his back. He falls to his knees and hears the clink of chains behind him and knows what is happening. This man took his mother and gave her a pale child that killed her, and now he is taking Akande as well.

"We have evidence, found this morning, of the theft of my silver. You are under arrest," drawls Chalumette, barely summoning the strength for his lie. "You fetched a good price. That money will buy a most handsome china set and more to please my Marie Louise." He pulls a locket out and waves it in front of Akande's unseeing eyes. "You see how fair she is? Mighty fair."

"Inch! Inch!" cries Akande desperately when he is trussed and thrown into the boat. His friend averts his eyes and all he can say is: "Thief."

"It's not true!" wails Akande, trying to lunge toward his friend but a young boy with a shark shovel prods him back, hissing: "Thief." They pass the surf without incident and reach the side of the ship.

"One more for you!" calls Inch. "It's all Chalumette could find. He's Nago, if you care."

This ship—oh gods, not this one. Last week there was an uprising on board. During the morning when the captives were brought on deck to be cleaned and fed, a few overpowered a sailor and grabbed his musket. They succeeded in killing two more sailors before they were subdued. Punishing the slaves was considered more important than profit and the four men and one woman deemed the instigators were hung from the foremasts of the ship by their arms. All through the night their cries reached the shore.

Cursed ship, thinks Akande in terror, remembering his callous bet with Inch over whether or not the wailing would stop before dawn.

"He's a good one!" Akande hears a white sailor shout as he is hauled onto deck. "Number 22," calls out another and even through his haze of terror that number doesn't make sense—slaves are given numbers in the order they come on board and this ship has been here for three months. But then his number does make sense—it's one of the dead men. One that died and gave Akande his place.

Shortly the ship is underway, the door locked above him and his whole life shut out. Stuffed down in the deep, dark hold, inside the literal jaws of Hell, Akande hears the boat creak as it sets off, the French sailors singing a departure song as they leave the African coast behind. Akande sobs in defeat. His only solace is that he has no one he cares about left onshore and for only that he counts himself lucky.

*

Akande knows this ship is bound for Les Cayes in the southern part of Saint Domingue. The stories he has heard come back to haunt him; slaves are considered fortunate if they sail to England, where they will work in houses, or even if they sail to the American Colonies, where cotton and rice plantations wait. But a slave bound for Brazil or the West Indies means the horrors of life on a sugar plantation and within that frightful world, Saint Domingue lurks as a place of particular darkness.

The decomposing bodies of the five rebels, still hanging from the foremast, sway above them in the mornings when they are let out to be fed and cleaned. Down in the hold, Akande suffers the stench, the competition for food, the rolls of the ship through strong storms, the sores where his chains cut deep. The terror of seeing no shore when they come on deck, their whole world reduced to water on all horizons. The freezing nights when his body shakes as though with rage and men shout for fire and blankets. The endless cacophony of voices raised in the deadly hollow of the ship, the cries for love and country and insurrection, the pleas and the deranged singing. Some men turn to stone, some to their gods, while others take out their anger in screaming fits of rage. The man beside him loses a leg and is thrown overboard.

Because of Akande's language abilities, the other men turn to him as a leader and he finds some comfort in giving comfort to others. He counsels his fellow passengers about their fate and dampens the terror of those who are sure the ship will sink. He corrects the frightful notions they hold—that they are going to be sacrificed, or eaten, or their brains pressed into wax and their blood taken to fertilize fields—while keeping his knowledge of Saint Domingue secret.

"How do you know so many languages, brother?" a man asks one night and Akande is silent a while. Finally he says: "I come from the coast where many travelers pass. My father," Akande lies, and tries to imagine that man—why had he never listened to his mother's stories?—"said I drank up languages as others might drink water."

None of his fellow captives recognize Akande as one who guarded the barracoons or rowed them out to the ship at the start of their own journeys. Or so he believes and hopes.

*

Akande survives the passage over and undergoes that terrible transformation of millions before and after: taken as a man from Africa, he arrives in the New World a slave, reduced to a piece of property, an animal but with nimble fingers and the ability to follow orders.

When the ship finally anchors and the captives are

hustled on deck, Akande feels something like relief. He's heard the grim tales of lands where the sun never shines and the water is so cold it becomes hard, but the air that greets him here is warm and dense, somehow familiar. From the ship's deck he is sold with six of his ship-brothers and two women, destined for a sugar plantation half a day's walk away.

Roped neck to neck they march in a lopsided gait through the town of Les Cayes, their legs feeling their way back to land and strength. In some ways, the town reminds Akande of Whydah: the glowering, heavy sky before the afternoon rains; the dull haze and crashing surf; the straggling houses filled with humanity of all different shades. He sees white women for the first time, their existence often suspected but never proven, their lower bodies hidden beneath long skirts. *My Marie Louise, so fair,* mocks Chalumette's voice in his ear. He thinks of that strange name that was his downfall and glares at every woman he sees.

They walk along cobbled roads that stretch for miles through seas of waving green and pass long, snaking stone structures that carry water through the fields. Houses almost as large as forts; carriages drawn by horses that cause some of the men to cower in terror.

Then night comes in all its glory. It has been two months since Akande saw the night sky and when he looks above him and sees the stars, same as the ones in Whydah, he knows then that he will survive. I will fight with everything that is left of my life, he vows, and one day I will be free. I must remember that however far a river travels, it never forgets where it came from. The same stars, the same water, and I am still me.

At the sugar plantation called Collet, he quickly impresses the whites with his French and the authority he gained working the barracoons in Whydah. He has worked for the white devils before; he will do so again. Quickly he escapes the back-breaking toil of the cane fields to work at the boiling vats. Out of the sun, but the heat from the cauldrons at the factory is like working in Hell itself.

Survive, he tells himself.

Slowly his health and his spirits recover. He doesn't become like so many of the newly arrived, their souls left behind in Africa, working through their days in a daze and dreaming only of running back across the ocean to be greeted by the embraces of their loved ones. Akande knows from his time in Whydah that no one comes back from these evil islands.

No one, ever.

His life in Whydah has prepared him better than most for this new hell: he is used to European clothes and food, used to clamor and noise, accustomed to being in the company of strangers and enemies, used to the vastness of humanity as well as its infinite inhumanity. When his mother tried to tell him about where and who he came from, she would always say that a person was like a plant—if you cut its roots, it dies. Akande never believed that but now as he eats strange food—cold white potatoes, greens fried in cocoa butter—he thinks of new foods and new roots and new places to come from and to be.

Gradually he learns to navigate the tricky world of the plantation. The men and women who work the fields are walking ghosts, their strength sapped from back-breaking labor. Luckier than them are the slaves who supervise the fields or process the cane, and those who do all the dozens of other jobs that the plantation, a small village unto itself, requires: making tiles and bricks, taking care of the machinery, caring for animals, overseeing the slaves' food, and working in the houses for the white men.

There are ten whites on this plantation: three brothers who run it for the owner, living back in France, as well as other men who count the money and oversee the slave drivers and keep the mills and crushers humming. The three brothers live in a large stone house set right in the middle of the sugarcane fields. Some dusky evenings they sit on the veranda and watch the men and women toil, and music, played on an instrument called a violin, floats around the exhausted slaves.

In the slave compound where almost three hundred souls are crushed together there are self-mutilations and suicides, as well as constant fighting: for women and resources, for scraps from the whites, for power and knowledge, for dominance and boredom, for old hatreds and traditional enmities that have followed the men from Africa. For more rice at feeding times, for a sliver of soap or a pair of trousers. Akande knows he is fortunate that he has six ship-brothers with him, for he only finds one old woman from his people amongst the Congos and Aradas that dominate. She reminds him of his mother. Among the other slaves there are also Creoles, men born on the island who know nothing of Africa. One man brags that he is the son of a son who was born out here; not an African but something new and strange, possibly powerful.

Inch would have said that these men from other tribes were not his brothers but as Akande adapts to plantation life he comes to believe any differences between them are erased by their suffering and mutual hatred of the whites. At night his dreams of freedom are nourished with elaborate fantasies of revenge that have grown to a monstrous size since the irons were first clapped on him in Chalumette's office. Akande imagines that they meet again, a chance encounter with the man now stationed in Saint Domingue. And his wife as well, that Marie Louise who demanded the fat dowry that had caused his downfall. And why not? No matter how big a sea may be, sometimes two ships meet.

Alongside his dreams of revenge, Akande has nightmares of meeting the men he never helped when he loaded them onto the ships. *I am Sola.* What would he do if they met again? What would Sola do? It is those faces he fears, even more than the whites.

The Collet plantation lies in the middle of a vast, flat plain, the sea on one side, then hills that become mountains on the other. Akande has never seen such high mountains and he learns that they harbor bands of *maroons*, escaped slaves who live beyond the reach of the whites and the gangs of pale brown men in blue uniforms who roam the plain on mules and hunt for runaways. There are hundreds of men in those mountains, and women and children, and also the descendants of Indians who lived on this island long ago.

They make their living by growing crops in the rocky terrain, or by cattle rustling and stealing from plantation storehouses. The slave patrols don't dare go too far into the mountains but getting there across the plains is difficult, a march of disaster and death.

Inside the boiling house, Akande stirs the vats and the heat rises and he stirs some more. The smell of the cane juice, once boiled, curdles into something dark and fearful. As Akande stirs and cooks, his dreams thicken and take shape like molasses. The mountains beyond beckon him with long, curled fingers that whisper: *Liberty*.

But first he will bide his time. The patient man feasts on ripe fruit, he tells himself; the impatient one eats green berries. Only when he is ready will he join them and make a new life for himself in the mountains. For now, he will bide his time and hide from his ghosts.

Alongside his new life, Akande is also given a new name. At first he hates it, the syllables harsh and alien to his ears but eventually he comes to like it. It is a name that allows him to push the shame of Akande deep down and far away to a place where no one will ever find it. I will never be that man again, he vows, and now, he is Appollon.

The Slave House
Almost noon

A cat chases something the length of the room. The noise rouses Brac, who wakes to see Jeannette watching him tenderly.

"You have looked too long," she teases gently in the half-darkness.

"Shit," he swears. He sits up and she giggles at his distress.

"Sorry, sorry." Jeannette strokes his arm.

"Goddamn!" He wants to swear at her or slap her, but finds he can't. Their eyes lock and again she gives him a wondrous smile, only for him. She runs her hands between her legs, as though to trap the memory of their lovemaking, then gets up and smooths her skirts. She kisses him softly on the forehead before she leaves.

Brac knows he has to follow. He grabs the lantern, now burning low, and kicks over a few of the pallets, his anger strong and misdirected. Monkeys, they wouldn't have the nerve. Not under his watch. Everyone knows what happened over at Allard's after the slave drowned the overseer in an indigo vat. There is no plot; all those rumors flying around the district and the drums La Fleur hears—just brigands and witch doctors thinking their *Vaudun* is powerful.

Brac decides he won't bother searching the other men's house, though he will tell Madame he has. He tosses another pallet over and imagines himself ripping it apart with his hands. Goddamn, but he wants her again.

Jeannette re-appears into the bright light of the morning, adjusting her hair covering. She descends the steps of the house and walks slowly past the slaves in the clearing. She doesn't look at anyone in particular—and certainly not at Appollon—but sings, in a language La Fleur doesn't know but that many of the slaves do, that the boar sleeps well.

When Jeannette was lying there with that man, she thought she could feel the knife poking up at her through the straw. Surely Brac felt it too? But a man befuddled with love feels nothing, Jeannette assures herself. Back in the kitchen she sits down, her ears alert for the sounds of Mercier or Madame Rose, coming to find out what took Brac so long. Oh Appollon, what have you done? Brac didn't find the knife but... Jeannette wants to believe it wasn't Appollon that killed the white but how could it not have been?

"The bread will rise high," says Flore, turning to her. "I can smell it. And I can smell other things," she says after a pause and Jeannette laughs.

"We all can," she says. She picks up the dough, soft and dense in her hands. "It's a good smell."

She lays the new loaves on a shelf where they will rise. The morning is coming to an end and soon the sun will be at its height. The slaves are still ranged under the apricot tree, the ground where they are sitting littered with white, silky leaves. Their ropes loop over and connect them together in unison, a fragile, eerie tableau captured before it breaks apart.

BOOK TWO

DAY

The Gardens
Noon

The sun reaches its zenith and the day rolls on.

"Where is Brac?" asks Rose, irritated. In the salon her guests and children are ranged in inactivity. Aimée on the floor beside her, mediating between a kitten and an injured lizard. Charles is daydreaming, Mercier appears to be sleeping and Madame Mathilde is staring vacantly at her lap, mechanically feeding herself guava sweets from a *bonbon* dish. Her brother Thoreau has rejoined them after his snit and is sitting in a corner, furiously scribbling away in one of his notebooks.

"Brac's taking his time," says Mercier, opening one eye. He stretches and sits up. "Being thorough, no doubt."

"Brac's coming, Mama," says Charles, looking out the back door. "And he's got a slave with him."

"Aimée, dear," says Rose, leaning over to touch her daughter. "I don't want you here now. Go to your room, play or read."

"But Mama," Aimée whines, "I don't want to be alone."

"Go!" says her mother in a voice that allows no disagreement. "But stay close to the house."

Aimée grabs the kitten and marches off, furious at being expelled. Again. Treating me like a child, she thinks viciously. But I know what happens in the pigpen and I know what's going to happen to the slave. Charles allowed to stay but me excluded, like a... young girl. Not fair. Aimée trudges along the veranda to her

139

bedchamber, throws the kitten on the floor and with a dramatic sigh flops down on the bed beside her Aunt Julienne.

Aimée was only five when her father's youngest sister married and left for the North province. But five was old enough to remember Aunt Julie, with her green eyes and soft hair, her pretty hands that played the piano. Kind and funny, too—nothing like she is now.

Aimée remembers her mother reading Julienne's letters that described her new life on a sugar plantation up north. The plantation belonged to a rich marquis of the great family of Choiseul, a man who preferred Versailles to the heat and inconvenience of Saint Domingue and who was happy to leave the management of his estate to his nephew, Julienne's husband.

Julienne's letters were full of the excitements of northern life: the glittering city of Cap-Français, with its theaters and opera and constant social whirl, their plantation an easy two hours' ride away on a straight, cobbled road. Steam baths and a linen market, public balls where women were expected to change their gowns several times over the course of one evening. The dancing school where she hoped to send her future children and the disciple of Mesmer she saw at the Vauxhall. Julienne sometimes included sketches of her pet squirrels and of the magnificent carriage and house that they had full use of in the absence of the uncle. She also wrote about their slaves escaping to the nearby Spanish territories and of mosquito nets made of silk thread and of the way the heat seemed to shimmer up from the ground, so much hotter than at Bayardel, and how she missed seeing the sea every day.

When the slave rebellion broke out last year, the Choiseul plantation was at the center of the violence. Everyone assumed Julienne was dead, along with her husband and baby son, but a few months ago she was returned to them. Alive, but barely, a vacant shell scraped clean by the horrors: her husband and baby murdered, then four months of captivity under the fearsome slave leader Biassou.

Aunt Julie had been like a slave of the slaves! Aimée can't think on it much—it all belongs in a box labeled "Up North" that she likes to keep closed—but in the wake of Julienne's return she does remember the silent tears of her mother. The doctors' visits and the whispers of pregnancy. The avid, bright eyes of their neighbors, poorly masked with sympathy, who filed through the house to catch a glimpse of the woman so debased by the blacks.

Since her return Julienne has spent her time in bed, sleeping or muttering about cleaning the marble floors, her mind unhinged and hidden away. It took the family a while to understand she was talking about the floors of her house, stained with the blood of her family. Now Julienne only gets up to use the chamber pot and once a week submits to a bath at the hands of the laundress.

Aimée has stopped wondering when Aunt Julie will get better and now accepts her as a silent companion whose presence gives some comfort if she wakes in the night. She has taken to talking to her, though Aimée is not sure her aunt can understand. Sometimes Julienne cries, silently, and Aimée wipes her face with a cloth.

"My mother is horrible," complains Aimée. "Treating me like a child."

Julienne's vacant eyes flicker.

"Treating me like a child," Aimée repeats, looking for some sympathy but knowing there will be none. She sits up and fingers a cubbyhole in the wall, risking spiders and bugs. Nothing—her little statue has not returned. She peers into the crevice but the hole guards its secrets. And apparently not her statue.

She looked for it two nights ago when Thoreau expressed an interest in the Indians of the island. "One has to wonder," Thoreau opined in his droning, high-pitched voice, "what effect, what syncretism if you will, the culture of those Ancient Naturals had on the slaves who now reside here? A special interest of mine—and yes, I know you are thinking that I have many special interests but alas, I have been both blessed and cursed with a mind over-curious yet decidedly capable!"

"And so I wonder," he repeated and Aimée saw her mother's eyes grow wide, as though fighting an urge to sleep, "what effect the original inhabitants, the Adam and Eve of this island had on the very first slaves. Surely they mingled together before the unfortunate demise of those Indians. And some of their material culture yet remains—at Corail I was shown several intact ceramic pots."

"Madame Nathalie, Monsieur Mercier's wife, has a large collection of artifacts," piped in Aimée, "and she is very interested in the Taino arts. She has cooking utensils, carvings and stone amulets." As well as the remains of a Spanish sword, rotten with rust, that spoke to the violence of the early conquerors.

Aimée is sure her statue is from those Indians. She found it last month in the cove next to the Bay d'Airdelles. The cliffs of this coastline are pitted with limestone caves, wonderful places to explore with Charles. Inside the cave they found old bones, all lined up in one direction, and the must of ancient air so dark and dry it felt untested by humans. Aimée knew instinctively that they were the first ones to enter in hundreds, perhaps even thousands, of years.

She found the statue, intact and round with curious amber eyes, peeking out from under a dried palm frond.

"We should leave it. Not disturb the dead," said Charles.

"But I like it," protested Aimée, and the mouth of the statue grinned in perfect agreement.

"Well, take one thing then," decided Charles, examining a tiny skull. "We mustn't disturb too much. This place is so... old."

About once a month the children visit their neighbors the Merciers. Aimée doesn't like Monsieur Mercier, with his cruel eyes and ugly way of speaking, but she does like his wife even though she is old and bedridden. Madame Nathalie's children are all grown up and don't live with her anymore and she smothers Charles and Aimée with kindness and sweets.

On their last visit Aimée sought a moment alone with Madame Nathalie and showed her the statue she'd brought, hidden inside a pocket. She hadn't even told Pomponne about it; their first secret. Madame Nathalie examined it and said it was probably fashioned by a runaway slave who sought refuge in the cave.

"But the cave felt so old," Aimée tried to explain, thinking of the eerie brown quiet. The bones lined neatly up, facing the sea.

"Perhaps a fertility goddess," mused Madame Nathalie, turning it over and unperturbed by its nakedness. "It reminds me of the statues slaves from the land of Benin carve. Regardless, you must treat it carefully."

Even as she swore she would take care of it, Aimée decided it was not female, that there was something universal about it. She hid the statue in a little hole in the plaster between the timbers in her bedroom and began to feel that the statue, though made by pagans, was watching over her and Aunt Julienne.

And now it is gone.

Her turtle *and* her statue. How unfair.

"Did you take it?" she asks Julie, even though she asked the same question yesterday and doesn't expect an answer.

Julie shakes her head but the faint trace of a smile appears. Aimée lies back on the bed and watches an enormous beetle make its way across a roof beam. She can hear the murmur of voices from the salon, traveling through the high ceilings of the house. Excluded, again!

Impatient, Aimée gets up and goes outside to sit on the front steps, unaware that her mother sat on the same spot just a few hours earlier. She stares moodily over the flower garden, down to where Plunkett's body was found. Now he is gone and it is almost as if he never was. How strange, how completely irrational, death is—to be one minute and then not the next. Who would teach them now? But Charles is leaving for France soon and though her mother is determined that Aimée will not be as uneducated as her grandmother or aunts, she already knows how to read and write well. Perhaps that is enough.

Aimée looks beyond the garden to the sea where a sprinkling of white caps dot the brilliant green-blue waters. She picks a curled petal off the step and crushes it angrily. I'm not just a silly girl, she thinks, and I know why Plunkett was outside last night. But then the thought comes to her, again, that if Plunkett was outside doing *that*, then there was no reason for him to be at the front of the house. What a funny place to be in the black of a hot, rainy night.

Pomponne sidles up behind her.

"What's happening?" Aimée asks. She always thinks it vastly unfair that Pomponne is allowed to go anywhere and everywhere, listen to everything.

"Brac came back from the quarters with old Joseph. Charles keeps saying they should send for Captain Bassompierre at Dame Marie, but the men are ignoring him. The rooster is quiet, for once." They both giggle; it was Pomponne who came up with that name for their strutting, opinionated guest, so awful that even the young girls feel free to mock him.

The two girls sit in silence, Aimée trailing her fingers through the dried blossoms that paper the steps, Pomponne twining Aimée's hair into a braid. The two young girls know where babies come from and the possibility dangles before them, tantalizing and ripe, that Aimée's father is also Pomponne's, and therefore they are sisters. Real sisters.

After Aimée's father died two years ago, notaries and lawyers descended on the plantation to divide up the estate. On paper and only for the future; for now, the plantation remains intact. The names of all their slaves were put into a hat and one by one the notary L'Epine pulled out names for each of her father's heirs: Mama, herself, Charles.

"But what if I don't get Pomponne?" Aimée wailed to her mother when L'Epine first proposed his system and her sobs doubled when Pomponne's name was picked by her mother.

"Shhh, don't mind," said her mother, her voice at once full of irritation and grief. Like it always was in those awful first months. "She'll be yours when you marry." Aimée doesn't always trust her mother but for now at least, Pomponne is safe here and she considers her friend her own.

Aimée is always surprised when she hears that there are Frenchmen who oppose slavery: Why would people in far-away France care about their slaves? And if Africa is really as awful as everyone says, then aren't the slaves better off here where they can be baptized and live under the eyes of God? Aimée hates to imagine Pomponne, so pretty and delicate, running around naked in Africa and unable to even speak French. It is much better that she is here with Aimée and will be forever. It's a thought that gives Aimée great comfort and she is sure Pomponne feels the same.

"What will happen to his clothes?" asks Pomponne, finishing Aimée's braid.

"Mr. Plunkett's clothes? I don't know," says Aimée in surprise. "Perhaps his son will take them?" She has seen his colored son, sidling around the plantation.

"His son is too skinny. And ugly," counters Pomponne.

Aimée agrees.

"Appollon would like them," suggests Pomponne. "Laurine could get the blood out."

Aimée nods. She knows that Pomponne adores the big slave Appollon, and decides that Plunkett's oversized green jacket and breeches would look well on him. Now that their house slave Mercure is gone, along with his livery, Appollon would be the only slave on the plantation to own such a handsome jacket.

"I'll ask Mama," says Aimée and then there is silence as the two girls contemplate the mysterious events of the morning.

"Mama told me his first name was Elijah," says Aimée eventually. "I like that name—we should christen the next baby Elijah. Though it sounds a bit English." A few years ago, Aimée took over the naming of the slaves and stopped the vogue of naming them after Roman and Greek gods, or even, when feeling particularly lazy, days of the week. Her mother called her a little prig—she frowns at the memory—but eventually agreed.

"There won't be a next baby," says Pomponne.

"What do you mean?" asks Aimée. "Of course there will be. Mama said Chereze might be with child again."

"She isn't."

"Well, fine, then," says Aimée, a little crossly. Recently there is a slight air of mystery about Pomponne, as though her friend is walking ahead of her and she is still behind, struggling to keep up. "Then we'll use that name for one of the Aradas. Mama said they are already baptized, but I'm not sure." The law prescribes baptism for all slaves but Aimée suspects her mother doesn't always comply. While she can't quite accuse her mother of lying, what are the rules if souls are at stake?

Pomponne shrugs. "Shall we go and see *Elijah* in the well? They tied his feet with a rope, we could winch him up."

"Mama said to stay by the house." And for once Aimée does want to stay close; the eyes she saw earlier in the swamp still haunt her. Perhaps the two slaves Mercier is chasing but why are they here and not in the mountains? Did those escaped slaves kill Plunkett?

"Then let's have a look at where the body was found," suggests Pomponne. "Maybe there will be a clue!"

They head to the bottom of the garden past the statue of the black Venus and reach the spot that Pomponne indicates.

"This grass is not wet," says Aimée, squatting down. The ground here, under the shade of the forest that rings the bottom of the garden, is still mostly damp but there is a dry patch where Plunkett's body protected the earth from the night rains.

"I forgot to tell you: I saw him when I went with Mama to the Azor's plantation, two weeks ago," says Pomponne casually. "I wonder what he was doing there?"

Another secret, thinks Aimée in annoyance. She touches the dry earth. "What time did the rains start last night?"

"I'll ask Flore," says Pomponne. "She knows everything about the weather. Or your mother—she is awake most nights."

Aimée didn't know that but she supposes it true if Pomponne says so. Her friend straddles both worlds of the plantation with the ease of a cat that is welcome everywhere, slinking back and forth in the shadows.

"They said his throat was slit like a pig's, so there must have been a lot of blood," continues Pomponne, considering the rectangle of dry earth. "But there is none. And if they fought there would be signs of a struggle."

"Do you think there was a fight?" Aimée half-remembers the men's voices cutting through her sleep last night. Thoreau repeating again and again something about a constitution before a revolution, or a revolution before a constitution.

"No. I think someone... crept up behind him!" Pomponne darts behind Aimée and reaches around and grabs her throat. Aimée screams and jumps away, landing on the patch of earth where Plunkett lay. She hops off to safety.

"Don't do that!" she says crossly. "You made me step on it."

"But you see it is possible for someone to come from behind. And cut your throat."

"But you were already beside me. If not, I would have heard you coming."

Pomponne's face is a blank mask and the thought comes to Aimée, new and unbidden: should she be discussing such things with a slave? She pushes the thought away—Pomponne is her *sister*.

"We should search around," Aimée continues, looking away from Pomponne's impassive face and the feel of those lithe little hands around her throat. "For clues."

Pomponne scuffles her feet through the wet foliage while

Aimée peers under bushes and pulls back bands of flowers at the edge of the garden. She pushes her way through a thick tangle of bell-shaped flowers to the path that leads to the graves—had Plunkett come this way?

And there, in the middle of an innocent patch of earth, sits her statue.

Aimée stares at it in astonishment and it looks back at her, its amber eyes larger now, its clay lips placid and terrible. It seems to say: *I am here. Just as death is here.* A small lizard darts across the path and sniffs at it before disappearing into the undergrowth. Aimée picks it up, gingerly, as though it might be hot or poisonous but the thing is as solid and heavy as usual. Though unnerved, there is a part of her that is happy to see it again.

Pomponne comes up behind her. "Your statue!" she says in amazement.

Something ill stirs in Aimée, for she never told Pomponne about her statue. She wants to ask how her friend how she knew but something holds her back. Fear, or perhaps even knowledge.

The Women's House
Noon

"What did we find?" asks Mercier, rising as Brac comes up the back steps. The old night watchman Joseph waits at the bottom of the steps, safely outside.

"Searched both of the men's houses but just the usual bits and bobs. A scrap of a pamphlet under Jacques's bed," Brac improvises, playing to his eager audience. "We'll, ah, put him in chains for a day. When the harvest is over."

Rose looks at him with scarcely concealed distaste. "Where are they now?"

"Who?" Brac looks around the room.

"The slaves," says Mercier. "Where are the slaves?"

"Still in the clearing. I have Joseph, the night watchman," he adds for Mercier's benefit, "outside and he didn't hear or see anything."

Rose rolls her eyes. Joseph is decades old and has only half a left leg; the idea of him vigilantly hopping around and guarding the plantation is a sincere fiction that would be funny were it not so tragic.

"If you have searched the houses, then there is no need to keep the slaves from working," says Rose in a careful voice. It is already gone noon: half a day's work missed.

"Commerce stops for no man, not even a dead one," chips in Thoreau, nodding.

"Fine, yes, we'll search the women's house, then we can

get them back out," agrees Brac. "Might even be able to get the mill going by sunset," he lies.

"Excellent, we shall all participate in this search," says Thoreau. "And we won't miss anything this time!"

Charles looks at his mother and receives a small nod. He follows the men out of the salon, accompanied by the dogs that tumble down the steps and bark around the watchman.

"Ah, young Charles, how good you should assist us! I always say trying times make men out of boys," says Thoreau, smiling at Charles. Charles nods uncomfortably and tries to avoid a hand on his arm. They reach the clearing, the slaves still corralled under the apricot tree.

"Get started," says Brac, pointing them into the women's house. "I've got to talk to La Fleur."

Charles nods and leads the way inside. The women's house is brighter than the men's, with windows open to the air, baskets and cooking pots piled neatly at the end of pallets. Here and there sheets or rushes divide the long space into separate quarters and there is none of the stench of urine of the men's quarters.

"How interesting," remarks Thoreau, pushing aside a frayed curtain. "They have attempted to make little homes here! The *nesting instinct* in the female is universal, even in such degraded circumstances."

"I suppose," replies Charles, looking around. It is his first time inside the women's house, a glimpse inside a life generally kept hidden. Where does Bridget, the slave he had in the pigpen, sleep? And pretty Zabeth?

"Well, let's get to work, men," barks Mercier. "Don't worry about moving things around, they can straighten up later."

Thoreau obliges and tips up a woven mat, only to be enveloped in a plume of dust. "Oh, my."

Mercier chuckles in derision and kicks over a woven basket filled with clothes. Charles moves to the far end of the house. Behind a yellow curtain he finds two beds, a chair and some clothes hanging from nails. Another door leading to the outside. He recognizes a pink dress of Pomponne's that had once been his sister's: this must be where Jeannette and her daughter sleep.

Charles fingers the soft organdy and wonders why Brac had not offered him Jeannette. He knows that Brac sleeps with

Jeannette on occasion but it isn't as if they are married. And Jeannette is the most beautiful slave on the plantation, even more so than Zabeth who is very young and largely agreeable. He pulls out a sheer muslin petticoat from a basket. Smelling faintly of vetiver, the sharp plant of the islands that is dried and burnt for its fragrant ashes, and so soft—

"Ha there, my boy," says Mercier, coming through the curtain and slapping him on the back. "Enjoying the small clothes? Remember those were your mother's at one point."

Charles drops the petticoat and darts back into the main cabin and almost collides with Thoreau, emerging from the darkness of another corner.

"Interesting," says Thoreau, holding up a length of rope hung with a series of white shell figures. "Some artistry in this, though of course very primitive." He raises the necklace to the light of a window.

"I don't think…" murmurs Charles, staring in horror.

"Give me that," says Mercier. He grabs the necklace from Thoreau, his eyes bright and alert. "Where did you find this?"

"Why, here," points Thoreau, taking a step back from Mercier's brusqueness. He points at a pile of loose palm leaves covered by a scrap of brown sheet.

"Who sleeps here?" demands Mercier.

Charles shakes his head. "Brac would know."

"I'm sure he would," says Mercier grimly. The necklace dangles menacingly from his hand: one large figure, two smaller ones. Black markings crudely painted on the faces. "This is evidence, right here." Mercier shakes the necklace at Charles, who backs away, feeling dizzy. The house is so hot and sticky and he has a strong desire to run away from the smell of the small lives suffocated in here. Are the slaves outside humming? Or is that just the throbbing in his head, now getting louder?

"My good man, what do you mean by evidence?" says Thoreau. "Surely the desire for beautiful things is common in women the world over—even the most naked of savages feel the need for adornment! It is similar to one I saw in La Leogane and I would make a sketch of it." He reaches for the necklace but Mercier whips it away.

"Oh, shut up," shouts Mercier. "I'm tired of you. This is

serious business, do you understand? Take it!" He thrusts the necklace at Charles then hurries out of the house, calling for Brac.

Charles holds it gingerly, wishing he didn't have to. It is heavier than expected and he sees that the heads of the figures are not shell but stone, white and smooth, red thread wrapped around the necks. The walls around him contract, threatening to smother.

"What is the matter with the man?" inquires Thoreau in a hurt voice. "He appears positively *deranged*, and it seems nothing I can do or say pleases him. Though why I should have any interest in currying his favor, I do not know!"

"This is not a necklace," says Charles slowly. "It's *Vaudun*, the slaves' magic." His father used to call it *comical conjury*, but still warned his son never to underestimate its power. I don't believe, but I don't disbelieve, thinks Charles, and his stomach lurches as a wave of nausea hits him. One large figure, two smaller ones…

"Fascinating!" declares Thoreau in delight, reaching for the necklace which Charles gladly relinquishes. "I have heard much of this magic of the slaves and of its origins! Some say it came with the Fon, a famously savage tribe, and the mingling of their magic with our true faith, while to be widely condemned, is nevertheless intriguing. If one is allowed to be interested in something that is completely wrong," he adds, almost as an afterthought. "And illegal."

Mercier returns with Brac. He grabs the necklace from Thoreau, who makes a small whoosh of protest.

"This is intent to murder, if not murder," Mercier says, shaking it at Brac.

"Clear as day," says Brac, nodding.

"Intent to murder," repeats Mercier.

"But I think it's of us," says Charles in confusion. "Mama, myself, Aimée." He points out the three figures, their sizes neatly matching his list. "Not Plunkett. He's not family."

Mercier shakes his head, his face alive and excited. "They don't make the distinction! One white is as good as another. Intent to murder, I say!"

Thoreau puffs. "Hardly! A necklace! Then is every fair lady a sorceress? Every pearl a death wish? It is somewhat like a rosary even, but perhaps with—"

"Who sleeps here?" demands Mercier, kicking the pallet where Thoreau found it.

"Bridget," says Brac.

Charles gasps before he can stop himself. He thinks of the pigpen, the feel of her soft body, small grunts of—what? What had she been thinking? Why would she want to kill him? Not because of that, surely? Luckily Brac does not appear to be making the connection—please God, and not in front of Mercier and Thoreau.

One by one, says a voice so clear and true he jumps but it is only Mercier muttering something about Thoreau going on and on.

The men crowd around Bridget's meager pallet, not even a basket set beside it.

"Recently purchased?" inquires Mercier. "It's often the new ones."

"Last year from the *Marta.* From Gaboon they told me, via Jamaica, and she only speaks English. If that. A dull one, but does her work. Strong," says Brac.

"Re-sales are always trouble," observes Mercier. "I only take fresh ones we can train ourselves."

Brac snorts. "You know Madame Rose, always looking to save a penny." He catches Charles' eye and shrugs.

"Well, then I believe we have our culprit, Messieurs," announces Mercier in satisfaction. "Good, quick work. A gratifying ending. And a dose of luck."

"Hardly luck," protests Brac. "Searching the houses was *my* idea."

"But…" says Charles, gesturing to the necklace. "It's *Vaudun,* prohibited yes, but it doesn't mean she killed Plunkett. I don't see—there's no connection! And no knife was found!"

"Not yet." Brac reaches down and scatters the dry fronds of Bridget's bed but reveals only the desiccated skeleton of a mouse.

"You're beginning to sound like a *Frenchman,* Charles," snorts Mercier. "This is clearly your family. We'll whip her accomplices out of her and those men will be punished too."

"But it's only a necklace and not of Plunkett!" Charles repeats. What Mercier is saying is wrong but Charles doesn't have the words to argue with the older man, not with Brac nodding in agreement beside him. But who is Mercier to take charge like this? It isn't even his plantation.

Apricots

"The whip," says Brac with relish, ignoring Charles. "Come on, let's go and tell her highness."

"This is preposterous!" protests Thoreau as the men exit the house.

In the clearing Brac beelines for Bridget, sitting at the edge of the group of women and hauls her away from the safety of the circle. He throws her on the ground in front of La Fleur, her ragged once-pink skirt riding high around her thighs.

"Keep her here," says Brac, kicking her on the side. Bridget grunts softly. "We're coming back for her."

"An outrage!" cries Thoreau, his voice a higher pitch than usual.

Charles turns away, shaking. Why would Bridget—or anyone else—want his family dead? If his family died, they would only be sold again and surely they know how kind his mother is? He looks back at Bridget on the ground and remembers the way he cleaved into her and they became one, the wetness and the wonderful ending that overcame him so quickly. She muttered something over and again, words he thought English or another dialect, but perhaps it had been an incantation or a spell. If they whipped her, would she tell what they did together?

But I've done nothing wrong, Charles thinks in confusion, hurrying back towards the house, followed by Thoreau still squawking in protest. And even if Mama finds out, what did I do wrong?

*

"Aaaah," whisper the women when Bridget is dragged from their group. Then they look to the ground and close their eyes, for they know well never to look danger in the face.

"Poor Bridget," whispers Mumbo, known for her tender heart; it is she who feeds the sick in the hospital when Brac forgets. "What will they do to her?"

"Don't worry about her," snaps Laurine. "We need to be worried for ourselves."

Jeannette watches from the shadows of the kitchen hut. What did they find in the house?

La Fleur walks over and kicks Bridget, who curls up some

153

more.

"*Bas tête*!" he cries in a terrible voice, as if she would ever look up.

BRIDGET'S JOURNEY

GABOON TO JAMAICA TO SAINT DOMINGUE
1787-1792

Bridget was born on the downward slope of western Africa, south of the Loango river but north of the Congo. The area is sparsely populated and slavers don't care for it much, though Cap Lopez, a day's walk up the coast, is often used as a refueling stop for slave ships coming from the south.

The *Marseilles* hangs anchor at Cap Lopez. Some of the crew are given a day off while water and supplies are loaded before the ocean crossing. A canoe of sailors goes inland in search of an elephant with six-foot tusks the locals claim to have seen. They don't find the elephant, but they do find Bridget, alone on the riverbank. They pick her up and pocket the two hundred *livres* the captain grudgingly gives them, saying he has a sixth sense and this one doesn't look like she will survive the passage over.

They throw her in the hold with thirty or so women bought in Luanda. Isolated from the beginning, it will be a long time before Bridget hears the soft sounds of her own language again, the way her name—Azinza—sounds like birdsong, or the lullabies that trill from the women as they croon their babies to sleep.

In Jamaica, Bridget is sold to a sugar plantation six days' ride from Kingston. On arrival she is branded with a series of intertwined *Bs* and that night she runs into the nearby woods and spends the hours huddled amid strange-smelling bushes, the moon the only familiar thing, crying for something, anything that she can understand. How can she be here, so far from her family, and how will she get home? Who are these people who have taken her? At dawn the dogs catch her scent and she is brought back. The wound where the dog bit her swells up and spreads down her arm. Bridget is chained in the hospital for a month, until the infection subsides.

As soon as she is unchained she runs again, knowing she will be caught but also knowing she can't stay. The cycle repeats itself until the manager, exasperated, sells her cheap to another plantation. Soon she is thrown in the dungeon there, the manager spitting that even the royal chain gangs will not take her.

Lying in mute misery on the cold stones, Bridget prays to her gods for a boat that will bring her home so she can see her family again. Or to at least to let her die and be reunited with them in the afterlife. But the strength of her sixteen years betrays her: blood still courses through her veins, her heart continues to beat, and her mangled arm heals. Though her soul is tethered by only the faintest string, her body refuses to give up.

Bridget is dragged back to the coast and sold with a batch of damaged slaves, all bedraggled, crippled or barely alive, some fresh from the ships, others fresh from other horrors. A motley bunch taken on in risk by a Portuguese trader who knows that no matter how decayed a slave may be, someone, somewhere, will pay a price.

A mosaic of actors feed the plantations of the ravenous New World, including many who operate far outside the well-controlled triangle of commerce that the French and the other European nations have set up. So many shadows exist: illegal trade, intra-Caribbean trade, up from Brazil, down again. Re-sales, fakes, leases and lending. Ships bearing neutral names, counterfeit papers, illegal cargo. A tangled, convoluted web populated by all manner of spiders, including Senhor Diego who buys damaged slaves cheaply and waits for the right moment. He sells mostly in the doldrums of winter, when fewer ships arrive from Africa, but his network of agents in every port city keep him informed of opportunity. Famine, epidemics, rumors of abolition—all increase demand. Hurricane years are especially profitable.

Though Senhor Diego claims to be Portuguese—the Portuguese have no colonies in the West Indies and are free of international laws—he isn't. In Montego Bay he buys Bridget and seven other barely-alive slaves. Two die on the brief passage to Saint Domingue but Senhor Diego is not overly concerned—a certain percentage of loss is expected.

On his boat, the only piece of luck in her luckless life comes for Bridget. One of the other slaves is an older woman named Polly, in Jamaica for almost thirty years, and marked by the thinness that comes from starvation. At once Polly recognizes Bridget and speaks to her in their language. To Bridget it is a sound sweeter than any music and a friendship springs up; thirsty for human contact, they lie on the deck entwined, whispering of their homes and memories. All of Bridget's tears, kept inside for so long, come pouring out.

Being on the water and speaking her own language helps Bridget's dreams return: the ship is blown off course, back across the waters and straight to the riverbank where she was taken. She will get out, free of chains, her skin smooth again, and walk back to the village where her mother will embrace her. Every mild storm, every surge of a wave gives Bridget hope, but instead the ship sails briskly over to Saint Domingue where demand for slaves is always strong and the government has opened the trade to all nationalities. Senhor Diego bypasses the poorer town of Jérémie and sails to Port-au-Prince.

"Ah, no, no," he complains in perfect French when the first visitor boards the ship. "Ah no, I have nothing for you. Go away!"

Monsieur Cartier tips his hat. "I have heard differently, my friend, but I will not bother you for several days. I am just making my interest known."

Senhor Diego spits, puffed full of false anger. "This time I have nothing that will interest you. I only have fine stock."

"Not what I hear. From Brazil?"

"Yes," Senhor Diego lies, "and some added along the way."

Monsieur Cartier gazes up at the sky. "Demand is strong. I will pay handsomely."

"Pah! Handsomely—we have different definitions of that word. For you it means no more than 10 *livres*."

Cartier bows. "An exaggeration, Monsieur, but I am not offended. I will be back."

And so he was; after ten fruitless days in harbor, Senhor Diego sends word that he would be pleased to welcome Monsieur Cartier again.

With sadness, Cartier inspects the men and women that remain.

"Oh no," he exclaims. "I would be a fool to take such dregs." He pulls one up and turns it around. "No, the yaws are too far spread. But I'll dispose of him for you, if you pay me for my troubles."

Senhor Diego grunts; at this point he needs to take what little money the slave-fattener will give. As some might fix worn-out shoes, Monsieur Cartier's specialty is restoring life to worn-out slaves. "I restore souls, not soles," he sometimes likes to say.

In the end Monsieur Cartier purchases the lot, including a blind child and a man with one arm, for only two thousand *livres*—a bargain when one healthy field hand might fetch three thousand. He only refuses an idiot Senhor Diego picked up free of charge in Gustavia and whose incessant shrieking has frayed the nerves of all on board. Unsellable, Diego has him smothered that night then taken to the city slave dump, situated conveniently next to Monsieur Cartier's slave-fattening warehouse.

There Bridget spends a month resting and eating, following the same principles one might use on a goose before slaughter. It is the best month of her life since she was taken from the riverbank—a soft bed with a straw mattress in a safe house and food, lots of it, twice a day: mounds of steaming leafy vegetables, chicken and pork as well, rice for those who might be missing it. Oil for her skin, lemons for water, sometimes chocolate in the mornings. Lots of sleep and then only light duties of cooking and laundry shared by all the women.

Cartier knows from experience that this luxurious regime helps even those who suffer from "heart sickness" to blossom. He inspects his wares daily and grunts in approval when he sees sheen return to skin, light to eyes and black to reddened hair. He tuts in sadness when yaws get worse or eye infections don't clear and he shouts in anger when, a day after his purchase, a slave expires in a dramatic fit of diarrhea, his wasting concealed with a plug of cork pushed so far into his anus that even Cartier's probing fingers had not discovered it.

Bridget thrives but her friend Polly does not. Polly's belly swells and she screams that a great pain is eating her insides. One day she is moved into the end house, where slaves beyond repair enjoy starvation and death.

"My name is Bintou," Polly whispers. Through her tears Bridget waves a palm leaf over her dying friend and whispers traditional words of mourning to speed Polly through to the afterlife, chants half-remembered from the village funerals of her youth. Then Bridget stops crying; she should have known her happiness wouldn't last. She wants to go with Polly and be done with this life once and for all, but even though her heart is full of more sorrow than one human can bear, her body still lives.

Cartier pays a master ironworker to skillfully connect the weal of the three brands that mark Bridget's shoulder, to make it look as though Johnson of Kelly of Babbit was really just the name of a single Englishman or plantation. "The British," Cartier would say, "are fragile men with brittle pride and they give themselves long names to proclaim their importance to the world!"

Cartier has Bridget washed, her hair braided and decorated with shells, then dressed in a snowy white chemise that sets off her dark skin and white teeth. He even rubs a smack of annatto spice on her lips. He has a reputation to protect, so he merely polishes; he practices no deception apart from the skilled work on the brand. He contacts the *Marta* in harbor, ready to sail for the Grand'Anse, and presents Bridget for sale. Cartier receives the satisfying sum of a thousand *livres*; even accounting for her care and board, an excellent return on her meager purchase price. He takes back the chemise and the hair shells, pockets the note—good for withdrawal at any bank—and takes himself off to celebrate in Port-au-Prince's finest rum shop.

The *Marta* sails to Jérémie where Bridget is sold to a white man with leering eyes and bad breath. She is taken to a shop where she is branded once again, this time *Fongravier,* and then they begin the trek over the mountains to her new home.

Here the hours are not too long and there is a general air of disorder. The white manager pulls her from her sleep sometimes, as does La Fleur and a few other slaves who like to pester the women. She is given a provision plot but mostly she eats whatever scraps the others do not, licking their bowls and occasionally stealing off at night to find mangoes or oranges in the hedges around the pastures. When other slaves try to talk to her, she doesn't respond; there is something dead inside her now, something that will never re-awaken.

Life continues and Bridget no longer has the strength to run. She just exists. She still dreams, occasionally, of a boat that will take her back to her family but now she also dreams of the hot, rich chocolate served in the fattening house and the meat they had once a week. And she dreams of her friend Polly and the feel of her arms around her, the way she smiled and the way she smelt, just like home.

The Salon
Past noon

While the men search the women's house, Rose and Mathilde sit in the salon with the heaviness of the afternoon draped over them. Rose settles on one of the sofas but next to her Mathilde sits rigid and ready, but for what she can't imagine. *Slouch*, Rose wants to shout, but of course she doesn't.

Rose tries a few polite sorties with Mathilde—*How does she like Saint Domingue? What does she think of the Creole women she has met?*—but after a series of abrupt answers she gives up. Rose is struck, and not for the first time, by the older woman's almost complete lack of social grace. So reserved and cold. Like a dried-up leaf, ready to crumble at the slightest touch.

Rose closes her eyes. The men will take care of everything—thank goodness for Mercier—and now all she has to do is sit and wait.

A noise startles her awake—had she been sleeping? One of the dogs wanders back in and settles by her feet. The room is so hot even the floors are sweating, a thin layer of slickness over the blue tiles. Rose looks at her guest, who smiles back with what almost looks like a leer.

"Your children?" inquires Mathilde. Rose blinks in surprise. Mathilde is pointing to a painting of Charles and Aimée done a few years ago, surrounding a baby in a crib. Crude, yes, but such is the talent out here.

"My Aimée and Charles," nods Rose.

"And...?"

"My daughter Aurore, who passed a few years ago," Rose says carefully. Saying the words out loud is still hard.

"Ahhh, truly I am sorry," whispers Mathilde and Rose hears some hint of humanity in the woman's voice. "And Aurore is such a charming name. Normally I would not countenance an unchristian one, but such is the fashion these days—a neighbor named their daughter *Agläe*."

"Her godmother's suggestion," says Rose. She senses the sympathy from the woman is sincere and notices a locket around Mathilde's neck, almost hidden in folds of soft tissue. We all carry our sorrows but in different ways, she thinks.

"And that poor woman in the bedroom," says Mathilde, widening her eyes. "What tales she has to tell."

"You have been speaking with Julienne?" Rose says, more sharply than intended. When had the woman been doing that?

"No, no, I have not," simpers Mathilde with a coy, strange smile.

"Would you care for a drink?" Rose asks, tired of the old woman and her nonsense. She gets up and takes a bottle from the bottom of a sideboard graced with goblets. "Taffia, a sort of rum, if you will. With fruit. You have had it before?" inquires Rose, pouring two glasses. That rum at breakfast that flooded her body with peace; she needs that again.

"No, I have not," replies Mathilde, then giggles: "My brother dislikes women drinking but he is not here!"

Rose smiles thinly and hands the woman her glass, downs her own then pours another. Mathilde nods her head and looks at Rose with a knowing, almost sympathetic air. Oh, no you don't, thinks Rose, settling back on the sofa. You think you know me, but how could you? I don't even know myself.

Rose fights the urge to close her eyes again and sink into the liquor's lull. This is how she often passes the long, hot afternoons: on the sofa with a drink and her daydreams, pretending the rest of the world doesn't exist. Once she had had passions and interests—the kitchens, the piano, her garden—but those pursuits gradually withered away beneath the corrosive apathy of colonial life, then were lost completely under the sorrow and the responsibilities thrown at her after Marcel's death.

I'm so exhausted. Too exhausted for all this. Though she knows it wrong, Rose sometimes finds herself envying the slaves: they are taken care of, clothed, and need only follow orders. Taken care of—like she once was. Rose's heart clenches for the thousandth time at the loss of her husband. Why did he have to die? So sudden and so needless, leaving her all alone in this horrible world.

She knows there are women who thrive on responsibility and independence—the Widow Yvonnet, vaguely related by marriage, is constantly buying land to expand her mahogany export business, and she remembers an old aunt of Marcel's cackling with glee when her husband died: *Free at last*, she said, choking with joy on her cracked ivory teeth. *Free at last*. But Rose is not one of those women and she often wonders why she ever chafed at her husband's dominion.

Bayardel was faltering in the years before Marcel's death. Rose knew of some of his struggles with the coffee wilting disease and a smallpox outbreak amongst the slaves, but she hadn't known the full picture of the straits they were in. After his death, reality was thrust upon her in a cold awakening and last year there had been barely enough money to pay Brac. And when a new overseer, a youth just arrived from France, decided that the colony was not for him, Rose was forced to take over the plantation books herself.

Mornings, once filled with minor domestic concerns are now given over to orders, messages, vets' and doctors' bills, the lock box getting emptier and the pile of invoices growing larger, the mess captured by the sad story of the account books written by a year of prolonged rain that rotted the coffee cherries on the bush. Money sometimes seems like a line of ants, each coin marching off in determination to points unknown and beyond her reach.

The more Rose is involved, the more she hates the plantation. It was so easy to skim along the surface and enjoy the fruits of this life without realizing the struggle and brutality beneath it. Just last week... Rose closes her eyes against the memory. News came of a ship docked in Jérémie and she jumped at the chance to replenish her stock. So few were the slavers coming this far south, and so dismal and so expensive their cargo, that the colony offered planters subsidies for their purchases. Still, the six slaves cost her more than 10,000 *livres*. It was all against the advice of Brac and against the ability of her account books, but without more hands they would never be able to re-plant the failed north field, struck last year with a mysterious wilt.

Everything went wrong, starting with the horror of having to board the stinking ship where the sale was made. Under sleeting rain, she struggled to negotiate with the English captain who conveniently lost his ability to understand French at key moments. Around them the constant wailing of the huddled savages, forced out into the lashing rain. The incessant whine of the ship's doctor who kept shrieking over and again *Bene! Bene!* for each emaciated, oil-slicked Negro that was paraded in front of her. The roar of the captain when Brac accused him of bringing in half-dead re-sales, voices raised in misunderstanding above the howling of the wind-whipped sea.

Pressured and anxious, Rose bought six shivering Aradas and hustled them immediately to the branding shop in town—if one of them ran on the journey back to Bayardel, unmarked, she would have no proof of ownership. Two of them died that night at the house she rented in town.

"Why couldn't they have died on the bloody ship," Rose raged in anger and tears, "rather than waiting to be purchased! Almost as if they did it on *purpose*." Then she made the mistake of looking at one of the survivors, straight into his eyes, and now she can't get his face out of her mind, nor the look of indefinable pain and confusion she saw there.

Rose takes a deep breath and opens her own eyes. Might it be possible to excuse herself and lie down in her bedroom? She considers sending for Aimée—her daughter has little exposure to the niceties she will need as a hostess, and she could take care of this dreadful woman. But no—Aimée and her sulkiness often have a way of making bad situations worse.

Besides, the men will be back at any moment and Rose is reluctant to cede her tenuous control over the events of the day. What if Plunkett had never come? Why didn't she just cancel this last week of lessons? Charles is leaving next month, as ready for France as he will ever be. What would the men find in the women's house? And—oh God—that visit from Monsieur Azor that she keeps forgetting about!

"Oh!" The glass slips from Mathilde's hand and red taffia

seeps ominously over the carpet under the chair. Blood, thinks Rose and remembers Plunkett's neck.

She sits up and rings the bell.

"I am so sorry," whispers Mathilde. "I don't know what happened."

"No, no," says Rose. "An accident." Pomponne skips in so quickly she must have been waiting on the veranda. "There has been a spill. Please clean it up."

"Such a pretty child," observes Mathilde as Pomponne sprinkles salt from the dining room over the stain and pats at it with a linen napkin. "And her fine clothes so charming. A lace petticoat! If she were darker it would be quite ridiculous, I saw one in Port-au-Prince—a Negress, very dark—but dressed like a lady. Looked like she should have been in a circus!" Mathilde attempts a little laugh.

"Indeed," says Rose politely.

Mathilde lowers her voice, as though Pomponne, not a foot away, would be unable to hear: "I understand that illicit contact between our men and slaves is a necessary evil, that helps prevent greater vices."

Rose blinks. What a subject for the old woman to latch on to! But perhaps not surprising: Europeans are always so interested in the carnal side of plantation life, imagining them to be like Turkish harems. Perhaps some places, but not here.

"At Petit Goave we heard a story," breathes Mathilde, her eyes black and somehow different, "about a father who was unable to resist his mulatto daughter. Resist—you know in what way!"

Rose stares at the woman and has the odd impression she is looking at a stranger.

"Overcome by his passion," continues Mathilde, "his passion for the *darkness* he saw in his daughter. His sons, also mulatto, strangled their father to stop him. But then they were hung, all of them, even the daughter who—"

"Yes, thank you," says Rose, wincing. "A sad and well-known story."

"A lovely complexion," Mathilde says, returning to the subject of Pomponne and suddenly looking normal again. "And such interesting hair. Child, can I touch it?"

Pomponne looks at Rose, who nods.

"Of course, Madame," Pomponne says. After giving the stain a last pat, she goes to sit by Mathilde on the sofa. "I'll clean off the salt in a few minutes, Madame," she adds helpfully.

"How extraordinary," says Mathilde, touching the end of one of Pomponne's braids, tied neatly with white ribbons. "Not as wiry as a Negress's but not as soft as ours. Something like horse's hair, I would say? A well-combed mane, perhaps?"

Rose stifles a smile; Mathilde sounds exactly like her brother.

Taking her cue from Madame Rose, Pomponne giggles and swings her feet back and forth. She is wearing a pair of Aimée's old slippers. Soon her feet will be big enough to do without the stuffing that currently keeps them tethered to her feet. She is the only slave on the plantation who wears shoes; even her mother doesn't.

"Now, is she a mulatto, or a *griffe*?" asks Mathilde, continuing to sound unfortunately like Thoreau. "Her skin is mild, lighter than a mulatto I would say. But a *griffe*, no I have it wrong—a *quateronne*?"

"Mulatto," says Rose shortly. "Her mother is a Negress—our cook, in fact—and her father... is white." Was white?

Sure enough comes the next question, breathtakingly inappropriate: "And who is her father?"

Pomponne stops swinging her legs. The identity of her father is one mystery she can't solve as she effortlessly slips between the two worlds of the plantation. Her mother refuses to say but she does hope it was Sieur Marcel, and therefore she is a *real* daughter of Bayardel.

"Mathilde, you are a welcome guest, but there are certain questions that are best left unasked in this house. Or elsewhere in the colony," says Rose coldly, when what she really wants to say is: *Go to Hell.*

"Oh," says the older woman, looking at Rose with pity and understanding. "Oh, I am sorry. I didn't—I—"

"Brac is my father, Madame," says Pomponne with what she hopes is a winning smile. "The manager here."

"Oh, of course. I mean, not of course, but—" Mathilde's cheeks are a reassuring red. At least the old woman has some delicacy of feeling, thinks Rose.

"Pomponne, finish with the stain then fetch another bottle of the taffia from the storeroom," says Rose, pulling a circle of keys from her pocket. "And lay out some bread and cheese for lunch." Her guests can't expect more than that; they seldom eat much in the heat of the day but wait for supper when the sun sets and night breezes return the appetite.

Rose gives Pomponne the key and offers her a quick, grateful smile. The child is extremely precocious and expertly managed Mathilde's pestering. Very charming and very bright—an unfortunate reason to assume that lout Brac is *not* her father.

The Salon
1 pm

"Madame, an outrage!" says Thoreau, hurrying in and accompanied by Charles.

"This man needs to stop now, Madame," says Mercier, striding in behind with Brac. "He risks contaminating the whole investigation." The four men clutter into the salon, bringing the horror inside, the room not big enough for their egos and animus.

"Go to the veranda," whispers Rose to Pomponne, not wanting the girl in the same room as Mercier. She sets down her glass and stands, slightly unsteady on her feet. "What is going on?"

"We found evidence!" says Mercier grimly.

"Hardly evidence!" says Thoreau, looking imploringly at Rose. "A trifling find, yet these men want to——"

"Be quiet, sir!" barks Mercier.

"I think they hate us, Mama," pleads Charles.

"Gentlemen, stop!" shouts Rose and the men fall into shocked silence. I must remember I am the owner here, she thinks, even though I wish I weren't. "There, that's better," she says calmly. "Someone tell me what is going on."

Mercier meets her gaze, a hint of a challenge underneath. "We found a *Vaudun* necklace," he says, too much satisfaction in his words. "We will whip the truth out of her and take the appropriate action."

"Barbaric!" shouts Thoreau. "To whip her over a *necklace*. Madame, as perhaps the only voice of reason here——"

"What—they don't whip men in France?" snorts Mercier. "If so, then things have changed mightily; I remember a man whipped so severely his spine broke and all for stealing half a ham."

"Yes, but with due process!" protests Thoreau.

"The due process is our decision," says Brac, speaking for the first time. "And it is decided."

"To whip, possibly kill—" splutters Thoreau.

"Despite the fairy tales you Europeans consume with such avidity, we do not practice wanton death here; if the slave dies, it is because it was necessary to make an example of her," snaps Mercier.

"*Vaudun,* though ridiculous, is a potentially terrible weapon," adds Brac.

Rose holds up her hand. "I must understand what you are saying. Where was the necklace found?"

"Under the slave Bridget's bed."

Rose looks at Brac. "Bridget?"

"Yes, purchased last September."

"Yes, of course." Rose frowns and looks at the men ranged in front of her: Mercier, flushed and excited; Brac, smirking; her son Charles—why had she allowed him to get involved? And Thoreau, worried and wobbly.

"But this makes no sense," Rose says slowly. "The woman speaks no Creole or any of the dialects. Brac, I remember you complaining about that."

"True," mutters Brac.

"Then how do you propose to learn her secrets?"

Brac shrugs. "She'll understand the whip."

"Yorick!" exclaims Thoreau. "Plunkett's son—we might press him into service as a translator? If he speaks the language of his father?" Thoreau then frowns, as though regretting his contribution to the plan.

"The woman is isolated," says Rose slowly. Though she distances herself as much as possible, she has spent nigh on twenty years in this colony and understands some of the relations between slaves. "I doubt anyone even talks to her. And how could a woman have done such a thing?"

"She's healthy," offers Brac. "Strong as a mule."

"I agree, Madame!" exclaims Thoreau. "Surely even in the Negress we must find evidence of feminine weakness. And what motive could this lone woman have?"

Rose stifles an urge to laugh. What motive indeed! Is the man a fool, blind or both? There are some eighty motives clustered in the clearing under the apricot tree, kept only in check by—by what?

Mercier flicks his hand at Thoreau, as though swatting a mosquito. "Keep out of this, sir, you don't understand how things work here. And we mustn't forget she is from Jamaica—all the more evidence!"

"Why is *Jamaica* evidence?" asks Thoreau, his voice rising in frustration.

"The devil Boukman was from Jamaica," says Mercier, referring to the leader of the northern rebellion last year. "Before he came to Saint Domingue and infected our lot. And the poisoner Macandal as well. Another nuance, Monsieur, that you might learn before you start meddling in our affairs!"

"But Bridget is no heir to those devils," protests Rose. "Surely someone hid the necklace beneath her bed, knowing it would be found there."

Mercier turns to Brac. "Any other Jamaicans in the lot?"

Brac nods. "Joseph, the night watchman."

"A-ha!"

"Joseph is ancient and has half a leg!" Rose shouts. She feels as though she has awoken into a hot, annoying nightmare. Such a delicate situation, yet these men are crashing around like a hurricane raging through a flower garden. "Stop this idiocy, it's neither Bridget nor Joseph!"

Mercier glares at her. "If you insist on flouting my will, I have a mind, Madame, to leave this house. But as a man of honor I cannot leave you alone, with only this fop of no sound judgment."

"Monsieur!" cries Thoreau, his eyes bulging at the insult.

"Certainly, we are grateful," Rose says, glaring at Mercier. "Truly," she adds, and she means it. She takes a deep breath. "I want to see the necklace."

Brac produces it from his pocket. Rose takes it and instantly sees her life—and death—in its crude shells and stones. Oh. She closes her eyes, remembering Mathilde's hollow voice from the morning: *It is beginning.*

"Mama, it's us. Not Plunkett."

"I can see that, Charles, thank you."

Rose hands it back to Brac, willing her hand not to shake.

"Outrageous!" says Thoreau. "To whip that woman over a *necklace*, when even the most basic questions about Plunkett's killer have yet to be answered. For example, what was the man doing outside at that time? Place? And his son—I understand patricide for freedom is a concern."

"Pish! Only a *Frenchman* would not be able to see the truth," remarks Mercier to Brac.

"Very well, *Monsieur*," says Thoreau, and Rose admires, just slightly, the sarcasm he places on *Monsieur*. "If this necklace is important, then surely there are laws for this situation—you cannot ignore the *Code Noire*!"

"Good lord man, shut up about the *Code Noire*!" shouts Mercier.

"I speak of the process of law!" Thoreau bellows back. Both men are breathing hard, their faces matched in crimson. "Is Saint Domingue not a civilized nation?"

Bulls, both of them, thinks Rose in despair.

"Monsieur," she interjects gently, laying a restraining hand on Thoreau's sleeve. "You can appreciate that the *Code Noire* inspires conduct but does not dictate. Similar perhaps to the Ten Commandments? Sometimes putting them into practice is difficult, or impractical."

Mercier strides to the sideboard and pours himself a glass of the taffia, almost pushing Charles out of the way as he does. We'll need another bottle, thinks Rose. And real rum, not this weakened red stuff. Blood. Where is Pomponne?

Charles pours a glass for himself, casting his mother a slightly worried look. She nods, distressed that she allowed him to go with the men; she should have kept him here in the salon.

"Savagery!" says Thoreau.

"Who are you calling savages?" demands Mercier, draining his glass and waving it with menace at Thoreau.

"You, sir, you! A savage!"

Rose takes a deep breath. "Enough, gentlemen, enough. I agree that necklace is… serious." Perhaps. Rose feels the fight ebbing from her, flowing over the tiles and straight out the door. She sits down, shaking. The easiest course of action would be to let the men focus on that unfortunate woman. "Perhaps interrogate Bridget"—what a farce—"but at the same time we can send the rest back to work?"

"Soon enough," mutters Brac.

"So they will whip her?" asks Mathilde, speaking for the first time, her face alive and avid. Rose suddenly feels nauseous and buries her face in her hands. I can't, she thinks; I just can't. She breathes in, out, then hears a carriage trundling slowly up the drive and the whinny of horses.

Monsieur Azor, arriving into the middle of a maelstrom.

The Salon
After 1 pm

A coachman in plum livery helps Monsieur Azor out of the carriage. Rose watches from the veranda in only partial understanding. Who are all these people, both down there and up here? Usually so routine, life is now turned upside down and the house is fuller than it has been since Marcel's memorial.

Behind Azor a young man emerges from the carriage. Possibly one of his sons. His remaining sons, checks Rose; we are all bound together by sorrow.

"Good day, Monsieur Azor," Rose says as they mount the steps. Though it has been many years, she recognizes him. A handsome man with silver-peppered hair and fine features, a face of unexpected calm and kindness. His son is a younger version of the father, though oddly dressed with a bright red cravat and what appears to be white trousers.

"Madame Fongravier." Azor reaches the top of the stairs and, keeping his distance, gives her a half bow. A safe choice. He looks at the men assembled behind Rose and at the flushed face of his hostess. "Is everything all right? I have interrupted something?"

Rose opens her mouth to explain, fighting an overwhelming urge to cry. Her chin trembles slightly and Azor averts his eyes in delicate understanding.

"A very trying day," Rose manages to whisper, thankful for his tact. She half-turns to the men behind her, their eyes questioning this pair of new arrivals of an unexpected color.

"Messieurs, this is the *Sieur* Azor, of the plantation La Fraternité," Rose says, emphasizing the honorary title not generally used for men of color, though with their recent equality who knows how they should be addressed? Nonetheless, it is her house and she will do as she will. "We had a visit today and I did not think to cancel."

"Would it be best if I returned another time?" suggests Azor.

"No, of course not. I cannot have you come all this way and leave without your business accomplished."

"And what is his business?" asks Mercier, standing as though to block the entrance to the house. And acting as if he doesn't know who Azor is; how could he not, after what happened in Jérémie?

"As I said, the Sieur Azor requested a visit. Please, do come in and let me offer you refreshments."

"What, you would have them inside the house?" demands Mercier.

"Yes, inside *my* house," Rose says, brushing past him.

Mercier reluctantly lets them pass and everyone reassembles in the salon, the son still hovering in the background.

"You are most welcome here, Monsieur, though I am not sure," Rose says to her guest, "that I can be of much service to you. I do not know the purpose of your visit…?"

"Ah, Madame," Azor replies, seeming to intuit her distress. "A minor issue. I came by to see Mr. Plunkett: I have some small business with him regarding the education of his son. The road to Apricots being washed away after the storm last month, this was the preferred meeting place."

Rose blinks. An odd explanation—here to see Plunkett?— but her relief is great that he has not come about the loan.

"Madame Rose has no time for social visits right now," snarls Mercier. "And what impudence, coming here like this! Just as we feared—you get the vote and then you come house calling again!"

Oh God, they mustn't start fighting, thinks Rose helplessly. Though given their history, how could they not? But Azor is looking at Mercier with something like amusement, no animosity or anger in his gaze. He pauses a moment, allowing the full rudeness of Mercier's words to sink in, then raises his shoulders. By far the most well-dressed man in the room, Azor is wearing a striped blue and orange silk jacket and his whole bearing proclaims wealth and dignity.

"As you say, Monsieur," Azor says easily, then turns back to Rose. "Yes, I wish to see Monsieur Plunkett, Madame."

"Oh, certainly. But, ah…" Rose pauses. "Mr. Plunkett is no longer with us."

"He has left?"

"Plunkett is dead," snaps Mercier.

"Is it true, Madame?"

"Yes," whispers Rose. "Unfortunately."

"My goodness." Azor sinks down into the nearest chair. He looks confused and Rose sees him patting his jacket pockets, as though searching for something.

"Charles, a drink for our guest, please. Mr. Azor is perhaps tired from his journey."

"Blanchelande said the gates of Hell would open when the woolly heads sit in front of their betters," says Mercier loudly to Brac, who laughs in ugly agreement.

"How did he die?" Azor asks, ignoring Mercier and Brac.

"Monsieur, he was murdered," announces Thoreau for the second time that day. He steps forward and makes a half-bow, aware of more snickers from Brac and Mercier. Thoreau does not know the proper mode of address for these colored men; he was never been introduced to any by his previous hosts. But he has an ingrained respect for handsomely tailored clothes, mellifluous speech and the aura of good breeding that this man, though the color of milky coffee, improbably exudes.

A swift intake of breath. "Murdered?"

Rose takes the glass of rum from Charles and hands it to Azor, who downs it without looking around. He hands it back and she goes to refill it herself, aware of the scoffing eyes of Mercier. My house, my rules, she thinks defiantly, and there is something in Azor that she immediately appreciates. Something solid. And the kindness in his eyes when he saw her distress… perhaps he will know what to do.

"Yes, most unfortunate," says Thoreau. "His throat slit, found at the bottom of the garden this morning."

"Who committed this crime?"

"It is unclear as of yet," says Rose softly. Strange—she would not think that this dignified and wealthy patriarch would care so much about a dead Englishman.

"No, it was a slave and we've found which one!" says Mercier.

"But that is terrible, Madame," says Azor, shaking his head and focusing his gray eyes on Rose. He is trembling slightly and Rose has the impression he trying to control something enormous within himself. "How dreadful for you. The authorities have been informed? This could be evidence of a wider plot?"

"No wider plot," says Brac stiffly. "Not on my plantation. And like Monsieur Mercier said, we've found the slave responsible."

"An internal plantation matter," agrees Mercier, "which we are taking care of."

"Debatable," says Azor. "These days even isolated incidents may be part of something larger and it is imperative the constabulary be informed, as well as the magistrate in Jérémie. Surely you, Monsieur Mercier, as leader of the Security Council, would agree."

Rose admires the way Azor coolly addresses Mercier, as though the man hadn't been the mastermind behind the death of his son.

"Ah, thank you, Monsieur Azor!" says Thoreau. "I have been saying all along that the authorities need to be informed and yet these men propose rough plantation justice based on the flimsiest of evidence! But forgive me; we have not been properly introduced. Monsieur, my name is Philibert Theophile de Moran de Thoreau and I am a representative of the *Académie Nationale de Bordeaux,* here at the invitation of the Saint Domingue Chamber of Agriculture." He offers a deep bow.

"A pleasure to make your acquaintance. Indeed, the constabulary must be informed," continues Azor. He has a measured, careful way of speaking. "A man—a white—has been killed and possibly by a slave. This is hardly a plantation matter, either in what concerns justice for the dead man or for the slave."

"I assure you we have more important things to do in these volatile times than worry about a dead *petit blanc,*" says Mercier dismissively. "We have a slave and we will whip any accomplices out of her. In due course, once everything is settled, we will inform the authorities."

"I disagree," replies Azor. "It is precisely because the times are volatile that we must enforce the rule of law."

"So you stand against the right of a plantation owner to punish his property as he sees fit?" exclaims Mercier in disbelief. "As an owner yourself, I would not have expected such stupidity! Surely you understand the value of freedom from interference?"

"Monsieur Mercier, I am in no way arguing against your right to punish your slaves—I was as shocked at the LeJeune case as the next planter," Azor says. A few years prior, France passed a law prohibiting the killing of slaves by their masters. Soon after, a planter LeJeune tortured two slaves to death and was convicted of murder in the colonial courts. But such was the wrath of slave owners—fiercely resisting any interference from France—that the verdict against him was quickly overturned. "I am merely saying that the authorities are better placed to determine the level of threat."

"I agree with you, Monsieur Azor," Rose says. Why had she listened to Brac and Mercier? *Of course* the authorities needed to be informed. "But... we could not spare a messenger, or the mule," she continues, aware of the paucity of her answer. We all try so hard to hide our real situation, and for what? "The harvest, there is a ship... we can't ... The warehouse roof is ruined, the tarpaulins are torn and the ship won't wait past Saturday and I can't—oh, I just can't..." Her tears are flowing freely now, casting the room into immediate and uncomfortable silence.

"Mama," says Charles, putting a hand on her shoulder.

Azor rises. He is a tall man and stands a good foot over Mercier, who backs off quickly to avoid the comparison. Thoreau notes again the expensive cut of his jacket and the sheen of his boots with their embossed silver buckles. Even the son—assuming it is the son—is finely dressed and what an interesting cut of cloth on his breeches; practically *trousers*, though the son is obviously no laborer.

"Madame, I understand the difficulties of the harvest and how hard it is to find a ship in these times," says Azor. "A proposal: First, my coachman will return to La Fraternité with a

177

message to prepare ten of my best to be here by sunup tomorrow. You may keep them as many days as necessary. I can also spare a carpenter for the warehouse—he will be able to fashion new shingles in no time. Second, my son Henri will ride to Dame Marie and alert Bassompierre to this situation; he will doubtless hasten here and help us determine the right course of action."

Rose stares up at her guest in amazement.

"Entirely unnecessary," mutters Mercier but even he appears cowed.

"This is not a simple plantation matter and a slave who deserves death needs to be handed over to the courts. You may proceed with your interrogations," says Azor, now looking at Mercier. "See what you can find out. But don't go too far."

"Are you telling me what to do, boy?" There was a time when a white man could strike a colored man—no matter his wealth or status—with impunity and it is clear that Mercier is wishing those times would come again. Rose can almost see his fists clench.

"I am sorry you do not agree with my course of action, Monsieur," Azor says softly, adjusting the lace cuff of his jacket, as though to emphasize its elegance.

"Ridiculous," says Mercier even as he turns to leave with Brac. "Come on, boy, I need you," he says to Charles, who follows obediently.

"Thank you, Monsieur Azor," says Rose, wiping her tears with a handkerchief provided by Thoreau. Strangely, she doesn't feel embarrassed; such an extraordinary day. And now everything is going to be all right. She feels free, weightless, delighted. Monsieur Azor is here and he will take care of everything.

*

Thoreau stays in the salon, happy to have found an ally in Azor and with no desire to follow Mercier and Brac. A sudden repugnance for the whole colony sweeps over him. Of course, punishment is an integral part of the balance of plantation life but to propose to whip a woman—and possibly to death!—for the mere possession of a necklace! Barbaric.

And such open hostility from that man Mercier! In truth, it

was all rather exhilarating. To be free of the social constraint of politeness, shouting at each other in pure anger and passion! Like... but Thoreau can't think of an appropriate parallel in his life. Is this freedom? he wonders, and motions to Mathilde for his notebook. She has been silent since Azor's arrival and is now staring at the colored man with what can only be described as ardent eyes.

"Henri, give Malachi my instructions," says Azor, seating himself again. "Then as I said, ride to Dame Marie for Bassompierre. It shouldn't take you long." His son looks less than pleased but exits without protest.

Such an educated, rational man, thinks Thoreau. But how extraordinary that Azor should be from the race that the great Voltaire called *biologically and morally deplorable*, a product of monstrous hybridity, descended from two species of man but belonging to neither! During his year in the colony, Thoreau had lightly imbibed the prevailing view of the whites that any concession to the coloreds was the beginning of a slippery slope, one that would end with wholesale equality for every human in the colony and implying the abolition of slavery. Thoreau is against their political ambitions and firmly believes that white blood is sacred; one drop, no matter how faint, fouls the whole. But how elegant and well-spoken this man is!

"Certainly, we must involve the authorities! And a good idea to get the magistrate out here to look at the body. An *autopsy*," says Thoreau. "A well-used tool of the French police— often a careful examination of the body can yield clues about the circumstances of death."

Rose looks puzzled. "Oh no, Monsieur. Even if we had sent for the magistrate as soon as the body was discovered, Plunkett will have to be buried today. In this heat we cannot delay for more than a few hours. Sundown at the very latest."

"Oh!" Thoreau absorbs this latest piece of colonial contrariety with a frown. "But a priest...? Surely...?"

"And where is the unfortunate Mr. Plunkett now?" inquires Azor.

"Down an old well," whispers Rose. "I have not yet made arrangements for his burial. I suppose I must tell Brac."

The Clearing
2 pm

In the clearing, Bridget lies motionless at the feet of La Fleur, now singing that she will pay for what she has done. He falls silent when he sees the men returning: Brac, Mercier and the white son. Mercier strides over to Bridget and hauls her away, down the path to the old pigeon coop next to the slave cemetery where the whipping post stands. Bridget hangs off him, no muffled cry or protest, her limp feet dragging on the ground. The boy follows. As they pass, Mumbo offers up a soft ululation of the kind she remembers from funerals of her youth.

Brac watches them go with sour eyes; he dislikes the way Mercier has taken over the interrogation. And Madame Rose, practically ordering him back to the fields—he will miss all the fun. "The rest of you are returning to work!" he shouts angrily and tells La Fleur and Louis to untie the men.

"All back now, hard work coming," sings La Fleur. The slaves shuffle up slowly, each untying the one in front. The women rise and shake their skirts, adjust their head wraps.

"We want something to eat," says Capidon, pointing up at the sky. "It is our eating time."

"No eating!" shouts Brac. "No time. Later." He glares at the offending slave and gives him a good cuff. That uppity woolly-haired man with his expensive coat, impugning his harvest skills with his offer of help! Just like a stuck-up colored to think he knows best, feeling themselves equals to the whites though they are hardly better than slaves. That striped coat that probably cost a pretty penny, and him lounging in the armchair where Monsieur Marcel used to sit and Madame Rose simpering over him like a convent girl.

He'll turn Azor's slaves away when they arrive. We don't need their help, Brac thinks angrily, even as he starts to plan how he will use them. Ten good hands would make short work of the remaining bushes and then they can finally get the mill going.

Scowling, he chews on a plug of tobacco and looks to the kitchen house but doesn't see Jeannette. The sun is beating overhead and he doesn't know where his hat is—probably left in the salon, damn it. He directs La Fleur to take the work gangs back to the fields and the women to resume their work at the drying and sorting platforms.

"You two," he calls to Capidon and Pierre, "Go to the cemetery and dig a grave for Plunkett. Then finish the tarpaulins! And you," Brac continues, flicking his whip at Appollon. "There's a carriage and horses need tending to up at the house." Brac spits out his plug and sniffs. He'll get the women settled then he'll check in on Mercier and the boy; it has been a long time since there was a proper whipping down at the post. He mounts his mule and heads off in the direction of the drying platforms, shouting at the women to hurry up.

*

Appollon rubs his neck where the rope chafed. Free again, the day to continue as before. He looks down the path where Mercier dragged Bridget. A man he knows well, a barbarian of the first order. Mercier's personal slave George once told Appollon that his master feeds mercury to slaves who are too old or feeble to work, deliberately hastening their death.

But Bridget—why was she chosen? She is a nameless waif on this plantation, never smiling nor understanding, surviving like an animal on the few scraps thrown her way. Three layers of branding on her chest to signal a runaway and a trouble maker. She must have been sold for a song—a song of madness that only Madame Rose could understand.

The very idea that Bridget has a part in what is coming

tonight is laughable, but perhaps the ignorance of the whites is a good sign. Though they claim to be so powerful, they cannot see what is in front of their faces, nor can they hear the drums that beat at night and foretell their doom.

Appollon is sure no word has been sent beyond the plantation to any of the white authorities; no horse saddled, no messenger posted. But troubling are the new arrivals—the carriage and horses that Brac mentioned. Again more strange happenings when usually the days are all the same, just an endless wheel of work, meals and sleep. First the dead white man, then Mercier arriving, and now another carriage.

Appollon slips inside the long slave house and finds the knife under his pallet, ignoring as he does the image of Jeanne and Brac together. The blade gleams in the semi-darkness. He sees it slicing off Brac's cock but for some reason the image doesn't excite him as it should. Maybe he'll just stab him, quickly in the heart; why spend more of his time on that dog?

Appollon heads outside with the knife secured under his shirt. He avoids the kitchens and at the stables hides the knife under an old barrel used to hold molasses; he'll come back for it soon. He fills two buckets with water and makes his way to the big house where he finds a magnificent carriage and two matching piebald horses. There is also coachman and a young mulatto wearing strange white trousers and a brazen scarlet cravat, pinned like a giant flower at his neck.

"Good day," Appollon says quietly to the coachman, setting the buckets down in front of the horses.

"Good day. Only you with the stables?"

There is a touch of something superior in the man's voice. Appollon nods. The coachman is young, perhaps the same age as Appollon, with handsome skin so black it almost gleams blue. Appollon notes the man's smooth hands and fine plum livery.

"Well, help Malachi untie the horse!" barks the young mulatto impatiently.

Appollon nods and keeps his head down; the young master is clearly annoyed, though at what or who, Appollon doesn't know. He untethers one of the horses and the coachman fetches a saddle from the back of the carriage. Appollon starts securing it but the horse whinnies and rears up at Appollon's strange smell, or at something darker.

"Bloody hell!" exclaims the mulatto, striking his whip on the ground. "Get away from my horse."

The coachman tightens the saddle and helps the young gentleman mount.

"Be careful with the carriage, this place doesn't look safe." The mulatto scowls before setting off down the driveway in a cloud of dust.

"Yassuh. Ride safely with the Lord," the coachman calls out after him.

"Where's he going?" asks Appollon.

"Dame Marie. To get the constable."

"Get the constable?"

"Ya, constable, their big man in care of laws, in charge of *constabulary*."

"I know what a constable is," says Appollon.

"Well, he's gone to get him then," says the coachman impatiently.

Appollon turns away. So they are fetching the authorities, inviting the outside in, bringing white justice to this plantation. Damn it! One hurdle cleared then another springing up as weeds after rain.

"I'm going too," says the coachman, starting to untie the second horse.

"To Dame Marie?"

"No, back home. Message for the manager—we sending hands to help with the harvest. You got troubles here?"

Appollon shrugs cautiously. The two men look at each other.

"Hard times all around, we can only trust in the Lord," Appollon says but there is no flicker of recognition in the coachman's eyes. "*The Lord*" is how they refer to Milord, the leader of what is planned for tonight. Was the coachman's call to the young master to *ride with the Lord* a sign, or just convention? There is no cross hanging around Malachi's neck.

"How many you here?" asks the coachman. He takes one of the buckets and drinks from it.

"About eighty," answers Appollon. The constabulary, coming here. He squeezes his head, the heat of the high day cooking his brain. This changes everything. What does he need to do?

"Just little place then," says the coachman. "We at over three hundred now at my place." He takes the hamper from the back of the carriage and rummages through it, emerges with a chicken breast.

"Yes, sure," says Appollon. "What is the name of your master?"

"Monsieur Azor. Not that runny rum fellow who left, he just come from France. But his daddy is in the big house, sitting with your people," says the coachman. "Monsieur Noel Azor," he repeats proudly.

"Right." Appollon nods. He knows of the Azors and remembers that Jeannette went there a few weeks ago. *To help with a party*, she said and he hadn't thought much of it at the time. Had he missed something? "Where is your plantation?"

"Took us more than two hours this morning, but you know that road nasty since the rains," says the man. "La Fraternité, by Les Irois, mighty big place, we got coffee, indigo, animals, everything. Our master a good man, plenty rich and he make money just by touching the air."

Far, thinks Appollon, almost down by Tiburon; their plan focuses on the coast north of there and back into the mountains. He doesn't remember seeing the coachman at the meetings with Milord, but men look different in the dark of the midnight hour.

"You know Milord?" asks Appollon carefully.

The coachman's eyes cloud over and his lips curl. "That *Vaudun* man from Les Platons come to try troubles down here?"

"Perhaps," says Appollon cautiously. A hand extended then quickly withdrawn, no harm done.

"No, I don't know no *Vaudun* priests, man, I keep away from that shit."

"Of course."

The coachman throws the chicken bones on the ground and heaves himself onto the remaining horse. He pats his pocket. "Got my papers if anyone thinks to stop a man in livery on a horse, a fine sight I make."

Appollon nods in agreement; the man does look rather strange on the saddleless horse in his full coachman's outfit.

"Look after the carriage."

"It's safe here."

Appollon watches as the coachman rides away down the drive. He examines the carriage: the color of an orange sunset, velvet upholstery inside, the wheels finely turned, the whole thing looking for all the world like a giant peeled mango fallen from the sky. Appollon unfolds one of the foot steps and sits down to stare at the big house not a hundred feet away. Why is that rich *colored* planter here? The coloreds are no friends of the blacks, with their trickiness and duplicity and one foot in either world. He shouldn't have said anything to the coachman; these days a pair of loose lip is more fatal than a pistol.

Appollon stands up and refolds the footstep, his mind humming with the disastrous news. Dame Marie is not far, so at most two hours before the constable and possibly the entire district militia arrive at Bayardel. The wrath of the whites, descending on them like a plague of locusts. This changes everything. I've got to get word to Milord, he thinks in something approaching panic. I've got to stop it. Stop everything.

Appollon looks up at the sky—brilliant blue, the sun past its height.

Is there time?

MILORD'S JOURNEY

THE NORTHERN PLAINS OF SAINT DOMINGUE
TO THE GRAND'ANSE
1791-1792

Milord walks through the storm-heavy night towards the woods known as the Bois Caïmans. The others around him are full of excitement and nerves but no one talks or smiles in greeting as more join them from the darkness. Silently they continue, slaves from a hundred plantations on the northern plains, converging on the Bois Caïmans.

When all are gathered, a woman dressed in white sacrifices a black pig, its flesh offered to the spirits and gods, its blood shared with all who attend. Milord drinks the salty goodness with a vicious thirst and feels power course through his body. The night storms and thunders, then mosquitoes flood the air but never bite—sure signs of the spirit of Macandal. The rain stops and their leader Boukman rises to speak.

Boukman's tall body grows in size until he towers above the assembled crowd, so high he resembles a sinewy tree, the flames from the fires that burn through the rain illuminating the scene as he cries out the sacred oath:

We swear to destroy the whites and all they possess
Let us die rather than fail to keep this vow

The men repeat the oath. The crowd disperses, each man armed with courage and the instructions that will set the massacre in motion: Kill the whites; kill any slaves who resist; torch the houses and fields. Milord returns to the Choiseul plantation, one of the finest in the district, where he has worked as a slave driver for eight years. When Wednesday comes, they creep to the overseer's house and enter with ease. Milord slashes the heads of Contois and his assistant, a boy recently arrived from France, then grabs the slave girl from his bed and casts her on the floor.

Milord is an enormous Fon, the scarification carved on his cheeks and body proclaiming his high lineage to the world; when he meets other slaves from his birthplace and they see his face, they prostrate themselves in front of him. Milord used to be a warrior but it has been many years since he has killed a man. Soon he remembers how easy it is: one chop to the head to immobilize or kill, then the fun can begin.

"Do you know why?" Milord screams in his old language to the split scalp of the French boy. "Do you understand?"

Next, they go to the big house. There they skewer the manager, tie up his wife and dash her baby against the marble floors. At other plantations there may be some mercy, but not here; this manager regularly starves his slaves to keep food costs down. They kill one of the house slaves who tries to defend the family, as well as the carpenter because no one likes him. The women start burning the sugar fields and they blaze easily as dawn approaches, the swaying seas of green turning to gold and orange then ashes. A group of field slaves attack the sugar mills, screaming in rage. Milord's group overtakes old Bonny on the road, looking to sound the alarm and they kill him too, then move on to the next plantation.

They converge on a houseful of cowering whites.

"I am a god!" howls Milord as he chops off an arm. "I create and I destruct with my own power!" Milord chops off another arm as the man screams in unholy pain, the sweetest sound he has ever heard and then he starts on the legs. All the rage of being forced into a life he never chose, of being denied his history and his lineage, subsumed under years of humiliation and hunger, comes rushing back through him.

Once again Milord is a warrior prince, a descendant of the great King Agasu, so fierce the griots still sing of him even though he is dead for hundreds of years. Milord takes up the man's leg and beats him to death with it.

The rebellion floods out across the plain in a monstrous wave of revenge. And so it goes from plantation to plantation, whites fleeing, chopped down in the road, the rebels converging then diverging, leaving behind a flaming wake of destruction until the entire plain blazes in fire and bands of rebel slaves are burned alive when the wind strikes too fast or they miscalculate their movements.

The beast of liberty and vengeance, unleashed.

"How sweet is your blood!" Milord screams and bites into the arm of the white woman they found hiding down a well. His laughter is crazed, his feast illuminated by the burning house behind them. "Your flesh is rotten but good!"

As the weeks pass, the rebels spread further to outlying districts. They coalesce into small bands, then larger ones and larger. Leaders emerge and their success draws more slaves to join them. Their ranks become fat with fighters and a powerful sense of invincibility that carries them from one victory to the next, the whites taking cover in the towns and the small forces of the government's army easily rebuffed.

Still the rebellion grows, so far and so fast it amazes even their most optimistic leaders. The winds of victory are behind them, pushing them forward: *We will take the world!* becomes their rallying cry. At night they sit in their camps— captured big houses or unburnt warehouses—and talk about the future. Once all the whites are exterminated, they will return to their destroyed plantations, claim the land as their own and be their own masters. Commandeer the boats out in the harbor, stuff the whites in the hold and bring them back as slaves to Africa.

Milord will remember those early nights in the camps as some of the happiest of his life. Everyone is together. Men, women and children from a hundred tribes in Africa and a hundred life histories—princes, farmers, soldiers, herders, adulterers, witch men, goldsmiths, griots, slaves and servants. They did not come by the same ships but now they are all sailing together. Some were born on the island and some have been so long in Saint Domingue that their memories of Guinée are faded and slight; yet others—the majority, perhaps—are raw and fresh from Africa. Regardless, all came together in a way that few are ever united in this life, the hatred of their masters their guiding force and the conviction that they will inherit this land their strongest belief. And though they have different gods, their prayers are all the same: *Deliver us from the white devils.*

Within a month, they are twenty thousand strong and control a third of the North Province. Boukman is killed in a skirmish but other leaders emerge, feeling their way back into the power so long denied them. Milord admires how the leaders imbue their men with the courage to fight: with their words they build a hate so strong it blinds the soldiers to their certain death. They use visions and prayers to persuade the slaves to seek glory in battle, assuring them that on their death they will return to Africa.

Milord soon loses count of the whites he has killed. Now they are in the foothills of Limonade pursuing a fleeing white, an older man whose slaves fought back for him. They killed about twenty of the resisting men, base fools who deserve to die for their stupidity. A Spanish priest, a prisoner from a nearby town and babbling with fear, is brought before the leaders.

"Tell me something so I don't kill you," says Milord; it can be fun to toy with the whites and break the tedious monotony of killings.

"He is a good man," says one of the slaves from this plantation, softly.

"Quiet, fool!" snaps Milord. "Or we'll kill you too."

"Please, please, I beg of you—don't kill me," cries the priest, snot running down his face. "I will tell you where they are hiding, the D'Orfeuille whites!"

After Milord kills the priest they search the old warehouse he named. It lies at the edge of the plantation, long disused and fallen under a tangle of green shrubbery. There they find a dead white woman, her body decomposing and her eyes already picked out by birds. Behind a thicket Milord finds two little ones and a baby huddled together, their clothes dirty and with the feral look of hunger. They stare up at him with wide eyes.

Girls, Milord thinks, though the whites sometimes dress their children the same when they are small. Not that it matters; one is the seed of more whites, the other the bearer. Milord kills them both with one blow of his machete, then considers the small baby in a moment of indecision. He could bring it back to the camp and have sport with it later. They have a growing menagerie of women and children as hostages, though some of the rebel woman are starting to defend them against the cruelty of the men.

The baby mewls at him, scrunched and red. Milord wipes his brow, looks around and coughs from the distant fires of burning cane. Then he turns and leaves, lopes back to the big house where doubtless by now they will have taken over the storehouses and there will be good drink. They have amongst their group a man who used to work for a very rich white. While they drink from the plundered caskets of sweet wine, this man likes to mimic his old master and prate on in an affected voice, telling the other rebels how this wine holds the faint taste of blood, this one notes of a burnt white, this one the subtle aftertaste of revenge.

The baby Milord leaves in the field; in the sun it will surely die by tomorrow.

*

Early in 1792 French troops take a rebel camp at Gallifet, one of the strongholds of the northern rebellion where two thousand slaves are camped. Believing rumors of the impending attack, Milord escapes the day before. He is not sad to leave; life in the camps is becoming hard and he is dismayed by growing talk of negotiating with the French for the return of the men to plantations, albeit under better working conditions.

Milord escapes south in the hull of a small ship captained by a free black. He lands at Jérémie then, dressed as a woman, makes his way to the misty mountains that divide the southern peninsula in two. The highest mountains on the island, rumored to harbor the descendants of the earliest Indians and, more improbably, snow. There Milord joins ten thousand rebels in the mountains at Les Platons, overlooking the plain of Les Cayes and under the command of two ex-slaves, Armand and Martial.

This insurgency grew out of a colored revolt in the area around Les Cayes. In that brief skirmish, both the whites and the coloreds armed their slaves and enlisted them in their fight. That rebellion was quickly put down but then the armed slaves from both sides took up the battle on their own. Now they are finishing the job the coloreds started: they have decimated the countryside, sugar and cotton plantations on the fertile plains and indigo and coffee in the foothills of the mountains. They have forced the area around Les Cayes into total anarchy, the countryside burnt and the whites cowering like rabbits in the town.

At the encampment of Les Platons Milord finds almost a thousand huts, set in valleys high in the fog. There is a hospital and a school for young children, training grounds for the fighters. Here Milord finds a return to the heady early days of the northern rebellion, when men could not stop talking of the future and he lives again through that wonderful moment when hate is replaced with hope. There is even talk of proclaiming Les Platons a separate, independent nation. *The Kingdom of Les Platons.* In Jamaica it happened so: several decades ago large groups of maroons, undefeated, signed treaties with the British that afforded them freedom and independence in exchange for agreeing not to harbor new runaways.

Soon after Milord arrives, the rebels soundly defeat a troop of eight hundred French soldiers sent to quash them. The newly arrived soldiers are unfamiliar with the heat, the rocky terrain and the way the slaves ambush them, shoot at them from hidden positions, retreat then return. So unlike fighting in Europe, where war is played out on formal battlefields and the enemy is clearly seen! "Dishonorable and ungentlemanly," complain the French soldiers and decide the slaves' way of fighting is just another example of their savagery. The rebels kill a quarter of them before they retreat.

The defeated French turn to negotiation and Milord sees again that same annoying spirit of conciliation emerge: some of the rebels want to return to their plantations and resume their lives again, albeit under better conditions. Those men argue that everyone has to work and so why not work for the whites, but under their own terms?

Milord's oratorial skills, his experience up north and the scars on his face that proclaim him a prince among his people quickly make him one of the leaders. He argues passionately against any compromise: "Why negotiation—we are so close! How can we ask for three days of work and no whip, when the whole world could be ours?"

"We want to go home."

"The French know they are losing control and that is why they negotiate," argues Milord. "But every town we take, every white or colored we kill, is one more step towards freedom."

"We want to go home." Life is hard up at Les Platons, with the cold weather and morning fog, the constant fear of pillage or attack, capture and gruesome death. In the early days many were caught up in the excitement but now regret their enthusiasm. Who were they to think they might create a new kingdom? They are just men and many do not want to be heroes.

"And how can we trust the French?" shouts Milord. "We know of their treachery!"

His words fall on deaf ears and when the rebels are offered amnesty by the government, several hundred take it: they will be granted their freedom in exchange for serving in the French army.

In disgust, Milord and other hardliners vow to extend the fight. After the heat of the summer dies down, Milord leaves Les Platons with a vanguard of twenty trusted men, most of them Congos with experience fighting in the wars that long wracked their nation. They make their way down the mountains to the hills behind Dame Marie and settle on the deserted Pellegrin plantation. From here, they will spread the fight: their goal is to take ten leagues of coastline south of Dame Marie to reach Tiburon, already in rebel hands. Then they will continue north around the coast to Jérémie and plunge the entire southern peninsula into chaos.

Included in Milord's vanguard is a Mandingo called Fraise—*Strawberry*—a man who once worked for the Royal Surveyor in Les Cayes. He brings with him a surveyor's map that shows the area around Dame Marie, all the plantations neatly marked in alternating colors of pink, blue, green. The whole like a pretty dish of candies; Fraise's old master was a thwarted artist, cursed by the rigidity of cartography.

Fraise unscrolls the map and carefully they select the plantations they need. Coffee trees, so abundant in the region, are planted in what the whites call a quincunx of five plants: one central bush surrounded by four others. Fraise knows his numbers and the power of multiplication. He chooses which plantations will be the centers of each quincunx and maps out how the rebellion will spread. They steer clear of those plantations too well armed or where they are not guaranteed of sufficient response. They know to avoid, for example, a plantation like Noel Azor's, rumored to have an arsenal and where too many slaves are loyal to their exceptional master.

Thirty plantations selected, spreading out by four to more than a hundred. Milord can't read but he knows the names, engraved in his heart: Bayardel, Fondin, Mercier, Gaultier, Yvonnet and so many more. From each plantation they choose a handful of loyal slaves to be privy to the plot. They want house servants or those that work in the trades; field slaves, especially the newly-arrived *bossales*, will be the foot soldiers but their generals are to be drawn from the ranks of *commandeurs*, carpenters, coachmen and butlers. Men who work in close proximity with their white masters are the ones most above suspicion.

It is hard for Milord to imagine that the colored squares on the map represent real land, hills and houses, boundaries and gates, but he likes looking at the Pellegrin plantation, well thumbed, and marked with an X. He imagines the pale pinks and greens, blues and yellows of the surrounding plantations turning to red as the rebellion spreads out, blossoming like an enormous crimson flower and engulfing the entire district in death.

Soon.

Around the Plantation
2 pm

From the kitchen Jeannette stares over the clearing, empty now: everyone back to the fields or at the drying platforms. Appollon slipping away without a word. Bridget taken off to the whipping post. Jeannette's throat tightens. The post is rarely used these days and she herself has never been tied there, but the stake is still stained with the blood of slaves long dead, some of whom died with their hands still bound to it. White savages. Monsters. Poor Bridget, but there is nothing Jeannette can do about it; pity is scarce in this life and there is none to be shared.

Cautiously Jeannette emerges from the safety of the kitchens and slips round the back to the poultry pens. These used to be stocked full of hens, geese, ducks and turkey but now only a few chickens, one strutting rooster and two startled quail remain. She grabs and snaps the neck of the scrawniest chicken, then pauses. There is a heavy stillness in the air today. Hurricane calm, Flore would say, like the one fifteen years ago that uprooted the last of the indigo plants and destroyed most of the old big house.

Back in the kitchen Jeannette plucks the feathers from the bird. She hacks up the carcass and throws the pieces into a pan on the stove where they sizzle in molten lard. She starts mixing the crust of the pie, the pastry crumbling under her fingers. Then she will chop the onions, garlics and wild potatoes, the spinach and parsley, season them with salt from the barrel and wild rosemary, simmer the sauce all afternoon until it sings with notes of extraordinary flavor. Beside her Flore is sleeping and the world is returning to normal.

Breathe, just breathe, and the day will bring what it brings.

A soft cooing from the poultry pens and she finds Appollon out back. They embrace and she feels his heart beating, too fast.

"What?" she asks, pulling away and looking into his face. She knows it so well, sees lines of fear and worry etched around his eyes, a clear map to his emotions. "What are you doing? What's happening?" Jeannette feels herself starting to tremble. "The dead white…?"

"Not my doing."

"But the knife," she sobs, worry rushing out of her and crippling her with relief. "You have the knife."

"I do, Jeannie, but everything is fine. Because of you. Thank you." Appollon averts his eyes. "Everything is fine, believe me."

Jeannette doesn't believe, not for one minute. She pulls him close, runs her hands over his back and feels the knots she wants to smooth out with the force of her love. There will come a time, horribly soon, when he might no longer be there for her to hold on to.

"Jeannie, I've got to go and see someone," says Appollon, pulling away. "The constable is coming here and… It can't happen tonight, not with the militia here."

Jeannette closes her eyes. So it was tonight. She guessed it when he returned from that meeting last Sunday morning, white paste covering his chest, his energy enormous and ready to spring.

But now it is delayed.

"Sorry, sorry," Jeannette murmurs, trying to keep the relief from her voice. Any delay means a chance it will never happen. "Where do you have to go?"

"To Pellegrin's," Appollon replies. "I hope he is there. If not…"

Jeannette knows who *he* is—Milord, the rebel leader from Les Platons.

"They'll miss you here," she whispers. "Brac is in a foul mood."

"It doesn't matter now."

Jeannette takes a deep breath. "We heard a carriage. Who

arrived?"

"Coloreds from the Fraternité plantation. Big ones—Azor. That's where you went on that Sunday, right?"

"I did," Jeannette replies. They are here, just as Pomponne said they would be!

"Why?" Appollon's voice is sharp and suspicious.

"I told you—a party. I helped in the kitchens." Jeannette buries her head in his chest, to hide her smile and the hope that is spreading through her. She hasn't told Appollon what happened at La Fraternité; she didn't want his scorn for her foolish dreams. And he hates the coloreds, almost as much as he hates the whites. "I saw old friends, made a few coins. It was nothing."

Appollon pushes her away, his eyes searching her face. "But the Azors are here now. Why didn't you tell me?"

"I only knew this morning," Jeannette protests. "Who came—the big master or one of the sons?" Perhaps she shouldn't be thinking of this right now, or perhaps this is the only time to think of it.

"I saddled up one of the sons—he's riding to Dame Marie for Bassompierre. The father is with the whites in the big house."

"What is the son's name?"

Appollon laughs. "How would I know? A young one. Spoke in a most high manner but those people always think themselves so fine."

Appollon strokes her head and gives her another kiss. "I've got to tell Milord the constable is coming. I'll be back in a few hours."

"Wait, you need to eat." Jeannette fetches a piece of chicken, dripping in fat.

Appollon eats quickly and kisses her.

"Come back safely," she says.

"Of course."

Appollon starts up the path towards the provision fields, heading for the hills and Pellegrin's charred plantation. Jeannette watches him until he disappears into the thick green foliage. All is silent again. No cries from the whipping post, yet. She offers a prayer to the gods for Appollon, and one for her daughter.

So it was supposed to happen tonight. Unbearable, to think that tonight might have been the night she lost Appollon and all her happiness. *I've got to stop this,* he said. But perhaps some things cannot be stopped. The wind, a wave, a wheel set in motion, the tides of the sea and the arc of history that is hanging over them.

Jeannette puts a napkin over the pastry and squeezes Flore's hand; the old woman grunts but doesn't open her eyes. She walks out behind the men's house to the hospital hut and peeks inside.

"Ah, go away," grumbles Joseph the watchman; he sleeps here before his night duties and this godforsaken day has already brought too many interruptions. Victor groans and Charlotte lies motionless; her jaw is so rotted she can no longer eat and is slowly starving. Only a few more days, thinks Jeannette, looking at her friend. Only a few more days, then death must surely release her. Or perhaps it will release us all.

Jeannette continues up the path to the wash house. "Have you seen Pomponne?" she asks Laurine. The laundress is staring into the sudsy water of a large copper tub, drawn from the stream that gurgles beside her.

"At the house, I'm sure," says the laundress shortly, not looking up. Laurine is plump and nasty; the others joke that her husband back in Guinée sold her to the slavers on the condition that she be taken to the farthest place on earth.

Pierre and Capidon wander over, bearing shovels and laughing.

"Why are you laughing?" Jeannette says, scowling. Capidon is her least favorite, always lying and whining, and she doesn't understand his friendship with Appollon.

"Why wouldn't we be laughing?" snaps Capidon.

"You know what's funny?" says Pierre. "That little scrap Bridget killing the white!"

"She's a deep one," remarks Laurine. "Never trusted her."

"She's hardly deep," says Jeannette, feeling the need to defend Bridget. "That poor woman."

"Eh, you be getting as soft hearted as Mumbo," says Laurine, shaking her head.

"Maybe she tired of being used in the pigpen," remarks Pierre. "But she didn't kill the white."

"Then who did?" asks Jeannette. Now that she knows it wasn't Appollon, she can openly ask and wonder.

"Dunno."

"If Bridget be smart, she blame it on the dead man's son," says Capidon. "He creeping around the plantation all week."

Jeannette nods thoughtfully. "I caught him yesterday trying to steal a quail. Who was feeding him?"

Laurine shrugs. "Probably Mumbo, she always feeding the weak ones. Or his daddy."

"What's that fat white like?" asks Capidon, nodding at Jeannette. "Why not him the killer?"

Jeannette shrugs. "Just a fat white. Pomponne calls him a rooster, says he talks Madame Rose's ear off when all she wants to do is sleep."

"I seen him poking around," says Laurine. "Up to no good. And trying to tell me how to wash his hankies!"

"Maybe the white children kill that man, don't want their lessons no more," suggests Capidon.

"Don't be silly," says Jeannette sharply.

"While they sitting inside with lessons, we got that turtle Pomponne tell us about," says Pierre. "Mighty fine shell it is. Fetch a good penny in Jérémie."

"What did you do with the meat?" asks Laurine with some interest.

"Drying in the candlewood trees. Sell you some cheap."

"The little whites will be unhappy," Jeannette remarks. "They were most excited."

"Just like that baby to cry over a turtle," scoffs Laurine. She and Aimée are locked in an ongoing battle over what Aimée considers, rightly, the deliberate ruin of her clothes. Every time the girl complains, another sleeve is rubbed worthless and another lace collar ripped.

"Master Charles, you know he was with Bridget in the pigpen," says Pierre, turning away from the triumph of the turtle.

"That hardly makes him a murderer," scoffs Laurine. "He's just a boy, spurting over his sheets every night."

"It's a sign," says Capidon solemnly. "One white die, then many more. The hand of Jesus or Ogun, reaching down from the sky."

Jeannette shivers at his words and they all fall silent. Eventually Laurine leans forward an inch and picks out a handkerchief from the water. "That fat man, he have a hundred hankies, using them all day and they not even dirty."

"Fah!" says Pierre, stretching. "Don't say you saw us—we going for a sleep before digging that hole. White man nice and cool down the well, he don't want to be moved is my thinking."

"Brac's in a foul mood today," says Jeannette. "If you don't get that hole dug you might be joining Plunkett down the well."

"Not after tonight," scoffs Pierre with a wide grin. "Not after tonight."

Jeannette wonders briefly if she should tell them that the plan is delayed. No, she won't get involved; Appollon can tell them on his return.

"I'm hungry," whines Capidon. "Give us a morsel from the kitchen. We can smell the chicken."

Jeannette shakes her head. "None to be spared. But give me a *sou* and I'll get you some milk."

"Don't you go sell me something you get free."

"Two *sous*."

"Bitch. You be glad you with Appollon otherwise you wouldn't like tonight," grins Capidon.

"Oh, shut up, you mean goat." Their easy hatred bothers neither; his threats are as plentiful as they are empty. "If you see Pomponne let me know," Jeannette says as the two men head off into the woods for their nap. She peers down the well at Plunkett's dark shape. A faint smell wafts up, fish baking in the sun. He'll have to be buried before sundown.

Jeannette wanders back to the kitchen and continues working on the pie crust. The plan for tonight delayed, perhaps never to come again. She thinks of Pierre and Capidon, laughing about the turtle, and of Laurine complaining about Thoreau. An odd man, certainly. He came into the kitchens yesterday with a measuring stick, jabbering about *nutrition* and beans and scribbling away in his notebook. She had pretended not to understand French then directed him to the provision fields and told him to look for Samedi or Dimanche, the twins who tend them during the day.

"Ah no, Madame," Thoreau said with a half-bow that Jeannette thought ridiculous. "I fear today is Tuesday and I cannot wait until Saturday to continue my important investigations. Science waits not for the slow nor the slothful!"

Jeannette presses the pastry, smooth and sticky, into an enormous ceramic tureen. She eats a piece of the chicken and peels off a few morsels for Flore but the old woman is still asleep. Should she make something for dessert? Madame had not specified anything. Jeannette thinks of the pudding of their earlier days—*Tropical Rose Soup*, Master Marcel called it and how much fun they had making it! Jeannette has a sudden desire to make it tonight, though she can't say why: sympathy or spite?

The last time Jeannette made it was after the death of Monsieur Marcel. Thinking to comfort her mistress she prepared it, but then... a dreadful scene. Jeannette was called by Brac to the big house and she went inside for the first time in many years. In the dining room she was greeted by the sight of her pudding, slung and dripping over the table and walls.

"How could you serve me this slop?" cried Madame Rose in a voice Jeannette had never heard before. "How *dare* you serve me this?"

Jeannette nodded, eyes downcast and breath held. She knew Madame Rose's rage was really about the loss of her husband but that knowledge might not keep her safe. Eventually, thankfully, her mistress subsided into tears and Pomponne set about cleaning up the mess. Jeannette slipped back to the kitchens, her heart beating so fast she thought she would choke.

"Poor Madame Rose," she said and Flore cackled in disbelief.

"Poor nothing! That woman is mad. She writes her own misery."

But Jeannette couldn't shake her feeling of sadness and pity. Madame Rose was so... defeated. Lost. So different from the young girl with laughing eyes and high spirits. Jeannette had seen her change, saw how the years had unfurled and sapped the life out of her, any remaining happiness snatched away by the loss of her baby and husband. Jeannette imagines the pain she would feel if Pomponne died, or Appollon. Whites feel just like us, she thinks, hard as it is to imagine they have hearts. They feel just as we do.

Jeannette decides she won't make the pudding. She has enough to do with the chicken pie and all the side dishes, and she can serve cream and fruit if they desire something sweet.

More importantly: Where is her daughter? The Azors are

here. Only the father, if the son has gone to Dame Marie but he'll be back shortly and what if it is the same young man that Pomponne talked with two weeks ago? It has to be, and if so that means he was as delighted with her daughter as Pomponne had so modestly implied.

Jeannette is considering going up to the big house when she sees her daughter in the clearing. She rushes out and grabs her.

"Where have you been?"

"At the house," says Pomponne. "Getting bottles and laying out the cheese and bread."

"You were a long time there. You stay out of the way?"

"Yes, the old hen dropped a drink so I cleaned that. Then the men came back and I left, but I listened."

"So you know that the Azors have arrived! Did you see which one?"

"Yes—the old man and his son—the one I spoke with last week," says Pomponne with some pride. "Henri has gone to Dame Marie but he will be back soon."

Jeannette stares at her daughter. Wonderful, and what a blessing that nothing is going to happen tonight! Maybe the white's death this morning was divine intervention, like Pierre and Capidon suggested: now her own plan, for the future of her daughter, can go ahead even as others are foiled.

"Go and change into your pink dress," Jeannette whispers. "Stay inside, out of the way until the Azor boy comes back." She gives Pomponne a sudden hug, quick and fierce. Her daughter is so innocent but events and times are moving fast.

"Yes, Mama," says Pomponne. She twists free of her mother. "What is Appollon doing? I saw him going up the hill."

"An errand," says Jeannette. "Did you eat?"

"Yes, cheese. What are they going to do to Bridget?"

"Never mind that. Don't think of it. Go!"

Pomponne leaves and Jeannette chops herbs, sets about simmering the sauce over the range, everything beginning to bubble together in harmony. Who would have believed it would happen like this? The Azor boy has come here and it must be for her daughter.

"Do you know what you are doing?" asks Flore, suddenly awake.

"I do." Jeannette glances over at the old woman but surely Flore can't know all her secrets hidden so deep inside.

"Child, the devil don't come at night wearing horns. But he do appear in your hopes," says Flore, closing her eyes again.

On the Veranda
2 pm

Rose sits in the salon, as alert as a cat before a mouse. A brief pause in the flow of words from Thoreau and she pounces: "As Monsieur Thoreau so modestly stated," Rose says, "he is here on a mission from Bordeaux. He has a particular interest in, ah, fertility and you may find, Monsieur Azor, that you have much in common."

"How wonderful, Monsieur, that you share a passion of mine! Indeed! As Madame Fongravier alluded, I am tasked by the *Académie* to propose *scientific* methodologies that may be used to improve breeding and infant mortality rates. Perhaps we might take advantage of this time as we await Bassompierre to discuss—?"

Rose rises, glad her little ruse worked. "If you will excuse me, I really must lie down." Wonderful happenstance, though she feels slightly guilty at leaving Monsieur Azor—who has been nothing but kind and helpful—alone with Thoreau.

Before going to her room, she checks Aimée's bedroom but only finds Julienne. She strokes Julie's head—she is often in danger of forgetting about her poor sister-in-law—and pours her a glass of water from the bedside pitcher.

Outside on the veranda she almost collides with Thoreau, waiting.

"Oh! You startled me. And Monsieur Azor?" Rose queries, closing the door of the bedchamber and trying to keep the irritation from her voice.

"Awaiting me, but not to worry, Madame, I excused myself with finesse. I really must take a moment of your time before you retire." Thoreau pulls a paper from his jacket and clears his throat. "This document—I found it in the satchel of Mr. Plunkett; indeed, I saw him take it from the cupboard in the dining room last Sunday."

Rose scans the paper. "Julienne's baptism certificate?"

"Yes, *Julienne Elisabeth Marie Fongravier*. I presumed a sister of your husband, or a niece, cousin? But what interest could Plunkett have in her baptism?"

"Sister. But I am sorry, Monsieur, I cannot speak to the significance of it," says Rose. Her head is throbbing and the lingering drink still clouds her mind. The closeness of the man is unbearable. What was Thoreau doing prying around in Plunkett's bag? A secondary question, perhaps, to why their tutor had seemingly stolen one of their family's documents.

"Compelling and curious, Madame, I thought—"

"Monsieur Thoreau, please forgive me. I am, ah, unwell," Rose says, gesturing to her stomach in vague intimation of female troubles. "Perhaps I can reconsider this matter later?"

"Ah yes, indeed, a thousand pardons! Madame, let me help you to your room!"

Safe with the door latched, Rose sinks down on her bed without even removing her slippers. Why did Plunkett have Julie's birth certificate? If indeed Thoreau was telling the truth? Her head spins. How did Azor know that Plunkett was coming this week? she thinks suddenly before sleep snatches her away, a thought she will forget on waking. She dreams of a very handsome man, offering her strawberries with one hand then taking them away with the other, and then of Julienne complaining that no one even remembers she was born.

*

"Forgive my absence, Monsieur Azor," says Thoreau, hurrying back into the salon. He notices his sister Mathilde is gone and vaguely wonders where. He smiles at Azor. The mulatto is a handsome man: Perhaps that universal law that generally makes the women of mixed race superb extends to the men as well?

Thoreau pours two glasses of rum from the sideboard; taffia he considers a woman's drink. Damnation that he had not thought to put on his best jacket! Instead he is dressed in a pale blue coat that has seen better days and is perhaps a little tight around the belly. Thoreau considers apologizing for his rustic attire but then decides he will redeem himself by changing into his best—cream silk embroidered with acanthus leaves—for dinner. Though he cannot admit it to himself, Azor's fastidious fashion invokes in Thoreau a subtle feeling of inferiority.

"Thank you," says Azor, taking the glass of rum. Thoreau settles happily on the sofa opposite and regards him with admiration. The way he calmly faced Mercier and his damned rudeness! Should he make common cause with Azor against his enemy? No, perhaps that type of intimate confession—hatred for another white man—might best come later.

"What an honor, Monsieur, to have found a like-minded companion! I have been somewhat frustrated by my hosts' complete indifference to my proposals and experiments. Perhaps you will help me put lie to the notion that slave breeding for profit is a myth."

"It is true what you say, Monsieur Thoreau," acknowledges Azor, inclining his head. "Most planters here have a short-term mentality that precludes any investment in improved breeding. Most prefer to see Mother Africa as a limitless source of bounty— a wasteful mindset."

"Indeed! Sadly short sighted!"

"I believe the unrest currently overtaking this island is the consequence of that blindness: instead of a more docile slave population, born and raised in captivity, too many slaves here have fresh memories of freedom."

"Ah, interesting, interesting," breathes Thoreau—that thought had not occurred to him but he will certainly adopt it as his own. "Now let me start with a question designed to frame the nature of the problem," he continues. "This is a part of the *scientific* method, whereby one starts broad and then works downward toward the answer by deductions. So first, an overview of the matter."

"As you are aware, no doubt," starts Azor, "a plantation is a closed environment where everything is connected and delicately balanced. For success in breeding, one cannot focus on just one area."

Thoreau sees that the other man has taken his words to mean that he, Azor, should begin. Thoreau considers interrupting; after all, he has far more to share—he has been investigating for nigh on a year!—but then decides that he is interested in hearing what Azor has to say.

"For example, one cannot focus solely on the health of the mother," Azor continues, "without considering the incentives for the midwives."

"Oh yes!" says Thoreau eagerly. "An understanding of the linkages is absolutely crucial!" He pauses, aware for the first time of just how much he wants the other man's approval. "I have a little hypothesis that I am working on, based on the minimum breeding space and optimal food intake, two factors I believe are vastly important."

"Indeed," says Azor, and Thoreau beams in pleasure. "And of course, one must find the balance between incentives and punishment. Many in Saint Domingue rely too heavily on the stick but an overly harsh environment will not produce the desired result."

"Ah yes!" agrees Thoreau. "Better conditions in general will surely lead to an increase in both the quality and the quantity of breeding!" He pauses, then plunges on: "The idea of a three-day work week, perhaps four days, seems a modest and favorable goal."

Thoreau holds his breath, watching Azor carefully and remembering the last time he espoused these moderate views. At Corail, with the cousin of Madame Rose. His natural tact run adrift from too much rum, Thoreau had made the mistake of expressing support for the idea of a reduced workweek. He was rewarded with an enraged host, dire threats and a hurried departure as he and Mathilde fled in the middle of that same night. Indeed, he feared for his life for there was no telling what an enraged Creole might do: the colony is littered with the decapitated corpses of men—some of them white—who espoused moderate views.

"Perhaps," agrees Azor and Thoreau exhales. "But then, if incentives are too freely given, the stick loses its power."

"Of course, of course. One cannot be too soft."

"When looking to optimize breeding, the stick is necessary in the early days when the balance is being created. The harshest punishments must start with those mothers found harming their children."

"Ah, yes, I have heard of that!" exclaims Thoreau, shaking his head. "How misguided those mothers are, to kill their young. Certainly, one cannot expect slaves to possess the maternal instinct as our women do, but surely they retain *some* fondness? Or if not for their children, then at least for their owners' profits?"

"I also take special care in my selection of midwives, who know it will be instant demotion to the field if an infant fails under their care. And no quarter is given if the infant develops lockjaw. I make a point of fifty lashes for any mother or midwife whose child dies of the dreaded *mal machoir*. Innocents may have suffered but my plantations have been free of trismus for nigh on six years."

"Incredible!" breathes Thoreau. "Near Port-au-Prince we visited a plantation where that dreaded disease claimed half of all births."

"Generally, not a disease but sorcery. A thin needle inserted through the soft fontanelle of the baby's head can cause that particular affliction."

What a fountain of knowledge the man is, thinks Thoreau, and it is only through steely determination that he prevents himself from gushing as much. An eager sip of rum, then he takes out a notebook from his jacket pocket, a little pencil attached, and starts to scribble. "If you permit me?"

"Of course. We track our females' monthly cycles—both to determine optimal breeding times as well as to uncover pregnancies," continues Azor. "At the first hint of pregnancy the woman is moved to a lighter job. If there is a miscarriage, we affix an iron collar that is worn until their next pregnancy is confirmed. One woman wore hers for four years before she managed to show again; harsh, you may say, but our rate of miscarriage now falls squarely in the median one might expect with the European female."

"Incredible!" breathes Thoreau.

"Additional precautions include banning alligator pear trees from the provision fields and ensuring wild ones are cut down: the bark is well known to induce flooding and abortion." Azor pauses and takes a sip of his rum, then remarks in appreciation on its taste. Thoreau swells with pride on behalf of his hostess. "But the stick must at all times be countered with appropriate rewards and incentives. We provide simple gifts for pregnant Negresses that provide pleasure and status: bolts of cloth, shoes, mirrors. Then rewards for live births and children who attain the age of twelve. You are aware, Monsieur, that the French Crown—ah, French *government* now!—provides pensions for fecundity amongst the white and colored populations?"

"Certainly, yes, as in France," replies Thoreau. Pensions for twelve children living, as well as for six. Though curious that the law also applies to free coloreds—why is the French government interested in promoting the growth of that particular group?

"We grant one day a week to a mother for each living child, so that when a mother has six children who reach the age of twelve, no more service is required."

"Ah, indeed." What joy to discuss this topic, finally, with someone who shares his interest! How remarkable that he should find intellectual harmony here, and with a *colored* man!

"We also encourage families. A minority view amongst my peers but apart from the obvious benefits to the mother, it encourages the fathers' attachment to the infant and by extension to the plantation."

"I saw such a thing on the Monville plantation," replies Thoreau. "I was shown three families, with nine, eight and seven children each! They seemed most happy in their domestic bliss but I was told they were all Creoles except for one mother."

"An important point, indeed; marriage on my plantations is only for Creole slaves that have proved their fertility; it has been my experience that *bossales* born in Africa do not have the right mindset. For those men, we make the women available in the evenings at the precise time in their periodic calendar, in what we call the breeding huts. That service cuts down feuds between the men though the women and girls are not overly fond of the practice. But their service in the hut is only required for about a week a month."

"Ah, how interesting." There is a lull in the conversation and Thoreau summons up the nerve to broach a topic he has been mulling over. "Here on this plantation, there is the Negress

Chereze, addled in the head. Yet Brac told me she is their most fertile breeder, which set me to wondering: Is there a connection between idiocy and breeding? That question then leads to the obvious next one: Is there a way to promote or encourage idiocy in the name of improved fertility?"

"An interesting idea, Monsieur Thoreau," says Azor. "Certainly, the ideal Negress is one who is both fertile and tractable."

"That needle in the fontanelle," breathes Thoreau, the idea hitting him as he struggles to contain his excitement. He feels as though he is on the verge of a great discovery: Newton and his apple! Galileo and his stars! He might even become known as the father of the enslaved Negroid race! "Some trial and error, certainly," he rushes on. "Experiments, yes, the needle into various parts of the skull until the right state of idiocy is obtained, and imagine the potential were the exact spot to be discovered—the spot that might remove all resistance, even from the male Negro, and render him docile! A castration not of the testes, but of the mind!"

Thoreau pauses, aware that he is sweating and his heart pumping rapidly. Just look what genius could be achieved when two great minds work together! With Azor's experience and his intellect, what might they not achieve?

"An interesting idea, perhaps," says Azor, raising an eyebrow and Thoreau hopes he has impressed the man. But then Azor moves on, without giving Thoreau's momentous idea the appropriate due. "Finally, my plantations are almost evenly divided between Congo and Ibo, two nationalities known to be good breeders, though because of my success in breeding my main plantation, La Fraternité, is almost three quarters Creole. I believe Creole slaves are far happier and less prone to acts of insubordination than *bossales*. You might say the Creole slave belongs to a race of subjugated men, not subjugated by force, but by the limits of their experience and expectations. And we can imagine that with each passing generation, they will be bred into further submissiveness."

"As animals may be domesticated!" exclaims Thoreau. "And then imagine if we could couple that careful selection with the small operation I was alluding to…"

"Interesting, interesting," says Azor with what appears to be genuine enthusiasm. Thoreau feels a rush of pleasure. When Azor finishes his rum, Thoreau leaps up to serve him another.

"Are your thoughts common amongst those men of your own race?" Thoreau asks, somewhat shyly, as he hands him another glass.

Azor chuckles. "Not entirely; we suffer from the same range of personalities, characters and flaws as afflicts the whites."

Thoreau wants to ask more but is unsure how to continue, at last acknowledging his feelings of inferiority to this man, to his intellect and to his clothes. He is reminded of the time he had the pleasure of dining—at the same table!—as the august Comte de Maurepas, the Minister of the Marine. Thoreau felt as though he were holding his breath throughout the entire dinner, served in honor of the man's visit to Bordeaux. Thoreau studied how the great man talked, ate, carried himself, even how he sneezed! Surely, he remarked afterward when he recounted the minutiae to his sister, that man could have been put in trousers, with a hoe in hand, yet still his breeding would shine through!

Thoreau decides to continue—certain improprieties can be excused in the name of scientific investigation: "On the subject of breeding, I am a follower of Buffon and his theory that the different races are, ah, different species." A commonly accepted viewpoint but the theory had one main sticking point: fertility. If black and white were truly separate species then their offspring should be as infertile as mules. "Is there any credence to the idea of declining fertility amongst those of mixed race?"

Azor appears bemused and Thoreau fears he has made a tremendous blunder. Too soon! He launches into an abject apology but Azor holds up a hand.

"Not to worry, Monsieur," says Azor mildly. "I am aware of that theory but I myself fathered eight children, six—five—of whom survive. And my wife, also a mulatto of similar parentage to myself, is one of eight sisters."

"But your grandchildren? The next generation?"

"Both my daughters are married and have children."

"Many?"

"Six between them, but they are as yet young."

"Ah, indeed. Interesting, interesting." Thoreau smiles

happily, believing he has made a new friend. "Perhaps we may enjoy my findings to date? Let me fetch my other notebooks that I might share the wealth of detail I have collected, including measurements and—"

Outside
2 pm

Mathilde silently descends the front steps and moves away from the house. She hears something calling to her, drawing her outward from her place of safety and into the afternoon. No one will miss her. No one sees her or even notices her and lately her invisibility has become a cloak she wears with some pride. She is a shadow, but not only in the night.

Mathilde searches the front gardens but the overgrown flowers in all the gaudy colors of creation confuse her; they are trying to tell her something she can't decipher. It was here that she saw the men last night but what that meant she doesn't know. And I must find the white horse, she thinks, remembering the animal that glowed through the blackness and whinnied when it smelt her.

Now around the side of the house, she stares at the orange carriage that brought the man and his son here. To Mathilde it seems to pulse like a giant heart, the house rising protectively off to one side. From the veranda she can hear her brother talking, as he always talks, and she takes a side path that leads her further away.

Mathilde's decision to come to Saint Domingue was hastily taken but not regretted, and it surprised even her. Back in Bordeaux, Mathilde turned sixty and started having trouble getting out of bed; she felt her age and as though she was not wanted in the world anymore. She tended the house, took care of her brother and listened to his endless talk, but never once did he think to ask about her, or her happiness.

Happiness—what a strange notion and not one that had worried her before. Mathilde never shirked from duty; as a child she was at the heart of a large and loving family, one that gradually shrank through death, marriage, adventure or career. Mathilde stayed with her brother after her parents died, keeping their house, making him comfortable. Then, after a lifetime of devotion, long past the age when she thought such things should matter, life began to seem empty and pointless. A little voice popped up inside and asked: Is this all?

All around Mathilde changes were afoot, leaving her breathless and disoriented: flying balloons, steam machines, inoculations, Mesmerism, a thousand new ideas percolating and bubbling and creating a whirlwind of change. Servants learning to read, magicians in the street. Jugglers and acrobats. Rhinoceroses and lightning rods. Gentle women disavowing corsets and dressing like maids. Men talking openly against the established order, against royalty and even the clergy; nuns turned out from convents and priests killed. When she was young in the middle of the century, things were simpler and slower but then the world starting turning faster and faster and yet she stayed the same, overwhelmed at the center.

Their neighbor Madame Magnon lived past ninety, so who was to say she didn't have another thirty years in her? And the houseflies were getting larger and one even talked to her; she had to get far away to ensure that did not happen again.

"I am coming," she announced to her brother, one winter evening as they were sitting in the parlor, a fire keeping them company as the wind whistled and howled off the Atlantic and through every crevice of the house. Thoreau spluttered and hawed, suggested a visit to their sister in Toulouse, then finally acquiesced: "How tender is your heart, dear sister, that you wish to accompany me and ensure my comfort!"

Mathilde curdled at the idea that it was from devotion that she wanted to come. Though she loved her brother, his endless self-absorption was starting to annoy her in a way it never had before. So puffed up and conceited, yet so fragile.

Mathilde began her preparations. She knew that women dressed scandalously in the tropics—even more scandalously than the new fashions from Paris!—but she would not give in to that dreadful looseness. Mathilde believed looseness in dress equaled looseness in morals and that could never be.

"Why not?" asked the fly, buzzing against the window pane.

"Because then everything would fall apart!" Mathilde shouted. She quickly flattened the fly with her hand and knew she must ignore the insects, no matter how seductive their voices.

At the last minute their departure was almost derailed by the news of the king's escape from Paris, then his capture a few days later.

"The king—fled!" said Thoreau with worry. "Brought back to Paris as a prisoner! But this changes everything!"

"It changes nothing!" snapped Mathilde. She didn't care about the king and his family.

"Perhaps there is not much I can do here," conceded Thoreau and she allowed herself to breathe again.

Finally they departed and Mathilde exulted as she felt the ocean spray on her face and the force of the ship surging forward. She reveled in the vastness of the ocean and in the feeling of freedom the wind and the water gave her.

Freedom! Why had she never craved it before?

In Saint Domingue the savagery of the colony awakened odd feelings. With every story of horror she heard, Mathilde felt herself swelling up. It was the blacks, she knows now; it is they who are feeding her soul and spirit. She was transforming, just as the world was transforming. At night she dreamt of becoming a bird, something free and vicious that would fly over the island and witness every scene of terror, even get inside the terror itself.

And there is something physical growing inside her, something about to hatch. Mathilde believes it is the spirit of the island, though a doctor might offer a more prosaic and sad diagnosis. It is feeding off the darkness and the evil of the earth that is all around her, but where the evil comes from she is not sure. And there is something on this plantation, that Mathilde felt from the minute she arrived, something that propels her outwards and into the shadows, searching for something she cannot name but only anticipate.

Whatever it is, she suspects it might show itself today.

Mathilde pauses at the top of the path leading to the kitchens. Down there is death, dead animals, the muck of ages, and yes, flies. To her right, the stables and more flies. She breathes in, out, then creeps on, feeling her way through a thicket of overgrown creepers.

The Road to Dame Marie
3 pm

Henri is in a foul mood; this is not an errand he cares for. Jolting along all morning in the carriage and now forced out again on horseback and all when there are far more pleasant diversions to be found. *Oh Madame Rose, I have a plan. I will save you,* Henri thinks sourly, remembering the way his father talked with that white woman. His father, ever the noble patriarch, ever ready with the perfect solution.

But Dame Marie is only an hour's ride. Plenty of time to get there and back and find that little girl. Pomponne—absolutely delightful. She has scarcely left his mind since their meeting and what a stroke of luck that his father was headed here today, to her plantation.

Henri rides along the coastal road that loops inward and up before breaking out with a clear view of the Anse de la Bossée, the next bay over. From this height he can see the town of Dame Marie tucked neatly in the next curve of the coast, twenty bright colored houses grouped around a river mouth, more cliffs rising in the distance. Wild sugar cane, planted along the edge of the road to prevent erosion, sways in the sea breezes. Henri passes a plantation boundary marked by lemon trees that release a light odor as he rides by.

This weather is what he missed the most in France. The walls of his school were like cold dungeons and the winters not to be borne. Even the summers disappointed: the heat thin and fickle, the sun always disappearing behind clouds or quick showers. Henri leans his head back and basks in the full force of the sun. He was happy to trade the cold mortar and stone of France for this lush greenery and heat; the drabness of that life exchanged for the brilliance of blue seas and sugar white cliffs. The water is enticing and turquoise, smooth. A good day for a swim. Perhaps on his return; if one disregards that unfortunate swamp, the beach at Bayardel is noted for its fine sand.

In France he often boasted to his friends of the shimmering colors of Saint Domingue, in such contrast to the grayness of French life. What a marvelous country it is: chalk and limestone and rich red earth all within the span of a league. Verdant lushness and the flowers and the fruit—ah, what delights to be savored! He laughs to remember how his French schoolmates imagined the West Indies: steamy jungles, lizards and cannibals, the colonists to be pitied as Robinson Crusoe might be, cast upon a desolate isle.

It is certainly good to be back, though the talk this morning with his father was rather distressing. Henri had hoped his father would give him some of his inheritance early but instead he suggested an apprenticeship, almost! How humiliating. And annatto—was there ever a sorrier crop? But no doubt still better than joining the Navy or Army in France, like many of his friends, or off to some soulless position in Paris where no one knows what is happening and the world has seemingly gone mad.

It is good to be back.

Up a bend are a set of fine plantation gates, carved cacao and coffee beans adorning the iron grilles and then some while later another set of gates, more modest this time, with a small rum stand set beside them. Ah, excellent! He thought this road too quiet to support the venture but a little rum would not be remiss on his boring errand. There are few sugar plantations in this area but many plantations still grow small fields for their own molasses and rum.

Henri dismounts and fishes a coin from his pocket.

"Not much traffic today," he remarks to the man who pours him a bowl.

"Very quiet these days," the man agrees. Black and elderly, with clouds over one eye.

"Durocher's?" asks Henri, motioning to the gates. There is

something familiar about the place.

"No, this is an Allard plantation," corrects the man. "Durocher's on the other side of the cove."

"Right." Henri drains the rum. "Good stuff."

"Nothing finer," says the man, pouring a refill without asking. "And would you like some crayfish, sir? Fresh caught this morning."

Henri notices a white-turbaned woman sitting in the shack's shade, in front of a fire shimmering in the heat.

"Yes, some would be good." All he's eaten today were those damn eggs.

The woman pulls a few creatures from a pail and drops them into a pot.

"And where are you heading this afternoon, sir, if I may ask?"

"Down to Dame Marie," says Henri, gesturing up the road. "I've come from Bayardel, the Fongraviers. A spot of trouble there and I'm to get the captain."

"What sort of trouble?"

Henri smiles. These little rum stands are notorious for capturing the passing gossip. "Murder, actually: an Englishman. Name of Plunkett. Lived in Apricots."

The news seems to strike the old man with some force and he looks away. A moment later he turns back and says carefully: "You'll not be finding Captain Bassompierre in Dame Marie."

"No?"

"We see everything on this road, as I am sure you appreciate, sir. Bassompierre rode by yesterday to Les Irois. Trouble, of a domestic sort, they said."

"Ah." Henri frowns. "He has not returned?"

"No. And I believe he may be away for some days."

Well that decides that, thinks Henri in satisfaction, taking off his jacket and throwing himself down on the grass in the shade of the shack. The pleasant meaty smell of boiling crayfish washes over him and he takes another draught of rum. Peace infuses him. The heat is cooking me, he thinks, and how pleasant it is to be cooked.

One thing about Europe—it was so crowded and noisy. Even in the countryside: a glass factory here, a braying of farm animals there. The clanging of church bells. The cries of the stage coaches that bedeviled even the quietest of roads. Certainly, the cities here in Saint Domingue have their share of noise but generally it's much more peaceful. Right now, all Henri can hear is the lapping of the sea and a wonderful silence, clear and high.

Antoinette—the girl his mother wants him to marry. Why not, he thinks, as the woman lays down a platter of crayfish. He sits up and tears off a tail. Perhaps the old man would give him a spread as a wedding gift—surely he couldn't have his son start a family without? And the Pages are wealthy, Henri is sure of it; Antoinette's dowry might put him in a position to refuse his father's ungenerous annatto offer. And she is pretty enough though her eyes are small and her teeth rather crooked. At least she has them; Henri shudders, remembering a whore with none he sampled in Nantes.

The man appears with a pail of water for the horse. "Will you be continuing on then, sir?"

"Don't think I will be," says Henri, tearing into another tail. "I'll probably just turn back."

"Dame Marie a long way to go for nothing," agrees the man, "and on such a hot day. Might I ask: When did it happen? And how? Talking of the trouble you mentioned."

"Last night, I believe. They found him this morning. Throat slit. Do you have some pepper sauce?"

The man hands him a pot of pepper oil with a few stubborn flies stuck in it. "Sounds a frightful business," he says, "but there's a lot of that these days. Troubles, I mean."

Never a truer sentence was spoken. *The troubles, the troubles*, Henri thinks impatiently as he dips the crayfish into the sauce and accepts more rum from the man. All that anyone can talk about. Surely the unrest can't last forever—France is sending more troops and now that the whites and the mulattoes are supposedly at peace, they can put the troubles down and behind them together.

Before his return, Henri hadn't quite appreciated the scale and scope of the unrest that was transforming Saint Domingue, most reports lost beneath the seismic changes happening in Paris. The simmering civil war between the whites and the mulattoes, the shocking slave rebellion up north that hasn't yet been put down and, if anything, appears to be spreading. And of course, such a pity about his brother Simon. Not that they were close; when Henri left six years ago his brother was a pompous man of twenty-five, always his father's favorite.

Henri finishes the next bowlful of rum. In truth, he is not overly worried about the future—he is confident that the curve of favor, freely given from the world, will circle back to him soon enough. If his father is going to be so miserly then perhaps he and Lucas, his twin brother, should go in on something together. And if Antoinette could bring—he squinches his eyes and hazards a guess—perhaps 50,000 *livres*? Was that asking too much?—then they could get a decent-sized plantation, one that would support a gentleman and not ask too much of him in return. Annatto! Henri thinks again in disgust. It is sugar he wants, sugar that gives the prestige and the dignity.

Henri finishes the crayfish and thinks he might have a few more and another rum, then sees the shack is empty: the man and woman gone and the fire quelled. Strange. After a short nap Henri gets up and stretches. He looks north up the road to Dame Marie then south, back the way he came. It's getting late and he still hasn't seen Pomponne.

"Come on, old girl," Henri says to his horse, "let's go get your master some sport."

The Stables
3 pm

Mercier contemplates Bridget, lying next to the whipping post. "That fop had a good idea," he muses to Charles, standing cautiously off to one side. "Plunkett's boy speaks English. He can tell us what the girl says."

Charles is already regretting following Mercier. This part of the plantation always gives him the chills; nestled at the foot of the hills behind, it gets dark before sundown and the disused pigeon coop smells of something indefinable but certainly not pleasant.

"Go find him," Mercier orders. "Plunkett's boy."

Charles leaves, glad to be gone. He doesn't like Mercier taking charge and treating him like a boy, there to do his bidding and nothing more. The path to the stables is deserted but from the direction of the east field comes faint singing—the slaves are back in the fields. Their singing sounds eerie today and a sense of dread mounts within him, a sense that something—everything—is about to go wrong. I'm like Aimée, Charles thinks in impatience, always with her funny notions and fancies.

Recently Charles has been trying to distance himself from his mother and little sister, move away from them into manhood. He has perhaps not been successful and often finds himself halfway, an awkward place to be. After a growth spurt last year, Charles started wearing his father's clothes. He remembers the first time he put on one of the jackets, a gray affair with ivory buttons, each carved in the shape of a fish. It fitted well around the shoulders but the sleeves were a bit long. Charles admired himself in front of the mirror then sniffed the collar—only a faint smell of damp and mold and nothing to spark a memory. He felt sadness, mixed with pride that this jacket looked fine on him. He was even experimenting with one of his father's wigs when Aimée found him and heckled him mercilessly.

Charles wore the jacket—he remembers his mother's sharp intake of breath when he appeared in it—last year in Jérémie when they attended a speech given by a returned delegate from France. That planter was with the delegation from Saint Domingue that participated in the Estates General at Versailles, then stayed on when events changed course. This man spoke of how they had argued their case for more independence for Saint Domingue in front of the National Assembly. He also derided the Frenchmen they met as *librarian liberals*, making pronouncements from the depths of their libraries without knowing the reality of life in the colonies.

After the delegate finished his speech Monsieur Mercier, the President of the Security Council, asked the planters to stay behind and discuss security measures for the Grand'Anse. Charles looked eagerly at his mother and she nodded, indicating that he might stay and speak for Bayardel. The rest of the audience filed out, the *petits blancs* grumbling at being excluded, the Widow Gaultier—owner of four plantations—shouting that she should be allowed to join the men. The planters laughed and Charles felt the first inklings of that satisfying power that comes from being a man, at ease and owning the public sphere.

After that meeting he returned to Bayardel full of vigor and enjoyed issuing directives and orders for his mother and sister. Rose put up with it for a few days before snapping at him that he was still under her dominion when living in her house, and confiscated the pistol he had taken to wearing around his belt.

Charles colors at the memory and scowls. His head is throbbing and he feels vaguely dissatisfied, but that might just be the rum, unaccustomed as he is to drinking it. His mother's look when he helped himself to a glass. Pride? Or disapproval? Pride, Charles decides: pride that her son is becoming a man. But why doesn't he feel more like one?

He finds Yorick behind the stables, sitting in the shade of a tree and staring at nothing.

"I'm sorry," says Charles awkwardly. He's never spoken to the boy before but he sees they are about the same age. "I'm sorry about your father."

Yorick scowls.

"I lost my father. Two years ago." Almost to the day, thinks Charles—the date is seared in his memory like a wall, dividing the happy times from all that came after.

No answer from Yorick. How ugly the boy is, a misshapen face with freckles and those slightly feral eyes. Yorick is wearing a large, floppy hat and waving a fly brush slowly up and down, swish, swish, swish.

"Do you speak English?" Charles demands, sour that his overtures at friendship were not returned.

"Some." The boy's voice is flat.

"Can you come with me?" Charles knows he should be giving an order, not asking.

"I don't have to. I'm free."

"Yes, but can you come with me? We need someone who speaks English."

"I'm free," the boy repeats.

"Well, my mother will make sure you receive something," says Charles in annoyance. "And you're not busy!"

Yorick contemplates him for a few more swishes of the fly brush, then gets up.

The mules whinny as Charles enters the stables. He selects one of the horsewhips, well suppled and oiled, from the neat line that hangs above the water barrels.

"Come on," he says to Yorick. Though a part of him wants to run to the house and never come back, he knows he can't: Mercier is waiting for them. An anchor reeling him in, pulling him back to the whipping post. He must remember the necklace, remember that Bridget can tell them about it. Charles thinks of his sister talking about drums in the night—Aimée kept complaining about them until their mother snapped and told her to stop making up stories. But what if it is all connected, the drums and the necklace and God knows what other evil from the slaves' *Vaudun*?

Charles thinks of the pistol under his mother's pillow and

of her annoying indifference to everything. Even to danger. What if something is coming, something that a pistol under a pillow could not stop? What if—God forbid—what happened up north last year happens down here?

The Veranda
3 pm

"My good man, I have quite a headache," says Azor to Thoreau, after listening blankly for what seems like two hours but is probably less than one. The alternative is to play dead but given the events of the morning that might be in poor taste. "I must excuse myself."

"Oh, I am so sorry."

"Yes." Azor rises, stifling a great yawn. "I shall lie down while we wait for the constable."

"Of course, of course," splutters Thoreau. "I shall take a walk, allow our conversation to percolate in the bosom of nature."

Azor lies back into the comfort of a hammock and closes his eyes but as soon as Thoreau is gone—down the steps to the front garden, muttering happily to himself—his eyes flip open. Elijah Plunkett dead? His throat slit! But this is a disaster and not possibly a coincidence.

Plunkett—murdered.

From his pocket Azor pulls out the letter that was intended for Plunkett. The letter that Plunkett was to take and sail with to the British colony of Jamaica. In Azor's other pocket: money to fund the little expedition. Such planning and preparation, so many promises made to his friends and co-conspirators. And now Plunkett is dead, utterly ruining what had hitherto been the smooth functioning of a perfect plan.

The letter is for Lieutenant Colonel John Chalmers,

stationed at Fort George near Kingston, just a day's sail from this tip of Saint Domingue. The letter invites British troops to occupy the Grand'Anse and protect the planters from the unrest that is infecting the rest of the island, as well as from the potential threat of France abolishing slavery. The letter is signed with the names of twenty men, all among the elite property owners of the Grand'Anse: Spechbach, Kanon, Boccolin, Allard, Yvonnet and many others.

In the past year, events in France have taken a worrying and radical turn as the National Assembly in Paris revealed itself to be more and more anti-commerce. The sober bourgeois of the early days have been replaced by patriotic hotheads, including bakers, printers and butchers—men who would scarcely know Property, and its importance, if it hit them over the head. This new faction is incompetent and greedy, issuing confusing decrees and endless taxes.

Last month two new Jacobin governors landed in Port-au-Prince, supposedly to restore order to the troubled colony but really to ensure that the recent decree granting the coloreds the vote and full citizenship was implemented and adhered to. Something Azor should be celebrating but he is far more worried about the rumors that they and their accompanying six thousand French troops are here to abolish slavery.

It has not happened so far but God knows what further directives might be coming from the mess in Paris! Abolition of all and everything seems to be the Revolution's guiding mandate— getting rid of the nobility, the monarchy, the clergy, and now possibly slavery. France will soon collapse under the weight of its own tyranny and if they are not careful, she will drag all of Saint Domingue down with her. Who could have predicted after three years of unrest, that Paris would turn out to be the true destructor of the colony?

A disaster, heading towards them at breakneck speed.

So far, the Grand'Anse has been spared but how long can they hold out? Daily there are rumors of plantation uprisings and foiled plots; Azor suspects a lot of hot air and steam but there may be grains of truth within. He has no fears for his own plantations— well run and well speckled with spies and with a virtual arsenal of illegally acquired weapons in the cellars. But still, a longer-term, more durable solution is required.

In recent months, Azor had developed an alliance with some of his fellow planters in the district, both white and colored. Tentative tentacles were extended, including to those whites who had expressed sympathy to him after the dreadful events of Jérémie. Azor even counts among the group some members of the Security Council of the Grand'Anse, though he was careful to stay away from that bullheaded fool Mercier. Mercier—a man who exemplifies all the worst excesses and ignorance of the archetypical white colonist come together in one body. Azor believes men like that are relics, unaware that the tides are shifting.

No, the men he approached with his plan were far more rational and could see that if the current slave economy is to survive, the whites need the coloreds, just as the coloreds need the whites. Together they are a group of men who understand that the needs of property trump the inconveniences of race, and that class is more important than caste. Their group even includes a free black, a cotton planter from the plains to the east of Jérémie.

To safeguard their future, they are appealing to the British for protection. Not an original idea nor even one that is unique to the Grand'Anse. After the northern slave revolt last year, there was much talk of asking for help from the Spaniards, who occupy the eastern part of the island, or the British, close by in Jamaica. The Governor had even appealed to President Adams in America but tensions with France were too high for him to assist. Currently there is a delegation in London, comprised of émigrés from the troubles in France who are also absentee property owners in Saint Domingue, asking Pitt to deliver them from tyranny, restore order and abate the onerous taxes the island's administration keeps issuing.

Out here in the Grand'Anse, they decided not to wait for London but deal directly with Jamaica, and just for their own district rather than the whole colony. Security and independence in one blow! Treasonous, yes, to be privately negotiating with a foreign power that is perilously close to war with France. But such are the times—the British may talk of abolishing the slave *trade* but they are not foolishly considering liberty for their existing slaves.

And Plunkett was tasked with delivering the formal

request.

Perhaps not the ideal emissary but he was English and a learned man with some limited powers of oration. In case Plunkett decided to simply disappear with the money intended for Lieutenant Chalmers, one of his sons was to be kept as collateral. Azor was to collect the boy today, in return for the letter and the funds.

Overall a risky plan but the risk posed by inaction was even greater. Azor and his co-conspirators calculate that the white and colored planters not involved in the plot would choose Britain over France without much hesitation. The *petits blancs* are the only real sticking point: without property to protect, many of them are ardently patriotic and hope to see their own marginal position improved by the so-called Revolution in Paris.

And now, all gone.

Azor squeezes his eyes shut and sways in indecision. He must find out who killed Plunkett, and why. He can't imagine it was a slave as that fool Mercier is insisting—but it is troubling that the woman they have is from Jamaica. Had the slaves heard of the plot to continue their enslavement and intervened at the nexus of the plan? Or had a radical Jacobin from amongst the *petits blancs* killed Plunkett to stop the misalliance with Jamaica?

Azor swings harder.

He is too fundamentally logical to believe that the killing bears no relation to the Jamaica plot. Had it been rash to advocate sending for the authorities? But no, Azor thinks, I need as many eyes on this as I can get and I am confident the plan lies tightly with me. But then what would explain Plunkett's strange death? The son—he should be here on the plantation. Does he have any light to shed?

Azor turns Plunkett's death over in his mind, pulls it apart, reassembles it in different ways but still nothing makes sense. He fingers the packet in his pocket, a cluster of pounds sterling and Portuguese *zolas* bound by a red ribbon. A sizeable sum, enough to outfit three decent schooners and pay for a company of a thousand men. More payment to come later and they proposed that the British might also seek profit from taking over any plantations abandoned before, or during, their occupation.

Azor rubs his eyes and stares out at the overgrown flower

garden, the statue of Venus rising amid a tangle of bougainvillea. The place is falling apart and Madame Rose—poor woman. Despite their fraught history—Azor can still remember his wife's ranting after that Fongravier girl's rudeness at their party, so long ago—he has a soft spot for this family and instantly on arrival felt a strong protective instinct toward Madame Rose.

Azor wonders why she is still single. This is no place for a widow alone; generally, women out here are quick to remarry. But perhaps the idea of remarriage is not to her taste. She had been so in love with her husband and his unfortunate death doubtless hit her hard. Regardless, one has to be pragmatic and know when to seek protection, no matter how distasteful. Azor chuckles; rather like their situation with the British!

Azor scratches his head, then scratches the head of a white cat who has wandered up to him. What a *ridiculous* situation. His mind slides back to the man who ambushed him the last hour. Is it possible that Thoreau's buffoonery is an act and that the man is in league with the patriots? Or the royalists? Or the anti-English? The anti-coloreds? This place is a bad joke wrapped up in a nightmare: so much animosity and so many competing factions—how can anyone keep it straight?

Azor closes his eyes. The best place for him is here, awaiting the constable. He knows Bassompierre to be a sound and genial man with occasional flashes of insight. Time will reveal all and there is no gain in useless puttering and agitation. He sways a while in the hammock, pushes off the cat when it tries to jump up. His mind drifts and circles back to the events of his arrival. Mercier and his vehemence, unable to give just an inch. The sheer hatred and savagery everywhere. The waste of it all. And for what?

We coloreds never wanted a revolution, Azor thinks sadly; we only wanted dignity.

Around the Plantation
4 pm

Safe in her chamber Rose sleeps, and on the veranda Azor soon falls into a troubled nap, the white cat draped over his legs. Charles leads Yorick to the whipping post where Mercier and Bridget and so many horrors await. From the kitchens Jeannette watches them pass by and knows that soon screams will cut through the air. Her sauce bubbles over the range and Flore lies asleep in her corner, dreaming. Out back in the poultry pen two anxious quail hide from the afternoon sun, while the rooster pecks around in discontent.

By the drying platforms the women labor, turning and raking the drying beans while others sort through endless piles for grit and stone that might hinder the mill. In the fields more workers harvest the remaining bushes. At the family cemetery Pierre and Capidon dig the hole for Plunkett's body, while by the wash house Laurine stares into her tub of water. The men don't tell her anything but she knows they have been going to Pellegrin's abandoned plantation and she guesses something is coming. La Fleur also senses something is wrong and he leaves the slaves and heads away from where he should be.

Outside, Thoreau is restless; he has not adopted the custom, fashionable—or necessary—in the colony of sleeping the afternoon away. There is too much to be done! Find the killer of Plunkett, of course, but also reflect on all the ideas generated by his talk with Azor. He paces around the flower garden in the front of the house then decides to explore further afield.

Mathilde makes her way cautiously through the woods. She feels no danger, only anticipation. She skirts one of the coffee fields and hears slaves talking to each other, hidden from sight by the coffee plants that rise over their heads. Still she pushes on through the fertile greenery, pulsing with life.

After the shock of finding the statue in the clearing, Aimée takes it and returns to the house. She places it on the table in her room, out in the open. It doesn't need to be kept secret, she decides, and she can't remember why she ever wanted to hide it.

Aunt Julie follows her movements, her eyes flickering when Aimée sets the statue to face her, just a few feet away. "It's okay," says Aimée, bustling around the room. "I've brought it back. It will keep us safe." As she often does in the afternoons, Aimée lies down beside Julienne and sleeps for a while and when she wakes up the house feels still and oddly silent.

In the women's house, Pomponne puts on her pink dress and lies back on her bed, satisfied and excited. She turns over memories of her meeting with Henri two weeks ago at La Fraternité. They walked almost three hours to get there, starting early in the morning to avoid the heat. On arrival, Jeannette went to help in the kitchens and as instructed, Pomponne circled the big house a few times and grinned in pleasure when a slave, working on weeding the steps, bowed to her. Thinking me a free woman of color! she thought in delight.

Pomponne had easily surmised what her mother wanted and she decided it was a dream she too could adopt. She also knew that there were very few things that could not be forgiven after a smile and she only hesitated a second before entering the house through an open windowed door. Inside the empty salon, she laughed in delight at the luxury and had been busy examining a porcelain flower—somehow finer than the real thing—when Henri came in.

They chatted, and his indulgent smile, and her muddy skirt, showed that she didn't belong but he didn't seem to care. She thought him vastly handsome, and after she wistfully described the cakes she had seen in the kitchen, he offered to fetch her one. He returned with a miniature cake, set with a jeweled sapphire candy.

"To match your eyes," he said. When she took her first lick of the butter-cream icing and crunched on the sugar jewel, the delicious sweetness jolted her and she closed her eyes in pleasure. When she opened them and saw the look on his face, she knew she had done well.

Now Pomponne lies on her bed, dreaming of their coming meeting.

Outside and down the well, Plunkett's body is starting to rot, just ever so faintly.

*

In the hills behind, Appollon runs through the heat of the afternoon up towards the Pellegrin plantation. He sprints along a path through thick uncleared land high into the hills. He runs effortlessly, his body strong and well adapted, sweat glistening and his clothes quickly wet. Once he pauses, thinking he hears something behind him. Nothing. Perhaps just the hollow creaking from a bamboo grove. He looks back down towards the sea, glistening in the distance, calm and smooth and hiding its treacherous currents.

A month of planning in jeopardy. He must get to the Pellegrin plantation and tell Milord the militia is coming to Bayardel, warn him before darkness falls and the signal is given and events start their irreversible course. Another hour of running and he emerges onto a dirt track, little used, that leads to the gates of the Pellegrin place. Finally the gatehouse, moss covering its sides and the roof collapsed. The gates are stripped of their iron rails and now they hang limp and half open; only the carved iron falcon that adorns the top still intact. Abandoned just last year but nothing is permanent in this country: the heat, the rains, the insects all conspire to quickly draw back to the earth any structure of wood or stone.

Sitting beside the gates is a young black boy, wearing a ragged yellow skirt.

"Get him, it's urgent," Appollon shouts, slumping down against a gate post. "Tell Milord to come quickly."

APPOLLON'S ARRIVAL

THE PELLEGRIN PLANTATION
SATURDAYS

Appollon sits on the floor surrounded by another fifty or so men, some known to him, others not. The Pellegrin big house is mostly roofless and the fine ceramic tiles, imported from France and lovingly laid by Madame Pellegrin half a lifetime ago, are now cracked and choked with weeds, the pattern all but lost. A painting of a man, perhaps Monsieur Pellegrin, still hangs on one wall, sooted and blackened but unmistakably French.

Milord stands before them, his followers beside him and dressed in white, wearing belts hung with bones. For every white killed—man, woman, child—they add another bone and some of their belts are so heavy they sag and clang when they walk. There is also a priestess named Romana with strange eyes and bristling hair who claims to be in contact with the great *loa* Erzili, goddess of the sea. Romana has with her an enormous snake, of a kind rarely seen on the island—a boa brute with markings of orange and white. There is also a monkey, once a plaything on an elegant plantation and now a screeching mascot.

Milord tells the men gathered before him about the northern uprising. He is a powerful orator with the instinctive gift of knowing what his audience wants, or needs, to hear. He tells the gathered men how slaves from all plantations came together, how Boukman inspired them, how magic and *Vaudun* helped them leap from victory to victory. Then Milord tells the assembled group about the rebels at Les Platons and how they defeated the French forces, news that sent thrilling ripples through the Grand'Anse.

"And the time is now!" Milord announces, glaring in triumph over the awestruck men. Appollon feels as though he is holding his breath and will never exhale again. "Everywhere the whites are struggling and from chaos a new world will be born. *Our* world—that is why the great *loa* Agwe sent us over the water to this land of riches."

One of the slaves—a carpenter from the Spechbach sugar plantation—asks: "What about a boat?"

"What boat?" demands Milord.

"A boat to take us home." Some of the other men sigh in sympathy. No! thinks Appollon. I'm not going back, not ever. This is my home now.

"Ha!" says Milord. "There are no boats, man, you are not going back."

"You Ibo always wanting to go home," mocks another man from the same plantation. Appollon thinks of the slave Babichon, dead for a year now, who used to shout every time she saw a boat out in the bay; no words, just a cry of sharp longing.

"I want to see my family," says the man, looking up at Milord.

"How long here?"

"Five years."

"What are you going back to, heh? Your sons are all grown up and have forgotten you. Your wives are with other men. Nothing is left for you."

The man gets up and stalks off, muttering angrily to himself, but he is stopped at the door by one of the men dressed in white. Once admitted to the group, it is only by death that they may leave.

Milord glares at those that remain. He has a lazy eye that wanders when he speaks; better to see all enemies coming, he likes to say. "When we are victorious, that man will want to stay."

Milord sketches out the plan they are forming and the gathered men start casting objections. To the slaves in the Grand'Anse, Milord and his followers are fearless beings whose roots in rebellion and murder fill them with awe. They are the ones who have done what everyone dreams of: they refused to remain animals and now, once more, they are men. But the idea of that happening here is too fantastical and feared and they seek comfort in immediate objections:

"My master has seven pistols."

"Ten whites on my plantation and they will all fight."

"Too many workers are loyal to the master."

"My owner is meaner than a snake and we are scared of him." This is from George, a slave on the Mercier plantation.

"The militia in Dame Marie is strong and Jérémie will send many more men."

Then one man voices what all are thinking: "It doesn't matter our numbers, we will never defeat the whites."

Appollon holds silent as beside him Pierre and Capidon murmur in agreement. *We will never defeat the whites.* He wants to cry out that they can, and will, but there is also a part of him that cannot imagine the whites fallen and humbled. But they are only men like us, and Appollon looks at the belts of bones around the men's waists. White bones but they could also be black bones. And if we are all the same underneath, what does that mean?

Milord lets the naysayers speak until they fall silent and the only sound is the faint drip of water, still falling from the roof after the night rains.

"We are part of something larger!" shouts Milord. "We may fail but eventually our brothers will be victorious. We are waves from the sea: one comes and breaks upon the shore but another is right behind and another in a never-ending line. Trying to stop us will be like trying to stop the sea and there is no god on earth or in heaven who can do that!"

The men are silent.

"Yes, we may fail, but we are doing this for our sons and for their sons after them," finishes Milord, softer now;

he knows the men need reassurance.

"We don't know who our sons are," objects one man bitterly.

"That is true," agrees Milord. "You may not know who your sons are but we must think of all the children on your plantations as ours—we are doing this for them."

Seated with the others on the floor and proud to be one of the chosen ones, as Appollon listens to Milord a great clarity falls over him. He knows then that this is why he was brought to Bayardel: to be a part of something larger, a pebble on the road that will pave the way to a better future. This is why his ship bought him here. And it's Appollon's destiny, he knows; Akande is the man he left behind in the old world, a man who did things he was ashamed of. Only Appollon can avenge his past.

*

Then at the meeting last Saturday, the fatal word: *Wednesday.*

The men murmur in appreciation; so soon. Appollon licks his lips and glances at Pierre and Capidon next to him. Since their first meeting a month ago he has felt tense and taut, a harnessed horse ready to run loose. And now he will be released. Soon—Wednesday is but four days away.

"The spirits have spoken," continues Milord, nodding to the priestess Romana. "Wednesday—the same night it began up north and here the moon will be bright to guide us in our work." The monkey, sitting on the arm of one of Milord's followers, shrieks as though it understands the significance of his words. Appollon looks up through the missing roof into the night sky and sees the moon, already so full and bright, but only getting bigger.

"Wednesday. But we must all act as one," Milord says quietly, taking up a twig from the floor. "One twig alone is easy to snap but gather enough of them into a bundle and they cannot be broken. Romana," he continues, smiling with evil on his face, "will now prepare her magic. She will anoint you with it and then you will be with us forever and protected from the weapons of the whites."

The priestess emerges from the shadows. A large woman, almost as tall as Milord, with deathly black skin and slanted eyes, reputed to be a *mambo* from Congoland. She pulls forward a trembling white kid, her other hand holding a curved knife that glints in torchlight. As she slits the animal's throat, she chants in a language Appollon doesn't know but the words still make his heart thump with strange intensity. Hope flows through him as the blood flows from the goat's neck into an enormous calabash. When the kid is bled, Romana discards it and pours white powder into the bowl, sand from the earth but also so much more, her incantations rising as she mixes it with the blood.

White to kill the whites, murmurs Milord and gradually all gathered take up the chant: *White to kill the whites.* From the wall Monsieur Pellegrin's face seems to smile at them through the light of the flickering lanterns, blessing their undertaking. Outside the wind whistles through the orange trees, while inside the men file up and Romana smears the mixture over their chests and arms. When she pastes his chest, Appollon shivers; there is something evil about her. About Milord as well and his whole band of followers, some wickedness lurking below the surface.

Appollon sits down again, his heart pounding. Carefully he touches the pinkish white paste. He doesn't believe in this talisman—he saw in Whydah how nothing could stop the bullets of the whites—but he knows this magic will give the others strength if they have none. But I am already so strong, thinks Appollon and suddenly he sees himself driving a shovel into a white man's back. A vision, so strong and true: just the force of his wishful thinking or has he seen into the future? He thinks about Brac and La Fleur, of the shovels and machetes in the storeroom, and of the way Jeannette always talks so fondly of her mistress.

When the last man is anointed, everyone falls silent and even the wind waits in anticipation. Together they repeat the famous words from the Bois Caïmans that launched the northern rebellion:

We swear to destroy the whites and all they possess.
Let us die rather than fail to keep this vow.

And then Milord gives them their instructions. When night falls on Wednesday, the Belleville plantation on the Anse d'Esnos will be first. The absentee landlord's manager slaughtered and the slave drivers too—none of them are trustworthy—and then a cotton field on the plateau above the cliffs will be set on fire. That fire will be seen for miles on one side and miles on the other: the signal that everything should begin.

Coordination is key; everyone must start together. Cooking pots to create noise and diversion, as well as real weapons from the storehouses where machetes, shovels and pikes are kept. If you don't know, use torture to find out where the weapons are—all whites are required to keep pistols, something the slaves know well. But the greatest weapons, Milord tells the men, are speed and surprise, more powerful than pistols or bayonets.

"Use the ways of the whites against you," counsels Milord, grinning as he speaks of his favorite pastime. "Gut them, flay them, chop them into pieces. They show us no restraint nor humanity. They call us savages, and so savages we will be! Any slave that does not follow must be killed. But do not let your sport interfere with your mission—keep your eyes on the larger moon."

At Bayardel, Appollon, Pierre and Capidon and a few others are ready. For the last month they have been digging a tunnel into the building where the shovels and machetes are stored every night and they know from Pomponne where Madame Rose keeps the pistol. Appollon knows Jeannette will want a peaceful death for her daughter's white friend; they will quickly kill the family and save their sport for Brac and La Fleur. And anyone else who utters a hint of protest.

Only once the weapons are secured and the whites are dead—"And no hostages, for there will be no negotiations"—will they light their fires. Not the provision fields but the coffee, cotton and indigo plants, even the cacao trees if possible.

"The flames will nourish your hearts and stay the

strength of the men that join you," says Milord, his eyes gleaming. "Everything that can be broken, must be: the machines, the drying platforms and warehouses. Erase the big houses from memory and above all torch the fields."

The women and children will corral the livestock and poultry and start for the hills while the men concentrate on destruction, working outward from the center of the quincunx to the adjacent plantations. When morning comes the men too will head for the hills; Fraise has calculated that by that time there should be more than two thousand of them. They will consolidate their positions in the stretch of rocky hills behind Pellegrin's, where Milord and his men have been working on fortifications. It is not as good a stronghold as Les Platons but Milord brushes off any objections: it is sufficient.

His men will block the roads from Dame Marie in the north as well as in the mountains behind. They will kill any whites trying to flee and soon ten leagues of the coast and inland will be engulfed by flames and in the hands of the slaves.

Wednesday.

In silence Appollon walks back to Bayardel with Pierre and Capidon, each man lost in their own thoughts. Four days. Tomorrow is Sunday, a day of rest and chores. But who can sleep with so much to do? Appollon feels as though he will never sleep again. A month of waiting, of wondering, of imagining and dreaming, and soon it will be Wednesday.

The Pellegrin Plantation
4 pm

A rustle behind him and Appollon jumps up; was he sleeping? He squints at the sun, now lower in the sky. Only a few hours before darkness and the signal fire is lit.

"What?" Milord squats beside him and Appollon can smell the rum on his breath. His left eye is looking at a point beyond Appollon's shoulder. "Why are you here?"

"Trouble at Bayardel. A white killed, found this morning and the constable coming with the militia." Appollon's voice is low and urgent.

Milord whistles. "I knew the signs were not good. Last night..." He lets the words hang in the air; his is a deliberate and careful style of storytelling, at odds with the mania that strains beneath the surface. "Romana prepared the entrails to summon the *loa,* but they didn't come."

"We have to call it off," says Appollon, relieved that the man seems to understand.

Milord sighs. "Or not. Now that our plan is fully cooked and ready to be eaten, every day we wait is another day that it can spoil."

Appollon holds his breath. If the plan goes ahead, Bayardel will be sacrificed.

"It is risky," says Milord slowly. "Some will not get the message and may rise up without the strength of numbers."

"Please," pleads Appollon, "the captain and his men, all

241

armed, on our plantation. And so many others there already. Mercier and that colored planter Azor."

"Azor?" Milord sucks in his breath.

"A personal matter, I don't know. It he to help?" asks Appollon, an idea occurring to him. Is there a part of the plan their leader Milord is not sharing? Could Azor be involved?

"No, you know we stay clear of the coloreds. But after what happened to his son in Jérémie, Azor is no friend of the whites…" Milord points up at the sky. "Only a few hours to sundown. You said the white was discovered this morning—why did you not come earlier?"

"We were roped."

Milord leans back on his haunches and they sit in silence for a few minutes. The boy in the skirt is off to one side, watching, and Appollon feels as if the whole world has stopped and is waiting. Please. He searches the man's face for the answer he wants. On Milord's high cheekbones are the deep inflections of ritual scarification, giving his face a fierce and feral look. A great man, thinks Appollon, aware that his destiny is in his hands.

Then the snap of a twig. Milord and Appollon turn, just in time to see someone step boldly into the open.

La Fleur.

"Fools!" spits the overseer. He swings a machete in front of him. "I know something is happening, I hear everything!" He motions them up with his machete. Once upright, Appollon sees a slight re-calculation in La Fleur's eyes at the height of Milord and at the scars on his cheeks, his necklace of human teeth.

"Who are you?" demands La Fleur.

"No one you know," replies Milord. "Is he yours?"

"Yes—the manager's dog. Not a brain in his body," replies Appollon as steadily as he can.

La Fleur chuckles. "Brainless, eh? I followed you and I know your plan. I will tell all!"

"Then why did you not listen and turn around?" demands Appollon. Though they are both unarmed, the presence of Milord gives him some courage. "Why do you show yourself?"

"Because I want you to know who betrays you. Don't worry, I'll kill you both before I leave." La Fleur glances briefly at the boy in his yellow skirt, still sitting on the ground by the gate.

He turns back to Milord. "I know you. You are the famous rebel leader Milord," he says in a mocking tone. "The reward I will get for you will be bigger than a plate of gold snatched from the sky."

"And I know you," says Milord, taking a step towards the enemy, no trace of fear in his voice.

"You don't know me," smirks La Fleur.

"Yes, I do. You are Jean Kina."

La Fleur scowls but a flicker of fear crosses his face. "I am La Fleur."

"You are Jean Kina," repeats Milord. Appollon nods. They all know the story of Jean Kina, a carpenter from a cotton plantation near Tiburon, known for his loyalty to his white master. He adopted his master's hatred for the mulattoes, and when troubles broke out last year around Les Cayes, Jean Kina fought with the whites against the coloreds.

Armed and trusted, with skills extending beyond the licking of his master's boots, Jean Kina proved an excellent leader and eventually commanded a troop of slaves who helped the government restore order. In gratitude he was granted his freedom but as an example to other slaves, Jean Kina refused his liberty. We do not need freedom, he preached, our white masters will take care of us. But he did accept a pension of three hundred *livres* and a medal.

The whites hold Jean Kina up as the expected product of their benevolent society, while the slaves see him as something to be envied, pitied, or feared. Appollon often wonders about men like him and of the plantations that produce them: fear can never build those bonds of loyalty. But no matter the kindness that Jean Kina might have experienced, how could he not see the rot around him? Or does he place his future with the whites because he knows the slave struggle is doomed?

"Jean Kina, the *bon nègre*," spits Milord. "He got his little medal because he is a good nigger. But that name is no garland of flowers: you are a man who hates himself."

It is as if he is deliberately taunting La Fleur, thinks Appollon in rising fear. He glances over and sees that the boy in the yellow skirt has disappeared. There are branches on the ground and what might be a piece of iron from the gates. Potential weapons.

"White dog!" spits Milord and again he advances, slightly, towards La Fleur. "Why do you not learn to love yourself and come with us?"

La Fleur laughs and swings his machete. "I do not hate myself! Others may tremble before you and your *bokors*, but I do not. Your magic powers, big man, cannot stop this machete coming to cut off your head."

"It is you that is going to die, white dog," says Milord calmly, one of his hands starting to twitch. He is now only a few feet from La Fleur. Appollon is well behind and could flee and save himself but he cannot leave Milord alone with the crazed *commandeur*.

"What, are you going to make the trees come alive and strangle me with their vines?" taunts La Fleur as a sudden gust of wind, the first, whistles across the road. "Those are your powers?"

"They are," says Milord, now stroking his necklace of teeth, his other hand still twitching. "White man's bitch."

"Meet your ancestors!" roars La Fleur, and raises his machete. Milord leaps back, and from behind the gate house ten men or more appear, silent and swift, each armed with their own weapon and their fearsome belts of bone. They surround La Fleur and one throws a bayonet to Milord. Appollon steps back, his heart pounding and his knees weak.

"Foolish dog," says Milord. "Now you see who is going to die."

La Fleur does look like a dog now, the whites of his eyes gloaming in fear. Milord motions and from behind a man steps forward and smoothly slashes La Fleur's shoulder, almost severing it. La Fleur falls howling to the ground.

Appollon steps closer to La Fleur, squealing and pawing at his half-severed arm. He gives him hearty kick on his side. "This is a big thing you have done," Appollon tells Milord.

"A thing that was needed," says Milord calmly.

"I wish I had a whip," says Appollon, looking down. Great bursts of blood are now streaming from the slashed shoulder socket. "I want to whip him. Before he is too dead to feel it."

La Fleur's eyes roll back in his head and he is growing quiet but Appollon knows he can still hear. And feel.

"Here," says a man, offering him a coiled horsewhip. One

of Milord's men, a short man with a thin nose who always looks vaguely familiar to Appollon. One of the men he helped put aboard the ships back in Whydah? Recently he has felt the spirits of those men he never helped swarming closer, calling for vengeance.

As Appollon takes the whip their eyes meet and he thinks he sees a flicker of recognition. Previously they met in the dark, in a world lit by torches—perhaps he never saw him clearly before?

"The dog will lead us into battle," chuckles Milord. "His head on my pike will show the other bitches what happens when they leave their brothers behind to suck on the teat of whites."

Appollon raises the whip high and with terrible whistling force brings it down over La Fleur. La Fleur shrieks and writhes in pain but the pool of blood around him means he doesn't have much longer. Again! Appollon whips until the man on the ground is a bloody mess, silent now, and he himself is howling.

"Enough, my brother," says one of the men, catching his arm and pulling him away. "Let us get his head before you ruin it."

Appollon steps back, shaking, covered with flecks of skin and blood. He picks a piece of flesh off his arm and puts it in his mouth; the flesh of my enemy. He swallows it, salty and mushy, and feels some evil pass through him.

One of Milord's henchmen starts hacking at La Fleur's neck.

"Now this man Appollon brings news of trouble at Bayardel, the captain and constabulary summoned. This…" Milord pauses. "Because of this we will delay."

Appollon throws his head back in relief. Thank you.

"The entrails yesterday…" says the priestess Romana, now appeared and holding the hand of the boy in the yellow skirt.

"Yes. It is not tonight. The new day is Friday." Milord looks over at the sun, now low in the sky. "We must spread the word before darkness comes." He points to one of his men. "You, straight to Belleville! You two to Moron then continue on to Fanchon's. At Allard's have two new runners alert the three west plantations. You, into the mountains to Beaumont and Sans Souci. You—along the coast road. Gaultier to Esnos to Anse des Irois. Tell them all why they won't see the signal fire from Belleville; tell them all that Wednesday is now Friday."

Appollon wanders off to the edge of the group and leans

over to catch his breath. A smooth, great relief flows through him. The uprising, delayed. They will survive. He retches, wishing he could vomit out all the worry of the day and the piece of La Fleur that he now regrets eating.

Quickly the men disperse and then it is only Milord and Appollon, watched by the priestess and the little boy.

"Thank you, my brother."

"You have proven yourself," says Milord. "I had my doubts. Your plantation is in disorder and we know you love the cook. And sometimes those with the most anger see only what is in front of them, not the future." Milord looks at him, both of his eyes seeming now to focus on Appollon. "But you didn't run away when you had the chance."

Appollon shakes head, astonished at Milord's words. "No, I have always been with you. I am no white rat," he says, trying to keep the emotion out of his voice. He motions to the now headless body of La Fleur, still bleeding over the dirt of the road. "I know what needs to be done."

Milord nods. "Then Friday, and we will meet in victory on Saturday."

"Friday," repeats Appollon. Friday, thank the gods. Time for the captain and his men to come and go and the moon will still be big and bright enough. He starts back down the mountain, stopping in a stream to wash his hands and shirt and rid himself of the pieces of La Fleur still flecked over him. Brac will want to know where his *commandeur* has gone but really, what will that change? The manager will keep his investigation for after the coffee is loaded on to the waiting boat. "Saturday," Brac has been shouting all week. "Saturday everything must be done!"

But Saturday will not come for Brac, nor any of the whites.

Appollon makes his way down the rocky path through a grove of old cacao trees covered with dense vines and creepers. He will be back at Bayardel well before sundown. He walks slower now, his breath even and measured, at peace. The plan delayed, everyone safe. La Fleur dead.

Appollon knows Jeannette will be pleased but the delay is only two days. Should he tell her that it is delayed longer, allow her another few days of ignorance and peace? *Jeannette* Kina, he thinks ruefully; she wants life to continue as before and is content working for the whites. But such feelings are more understandable in a woman, content as they are with small dreams and yearning for safety and security over the glory of an uncertain future.

The Whipping Post
4 pm

The slave cemetery is a desolate patch of land, circled with thorny acacia bushes to keep the wild pigs out and away from the rotting flesh they covet. There are no headstones, only the occasional stick or wooden cross to mark where bodies of the dead lie. Uncleared hills rise behind, and the tall pigeon coop, empty now, throws it in ever more shadow. Next to the pigeon coop, the sentinel of the whipping post.

Charles, trailed by Yorick, makes his way there and finds Mercier, and Brac on his mule.

"You want a go at her? Before we begin?" Mercier jerks his thumb at Bridget.

"Nah, not as young as I used to be," replies Brac, thinking back to the morning and the way Jeannette moved her buttocks towards him. "And I've had her. You know who else has had her?" He laughs and points at Charles. Yorick smirks and moves away from Charles, closer to Mercier.

"Huh!" Mercier scratches his chin where dark stubble is already shadowing his face. "So Master Charles Fongravier is a man. Congratulations, boy! Can't have you leaving for France without some fond memories of home, can we?"

Charles doesn't say anything. Perhaps it is all right; he is among men and as long as his mother doesn't find out...

"How was it?" demands Mercier.

"How was what?" stalls Charles.

248

"Ha! Does your mother know?"

Charles feels a blush creeping up his neck and turns away.

Mercier laughs, a nasty bark striking through the stillness. "Bashful, are we? I can remember my first time. God, does one ever forget? What's that?" he says, losing interest in Charles' sexual escapades and pointing at a drooling figure tied to the cemetery gate.

"That's Lubin, he's not of right mind," says Brac.

Mercier takes in the bowl on the ground in front of the wretched man, the spilled water. "Do you know what one does with a slave that has outlived its usefulness?" he says, raising his voice. "Chop it up and use it for hog feed."

Brac snorts. "Not with Madame Rose in charge, I'll tell you that!"

Lubin makes a faint *mwooo* sound and Charles wonders if he understands. The slave has been like this since last year when he was hit on the head by a falling ladder: wild-eyed, staring, with an endless supply of drool sliding over his chin and chest. Like Aunt Julie, Charles thinks suddenly, disliking the comparison.

"Right," says Brac with some reluctance. "I've got see how things are getting on in the south field. Can't find that damn La Fleur. You get started and I'll be back."

"We'll be here," says Mercier, turning back to the business at hand. He drags Bridget's arms up to the stake and ties her hands to the iron loops. She hangs off the stake, only half supported by her feet. Charles sees her soles, pale and curled.

"We'll make her sing, eh boy?" Mercier grunts. "Good to do some physical activity, makes one feel a man."

"This is Brac's work," says Charles softly. They don't often use this post anymore, Brac preferring to tie the men to the apricot tree in the clearing. His father sometimes whipped slaves here but only when it was a matter beyond the usual laxness in fieldwork; something like theft, or... Charles closes his eyes against a certain memory and when he opens them Mercier is holding Bridget by the hair and running one hand over her back.

"No, you can't leave this to the managers. This is your responsibility. Can't call yourself an owner if you have never punished one."

Charles stares at the man, dreading what is coming. He

feels as though he being carried forward by a fast-moving river, heading straight for a waterfall, the sound of thunder rushing ever closer. What if he just runs away now, back to the house? But even as he thinks it, Charles knows he cannot. This is his life; he must do this to spare his mother.

Mercier jerks back Bridget's head. He takes a small knife from his pocket and slits the back of her blouse and pulls it off in one motion.

"Oh, you shouldn't have," says Charles before he can stop himself. His mother is forever complaining about the slaves and their never-ending need for new clothes.

Mercier chuckles. "She won't need clothes where she's going. Come, you do the skirt."

Charles takes the knife, his hand trembling slightly. Carefully he cuts away at the band of her skirt waist until it falls around her, revealing her buttocks and her legs, long and scarred, her thighs shaking slightly. Before he can stop himself, he runs a hand over her buttocks, smatters of memory from that dark night in the pigpen coming to him, the feel of her skin so smooth where it was not welt by whip scars. To his horror he feels himself stiffening and he backs away, stumbling in his haste.

"Ha!" says Mercier in satisfaction, as though Charles has confirmed something for him.

Oh, why did I ever come, Charles thinks in a panic, longing for the salon and his mother and the safety of female spaces. He should be back there, not out here with gibbering Lubin and the lunacy in Mercier's eyes. And Bridget, naked and trembling before him. *God, does one ever forget your first?* Charles decides he doesn't want to be a man, if this is what being a man means.

"Look at her back." Mercier traces his knife over Bridget's scars. "Three brands on her shoulder. This one was a troublemaker. Weren't you now?" he says, grabbing her under the chin and forcing her head to him. Bridget's eyes stay closed but suddenly then she spits up at him with surprising force. The gob lands on Mercier's arm. He laughs and stabs her neatly on the shoulder and she shrieks out, horrid and high.

"You see? You see how stupid they are?" Mercier says, breathing quickly. "She should be begging for mercy to make her death quicker and sweeter, and instead she spits in my face. They never learn. Beasts."

"Death?" says Charles, watching the rivulet of bright blood run down Bridget's shoulder. "But no, we just... We want to know if she will confess!"

Mercier laughs and grinds his thumb into the little wound. "Maybe not by the whip, perhaps later, but either way we'll finish this business ourselves. This is my right, *your* right. You understand that, don't you?"

Charles doesn't answer. In the gloom of the small valley, Mercier seems to be growing taller, his face darkening, and Charles feels something like fear. Who is this man? And why is he here?

"Give me that."

Mutely Charles hands Mercier the whip.

"Just a horse whip? No knots? I would have expected better of Brac." Mercier examines the whip and shrugs. Then, to Charles' horror, hands it back to him. "Go on boy, you start. Did your father never teach you how to trim a slave?"

Charles winces at the crude expression: trim a slave means whipping them until pieces of skin come off.

"Did he?" shouts Mercier.

Charles glares at him. "No, never."

Mercier laughs. "I had my Pierre trimming from the age of ten—builds character! But your father was soft like a woman, under your mother's thumb."

Mercier's open contempt shocks Charles. "Don't talk about my father like that!"

"You're too soft," smirks Mercier, shaking his head. "You'll thank me later."

"For what?"

"Fool!" says Mercier. "How else do you think they are kept in line? Once we've got her confession, we'll bring her back to the clearing for the others to watch the final scene. Can't have them here now, shouting in their piggy gibberish and influencing her, but they need to see the end. You," he says looking down at Yorick, now squatting by his side. "Ask her in English where she got the necklace."

Yorick does but there is no answer from Bridget, no flicker of recognition.

"She didn't have help, I mean I don't think… she didn't do anything," protests Charles. Without wanting to he looks to Yorick for help. The boy grins back at him; no quarter there.

Mercier chuckles and shakes his head. "You sound like your mother."

"Perhaps," says Charles defiantly. He imagines lashing out at Mercier, curling the rawhide around his legs and tripping him up.

"Get started!"

Charles takes a deep breath and lifts up the whip, brings it down on Bridget's back. She flinches and utters a short, sharp cry.

"A sorry start," snorts Mercier, "but not to worry, we have plenty of time. Put your body into it and make it count! You know their skin is tougher than ours."

Charles holds his breath and swings again.

Bridget screams again.

"Ask who helped her!"

"Who help you?" cries Yorick in English and Bridget howls back at him in a language that no one on earth understands.

"Again!" roars Mercier.

A whistling sound this time, then a sharp crack and a piercing cry from Bridget, writhing away from the pain.

"Who knows the necklace?"

"More!" commands Mercier.

Charles does and soon he finds himself whipping her so quickly that the whistle of the whip and the cracks as it strikes flesh meld into one. He is reminded of the way piglets squeal when they are scared or slaughtered, so high and heart-rending. Mercier laughs as each welt rises.

"There you go, work yourself harder! That's my boy!"

The whip splices through the air and uncoils on Bridget's legs and back and buttocks.

"Who help you?" Yorick shouts and Charles continues to whip, calmer now, in long steady motions. Whistle, crack, scream. Again. It wasn't her in the pigpen, he thinks. Whistle, crack and the scream, fainter now. As the sun starts to set behind the hills, Bridget's cries grow softer until she is making nothing more than the occasional grunt.

Charles stops and leans over, his breath heavy, his stomach

lurching, unable to look at her. It wasn't her in the pigpen. How could it have been? She isn't even real.

*

Mathilde hears the cry, high-pitched and feral: the sign she has been waiting for. She heads towards it through a banana grove, the green bunches like grapes for giants and everything out of proportion—the fruit too big, the ground too far away and the heat like a sticky beast riding her back.

From behind the trees, she watches. The young white one with the oddly shaped eyes. That man Mercier, so virile and crude who brought all the horror with him this morning, egging him on. Behind them a tied slave, drooling at the mouth. The distasteful colored boy, sitting on his haunches and laughing. The naked woman, strung up.

And I—in the shadows, Mathilde thinks in exultation. No one sees me: I am night, but in day.

The colony is alive with savagery and its constant presence has awakened something in Mathilde. From the beginning, the stories of atrocities committed by the slaves in the uprising up north fed her imagination and grew her desire: men tied to trees and burned alive; women subjected to horrors beyond a civilized man's capacity to imagine; a man bound between two boards and sawed in half, alive. White hands chopped off and stuck in the mud, left to mock rescuers who came too late. Eyes taken out by corkscrews and a man nailed to a gate, his limbs lopped off one by one. Infants impaled on stakes and captives roasted alive; one poor soul hung by a hook through his chin and left for two days before he expired.

Mathilde fingers her stomach, large and throbbing, and wills the growth to life—not the child she never had but the new presence that she has begun to think of as the fruit of this new world. A pineapple or a giant apricot. She can feel it, hard and round, and she knows that it is driving her forward, compelling her to places she should not go.

She stares at Bridget's naked back, crisscrossed with red lines and open sores. Her cries are growing fainter and fainter but the boy is still whipping, Mercier still spurring him on, the colored boy still shouting. There, thinks Mathilde, I am bound to them in their savagery, but they don't even know I am here. Her excitement sprouts wings and threatens to take flight.

A crackling in the leaves behind, soft footsteps over the dried banana fronds, and when she turns she sees it is *him*, the blackness that is coming for her. That has been coming all along.

*

Nearing Bayardel from the hills behind, Appollon hears the screams. It must be Bridget, the slave chosen to be sacrificed to the whims of the whites.

He skirts the slave cemetery, passes behind Lubin lolling at the gate—what will happen to him when the uprising begins?— and slips into a banana grove beside the crumbling pigeon coop. He sees Bridget hanging off the whipping post and the young white putting his force into her when all the world knows what happened last week in the pigpen.

An immense sadness fills Appollon as he watches the boy flay Bridget alive. These whites like to call the slaves savages but their cruelty is unlike anything else, no humanity to be found in their pale, grotesque bodies. He remembers Chalumette's icy eyes, the joy that man took in taking everything from a boy who worked for him in loyalty for so many years. Akande's life, gone, in a snap of his heartless fingers.

The cruelty all around him on the sugar plantation in Les Cayes: men starved to death, hands cut off for slipping bites from a sugar cane, only taken to sustain them in the heat. The barbarities inflicted by the whites on the slaves up north in the wake of the August revolt: gallows and a wheel erected in Cap-Français, lines of chained blacks paraded through the streets on their way to death, captured rebels but also innocent women and men caught in the hysteria. Random killings of faithful household servants and innocent field hands who stayed, chopped to pieces by white mobs and tossed into the streets for the wild dogs. Heads on pikes and babies torn from their mothers and stomped to death. Slaves who helped their masters escape through the chaos of the countryside, only to be gutted alive once they reached the stronghold of the city.

And these men attacking Bridget, even though Appollon is

sure they know the broken girl had nothing to do with anything.

Gradually the cries wither away to indistinct moaning, and Appollon knows that soon it will be over. He stares with hatred at Mercier, standing triumphant as he encourages the white boy and shouts at Yorick, who shouts back in a strange language. Perhaps it is good that everything is delayed—let this man be killed on his own plantation. He knows George, Mercier's slave, is relishing the night that is coming for his cruel master; he must have something special planned.

Appollon becomes aware of someone else in the banana grove: the old white woman who arrived with her brother a few days ago. As far as he knows she has not left the house since her arrival but now she stands not four feet away, unaware of his presence, watching the whipping while one hand slowly rubs her belly. On arrival, Appollon helped her from the carriage and observed her with furtive interest; there are few old whites here and their finely wrinkled faces and sunken cheeks are things of interest and disgust for him.

Appollon holds his breath but the woman remains unaware.

Bridget falls quiet, her back and legs now clothed with a covering of blood. The boy slumps down, sweating and exhausted. Mercier is staring at Bridget, breathing heavily, a look of elation on his face.

"Good work," he says to the boy. "But get up and stop mewling like a girl."

Charles casts him a look of pure hate then flings the whip down and runs off, his face streaked with tears. The old white woman makes a strange sighing sound, her gaze still on what is left of Bridget. Appollon steps forward and when she half-turns at the noise behind her, he thrusts his face forward, opening his eyes wide and terrible and becoming her black nightmare. Her eyes bulge and she faints onto the ground.

Appollon looks down at her. She'll never be able to identify him and besides, that's not going to matter soon. He takes off for the stables, leaving Mercier behind in the clearing, still staring at Bridget hanging from the post.

*

From sun-dappled water the boat comes ashore at the gentle beach. Bridget smiles and gets out; she knows the way she must go. Away from the river, along the path etched through the forest to the fields. Closer to her village now, the bleating of goats and smoke from the evening fires ushering her forward.

At the edge of the fields she finds her calabash where she left it. She looks to the left and then to the right. This is the place where everything went wrong, where she made that fateful decision to go down to the river and bathe. The sandy bar where she fell asleep, then woke when the sun was too far down and she was too far away.

Bridget picks up the calabash and balances it on her head, glad the water has not spilled. She continues through the fields towards her village, memory lighting the way. Back towards her future, the one that was taken from her when she fell asleep on the riverbank.

Soon she sees the huts, the curl of smoke and the earthy smell of *foufou* cooking slowly. When she reaches her village, they are all gathered in the form of jubilee to greet her back. Everyone she knows is there, clapping and ululating, and there is her mother and father and her two younger brothers—grown now but she knows them instantly.

Behind them is Issambo, a young man she once flirted with, and beside him, curious yet excited, is a young girl with her own almond eyes and his smile peeking out at her. More of her future, taken from her when she went left towards the river and not right towards the well.

You've come back, whispers her mother, embracing her.

We have missed you, says her father.

Welcome, says Issambo, stepping towards her and taking her in his arms. Bridget sinks into his embrace, peace and happiness restored as he breathes everlasting life into her body. Around her are the spirits of the taken, of the dead, of the drowned that line the ocean path from Africa to the Americas, numberless souls interred in nameless graves, all free now and they curl around and caress Bridget—now once again Azinza—and she beams up to the sky and lets herself be enfolded by all the light and love of the world that, finally, endlessly, pulses around her.

The Indigo Fields
4 pm

When the afternoon is quiet again, Aimée wakes. She leaves her sleeping aunt and goes out onto the veranda, peeks in the salon, but finds the room empty. Her mother must be napping, but where are Charles and Pomponne? Their guests?

Hungry, she takes a piece of cheese from the table in the dining room. Through the window she sees a colored man she doesn't know, lying in one of the hammocks. She frowns and leaves the house, makes her way towards the kitchen.

"Where's Pomponne?" she asks Jeannette. The deep, rich smell of the sauce, flavored with wild rosemary and thyme, fills the kitchen. The clearing beside the kitchens is empty, as deserted and desolate as the big house.

"I don't know," replies the cook, not looking at Aimée. "An errand for Madame Rose? So many people in the house today."

"There are," agrees Aimée, hesitating at the door. "Though no one is there now." Except that strange colored man in the hammock. "What are you making?"

"The most delicious chicken pie the world has ever tasted," says Jeannette, gesturing to the enormous crock where the sauce bubbles. Her hands are dusted with flour and she is rolling pastry, cutting long strands of pastry to lattice the top crust.

"Smells good," says Aimée.

"It does."

"If you see her, tell her I am looking for her." Everything seems slightly unreal today, thinks Aimée as she wanders out into the clearing. The man, dead. The turtle, gone. And her statue... it's return unnerved her, more than she cares to admit. Is someone, or something, playing a trick on her? Pomponne's lively mind is always inventing new games and trickery but how did she know about the statue in the first place?

Everything so strange, and yet life goes on.

Aimée walks past the hospital—avoiding the groans from within—to the wash house, next to the old well where Plunkett is hanging. She finds Laurine staring at the sudsy water.

"Be careful with my lilac dress," says Aimée, peering anxiously into the great copper tub. "The lace collar is delicate."

"Don't be standing and watching water," says Laurine sharply. Laurine's hands are plump and swollen, as though they have been resting in the water for hours.

Aimée frowns; she doesn't like the surly laundress who always scrubs holes in her skirts and ruins her lace. And complaining to her mother doesn't help—Aimée suspects her mother is as afraid of Laurine as she is. After checking the stables—still no Pomponne—she takes the path to the old indigo fields. Her favorite place on the whole plantation.

Indigo plants blossom with pretty pink flowers but it is the leaves that make the blue. They are boiled in giant stone vats lined with lime that now crumble beside the abandoned fields. A long warehouse, roofless, flanks the vats; thick blue cakes of solid dye were stored there and the stones floors are still blue, as are the sides of the vats. Inside the vats linger faint traces of the nauseating scent that used to steam up from the ugliness of the fermenting leaves before the beautiful blue dye emerged.

Indigo sucks life from the soils and now the fields are empty, desolate, gorgeous. Old Flore claims these fields are cursed—she says it was once an Indian burial ground, before the whites came, and that was why the indigo never prospered here. The earth holds the ghosts of blue sorrow, Flore once said and like many of the slaves who worked the vats the soles of her feet are blue forever. Sometimes Aimée thinks she hears voices here, in a language she can't understand—from the ghosts of the long dead Indians, perhaps—but the words are always welcoming and warm.

Aimée checks around but no Pomponne. She sits on the steps of a vat and tries to remember the last time they had all been here, the three of them: herself, Charles, Pomponne. More than a year, she is sure. Before her father died? Yes, that might be it. Two years, then.

The coming future is all that is bleak to Aimée. Once Charles leaves for France, she knows the easy freedoms of her days will be over and there will be no more ramblings through the countryside, no river or sea excursions, no explorations that were only permitted because it was the two of them. Though terribly condescending, Charles is also funny and she loves him and the secret world they created together.

I want a lightning bolt, Aimée thinks sadly. Her favorite fantasy: a great bolt from the skies that will stop everything, including time, and keep everyone in place forever just as they are now. Aimée would be twelve forever and most importantly Mama would always be Mama and she would be happy again, and Charles would never grow older or go away and she and Pomponne would always be together. Something, anything, to stop the troubling business of growing up and changing, and all the menace she can't help feeling in the air. Perhaps the lightning bolt should have happened before her father died, a time Aimée remembers as mostly happy.

But instead of a lightning bolt, a tiny hummingbird stops and hovers in front of her, interested in the ribbon in her hair. Aimée picks a pink flower growing out of a crack and crushes it under her fingers. A great-grandchild, or more, of the plants that used to be carefully tended and grown here. The pink stains her fingertips. Plunkett had ink-stained fingers, the mark of a notary or a writer. She wonders what she should do with the rest of her afternoon.

A small banana rat runs along the top of the vat then scampers off when it sees Aimée. She thinks of the eyes she saw in the swamp, peeking through the mangrove roots. What if the man who killed Plunkett is here, hiding in the warehouse or the woods? She looks nervously around her. Her could be watching her now! He might come upon her, all alone, and ravish her. Aimée isn't quite sure what *ravish* means, only that it involves loose hair and a leering man. And then he might kill her, like he killed Plunkett, run his knife over her neck and garnish it with a bright red ribbon.

A crunch of steps from the forest and a fear like Aimée has never known rises within her.

Thoreau walks into the clearing and the world stops.

"Oh!" Aimée lets out a frightened squeak then immediately regrets it. He must not know she suspects. For suddenly she does suspect. He is a stranger as Charles said, appearing out of nowhere a few days ago. Arguing last night with Plunkett.

"My little Aimée," says Thoreau, advancing toward her with a tree branch in his hand. "A pleasant surprise. What brings you here?"

Aimée notices he doesn't seem at all surprised to see her. Almost as if he were *following* her. Thoreau comes closer and she tugs her skirt over her ankles. Should she stand up?

"I was with my brother," she says, looking behind him at the path back to the house and safety. "He's with Mercier and Brac—they'll be coming back this way soon."

Thoreau chuckles. "No, I am afraid not, demoiselle. The path to the whipping post avoids these fields altogether. Even though I am recently arrived, I find myself quite the expert on this place. But this is the first time I am seeing the old indigo factory. For I assume this is what this is?" He gestures around at the disused vats and storehouse.

He sits down on the step beside her. Aimée's heart is beating so loudly she is sure he can hear it too. Should she run? Scream? The south coffee fields are not far and there she might find Brac or one of the drivers.

"Ah, indigo," thrums Thoreau, also picking a pink flower from the stone wall. "A fine crop. A *romantic* crop. Do you know why I call it romantic, my child?"

Thoreau leers at her and Aimée smiles timidly back.

"No?" says Aimée, unsure of the right answer. If he wants to ravish her then why had he killed Plunkett? And he doesn't look like a depraved criminal, though she's not sure what they look like. But surely a murderer would not be so... dapper? And mannered? Her only salvation might be to keep him talking, like Scheherazade in that tale. "I'm not sure—"

But Thoreau is not interested in her answer, only in the assurance of an audience. "*Romantic* because indigo belongs to one of the seven colors that Newton described on his optical spectrum, linked to the seven notes of the music scale and of course seen in rainbows—a happy marriage between nature and science! And speaking of nature and science, one must ask who was the first man to extract blue from the green leaf? How did he know? How incredible, how outrageous are the advances that have led us to these modern times!" Thoreau continues, lost in his own words. "Imagine what else is left for us to discover!"

He drones on and Aimée feels a tug of impatience: surely if he had devious designs, he would not be lecturing her right now? When Thoreau pauses after comparing indigo to blue gold, she takes the opportunity to ask him why he is not with the other men.

A strange look comes over Thoreau's face. "Ah, yes! I could not stand to be in the room a minute longer with that Mercier, and though normally I would not miss the chance to witness a punishment, I simply cannot abide the man." He stops and glances at Aimée. "Perhaps I should not talk thus of a man I know to be a family friend, but—"

Aimée shakes her head, happy to be in agreement. "Oh, no! I don't like him either."

"Good, well," says Thoreau, nodding. "A most unrefined man. So I stayed behind and had a most interesting talk with Monsieur Azor. A mulatto but most knowledgeable! I must say the conversation fair inspired me. I took a walk to gather my thoughts and happened upon an alligator pear tree and cut off a branch, to inspect the bark…" Thoreau trails off, as though embarrassed.

"Oh, where did you find a tree? The fruit is delicious."

"The fruit is edible?"

"Oh yes! Green, rich and creamy. Like butter."

"Indeed, I did not think to sample the fruit." Thoreau waves the stick around the clearing. "Rather desolate, here."

"Peaceful," Aimée agrees, sure now the danger is past.

"A good place for thinking," says Thoreau. "Monsieur Azor quite filled my head with thoughts for future experiments! But I suppose I should focus on the conundrum at hand."

"What's a conundrum?"

"A mystery or puzzle. In this case, the murder of Plunkett. We must ask: Who would want to murder him? An inoffensive man, really, despite our little disagreement last night. The answer, I am convinced, lies not with that unfortunate slave and her necklace but rather in the question of *motive*."

"Oh, I agree—it wasn't a slave. Where would they get a knife?"

"But they have knives of their own?"

"No, only pruning saws, and machetes when they clear land, but those are always locked up. Only Jeannette in the kitchen has knives. Oh!" Aimée remembers the knife that went missing last week.

"So many questions and puzzles," Thoreau says. "For example: What was Plunkett doing abroad at such a late hour?"

Aimée giggles then catches herself when she realizes the man is serious. "Oh! But..."

"But what, my dear?"

Aimée feels the beginnings of a blush. How is it possible this man doesn't know? Doesn't he make such visits in the night? Thoreau is looking at her quizzically and his understanding rises with the color in her cheeks.

"Ah! Forgive me, my dear, an indelicate question! But of course! At La Farge the number of little half-castes running around was quite astonishing. I—" he stops. "Quite. Well. Then perhaps I was not the last person to see him alive. This gives us our first line of inquiry?"

"Yes?" Aimée asks, glad he understood.

"Certainly. We need to know who the man was visiting. Had he yet to visit her? Or was he returning from his—ah—visit? But no! This is no line of inquiry to be discussing with you, my dear, you are far too young."

"I'm not so young," Aimée protests, then pauses; young ladies are more likely to be ravished. "I mean I am a child but I'm not."

"Well, that is one line of inquiry," says Thoreau after a few moments. "There is another... I am not sure I should be sharing this with you but your mother was disinterested and perhaps you might be able to shed some light on this document."

Thoreau fishes a paper out of his pocket. "I witnessed Mr. Plunkett take this—steal it, I believe—from a cupboard in the dining room last Sunday. It might be connected to his death."

"But that's Aunt Julienne's baptism record!" says Aimée in

surprise. "She was—is—my father's youngest sister."

"Yes, your mother confirmed as much," says Thoreau. "But what interest could Plunkett have in this document? Your mother was equally nonplussed."

Thoreau reads the flowing script aloud: *"This is the baptismal record of Julienne Elisabeth Marie Fongravier, born April 5, 1760, baptized at the Church of Notre Dame, Dame Marie Parish on September 13, 1765. The godfather Jerome Nicholas Pommier, the godmother Dame Elisabeth Nebout Fondin. Signed and witnessed here on this day in Dame Marie Parish...'* And followed by a series of signatures. There is a clue in here somewhere, there must be."

"I don't know," says Aimée, uncertainly.

"Where is your aunt now?"

"She's here," says Aimée, taking the document and reading it again. So poor Aunt Julie is thirty-two, though she looks younger. What had she been like at her baptism? Happy and never knowing, when she squirmed as the priest chucked water over her head, the frightful future that was waiting for her up in Limbé.

"Here, in Saint Domingue? Or in the Grand'Anse?"

"No, here in our house."

"In the *house*?"

"Yes, she's... well, it's hard to explain. She was living up north and lost everything in the rebellion last year and she came back and... she's not right in the head. Mama doesn't like us to talk about it. Her."

"My goodness. You mean she is here at Bayardel?"

"Yes, we share a room. It's all very sad."

"Well, certainly! But such an astonishing revelation..." Thoreau trails off and shakes his head, then turns again to the baptism certificate. "There has to be something here! *Godfather, Jerome Nicholas Pommier. Godmother, Dame Elisabeth Fondin.* And their signatures below, as well as those of the parents and the notary. Do you know the godparents?"

"The godfather must be Madame Nathalie's father. Madame Nathalie Pommier, she is married to Mercier. And then Madame Fondin is a cousin of my father's. Was—she's dead now. She married five times," Aimée says with a giggle and tells the old family joke: "On her fifth marriage, the priest asked whether he needed to bother saying anything, since she knew the words so well!"

"Ah, indeed, how…" says Thoreau. "And Jerome Pommier?"

"I am sure he is dead too. Madame Nathalie is very old."

"How interesting—a Mercier connection." Thoreau pauses, then plunges ahead: "I feel there is some connection between Mercier and this mystery. I have a gut, not my physical belly, but that which is known as the *intuition of the senses*, a hunch that is not based on provable evidence yet by design is true." He pauses again. "Is there a claim a godparent can make? This aunt of yours, is she to inherit any part of this estate, or others?"

"Perhaps part of it," says Aimée doubtfully. "But that would have all been settled when she married."

"And the husband lost everything in the rebellion?"

"Probably," says Aimée. "But her husband wasn't rich, he was just managing the place for his uncle. *He* was a grand marquis."

"I wonder… does this imply that Mercier has some claim on this plantation?"

"I think he offered to buy it," says Aimée. "After our father died?" She vaguely remembers a tense conversation and the end, for a while, of their monthly visits to Madame Nathalie. "We should show this to Pomponne, she is very good at solving puzzles! But I can't find her anywhere."

Thoreau points to a particularly ornate signature scrawled at the bottom of the document. "Who is that?"

"L'Epine, the notary. He lives in Apricots."

"Ah—that delightful sounding town, Apricots, also where our Mr. Plunkett lived! They knew each other?"

"Yes," says Aimée. "Apricots is only about twenty houses. He—the notary L'Epine—came when we settled my father's will. He probably does all our family's papers."

"More connections! Very interesting… And you see these signs by the men's signatures—the dots and dashes mark secret societies. L'Epine and your grandfather, you see they have the same marks but this Jerome Pommier has none."

"Oh, I didn't know that," says Aimée.

"Ah!" says Thoreau, suddenly standing up. "There might

be another letter, or a clue of a different kind, on Plunkett's person. He might have taken other papers and retained them on his person."

"Yes, there might be a clue on the body! If he is still down the well, we could winch him up," Aimée says, thinking of Pomponne's offer from that morning.

"An excellent idea!"

*

"Is the body still down there?" Aimée asks Laurine, sitting motionless in front of her tub.

"Huh."

"Is the grave ready?"

Laurine scowls. "Maybe."

"Well, who is digging the graves?"

Laurine considers for long while. Remarkably unpleasant woman, thinks Thoreau, examining her covertly but anxious not to catch her eye. He had quite the run in with her a few days ago about some missing handkerchiefs. Perhaps she is a Mondongue, well known as the most fearful of all Africans and prone to cannibalism; at Trou Bon Bon, near Apricots, there was a well-documented case of a Mondongue Negress who relished eating her babies after birth!

"Pierre and Capidon," says Laurine finally. "They dig."

"Are they finished?" asks Aimée.

Another scowl. "Don't know."

"Well, where are they?"

"I'll get," says Laurine and rises slowly, hissing something under her breath. She waddles towards the stables and Aimée looks anxiously into the water.

"Ah, I wonder if my handkerchiefs are in there," says Thoreau, peering into the sudsy mess, the acrid smell of lye almost swallowing his nose whole. "That looks like one. I tried to ask her yesterday but she was quite vicious really." He reaches his hand in then retracts it quickly as Pierre and Capidon appear, followed by Laurine.

"Ah, good, you two. Wonderful, yes," says Thoreau, greeting the two men. He points at the well: "Now, if you could winch the man up?"

The two slaves stare at him dumbly.

"Winch? Yes, WINCH." Thoreau mimics a winding wheel.

"Oh, they understand," says Aimée. "They're just being annoying."

"*Lev-li*," barks Laurine tersely.

Capidon and Pierre roll their eyes and slap their heads in an exaggerated display of delighted understanding.

"Jolly little fellows, aren't they?" remarks Thoreau. "They have a certain '*native naiveté*' that is not without its charms." He smiles at them and is gratified to see his smile returned a hundredfold, the two men positively beaming. How wonderful, this state of childlike happiness that is well known to be the natural disposition of the Negro! Though, if Thoreau is to be honest, evidence of that happy natural state has been largely absent on his travels so far.

Nonetheless a wave of bounteous magnanimity surges over him—he is here to help these pathetic creatures! Perhaps he should even interview some himself! In his time on the island, Thoreau has not actually been very close to the slaves—field slaves, at least—and has certainly not conversed with any. Now Thoreau imagines a pretty little scene, him inquiring as to their general feeding and sleeping habits, their gratitude for his interest in them.

Capidon and Pierre pull up the body and deposit it on a stretcher of wood lying by the well, there for just that purpose.

"Oh," says Aimée softly.

"Oh, my dear," says Thoreau, averting his eyes. Plunkett is beginning to smell, the top of his head wet and his face, a dull grey color, swollen and faintly wild. "Perhaps this was not a good idea…."

"No, I'm all right," says Aimée, backing away.

Laurine comes over to look. Pierre lifts one of the legs to an awful cracking sound, which causes the three slaves to dissolve into loud laughter.

"Now that's enough of that!" raps Thoreau, keenly indignant on behalf of the dead man. The thought of rifling through Plunkett's clothes doesn't appeal but it must be done. "We should take his clothes off," he decides and Laurine bends down, complaining about her knees. With some difficulty she forces Plunkett's green jacket, its front brown with blood, off from his rigid limbs. She hands it to Thoreau, who holds it up between two fingers, checking the pockets with his other hand. Nothing.

Thoreau looks around, wondering what he should do with it. "I suppose his son will want it?" Instead Laurine takes it and flings it into the laundry tub.

"Oh, not with my lilac dress!" shrieks Aimée. "Those are his *dead* clothes and they smell."

"Leave the breeches!" raps Thoreau as Laurine starts on the buttons at Plunkett's crotch. "Let me, ah," he leans over and gingerly pats the sides of the breeches and his chemise but comes up empty.

"Nothing there," Thoreau says with a frown.

Pierre and Capidon start talking, animated and excited.

"What are they saying?" Aimée asks Laurine.

"They talking about his neck."

Everyone peers at the neck.

"Oh—is that his neck bone? It's so white. And horrible," gasps Aimée.

"Bone," nods Laurine.

"No, I do not believe it so," objects Thoreau. "Yes, it looks like a bone but if I remember my anatomy correctly the neck does not have a bone as such. The spine is at the back of the neck, not the front, and so not visible per se... But there is indeed a white... what is that?" Before he can stop himself—his curiosity, though laudable, does lead him to surprising places!—Thoreau puts his fingers into the dead man's neck. A sensation of reaching through a ripe peach, not overly solid. He grasps the white thing and it comes out easily. He holds it up in front of the little group.

"A piece of limestone?" Thoreau queries. He dunks the bloody stone in the suds basin, to more shrieks from both Laurine and Aimée. Now clean, it is revealed to be a white stone about the size of a walnut.

"How very curious," says Thoreau. "A stone and there are markings on it. Part of your magic, then?" he asks Laurine, holding it up. She stares at it and shrugs. Capidon and Pierre waggle their heads, then start wailing and rolling their eyes, miming that they refuse to touch the thing.

"They're only acting, I think," mutters Aimée. "But there is something familiar about the stone, it could be *Vaudun* or..." she trails off.

"Very curious," says Thoreau, pocketing the white amulet. "So. Well, not much to be found here, unfortunately." He looks around, slightly uncertain as to what to do next. "I suppose—we should assist with the burial?"

The slaves lift the pallet with the dead man on it.

"*Nan lakou a cochon,*" directs Laurine.

"I heard that!" snaps Aimée; the *lakou a cochon*—the hog yard—is what the slaves call the white family's cemetery.

The small procession makes its way towards the big house. They circle the enormous carriage then skirt the flower gardens and enter the woods at the bottom. They follow the path that leads to the tombs and soon come to a neat clearing on the hillside with magnificent views over the bay, five small tombs placed at odd angles and one large fresh hole awaiting Plunkett.

"Goodness, what a lovely spot!" exclaims Thoreau. Even though he has been here a year and is now somewhat immune to endless vistas of turquoise sea, white sands and impressive cliffs, the rugged beauty of the island is still not lost on him.

Pierre and Capidon dump the body into the hole and immediately start shoveling the earth back in.

"Goodness! Stop!" cries Thoreau, leaping forward. "We should say something. A few words?"

"It's all right," says Aimée. "The priest will come later. That's when his family will come, if they want."

"So strange, this quickness," protests Thoreau. "Indecent almost! And for the man to be buried here, so far from his home... your mother explained it was because of the heat but it feels most improper."

"It happens," says Aimée. "You see there—" she motions to one of the stone tombs, a miniature house that Thoreau now understands is just a brick covering for the body, buried deep within the earth, "that was a friend of Father's. He was visiting and had an attack of apoplexy and died. He only lived a few hours away but still had to be buried here. His wife used to come and visit but she doesn't anymore."

"Indeed," says Thoreau, feeling a momentary flash of pity for *Calixte Dufour, 1726 - 1785.* How awful, to die so far from home and be buried in a stranger's yard! "Well then, I say proceed," he says, nodding to Capidon and Pierre, his earlier infatuation with them somewhat cooled by their callous approach to the body of Mr. Plunkett.

"Is the hole deep enough?" asks Aimée. "If it's not deep enough before the bricks are put on, wild pigs will get at the body. It used to happen all the time in the slave cemetery before Grandfather grew the fence."

"Oh, goodness," says Thoreau, feeling rather green and leaning against said grandfather, *Marcel Mathurin de Fongravier, 1698 - 1778* engraved on one side, with *Francine Pelagie Yvonnet, 1720-1780.* "I'm afraid I can't help you there, dear."

Aimée peers in to the dark hole and sees Plunkett turned on his side, his neck at an odd angle. "It looks deep enough," she says doubtfully and backs away.

"A lovely place," says Thoreau in his musing voice, looking in determination away from the grave and out towards the generous expanse of the bay. The water is smooth and glassy, some of its earlier turbulence gone. "But lonely too. Makes one think of the loneliness of dying in a foreign land, so far from where we belong. Yet no matter one's station in life, the Dance Macabre unites us all."

How extraordinary that he and Plunkett had been engaged in lively conversation just last night and then pop! a bubble bursting, the man's life gone and never to return. The thread of his days, snapped. Thoreau mops his head, aware of the beating sun and his exposed position, the white glare reflected from the water below. He spies what he thinks is a flash of lightning in the distance. But it won't rain again, he thinks, unsure where his conviction comes from.

Capidon and Pierre finish filling the hole. They pat down the fresh earth for what seems like an overly long time before they stop and look at Thoreau and Aimée.

"Well, I suppose that is that," says Thoreau. "Our duty towards Mr. Plunkett done, I suppose we should head back. Perhaps consider our next step? It is getting late." The sun over the water is now hanging lower in the sky and the light has softened to faint shades of amber.

"Yes," says Aimée. "But I do wish we could find Pomponne! She does love a good mystery and she's as sharp as a knife. She would be able to help us."

"Indeed," says Thoreau but privately he is reluctant to be allied with yet another young girl. If truth be told, it feels slightly humiliating to have Aimée as his only confidante, even though the young women of this colony are reputed to be rather mature in comparison with their convent-cloistered counterparts in France. It is well known that girls here grow up fast and that Creoles are generally oversexed from birth, no doubt on account of the sun.

Thoreau thinks again of Aimée's astounding revelation that her aunt is in the house. These colonials and their proverbial monsters in wardrobes—actually true! How dreadful but he has heard of the frightful horrors suffered by the female hostages— it is perhaps no wonder she is unhinged and kept hidden. That sort of shame, a mountain high, is best left undisturbed.

The little party is making its way back through the woods when suddenly Aimée stops.

"Wait!" she exclaims. "I remember where I've seen it before! The white stone from Plunkett's neck—the very same one!

"

The Flower Gardens
5 pm

Dusk is approaching by the time Henri arrives back at the plantation and rides to the stables. No one to even help him dismount, he thinks in disgust. He tethers his horse and looks around, shaking his head. What a place!

Henri considers going to the big house and informing his father that Bassompierre was not to be found in Dame Marie. But no, he is reluctant to give up the free time that this unexpected turn of events has provided: they still think he had to go all the way to Dame Marie before finding out his mission was futile. If he announces his presence, he risks being sent off on another errand. Another errand to save precious Madame Rose.

First, Madame, I send my coachman to La Fraternité for twenty slaves, guaranteed to be here tomorrow at sun up. Second, Madame... like a regular ministering angel, thinks Henri in scorn. His father still trying to curry favor with the whites, even after what they did to his family.

Not me, decides Henri, never me.

He wonders, since all roads these days generally lead not to Dame Marie, but to sexual thoughts, if his father had ever slept with a white woman. Sex with a real white woman, not some light-skinned *sang-melé* of the famous Madame Josephe brothel in Les Cayes, her black ancestry so faint as to be negligible. Henri was most distressed to hear—from his cousin, a great connoisseur—that the place was shut because of the troubles. Just his luck the

271

damned war had to intervene when he is now of an age to enjoy such matters!

Henri was only twelve when he sailed for France, too young to have done much but he found he could entertain his sex-starved French classmates for hours on end with tales of brown delights as bountiful as blackberries on the roadside bushes in France.

Of course, he, Henri, had had a white woman: as the boys at school grew older, more and more of them returned from summers at the family home with stories of trysts with maids or the village slut. In Bordeaux after school, Henri had enjoyed quite the delicious dalliance with the daughter of his tutor.

Certainly in France white women were no prize. But out here? Never. Here the white woman is transformed into an untouchable prize, strictly off limits to those with African blood. But ah, what a triumph it would be and Henri can feel himself growing hard at the thought. The attraction isn't only their silky hair or their pretty eyes but more the joy of the forbidden fruit. He imagines bending a white woman to his will and over his bed, using her body like the whites use their women.

Henri stops a safe distance away from the big house, mindlessly scratching at his hardened crotch, thinking of the breasts of Antoinette—the girl his mother hopes he will marry—and how they rose and fell as she played the piano. No one is on the veranda but Henri can hear the earnest, high-pitched voice of the French fop.

Henri's ears are cocked, his head pleasantly rummy. Which way wither the delectable Pomponne? The kitchens! Her mother, if he remembers correctly, is the plantation cook. I'll follow my nose, he decides, grinning at his own humor and sets off in the direction of a delicious smell.

And here we are.

"Hello," he says, peeking into the dark kitchen house. A kestrel screeches just as he speaks and the woman inside jumps.

"Oh!" She comes out, wiping her hands on her apron. What a looker—no surprise her daughter is so delectable.

The cook smiles, tentative and hopeful. "Would you be Master Azor, sir?"

Henri laughs inside; he knows her type and he knows her

desperation.

"I am." Henri makes a small bow. "The mother as beautiful as the daughter."

The cook gives a quick curtsy, trying to hide the pleasure from her face. "None as beautiful as my daughter."

"Indeed. She is a well-kept secret."

The woman laughs, a little nervously. "She would be very pleased to see you again."

"And where might I find her?"

"If you wait in the front garden, sir, by the statue, I will make sure she finds you."

Henri gives another half-bow, doffs an imaginary cap and takes his leave.

Jeannette watches him go, holding back a frown and a sudden feeling of misgiving—there is something a little odd about the young man and her first impression was not pleasant. The way his shadow cast across the kitchen and that bird's cry, before she even turned around and realized it was him.

But no, she's just being silly. Henri is handsome and well dressed and charming. And the garden is the perfect place—it sends the right message of propriety and decorum, his father and Madame Rose only steps away in the big house were he to get any wrong ideas. Jeannette hurries over to the women's house where Pomponne should be dressed and waiting.

*

Narrowly missing the party returning from the cemetery, Henri finds the gardens and sits himself on a bench. The rum is beginning to wear off and he wants another drink. Should have asked the cook. A beautiful woman, as beautiful as he had heard. Henri is sure she has been used by half the district but certain women, no matter how worn they are, never lose their charms.

But her daughter—Henri could tell by the eagerness in the mother's eyes that Pomponne is a fresh one. He chuckles; a mother's love can blind the truth.

"Ah, my little friend!"

Pomponne walks shyly down the path. Her pale pink dress—the color of the lip of a conch shell—shimmers against her skin and sets her blue eyes glowing. A doll, a perfect dusky little doll, Henri thinks in delight. And all for me.

"And how are you?" he asks.

"I am well, thank you, Master Azor." Pomponne curtsies and looks up at him shyly.

"Do call me Henri."

Pomponne bites her lips and nods.

"Well, these are beautiful gardens," Henri says, rising and offering her his arm. Beautiful gardens, my ass—just clumps of overgrown everything and that distasteful black wooden statue like a slave standing in the middle. Flowers run amok and weeds everywhere. Does his father need to send for a gardener as well?

Cautiously Pomponne takes Henri's arm; she has never held the arm of a man before but it feels good, solid and firm, not soft like her mother or Flore. And they are in the gardens, under the watchful eye of the big house. It's not yet evening though the afternoon has turned dark and still and the sun will set shortly. Henri is not wearing gloves and she sees hair on the back of his hand, dark and curly.

"Madame Rose bought these from France, many years ago," Pomponne says, pointing to a yellow rose bush almost strangled by a vicious heap of hibiscus.

"Indeed. How pretty. And what flowers are these?"

Pomponne relaxes slightly, enjoying his attention as they walk around, answering his questions about the flowers. And his clothes are very fine and he is charming too. There is a faint smell of something unpleasant coming off him, dark but so thin she is not sure it is even there.

"And these are gardenias and here pink plumerias and this hibiscus bush is supposed to be older than Madame Rose," Pomponne says. "Frangipani and these we call them bell flowers, they smell ever so sweet at dusk."

"And how is Madame Rose?" asks Henri, stopping by a mimosa tree with spiky flowers, its sugary rich scent unfolding as evening approaches.

"She is a good mistress. Very benevolent."

Henri chuckles. "You and your words, you clever little thing." When they chanced to meet at La Fraternité she had told him wistfully about the *armada* of cakes her mother was helping to prepare in the kitchens. And then he went and fetched her one.

"So tell me, which is your favorite flower?"

Pomponne points to a sweep of orange bougainvillea and Henri plucks one and tucks it behind her ear. She holds her breath at his closeness and at the way his hand pats her head, then casually chucks her chin. "Not blue like your eyes but this one matches your lips."

"And what is down there?" Henri asks, stopping at the bottom of the garden near where Plunkett's body was found that morning.

"That leads to the family graves."

"Well come on," Henri says. "I'll wager there is a good view from the hillside."

Pomponne hesitates; the edge of the forest is thick here but the graves are only a small way away and the view is beautiful. Henri is smiling at her and she thinks him so handsome. *Ever* so handsome; perhaps she is in love? His arm is outstretched to usher her through and so in she goes ahead of him, the path already dark inside the woods at the tail end of the afternoon. They pass the clearing where Aimée found her stupid statue.

Behind her comes Henri. Pomponne's ears, ever so sensitive to life, notice that his breath is quickening and when she hears that she knows she has made a terrible mistake. But she can't stop now and here they are in the clearing with the tombs, right on the edge of the cliff, the sea spread before them. The sun, starting to set in the west, sends orange shards over the calm waters.

"Ah, what a sight," says Henri, coming to stand beside her. Pomponne stares straight ahead. She holds still, as prey might; perhaps if she doesn't move, her predator will forget where she is. A flutter of birds soar out across the sun-dappled sea and her fear mingles with the beauty around her. She has a sudden urge to fling herself off the cliff that she might be saved and rise up like a bird.

"Lovely sunset," Henri observes casually.

A dead fish, that's what he smells like and the smell is getting stronger now. Pomponne can't breathe.

"And what's that—for the Englishman?" Henri gestures to the large hole, once black and cavernous but now filled in with Plunkett. The smell of fresh earth, piled neatly over the cavern, the earth where all living creatures are disturbed. Pomponne breaks into a sprint, back through the dark wood towards the house and safety. But Henri is right behind her. One hand around her waist and another on her throat, cutting off a cry that only the setting sun can hear.

Henri picks her up, laughing.

"Look at you kicking and squirming. Now how did your Mama know that's how I like it?"

He wrestles her small body back to the clearing. Like a fox, he thinks for no reason; so abundant on the grounds of his school in France and he always thought them such elegant little creatures, of much more interest than cats. I should have brought one back with me, he thinks as he throws Pomponne on the ground and straddles her and then his thoughts turn from foxes to the smooth virgin place between her thighs.

BOOK THREE

DUSK & DARKNESS

The Clearing
6 pm

Dusk comes quickly on the island, falling in soft waves that banish the harsh glow of the afternoon. The wind picks up slightly but still heat pounds forth from surfaces the sun scorched the day long.

Arriving at the stables, Appollon sees the piebald that the young colored man rode to Dame Marie. So, he is back; does that mean the captain is come as well? Appollon listens but there is nothing to indicate the constabulary is on the plantation. If they were, they would already be turning the slave houses inside out and wreaking their havoc.

The mules whinny at him in greeting and mindlessly he fills their troughs. He fills a bucket with water and pours in some medicine then quickly washes out the mules' eyes, oozing from distemper. All feels quiet and calm, no sound from anywhere, as though the plantation is setting in quiet alongside the sun. Appollon hesitates then heads for the kitchens where the smell of a savory sauce greets him. Jeannette comes out and falls into his arms in relief.

"I got there in time." Appollon kisses her and smells the wild rosemary she has been chopping. He picks a scrap from one of her hands and eats it. "It's not going to happen tonight."

"Oh, thank the gods. And you—are you fine?" Jeannette is looking at his shirt, dry now but still covered with blooming pink stains where he tried to wash out La Fleur. "Is that blood?"

Appollon doesn't answer, just exhales and looks around.

He can hear the calling of one of the gangs coming back from the fields. "I'm hungry," he whispers. "Get me something before I go back to the stables, I've got to get the animals in and fed. I see the Azor boy returned from Dame Marie—with the captain?"

"No captain," says Jeannette, coming back with some bread and peas in a gourd. "But the boy is here, I saw him…"

"Why? What business in the kitchen?"

Jeannette looks away. "Nothing."

The south field gang start returning to the clearing, Michel singing and Jean Pierre carrying a giant crab. He found it earlier under a coffee bush and blinded it—without eyes, the crab did not move. Now he brings it home for his evening meal, calling out that he will share it with anyone who will cook some beans for him.

"You should go," says Jeannette, pushing Appollon away. "Brac has been by twice, looking for La Fleur." She looks at his shirt again but Appollon shakes his head; he can't explain now. He finishes the food and kisses her goodbye.

"Later tonight?" she pleads. "We have so little time."

"Of course."

"You!" It is Brac, riding behind the men returning from the fields.

Appollon turns around, crossing his arms to cover the stains on his shirt. Shit, he should have changed. Jeanette slips back into the kitchen.

"Is the captain come?"

"Master Azor's horse at the stables, but no other."

"Don't call the woolly-haired mutt *master*," barks Brac. "And where were you when the boy came back?"

"Fixing the pasture gate," Appollon improvises. "Perhaps the captain's horse is by the big house?"

Brac snorts. The two men glare at each other, the hate between them palpable and pure. Friday, thinks Appollon and lowers his eyes to the image, so appealing, of Brac lying impaled on a stake. Or his life bleeding out from where his cock once was.

"La Fleur—has he been by the stables?"

"Didn't see."

Brac spits in disgust. "Left the east field unsupervised." He looks around him. "If you see La Fleur tell him he's in trouble. We'll have ten more hands tomorrow and once we get the mill going, we can pack and load the bags immediately. Those mules better be ready."

Appollon watches him depart. Once it becomes clear that La Fleur is gone, Brac will be suspicious; he knows his faithful overseer would never leave of his own accord. Appollon shrugs. And then what? All will happen as it will happen, but he doubts they will find the body before Friday.

Appollon watches the men filtering back from the fields. He must tell the others that the plan is delayed and then he will have done his part and there will be nothing to do but wait for Friday. He sits down on a log by the furthest house to wait. Dusk always makes him think of Whydah and his heart twinges unexpectedly. A magical time, when the lights of cooking fires began to burn against the deepening sky, the ocean finally quiet, the smells of food filling the air and soft light heralding the tranquility of the night to come. His mother used to burn a candle every evening at this time and pray to her gods, her soft voice murmuring the words.

Though Appollon tries to turn away from his memories, recently he has been thinking of the past more and more. His mother, lying on the birth-bed, dying but still lifting her hands and stroking his head, telling him not to worry, that his ancestors would care for him. Chalumette's laugh, the brightness of the sea visible through the window when the irons bound his arms for the first time. Even snippets of the ocean passage, two months of hell Appollon had squarely pushed down into the deepest crevices of his mind. Why is his past clamoring to be let in at this time, when all he wants to do is think about the future?

*

Jeannette lights a lantern against the shadows and gathers a pile of eggs. She cracks them into a bowl, one by one, stopping every now and then to stir the sauce still bubbling over a flame. She isn't ready to tell Appollon about Pomponne and Henri Azor. Something holds her back—he might be scornful of her for caring about such a thing with the uprising just around the corner. She whisks the eggs furiously.

Pomponne should be coming back soon and Jeannette

imagines what her daughter might tell her—were words exchanged, promises made? A plan for the future? Such a nice young man and so eager to see her daughter again. Only a faint trace of something darker… but no. Pomponne is probably at the big house and Madame Rose has set her to pouring drinks for the guests. Jeannette's heart tightens at the thought of her daughter in her pink dress, serving in front of the Mercier man. But Aimée and Madame Rose are there—they will protect her.

Outside a hundred bats awaken to the coming darkness and swoop through the yard. More slaves troop back from the fields, the setting sun signaling their work is done for the day. The women return from the drying platforms and the sorting lines. Some lie down in the clearing to wait for the coolness of night before entering the sleeping houses, while others wash at the stone troughs and drink water in great gulps from calabashes pulled from the well.

Night falls quickly in the tropics and soon darkness will surround them. This precious hour of dusk is for cooking and eating and when the plantation is in darkness they will sleep. The great events of the outside world largely pass them by; their world is small and they cherish this hour of humanity. The women busy themselves preparing food while others go off to their provision plots to gather beans or cassava for the evening. There are informal arrangements amongst them; some women cook for a few men, others for just one. It is always a matter of great interest to see who is sharing which fire.

Julien and Sans Quartier kneel facing the setting sun as Michel calls on all to join him in evening prayers for Jesus; no one does. Thom and Jason head off to hunt wild pigs with their bows and arrows. Back in his village near Luanda, Thom was Gougou, known far and wide as the best shot in his village; even in twilight he can hit a bird from fifty feet. Jean Louis goes off to find a pineapple he promised to Zabeth, who is so pretty and has a sweet tooth. Gros San Quartier slumps down beneath the giant apricot tree, too exhausted to move from the fever that has wracked him all day. Rosalie lies down beside him, her giant goiter pulling her head over to one side; though they were moving slowly all day— especially when La Fleur left them alone in the afternoon—she couldn't keep up. Her limbs feel detached from her body and she stares up at the orange sunset and the vast sky above her. Death is coming soon, she is certain of it. No matter how hard this life everyone wants to live, she thinks, and blinks back tears.

Louis, the second *commandeur*, collects the shovels—from Pierre and Capidon, from the women tasked with turning the dried coffee beans—and brings them to the storehouse. Normally he would count them with La Fleur before locking them up but Brac has been complaining all afternoon that La Fleur is missing. Louis hesitates, then places the shovels by the door. At the back of the storehouse he checks the hole that they have been burrowing for weeks, hidden under a pile of bamboo. Inside the storehouse are the shovels but also some twenty machetes. Tonight, he thinks, covering up the hole and heading back to the clearing. Tonight, when darkness falls and the signal comes.

Appollon catches him. "Not tonight."

"What, man?"

"Not tonight."

"Ai-yeee." Louis lets out a long sigh. "Why not?"

"Why do you think?" says Appollon, gesturing in the direction of the big house. "That dead white man, the constable coming."

"Stopping everything for that?" Louis sounds annoyed.

"Yes. But Friday, it's coming again. You tell Pierre and Capidon. And Laurine too—I think she knows and we don't want her bitter mouth setting something off."

"Right."

Appollon watches Louis depart, shaken by the man's doubt. *Stopping everything for that?* But it was the right thing to do and besides, Friday is but two days away.

The young twins Samedi and Dimanche come bearing bundles of firewood balanced on their heads. They drop them under the apricot tree and the clearing starts to fill with small fires, plantains and cassava ground, beans quickly shelled then settled in pots over the flames. The air is subdued tonight and no one asks about Bridget. Louis makes the rounds and murmurs to the few that know that they will see no fire tonight.

"What you mean, no fire?" giggles the spy Garifou, suddenly appearing.

"Get away from my fire," hisses Laurine, using a stick to

flick embers at him. She places a grill over the flames and balances a few yams on it.

"Heh, I can stand where I want," protests Garifou nervously. "There be fires all around?"

Louis pushes him away, then sits down beside Laurine and Capidon. They look at each other; a tense day of waiting and for nothing.

"You bring me one, I'll cook it for you," says Laurine in a sudden and uncharacteristic burst of generosity, motioning to the yams that are starting to smell mighty fine above the warm embers.

Mumbo prepares a cassava leaf stew for Giep, half-blind from an eye infection but still able to work the fields, and for the ones in the hospital. While the thick stew settles, she slips off into the darkening woods and makes her way to the slave cemetery. She lays a few plantains on the ground for Lubin and checks his water bowl. She jumps; someone is coming out of the woods behind her.

"Hela," she says to Rosalie. "What are you doing here?"

The other woman gestures over to Bridget. They look at the body, cut down from the whipping post, naked and half-flayed.

"Oh, poor woman," breathes Mumbo.

"But where?" says Rosalie, looking around. Then she sees them and sighs in pleasure. She gathers up the skirt and blouse, notices the straight cuts in the cloth and shivers. But easy enough to fix.

Mumbo stares at Bridget, feeling sad as she always does; other people's sorrows seem to flow into her and fill her up. Even when she was young, before she was taken to this life, it was the same: as though she could see inside another person and right into their sadness and grief.

Back in the clearing Laurine calls her over.

"She dead?" Laurine barks and Mumbo nods, trying to keep her tears back. She tried to get Bridget to speak, to learn the language, to be a friend. But she failed.

"I got her clothes," announces Rosalie in triumph and heads off to secure them inside the house. She'll fix them then sell them in the market down in Dame Marie.

"Well, Bridget dead," announces Laurine loudly to the rest of the clearing. "And the constable—the big law white man—is coming here. So what are we going to tell him? About Bridget?"

Most of the slaves look away.

"Who whipped her?" asks Victoire.

"That man Mercier. Or Brac or the white boy. Maybe all three. It don't matter, we all know this is not allowed."

Her words are met with silence and a few shrugs, though Perrine does stop pounding her calabash of cassava.

"Brac'll do the same to you if you tell the constable," Marie mutters finally.

"No need to tell him, we just show him the body! Clear she was whipped to death, right Mumbo?"

"Yes," whispers Mumbo; timid and fragile, she hates to be the center of attention.

No one else says anything. Jean Pierre cracks a leg from his crab, roasted by Porozina, and declares he's never had a finer one.

Laurine scowls. "What, we all pussies too scared to talk to the constable?"

"Now not the time to do anything," counsels Louis.

"Eh, cowards, all of you," says Laurine in disgust, pushing Louis' yam into the fire and blackening it until he cries out in protest. Mumbo takes a bowl of stew to the hospital. On the way she passes Pierre carrying an enormous tortoise shell, almost too heavy for one man to manage. He brings it to the clearing and proudly shows it off; the others sigh in appreciation and envy.

"I should go now, run to Jérémie and sell it. Take my strokes when I get back."

"Not the time," hisses Capidon under his breath. "No one should be leaving now."

"But what if I don't get a chance later?" whines Pierre.

"Bigger things," snaps Laurine. "Look at you worrying about your turtle shell and few coins!"

"Not a few coins!" protests Pierre. "We talking maybe fifty *livres*, maybe more!"

"What bigger things?" comes a whinging voice.

Laurine lashes out with her stick and catches Garifou on the side of the head. "Get away from me, you creeping turd."

Samedi and Dimanche take bundles of sticks to the warming hut where they are tasked with the evening fire. They unlatch the door, and when they enter the four Aradas immediately take up their keening, shouting frantic questions at them. Madeline,

284

also Arada and only three years in the country, comes over to talk to them as she does most nights. Brac should have gotten them working by now but he hasn't had the time or the patience and they are still cooped up, terrified and anxious.

"Tell them to shut up," cries Gros Sans Quartier, trying to sleep on the ground. "Tell them the whites are going to eat them tomorrow." In their ignorance, the newly arrived are a constant source of fun for the older and more experienced slaves; hardship does not always create camaraderie.

"Ha, wait until they come out and we show them the wheel trick, that'll be fun!" says Lundi. Many of them never saw a wheel before arriving, and the carts—not to mention the horses and mules—are sources of great fascination and terror.

"Oh, wait!" cries Lisette, dashing into the women's house and coming out with a small hand mirror. She has a green thumb and her cucumbers grow to twenty pounds or more; on Sunday she rolled two to town and got two *livres* for them and purchased this mirror. "Let's show them this!"

Several of the men and women laugh and crowd into the hut to see the Aradas' reaction.

"Don't worry," counsels Madeline as the men howl in horror. "It's like water on a pond, captured by the whites' magic in this circle."

Lisette watches proudly. She remembers when she was first brought to this island and how she marveled at mirrors which felt like the most superior magic of the whites; now she owns one herself.

Felicité cooks plantains and beans for Sieur Jean, and soon he is playing a tune on his roughly crafted flute, sprinkling warm notes over the clearing. Two men fight over a pair of trousers while Suzette concentrates on making a basket from the bamboo she gathers on Sunday. Her mother taught her and now weaving the sticks gives her a paltry peace and some connection to her life before; perhaps her mother is doing the same, weaving a basket under the same stars back in her village. Others lie on the ground staring up dully at the sky, Aume moaning about her yaws and scratching away. Sans Souci feeds Chereze the sardines he caught in the river last Sunday, dried on the roof; pleased with this treat, she is sure to lie with him tonight. Manon takes a handful of coffee beans, filched from the drying platforms, and starts roasting them. Soon the sharp smell of fresh coffee competes with the bready smell of roasting cassava and pot beans.

"How your fingers then?" whispers Jacques to Venus, taking her hand and covering it with kisses. She is less than a year here, bought from the same ship as Bridget but her resilient young soul adapted and now she has found love and the comfort of another human. Next to them Marie Jeanne lies on the ground, exhausted and sobbing and in the grip of a vicious fever; she can't go much longer. Brac's got to let me go to the hospital tomorrow, she thinks. Please, mercy, he's got to. I can't get up. Mumbo wheedles a cooked plantain from Porozina and lays it beside her but she is too weak to eat.

Ernestine, Brac's woman, wanders along to sneer at the field slaves. She is drinking from a bottle of brown rum and leading a little pig around on a leash, parading her wares. If Madame Rose refuses to give her fifty *livres* for it, she will sell it next week at the market.

"Hey, you hiding La Fleur under that thick ass of yours?" cries Pierre when he sees her and everyone laughs. Ernestine ignores them and makes a circle of the yard; she knows herself superior to the other slaves and dislikes all of them.

Followed by his mangy dog, Joseph the night watchman comes down from the hospital where he has been trying to sleep all day. As is the custom Jeannette feeds him some bread, dipped in sauce, before shooing him out. She sees Ernestine swanning around and grimaces. It will be a full house tonight and that woman never helps when needed. And where is Pomponne? Who will set the table and bring the plates in?

"Hela, you missed something last night!" Louis calls out to Joseph when he re-emerges from the kitchen hut, munching on his heel of bread.

The old man shrugs. "Nothing to see." He spends his nights by the plantation gates down on the main road, sleeping under a makeshift shelter of palm leaves. He likes it down there with his dog; after a lifetime of working the fields he now has an easy life, staring at the skies and watching the stars change, night after night.

"So the killer of that white man didn't come in by the main gates?" laughs Neptune.

"I already told Brac that," says Joseph with a shrug. He calls to his dog and together they set off down the hill.

"We shouldn't care about white man's killer," mutters Laurine, scooping the yams off her grill. "We should care about Bridget's killer."

The Big House
6 pm

Up in the big house Rose wakes suddenly, her sleep snapped by a feeling or a shadow. The last of the afternoon sun peeks through the shutters and she is aware of a sheen of sweat on her body. She splashes water on her face and changes into another light gown. In front of the mirror she re-pins her hair and pinches her cheeks. These days Rose mostly avoids looking at herself, and at the little lines that are beginning to appear around her eyes.

Rose leaves the peace of her chamber and moves towards the salon. The faint cries of the slave being whipped disturbed her sleep but everything is quiet now. The salon is empty but in the dining room she sees Thoreau and her daughter looking through a sheaf of papers, Plunkett's satchel on the table beside them.

Rose stands in the doorway, aware of a certain intimacy between them. She blinks, as though to understand the little scene better: perhaps Aimée is sharing her lessons with Thoreau?

"Aimée, where have you been all afternoon?" Rose's voice feels tired and unused and she is aware of a persistent throbbing in her head.

"We assisted at the burial of Monsieur Plunkett," announces Thoreau.

"He's buried already? Who told you to do that?"

"You did, Mama," says Aimée. "This morning. You told Brac?"

"I hope we did nothing remiss, Madame," says Thoreau,

rising. "I found the haste most strange myself but it was per your instructions."

Rose feels her way back through the events of the day but comes up empty. "Yes, yes of course. Aimée, do you know where Pomponne is?"

Her daughter shakes her head.

Rose decides to light the house herself. She picks out a flame from the constant oil lamp in the corner and glides around, lighting the candles and lanterns. She feels ethereal and odd, as though she is floating; perhaps still affected by the taffia from earlier. For reasons of economy usually only a few candles and lanterns are lit—wax and oil are imported and expensive—but Rose decides to light them all. On this evening of all evenings, everything must shine. And she must light the way for the captain who is coming. Is it strange he has not yet arrived?

On the back veranda Rose finds Monsieur Azor, still deep in a heavy hammock sleep. The poor man probably needs his rest after talking to Thoreau. Rose picks up his hat from the floor and places it gently on his chest, noting his smooth, kind face, aware that she is looking at him as a man. A sudden keening, from over by the slaves' houses and Rose whips her head around as though stung. She moves guiltily on.

Everything lit, Rose returns to the salon and refills the decanters from the bottles stored under the cabinet. Pomponne brought up a few bottles earlier but they will need more from the cellars. God knows with this day, everyone needs more.

Rose takes a small glass and sinks down on a sofa to savor the silence. How extraordinary, after all the events of the day, that everything is so quiet now. The plantation feels positively... deserted. But Azor is outside, resting in the hammock and Thoreau is in the dining room, safe with her daughter. The boy Yorick, Rose thinks, remembering Plunkett's satchel on the table; I need to get his things to the son. After the captain comes. A mantra for the evening: When the captain comes, all will be well.

Rose watches the sunlight spread longer and longer through the open salon doors as dusk settles in. The darkness creeps closer. Once the sun goes down everything will be over. She shivers. Then the heavy tread of Brac's boots coming up the back veranda and breaking the calm.

"Good evening," says Brac and makes a small formal bow. He usually comes at this hour to report on the day but it seems odd to Rose that he would come today. Then she remembers: the ship. The four days that have now become three. Saturday.

"The Aradas in the warming hut," says Brac, jerking his thumb back in the direction of the slave cabins and the faint keening. "The others always get them going."

"They're not out working yet? Surely...?"

"I've had no time!" Brac snaps. "They've got to be heavily supervised and I just don't have the time or the men."

Rose stares at him, aware of the accusation under his words.

"Tomorrow, at the latest," he concedes.

"What else?"

"Right. We'll aim to set up the mill up tomorrow and work through the night. They'll cause a stink but we have no choice."

"The tarpaulins?"

"Taken care of," Brac answers and Rose knows he is lying. He looks hungrily at the sideboard where the rum sits. She doesn't have the strength to resist but instead nods and he goes to help himself.

"Right, well that is taken care of," announces Mercier, striding into the salon.

Charles follows and Rose sees that something is dreadfully wrong.

"The slave confessed," announces Mercier. He looks around the room. "Where is the constable? I thought to share the good news."

"She didn't confess!" says Charles. "She said *nothing*."

"I was there, I heard it too," remarks Brac.

"You were *not* there!" Charles is trembling and Rose notices what looks like blood on his shirt. She feels mildly sick.

"Nonsense, boy," says Mercier with a smirk. "You heard how she screamed in agreement when Yorick questioned her."

Charles opens his mouth but finds he cannot talk. He killed that woman, he knows it deep in his bones. How does one die from a whipping? Which stroke killed her? When she finally stopped, he ran away from Mercier and the horror, stumbled into the safety of the pigeon house. Mercier followed, hauled him up and cuffed him over the head, called him a milksop.

"Charles, are you all right?" asks his mother softly.

"No, I am not." He goes to the side table and pours himself a rum, knowing his mother won't stop him. He downs it quickly then points at Mercier: "That man—that man made..." Charles trails off, looking to his mother and wishing she could help. But how can she? She can't erase what he did.

"Watch how you talk to your elders," says Mercier swiftly. "The boy needed guidance, is all, and I will not be reproached for providing the hand that a father might."

"What did you do?" asks Rose, amazed at how calm her voice is.

Mercier raises an eyebrow. "I assure you, Madame, nothing that your Marcel would not have done. Or *should* have done."

Rose looks resolutely down at the small glass in her hand. Small, yet comforting. She doesn't know what she wants to say. The smirking closeness of Mercier; the blood on her son's shirt; the way he is trembling.

"Charles, please change your shirt," Rose finally whispers but he doesn't seem to hear. She stares at him helplessly.

"Where is Bridget now?" Rose asks Mercier, looking away from her trembling son.

"We left her recovering from her stripes," says Mercier. "I'll have one of those, Brac, before the boy drinks it all."

Brac nods and pours him a drink.

"You're lying. She's dead," says Charles flatly.

"Nonsense!" says Mercier. "She was alive and well when we left her. She confessed, we stopped the discipline. She is resting now and we should leave her until the constable comes. One can't be too harsh—there must be a balance."

"She's dead," repeats Charles, sounding perilously close to tears.

"If that is indeed the case, then you have only yourself to blame. *I* scarcely touched the whip."

"You're evil!" shouts Charles. "She said nothing!" He rushes out the back door, almost colliding with Azor.

"Is everything all right, Madame?" asks Azor, entering the salon. "Your son appears upset. I heard shouting?"

"I don't know," says Rose. A part of her wants to run after

Charles but another part of her is glad he is gone, away from the sickening malevolence of her neighbor. Why was she so eager to push her son into the ugly world of men? He'll get there soon enough, on his own.

"He'll be fine," says Mercier, taking a glass from Brac and sitting in the armchair that Azor had claimed earlier. He adds under his breath: "Randy and wants a poke, no doubt. Common after a whipping."

"Monsieur!" Rose gapes at her neighbor. Mercier smirks and stretches one leg out.

"Ah, Monsieur Azor—your nap went well?" Thoreau appears from the dining room, followed by Aimée.

"Yes, thank you."

"Mama, what's the matter with Charles? Where did he go?"

"Nothing, dearest," murmurs Rose, pulling her daughter down on the sofa beside her.

"Hammocks! Devilish contraptions, I consider them agents of sloth and indolence!" says Thoreau, smiling at Azor. "But a godsend when one is tired!"

"Yes, certainly." Azor looks around. "My boy—Henri should be back by now? The constable?"

On cue, Henri enters. Rose feels dizzy and twirled around. All these comings and goings—like we are in a play. Enter stage left, the villain, she thinks, and remembers the amateur theatricals they used to perform at the meeting hall in Jérémie. She once played Suzanne in *The Marriage of Figaro*. And here she is again at the center of a play but she is not moving. Is she the heroine or just a piece of furniture?

"Ah, there you are, son," says Azor. "And Captain Bassompierre?" Everyone in the salon looks outside but there is no clatter of men or horses, nothing to herald that the cavalry has come to save the day.

Henri shakes his head, a pained expression on his face. His cheeks are flushed, almost the color of his scarlet cravat, and Rose notices one of the buttons on his jacket is ripped and now hangs off it like a little peapod. "I rode all the way to Dame Marie, Father," he says. "But when I arrived, they told me that Bassompierre had gone to Les Irois yesterday."

Silence as the room absorbs the news.

"Are you sure that's what happened?" Azor asks slowly.

Henri nods and averts his eyes. "Yes, Father. Uh, they think he might be returning this night," he adds after a little pause. "Someone could wait on the road to stop him if he does pass by?"

"Not a bad idea," says his father.

Brac looks doubtful. "It's almost dark; were Bassompierre heading back to Dame Marie he would have passed by now."

"It's barely dusk," protests Rose. "They could have set off from Les Irois an hour ago! And with his men he needn't be in a hurry to get off the road."

"Indeed, full moon tonight," chips in Thoreau. "Could be traveling late."

"I'll tell Joseph to stop the carriage," says Brac.

"No, he'll only fall asleep," says Rose quickly. "What about La Fleur?"

"La Fleur is not to be found," grumbles Brac. "I'll put Appollon out there. Good Creole, he'll be able to explain the situation."

"Well," says Mercier, "I do not see why we need the constable. The matter is taken care of and in a most satisfactory manner. I dare say we can all be going on our way."

"Taken care of?" queries Thoreau.

"The slave confessed. She did it alone."

"But surely if the slave confessed, the constable will want to talk to her?" says Thoreau. "Administer the appropriate punishment?"

Mercier shrugs.

Brac leaves on his mission and the little group coalesces rather awkwardly: Azor, Henri, Mercier. Aimée on the sofa. Rose realizes Mathilde is missing and has been for a while. She leans over and whispers to her daughter: "Aimée, we must find Pomponne and get ready for dinner. I had to light all the candles myself. Go and find her."

To Rose's surprise, her daughter looks to Thoreau as though for approval. Her gives her a quick nod. Rose thinks back to their earlier conversation in the dining room; her assumption that they were talking about lessons was perhaps… ridiculous. Gratefully she accepts another glass of rum from Azor.

"We really must find Pomponne," she repeats, smiling up

at him as her daughter leaves. Exit stage right, thinks Rose with a giggle.

Then Thoreau is upon Azor, grabbing his arm. "I would talk with you, sir. Two minutes, nothing more. Something of importance to say."

The Veranda
6 pm

Thoreau deposits Azor in a corner of the veranda, then hurries after Aimée on her way to the kitchens. Azor shakes his head; really, has the man not taken enough of his time today? He sees his carriage sitting like a magnificent peeled mango in the middle of the driveway, now illuminated by the setting sun. He is sure Henri is lying, but why? If he did not ride to Dame Marie, was it just laziness or something else?

"Magnificent," remarks Thoreau, coming back with Aimée. "Such sunsets cast the whole of the sky as a canvas for God's paint."

"A beautiful country. And this house has a wonderful vantage point," agrees Azor. The Frenchman's words evoke a sudden and unexpected sadness in him. It is true this country is magnificent and never more than at this time of dusk when the sea is calm and the sky a riot of colors contrasting with the white of the limestone cliffs at the other end of the bay.

Thoreau straightens up and offers a half-bow: "Monsieur Azor, we seek your counsel and help."

"Monsieur," says Aimée politely, "we may have uncovered some things related to the death of Mr. Plunkett but we don't know what they mean." She takes the white stone out of her pocket and lays it in the palm of her hand. White against pink and looking larger than it did when they took it out of Plunkett's neck.

"Yes, indeed!" says Thoreau, nodding eagerly. "We found

this in Plunkett's neck. We believe it a *Vaudun* stone but the slaves denied it, though of course they might if not—"

Aimée, emboldened by the events of the day, interrupts. "Monsieur Azor, I saw this stone before. At the house of Monsieur Mercier. You know his wife, Madame Nathalie?"

Azor nods.

"She has a collection of Taino objects that she used to show me when I visited. And I remember a box with stones in it and one was this stone. The same one, I am sure of it!"

"And yet it was in the neck of Mr. Plunkett!" says Thoreau, casting worried eyes back to the salon doors.

Azor whistles, low and surprised, and takes the stone from Aimée's palm. He holds it up to the light. "This stone was in the neck of Plunkett?"

"Yes. His throat was, ah—slit, and in the, ah, slit there was this stone. We thought at first a bone but there are no such bones in the front of the neck."

"Interesting." Azor turns the stone over; on one side are faint etchings and a cross in the shape of a man. "A stone from the house of Monsieur Mercier, found in the neck of Plunkett?"

"And that is not all," says Thoreau eagerly. "We have here the baptism certificate of an aunt of Miss Aimée's. I saw Mr. Plunkett take it last Sunday from the cabinet in the dining room. Like a thief he was, a furtive air about him."

"The cabinet where we keep our family papers," adds Aimée.

"We checked his body and bag but this paper appears to be the only one of interest to him." Thoreau shows Azor the document. "And as you see, the godfather is Jerome Pommier—the father of Madame Nathalie. Mercier's father-in-law! Another connection that perhaps points to the guilt of the man? Some motive? An inheritance at stake, a land claim?"

Azor takes the certificate and reads it. He shakes his head, unable to speak, aware the Frenchman and the white girl are watching him.

"Please, a moment," Azor says, turning away to look out over the flower garden, rapidly descending into darkness with only the orange gardenias emboldened by the setting light. The significance of the birth certificate is instantly clear to him. Azor feels a wave of immense relief: Plunkett's death had nothing to do with the Jamaica plot. Instead, a clear case of blackmail and Mercier most likely the killer. The rumors about Mercier's wife—from long ago but still somewhat current in Azor's own community—must be true.

And so Plunkett's death was just an unholy, unlikely coincidence. He chose badly and now he is dead and the Jamaica project is jeopardized. What a confounding, confused mess up.

"I heard the rumors but could scarce contemplate any kind of kinship with that man," Azor says thoughtfully. He hands the paper back to Thoreau.

"Kinship? Whatever to you mean?"

Azor looks at the eager faces of his audience. What a delicious chance to ruin the man—an extraordinary day, fraught with unexpected disasters but also now with unexpected pleasures. Mercier, with his airs and his fanaticism, his role in the Jérémie horror and the death of Simon. A dangerous man created by a system that prescribes no limit, a man who believes himself impervious to justice. And that man has a secret. A dangerous, life-threatening secret.

"I know what this means," says Azor slowly. "And it gives our man Mercier a motive. And that, coupled with the stone, points to his undoubted guilt."

How very astonishing, yet strangely exhilarating.

MERCIER'S JOURNEY

MERCIER PLANTATION TO BAYARDEL
OCTOBER 1792

Mercier sits all evening, drinking deliberately from a bottle of brandy he was keeping for a special occasion. On the surface, just a regular evening: the soft swish of the palm fan waving back and forth; the quiet ticking of insects fluttering around the lanterns; the steady sounds of the grandfather clock.

Mercier stares at his wife, her face and features drawing him in against his will.

"What is wrong with you?" complains Nathalie from across the room. After a stroke six years ago she now spends her days in a rolling chaise, her time divided between the salon, veranda and bedroom. A small, constricted world; she reads, writes letters to her family scattered around the island and back in France, and lives for the few hours of companionship from family and visitors. Her faithful slave and maid Yoyo waves a fan over her mistress and behind Mercier a *negrillon* performs a similar function. "Why are you staring at me?"

"Nothing, nothing," answers Mercier. He glances at the clock. His wife usually retires by ten, when the last hint of heat has passed and coolness beckons. Mercier goes to bed at the same time but tonight he must stay up.

Their daughter-in-law Monique sits reading beside them; her husband—Mercier's youngest son—is now Deputy

Commissioner in Jérémie but she prefers the coolness of the hills and proximity to the hot springs on Delahaye's land. Seven months pregnant but already huge. The girl is silly and rather plain—Mercier can forgive many faults in a female, but not plainness—and according to her, twins run in her family.

Mercier continues trying to read the newspaper. From Paris, reports of mobs attacking the Tuileries and the *Capets*, as the article refers to the royal family, moved to the Temple where they are now prisoners of the National Assembly. Mercier thinks of the conversation he had with Gaultier last week; his friend insisted that they should not be surprised if the king were executed. *Executed*. Seismic news but he can scarcely concentrate.

"Are you coming to bed?" Nathalie motions to Yoyo to stop her ministrations. His daughter-in-law gets up, yawning and complaining of her aching back.

"No. I'll continue reading," Mercier says, gesturing to the newspaper. His wife says nothing; her disability has given her an indifference to the outside world and she can't bear the news of horror and turmoil, both about France and Saint Domingue, that seems to arrive daily.

"What do you think—" Mercier says suddenly, then pauses; it has been a long time since he engaged Nathalie in conversation other than over the trifling matters of their widespread family. "Those stones in your Indian cabinet, what were they used for?"

Nathalie squints at her husband, surprised by his interest. "No one knows," she says slowly. "There's no one left to tell. I found most of them on the beach, years ago. Money perhaps, or some sort of talisman. Like our crosses."

Mercier grunts; just like his foolish wife to equate the dribbled carvings of the pagans with their Christian crosses.

"Don't ask if you don't like the answer," Nathalie snaps. "And why do you stare so much? You've been looking at me strangely all evening. All month," she challenges. The love and companionship of their early marriage has long since disappeared and now they are bound only by their shared house and children.

"No, I haven't!"

"Good night," Nathalie says, motioning for Yoyo to push her chair to the bedroom. Monique follows, still complaining about her back. Mercier continues drinking in careful, measured sips. Soon the clock strikes ten; he will leave in another hour.

His meeting with Plunkett is set for midnight at Bayardel.

*

Mercier first became aware of the danger to his life a month ago, after a meeting of the Security Council in Jérémie. In earlier and happier times, the meeting hall hosted balls, suppers, amateur plays put on by the local society, and occasionally grander treats from afar: an opera from Le Cap, a violinist from France. But that night the men are gathered there to speak of far more serious matters. Their subject is the ever-contentious issue of arming the slaves: Would it help prevent the unrest that is pulsing at them from the south and east, or would it merely hasten their downfall?

Mercier is firmly in the latter camp and argues passionately against the fatal error of putting weapons in the hands of slaves that could then be used against their masters. Others argue that their slaves are loyal and that the only way to defend the Grand'Anse is to turn each plantation into an armed fortress. They must hold on to the countryside and not be like the planters around Les Cayes who fled to the city and lost control of the plains.

In the end the vote is split down the middle. Frustrated, Mercier declares nothing will be decided that night. He stays behind with a few other planters, friends of his, and the three of them complain into the night. They all believe very strongly that *they*—planters of property—are the foundation of Saint Domingue, the very engine of the vast export machine, yet increasingly they are ignored while other groups take favor ahead of them: the *petits blancs* and their support from the revolutionary government in France; the coloreds being handed the vote and equality with the whites;

the new Jacobin governors' penchant for negotiating with the slaves, and those damn rumors of emancipation. All these changes threaten their perceived status, and through a long night of cigars and rum they complain about all and everything with aggrieved entitlement.

It is approaching midnight when Mercier finally takes to the streets and rouses his slave George, sleeping on the steps. His head full of indignation and liquor, they head to the house of his daughter to spend the night.

Plunkett approaches from a side shadow.

"Monsieur Mercier," he calls out softly. "This is Elijah Plunkett."

"I know who you are," says Mercier, stopping. His voice holds no friendly intent; Plunkett was at the meeting earlier, one of a group of raucous "patriots" who tried to derail the agenda, demanding representatives of their class be admitted to the Security Council. Some premonition makes Mercier wave George off and the two men face each other.

"I would speak with you about a matter?"

"Why do you choose this hour to approach me?" demands Mercier, but as softly as he can—voices carry in the humid, dense night. They are standing in an orb of light from a public lantern and from a few blocks away Mercier can hear the faint lapping of the sea.

"A private matter," stresses Plunkett in his oily voice and Mercier remembers the stench of scandal that swirls around the man: theft, blackmail, illegal trade with the Jamaicans. But Plunkett is still mired in poverty and unsuccessful at all his endeavors, legal or not. As a self-made man—he is apt to downplay the role of his wife's dowry—Mercier has nothing but scorn for men like Plunkett. To fail in this colony, where riches sprout like rushes, where the land is yours for a little risk and the taking. To fail here points to more than just bad luck—it points to a defect of character.

From his contemptuous perch, Mercier feels the *petits blancs* have only themselves to blame for their marginal position; anyone with a little gumption would have figured out a way to pull themselves off the bottom and into the planter class. Hard work and an enterprising spirit are all that is required! And now this lowly class of losers seeks to make themselves masters of the colony, and with the backing of France.

"Well, what is it?" Mercier demands, slightly uneasy at the way Plunkett is looking at him.

"A document—I give you this copy," says Plunkett, pulling it out of his pocket. "I stress this is a copy, and I know where the original is."

Mercier takes it with a grunt.

"Read at your leisure and we will talk tomorrow," says Plunkett smoothly, then disappears into the inky night without so much as a farewell.

At his daughter's house Mercier takes to his room and reads the document by candlelight:

This is the baptismal record of Julienne Elisabeth Marie Fongravier, born April 5, 1760, baptized at the Church of Notre Dame, Dame Marie parish on September 13, 1765. The godfather Jerome Nicholas Pommier, the godmother Dame Elisabeth Nebout Fondin. Signed and witnessed here on this day in Dame Marie Parish, signed...

Mercier sees the significance immediately and stifles a gasp. His wife Nathalie's father is listed as Jerome Pommier, not *Sieur* Jerome Pommier. A small slip, deliberate and significant. As part of the gradual hardening of the laws concerning the free coloreds, a statute passed in 1762 banned them from using the honorific *Sieur*—Sire. That honor was henceforth reserved exclusively for whites, and the same law also decreed that non-whites must have their racial classification listed in every official document: mulatto, *tierceron, quarteroon, griffe* and so on.

This notary L'Epine hadn't specified that Jerome Pommier was non-white but the missing adjective was his way of complying with the law. As Mercier stares in horror at the space between the words *godfather* and *Jerome*, a few little memories surface: his father-in-law refusing to ratify his will, even when it was clear death was imminent; refusing also to be witness to a cousin's marriage. The old man did witness his daughter's marriage but Mercier and Nathalie married in 1755, back when a plantation and some appearance of wealth was sufficient to merit the honorific *Sieur*.

Then why had the bugger agreed to be witness in 1765?

Mercier takes a deep breath and stares at the incriminating paper. Jerome Pommier. So it is true; perhaps he had known it all along. Nathalie was born in Port Salut— the oldest town on the Southern peninsula, established in 1726—and he remembers her saying that in her childhood, she was one of only five white children in the whole district. Mercier's lip curls. She was not—there were only *four*. Nathalie's mother was born in France and Mercier remembers a small, fair-haired woman. But Jerome, her father, was born in the Port Salut area. It was doubtless one of his parents or grandparents who mixed with an African.

The earlier part of the century was a different world, a time when many white men came to the colony as indentured serfs, when pirates became buccaneers and then became planters. A time of few white women and also a time when a child born to a white man and a slave automatically became free on their majority, their mothers as well. A time when it was guessed, and even accepted, that most families in the area had African blood in them.

The colony had been so different then. Constant fires and the smell of burning wood as hillside after hillside was cleared; whole work gangs wiped out by fever; the mountains filled with wild cattle left over from the buccaneers who had made their living from the meat and leather in the previous century. No roads, only leaking boats to sail the coast and stake claims. When he first arrived, Mercier remembers being vividly shocked at the number of men of mixed blood who thrived alongside the whites.

Before settlement increased and the long arm of French bureaucracy intruded, it was a relatively simple matter for free colored men to declare themselves white. The first census of the area in the 1750s simply counted all plantation owners as white and it was easy enough to carry on with the pretense, as long as they looked the part.

So it happened, Mercier knows it did: non-whites passing for white. And his goddamn father-in-law had been one of them. He slumps back in horror. From downstairs comes the sound of a crying baby, then the smooth notes of an African lullaby. One of his grandchildren.

His children. Oh God.

Most whites—then and now—recognized half-siblings from the dark side of their father or grandfather's beds. Nathalie had a brood of colored cousins who took the surname Pomme when the law forbidding coloreds from taking European surnames came into effect. They were her grandfathers' children, if Mercier remembers correctly, so perhaps that man was the harbinger of the hidden stain.

Almost forty years since they were married. So long ago, and it never occurred to him that the lovely twenty-year-old with the laughing brown eyes and curly black hair was anything but white. Mercier searches his mind for sneers, innuendos or rumors, but comes up short. But perhaps he should have known: a pretty young heiress like that, at a time when white women were mostly the scrapings of the Paris gutter, sent overseas as punishment. And yet Nathalie chose him, a lowly surgeon with not much to commend.

The more Mercier pursues that line of reasoning, the more sense it makes. An heiress but still unmarried at twenty and he could not recall any other suitors. He had thought her genuinely in love with him, in awe of him even, but perhaps that was only female artifice.

Jerome. Mercier remembers his father-in-law, but only vaguely. Short, stooped, curled black hair, his skin pale though with an olive hue from working the land alongside the slaves as was common in the early years. Perhaps his father or grandfather had knowingly contracted a marriage with a woman from a good colored family; indeed, back in the day marrying a wealthy free colored or black was a common way for a white man to establish himself. Mercier himself had never considered such an abomination and was proud to have allied himself with a white family with such long roots in the region.

Instead he was just a fool, blinded by his sheer good fortune that this great heiress—as he thought of her then—had consented to marry him. Did Nathalie know of the indelible stain she carried? But no, that betrayal was too great to even contemplate. Greater even than if she had been unfaithful to their marriage bed.

I stress this is a copy, and I know where the original is, said the vile Plunkett. Mercier burns it anyways: what if someone else were to find it? His hands are shaking so much he almost sets his shirt on fire but soon the fateful paper is reduced to a pile of ashes—as his future will be, if this thing ever comes to light.

I've been a fool, he thinks as he lies in bed, staring into the darkness through the longest night of his life. Such a fool. Taken for one, wedded to one. He thinks of his three children and two grandchildren. The next child coming. All with the blood of Africans! Now, can he even think of them as his own? Mercier is a man who looks to his children mostly for pride and for confirmation of his social status. His paternal instinct, already weak, threatens to wither almost completely under the scorch of this terrible knowledge.

And it is not merely personal shame and revulsion: the economic and social consequences for his family are enormous. He would be kicked off the Security Council and his son stripped of his commission—it is forbidden for those of mixed blood to occupy such a post. His daughters risk being cast out by their husbands, their ancestry sufficient grounds for divorce.

And even if Mercier could prove somehow that this one birth certificate was in error, if the affair was dragged through the courts they would doubtless find, scattered all over the Grand'Anse, further evidence, overt or subtle, that the Pommier family supports the indelible stain of Ham.

Then a thought strikes Mercier: the recent legal equality of the coloreds, as decreed by Paris! Might his salvation come with those laws he had long opposed? But no, salvation does not lie there: edicts from far-off France are generally ignored, especially here in the Grand'Anse, and Mercier remembers the raucous laughter at a Council meeting last month when they reviewed the application of a free black planter to join them.

Never.

Nothing will be left for him, except public humiliation and mockery.

The next day he finds Plunkett waiting for him outside the house. Mercier drags him back upstairs to his chamber, ignoring his daughter's pleas for them to sit and take chocolate in the courtyard. He shouts that she should leave him alone; he is so filled with disgust that he can't even look at her, afraid of what he might see there.

"How did you come upon it?" Mercier demands, gesturing to the pile of ashes. When Plunkett just smirks, he knows then that it truly was just a copy.

"A friend in the notary's office," says Plunkett coyly. Notary offices hold copies of all the marriages, deaths, and baptisms, while the church keeps another set, and yet another set goes to Versailles. Paris now, of course, and doubtless inaccessible given the upheavals. And then God knows how many more are floating around; for a small additional fee, families often had copies made to keep at home. Was there a copy at Bayardel? Why hadn't that luckless girl Julienne taken it up north with her when she married?

"And as you know, it is part of the public record for *all* to see," smirks Plunkett. What a cur of a man—as if he doesn't live in open filth with that slave woman and his six half-castes.

"And how did you know to ask for it?"

"One hears rumors."

"From who?"

"You appreciate I cannot reveal my sources. But I must also assure you that no one else knows of this. The secret remains with me."

Mercier snorts.

"It remains with me," repeats Plunkett with a hint of protest in his voice, as though Mercier were impugning his professional integrity. "I have done this before; you'd be surprised how many dark secrets our white families have—it has proved a lucrative trade."

For a moment Mercier is tempted to ask who—he has his doubts about Maffranc, with his flat nose and freckles— but stops himself. Instead he barks: "What do you want?"

"A reasonable sum," says Plunkett, small hands smoothing the front of his jacket, the gleam in his eyes growing stronger. "I am not greedy. Simply money I need for an upcoming business venture. Fifty thousand *livres*."

Fifty thousand *livres*, the price of twenty-five slaves or fifty hectares of land!

"Are you mad? Who has that kind of money now?"

"Fifty thousand," repeats Plunkett.

"No!" swears Mercier, making them both jump and causing Plunkett to hold up a cautioning hand and gesture to the floor below. "No, you cur. I'll give you twenty," and even as Mercier says it, he can't believe he is bargaining with this man. Accepting this blackmail, which means accepting this curse.

Plunkett considers, rolling his head to the left and then to the right, his eyes fixed on Mercier.

"Twenty thousand," Mercier repeats. Last year was profitable and he could sell his neighbor Fondin that piece of land he has long been coveting. Delay the payments on the new wet mill.

"Fine," says Plunkett and offers Mercier a wide smile. "And my assurances, Monsieur: this demand for payment, as long as it is agreed upon and the money delivered, will be my last. I wish I could give you some proof of this, from past clients, but discretion prohibits it."

Mercier wants to jump across the table and smash the man's head against the floor, spread his oily guts over the tiles. Instead he nods grimly.

"I shall be at Bayardel next month, the last week of October," continues Plunkett smoothly. "Your neighbors the Fongravier are the repository, as you might have guessed, of the copy—perhaps we can meet there? And I suggest a secret meeting; the fewer people that connect you to me, the better for both of us."

Mercier grunts even as he is already resolving to wreak revenge on Plunkett—a month will give him the time he needs. He returns to his plantation. Back home he finds he can no longer look directly at his wife Nathalie, only study her when she is absorbed elsewhere. Though now pure gray, she once had curly black hair and is there a certain... wideness... to her features? Or is he imagining things? Mercier considers confronting her but guesses she doesn't know, and it is a conversation he cannot bear to even think about.

He finds himself developing an irrational hatred for her. Or at least for her father: Why on earth had Jerome consented to be the godfather at the baptism of that lost woman? And stupid enough to attend the ceremony and sign the document?

Mercier has done the fevered calculations. Even if Nathalie's father had but one African grandparent, or even great-grandparent, it didn't matter: still the stain survives and can never be erased. Mercier drops a grain of ground coffee into a glass of water. For a few seconds the brown kernels bloom but then the whole is lost in the abundance of water. He downs the glass and cannot taste the coffee but it doesn't matter: it is there.

"Your father," Mercier asks one night, into the flickering candlelight between them. "Did you know his family well? His parents?"

"No, most of my father's family died when I was young."

"Pierre is so proud that his mother's family is one of the oldest in the district," says his daughter-in-law Monique, shifting in her chair. Mercier looks at her enormous belly in fearful disgust, feeling it about to spew forth a great quantity of babies with tell-tale African features. Everyone knows it could happen thus, even generations after the fact. But wait—Monique had two still births and for one crazed moment Mercier has the idea to dig up the graves and examine the infants to see if the danger is real.

"It is true, Monique," says Nathalie proudly. "My

father was born in Port Salut, long before it became a town. When I was growing up, I was one of only five white children in all the district."

Mercier throws his glass of rum on the floor, dashing it on the tiles and eliciting a terrified squeak from Yoyo, sitting beside his wife.

"Good lord, husband," cries Nathalie. "What on earth is wrong with you? I saw you throw that glass as though *on purpose.*"

*

Now the night has come. Mercier finishes his brandy and around midnight George silently saddles his horse; he never inquires as to his master's midnight runs and luckily there is a certain young woman over on Mercier's other plantation that has been occupying him for many recent nights. The perfect cover. Mercier takes a back path that avoids the main coast road and when he reaches the edge of the Bayardel plantation, two dogs come bounding up. They recognize his smell and Mercier feeds them some crab meat, in his pockets for just that purpose.

Mercier tethers his white horse to the remains of an old fence and leaves his lantern and jacket behind. The moon—just a night away from perfect fullness—lights his path and he makes his way to the place where they agreed to meet. Plunkett is at the bottom of the garden, staring up at the big house. Mercier comes up quietly from the side.

"Ah," says Plunkett, seeing him and taking a step back. "I was beginning to think you weren't coming."

"I'm here," hisses Mercier.

"So, you have what we discussed?"

"I do. And you?"

"No," says Plunkett, holding up empty hands. "I thought it best to receive payment first and count the money. You come by tomorrow and I will give you the document."

"That was not our agreement. You were to bring the certificate and burn it in front of me."

"It is for my protection," says Plunkett with a smirk.

"You have a reputation as a dangerous man."

Mercier wills himself to stay still. Nothing has changed.

"So..." says Plunkett, smiling at him through the moonlight. "You have the money?"

"I have it here," Mercier replies. He reaches into his pocket and draws out a brick. Before Plunkett can see what it is, Mercier steps forward and lands it with a thud on the side of the man's head. Plunkett falls to the ground with a surprised grunt, not dead but the blow enough to stop his senses. Mercier puts the brick back in his pocket and from the other pulls out his knife. He looks around but nothing stirs.

He kneels down beside his prey. Plunkett's eyes open in surprise. "The tide?" he murmurs in a weak voice, his arms twitching as Mercier draws his knife across his throat. Trained as a surgeon, Mercier has cut through flesh many times and though it has been years, his cut is smooth and deep. Plunkett's eyes bulge and he tries to gurgle something but the wound is too deep. Mercier jumps back as the man's life blood spurts out onto the earth around him.

When it has lessened to a trickle, Mercier rolls back the sleeves of his chemise and kneels down again, this time with the white stone he took from his wife's curio cabinet. A nice addition to the plan and one that would point a finger most squarely at the slaves and their *Vaudun*.

He places the stone carefully inside the man's neck, leaving it visible, then turns the body over. He sprinkles the back with white powder—just flour—that some Africans like to smear themselves with when they dance to their pagan gods. Mercier stands up and looks down in satisfaction at his handiwork, then feels the first drops. Ah, he had not considered the night rains. They will wash the flour away, so the stone is ever more a clever idea.

He checks Plunkett's pockets but finds nothing. If a copy of the certificate is with the Fongravier family papers and no one else knows about this matter, then it is as good as buried; God knows Madame Rose has other things on her mind these days. Mercier finds his horse where he left it and starts back on the moonlight ride.

At home the lights on the veranda are still lit and for a moment he considers sending George to get him a slave—there is a certain warm Ibo woman, older than he normally likes, but she never seems to resent his visits and often caresses him and murmurs sweet things; he is beginning to think she cares for him.

But no; the killing has not excited him. Instead it has made him sad in a way he cannot pinpoint or clearly understand. The soft grunt as Plunkett fell to the ground and his eyes, flickering wide when he slit his throat. The strong smell of rum on his breath, even after dying. And above all the fact that Plunkett's death, while momentarily pleasing and ensuring this affair does not become public, does not solve the central tragedy: his wife has African blood, as do his children. Plunkett had given lie to Mercier's whole life and now he feels an awful hollowness, one that may never be filled.

Back in the house Mercier doesn't join his wife in their chamber but instead takes a seat again in the salon where the grandfather clock tells him not two hours have passed. Outside it begins to rain, heavily. With true abandon, Mercier downs the rest of the special brandy. My hands aren't even shaking, he thinks in disbelief. I just killed a man, a *white* man, yet I feel nothing. Is it because Plunkett so definitely deserved to die that he feels not a single qualm?

Mercier slumps back in his chair. It doesn't matter how he feels, he decides; this had to be done. The future of his family is far more important than that thug's life. Eventually he gets up and staggers to his room. He'll ride back to Bayardel in the morning and make sure Madame Rose is convinced it was a slave, then let events unfold from there.

The Salon
7 pm

After Azor reveals to Thoreau and Aimée the significance of the birth certificate, the two men decide that the best course of action is to wait for Captain Bassompierre, hopefully on his way back from Les Irois. They will stay as long as necessary; they will not leave Madame Rose alone with Mercier, nor will they tell her what they know—both men feel Madame Rose has fragile nerves and must be protected from the truth.

"Yes, Mama is very delicate," agrees Aimée. She herself feels very grown up and important to be the keeper of such a secret, one that even her mother does not know. And not even Charles!

"The imperative," instructs Azor as they huddle on the veranda, "is to maintain a semblance of normalcy. He tried to make us believe that the culprit was the slave and he must not know that we suspect—or know—otherwise."

"A dangerous man," adds Thoreau.

"And we must," Azor continues, "keep him here at Bayardel. Once he is back on his plantation, he could deny everything or pay off the authorities. But here, in front of all these witnesses, he is trapped."

Aimée hurries off to the kitchens to find Pomponne while the two men go back into the salon. They find Mercier and Rose sitting quietly, watching Henri tease a cat that appeared hopefully as mealtime approaches.

Azor seats himself beside Rose, and Thoreau bursts into a nervous babble about a fellow member of the *Académie*, killed by his manservant. Occasionally he nods and even once winks at Azor. Good God, groans Azor, tasking that man with keeping a secret is as futile as trying to pin a wave on the sand. He glances at the clock, ticking away on the sideboard. It points just past seven. *Come on*, he exhorts silently, *come on, Bassompierre.*

How extraordinary that Mercier, seated opposite him and listening in bemusement as Thoreau waffles on about the facial shape of the accused manservant, is a murderer. And what strokes of luck that Thoreau saw Plunkett steal the paper, and that the girl recognized the amulet. Two pieces of evidence that firmly trap Mercier in a well of guilt no matter how he might try to explain them away. How strange that Mercier's fate should turn on such small grains of action and consequence; they might never have come to light and Mercier would have succeeded with his plan and deception.

How curious life is.

Azor settles back and reflects on the significance of what Aimée and Thoreau uncovered. He knew the notary L'Epine—father of the current notary—who prepared the baptism certificate back in 1765. Especially in the early days, there was a great deal of leeway on the part of notaries in their approach to dealing with the legal changes. A huge difference between a local, sympathetic notary versus a stickler for the letter of the law freshly arrived from France. If a bribe or just good standing and friendly relations allowed it, missing manumission papers could be overlooked, or an honorific inserted where none was allowed. Azor wonders why Jerome Pommier agreed to stand witness at the baptism and what had transpired—or hadn't, in the case of a bribe—between him and L'Epine that had resulted in the *Sieur* being dropped and the evidence of his ancestry locked in for all eternity.

Notaries are privy to all sorts of details about the families whose records they create and hold. Perhaps this L'Epine had challenged Pommier's status—that of a white man—and demanded a bribe before he would add the honorific on the public document. Pommier might have stood his ground and blustered, confident that the man would not follow through on his threat, or perhaps confident in the history of his family and their decades of "whiteness." Hard to say, really, what had resulted in the sad affair of the baptism certificate.

Regardless, somehow Plunkett found out and sought to blackmail Mercier. And for that he was killed, his neck slit as though he were a goat. Azor is not surprised. He has been around men like Mercier all his life, and indeed he is one himself: men who live like potentates on their plantations, dangerously infected with omnipotence, their word as law. 'God is too high and Paris is too far,' joke the planters, smug in their fiefdoms; an attitude that breeds the arrogance that makes it easy to kill anything, or anyone, that might inconvenience them.

"And the manservant's guilt was proclaimed in the shape of his forehead, low and thick," finishes Thoreau. "Almost like yours, Monsieur!"

"Why would you say such a thing?" replies Mercier coldly and with disinterest.

Azor pats the letter in his pocket, the heavy wad of money on the other side. So... their Jamaica tentative scuppered by this bizarre confluence of events. Azor should have paid heed to the rumors that swirled around Plunkett and chosen a better emissary for the job. Hindsight, the bane of history, he thinks with a sigh. One of the other planters involved in the Jamaica plot—Kanon, who grows coffee up near Apricots—once suggested he go himself. Kanon was confident he could make the journey undetected and he has a slave, purchased from Jamaica years ago, that still speaks English and would serve as translator.

Azor sighs; perhaps that is the alternative. Tomorrow he'll take the boat waiting in the bay, that one that was there for Plunkett, and sail north to Apricots. Visit Kanon in person, inform him of the change of plans and see what can be salvaged. Azor glances at Henri; his troublesome son can return to La Fraternité alone.

The clock chimes seven. Mercier shuffles his feet impatiently. "I think it's clear the constable is not coming," he announces, cutting Thoreau off in the middle of a sentence about ear shape and executions.

The clock revives Rose and she sits up, remembers her duties as hostess. "I am sorry, Messieurs, that I did not make this clear before. Supper is being prepared and I trust you will all stay?

My cook is preparing a delicious chicken pie alongside other dishes."

"Certainly Madame, I think the events of the day warrant a meal taken together," replies Azor. "We shall not leave before knowing our hostess is in good hands, and certainly not before we have partaken of your hospitality so generously offered."

"Thank you, Noel," says Rose warmly, using his Christian name. A slip she does not recognize but one that leaves everyone else in the room temporarily speechless.

Henri talks into the stunned silence, nonchalantly but there is an undercurrent of urgency: "I think we should get back, Father; it would be best if we left."

Azor shakes his head. "Malachi has not yet returned. And we will wait until Bassompierre comes."

"And Monsieur Mercier—you will stay as well?" asks Rose. Safety in numbers, she intuitively understands, aware of the deepening night outside.

"Well, ordinarily I would not share a table with such a man," says Mercier, pointing to Azor. "But this has been an extraordinary day and..." He trails off, indecision riddling his features.

Thoreau jumps in. "How wonderful, Monsieur Mercier, that you would stay! We must bury the hatchet. Loom the seam, so to speak, solidarity amongst all men! Perhaps raise a glass in memory of poor Mr. Plunkett?"

Everyone turns to Azor and eventually he speaks. "Monsieur Mercier, I know we have had our differences in the past," he says, "but I daresay we can put those aside in the interests of our hostess?"

Henri snorts.

"Oh, what fine sentiments!" exclaims Thoreau. "Never have I agreed more fully!"

"Very well," says Mercier. "I'll stay. As the senior male around here, it is my duty to ensure that you, Madame Rose, are well taken care of."

Rose beams, delighted to see the petty squabbles of the day seemingly set aside. "Excellent, Messieurs, I am so glad." Champagne, she thinks, I'll get out the champagne and perhaps even the last barrel of Bordeaux. But where is Pomponne?

*

With every movement from outside, Jeannette's heart trips but it is never Pomponne. In the clearing the slaves are still cooking and eating, the peaty smell of their fires filling the almost-dark air, the smell of *igname* overtaking the savory sauce of her pie. She spoons the sauce, bubbling for hours, into the crust; later, she will lattice the top and get it into the oven—the secret is not to overcook it, all the crust needs to do is crispen around its treasure. Flore finishes shelling a pile of peas and Jeannette turns her attention to the side dishes: carp stew, an omelet, a mound of steaming vegetables.

People keep coming into the kitchen, looking for a pinch of salt or a handful of peas, a touch of lard, but she turns them all away with impatience: "Too many up at the big house tonight! Stop pestering me—there's work to be done."

But it's not the number of guests that is making her anxious.

Something rustles at her feet in the growing darkness inside the kitchen—not a kitten. She lights another lantern and the flames give a ghostly half-glow to the hot room.

"The rain," says Flore, flexing her fingers and feeding herself a raw pea. "There will be more rain tonight. You tell Brac he needs to get the tarpaulins out."

"No," says Jeannette shortly. The drying coffee be damned, she'll not take on Madame Rose's worries. She has her own worries—something is wrong, she can feel it, long lines of tension snapping at her nerves, the shadowy outline of a huge mistake hovering at the edges. Where is her daughter? The kestrel that screeched so awful and loud when Henri's shadow fell over the doorstep—why did she not listen? Her heart quickens with dread and her hope is not strong enough to overcome her misgivings.

"That poor girl this afternoon," says Flore, turning her milky eyes to Jeannette. "I heard her death cry. The moment her soul left her body, so faint I doubt even the men whipping her heard it. But I heard it, soft like a *shoushh…*"

"Her suffering is over," Jeannette says, mixing cheese and cream for the omelet.

"Mama wants to know where Pomponne is," says Aimée,

entering the kitchen. "The table needs to be set! There are so many people in the house tonight."

Jeannette whirls around. "I don't know where she is! Have you seen her?"

"No! I've been looking for her all afternoon."

"She—" But what is the point of lies now? "She was in our house," confesses Jeannette, speaking in a low, urgent voice. "I told her to hide there." She improvises: "From Mercier. Then I sent her out to the flower garden but that was just before the sun began to set and now it's almost dark. She should be back by now! Is she not at the big house?"

"Why did you send her to the gardens?" asks Aimée curiously. She sticks her finger in the sauce and licks. "Mmm, delicious."

Jeannette shakes her head. "Is she still there now? In the flower garden?"

"I don't know."

"Can you go and look for her? I'll finish this dish then I'll go and set the table. How many are staying?"

"I think all," replies Aimée. "Eight of us."

"Please?"

"All right," says Aimée reluctantly. She leaves the kitchen and starts up the path back to the house. Her mind whirls with everything that Monsieur Azor told them: about the baptism certificate, about Mercier's wife and father... She didn't understand all of it but she knows Thoreau and Azor are convinced of Mercier's guilt. Monsieur Mercier, a murderer! Killing their tutor! It makes no sense.

A movement in the bushes and Aimée starts; she dislikes this part of the evening the most. A lonely time of change, poised between night and day when life moves only in shadows. But she mustn't fear because the murderer is no longer on the loose but back in the house with the men and her mother.

"Pomponne? Charles?" she calls out softly but the silhouette of a woman, black against the indigo evening sky, emerges. Mathilde, Thoreau's dried-up old sister, creeping out of the bushes.

"Oh! Where have you been?" Aimée asks in astonishment before she can stop herself.

The woman laughs. "Don't be curious, it's not polite." She moves closer. "I have seen it." She smiles at Aimée, reaches out and takes her by the shoulder. Aimée shudders under the dry touch. "I have seen the blackness."

"I, I'm sorry," Aimée stutters, backing away. There is something gleeful and mean about the old woman and she knows she has to get away, now.

"I have seen it and it is true, the blackness is everywhere." The woman is rubbing her stomach and Aimée sees her cap is askew—gray hairs sticking out in abandon—and dried leaves on her sleeves. The woman, usually so prim and proper, does not seem to care. "The blackness is *inside* me."

"I need to find someone," squeaks Aimée and bolts up the path towards the house. She skirts to the left and checks for Pomponne in the giant mango carriage sitting on the gravel but her friend is not there. The front of the house faces west and the last brilliance of the sunset still illuminates the flower garden.

Aimée pauses, uncertain.

"Pomponne?" she whispers. Through paths of hibiscus and bougainvillea she walks cautiously, skirting the statue of Venus that watches over her. "Pomponne?" The bench where she might have sat but there is no sign of her. Aimée nears the bottom of the garden, down where Mercier murdered Plunkett. And I am out here all alone and it is almost dark.

How silly for Pomponne to go missing at a time like this! Thoreau, a *sleuth-hound* as he called himself, seeking out the clues to solve the crime and together he and Aimée solved it! But Pomponne also loves mysteries and they might have solved it sooner, for surely Pomponne would have seen the significance of the birth certificate right away.

Aimée hesitates at the path that goes through the woods, now dark and faintly menacing. Resolutely she inches her way in, leaving the last rays of sunlight behind. She comes to the place where she found her statue.

Thank God, no statue.

But she won't go the graves, she decides. She remembers how Plunkett looked in his hole, half-turned on his side before they started shoveling earth over him. Some slaves believe in *zombis*, dead men who have displeased the gods and will be kept in Saint

Domingue to toil on plantations for eternity. Most slaves believe that death releases them back to Africa but *zombis* never return. Aimée has a sudden image of Plunkett, sure of having displeased some god, clawing his way out of the damp black earth and coming for her.

She turns and runs out of the woods, back to the safety of the flower garden. She looks behind but nothing follows.

*

Jeannette finishes the omelet, puts on a clean apron and fixes her head wrap. She hurries away, ignoring Laurine who has come to complain about Ernestine and her salty airs. At the back steps of the big house, Jeannette pauses and breathes in the smell of lemon wax, used on the wooden floors of the veranda. A smell that brings her back to childhood.

Cautiously Jeannette ascends the steps and hears the faint voices of the whites—well, of the fat Frenchman at least. She enters the back of the salon and sees a full house: Madame, Mercier, Thoreau, and an older colored man dressed in an orange and blue striped jacket and looking very much at ease. And the boy Henri sitting in a chair with his legs splayed out, drinking. Something inside her tightens.

No one notices Jeannette; they pay her no more heed than were she a fly. She slips into the dining room and from the sideboard takes the linen cloth and unfurls it over the table. She takes the plates from the cabinet, her fingers trembling and her heart beating in worried time. She peeks out again; Henri is still slouched in his chair, smirking.

Eight soup bowls, eight dinner plates—there are eleven sets left of the original sixteen and if she wants to, Jeannette can remember the occasion of each breakage. She runs her hand over lambs in a pasture, a pretty shepherdess painted on the china. Alongside each plate she lays the silver cutlery and the napkins. Bottles of wine, filled earlier from the barrels in the cellar.

Jeannette can hear the Frenchman talking, but she can't understand his words. Everything is wrong in the house, everything too bright and the voices too discordant. Nothing happening as it should: ripe leaves falling from trees, water running uphill. Sound boats sinking in the sea. And that boy out there with that red cravat, his pale ugly face holding all the horrors of the world.

Aimée slips into the dining room. "Pomponne's not in the garden," she whispers, worried. "I don't—"

"We need to tell your mother she is missing."

Aimée hesitates. "Let me check the rooms, first. Perhaps she fell asleep somewhere?"

Jeannette chokes down a sob and nods, twisting her apron in her hands.

The Bedroom
7 pm

Aimée goes first to Charles' room; Pomponne wouldn't be there but she's also concerned about her brother—where is he? Why is everyone missing? She peeks into her mother's room then the room that Thoreau and his sister are sharing. A black shawl is laid out on Mathilde's bed and Aimée thinks of their strange encounter and shivers.

"There's blood everywhere, we've got to get it out," hisses Julienne when Aimée enters her room.

"Oh Julie, not now!" says Aimée. "Pomponne is missing."

"She's here," says Julienne, pulling back a bedsheet to reveal a curled-up Pomponne.

"There you are!" exclaims Aimée, exasperated but mostly relieved. "Mama is looking for you! And your mother is worried."

"There's blood, stains, how can we get it out?" wails Julienne. Pomponne is wound tightly into a ball, her eyes closed. In the half-light of the chamber, Aimée sees Pomponne's pink dress, the skirt bunched up and stained with mud or blood.

"Pomponne, what's wrong?" says Aimée, unable to take her eyes off the skirt. "What happened? Who? Mercier?"

Pomponne doesn't stir, just moans slightly.

"The blood!" hisses Julienne.

"Oh, Pomponne." Aimée climbs onto the bed beside Pomponne and wraps her arms around her. Her friend is hurt but Aimée doesn't know what to say or do to make it better.

"My mother is going to be so angry," whispers Pomponne.

"What happened?"

Pomponne rolls over and stares up at Aimée.

"She'll never get the blood out!"

"Oh, shut up, Julie," shouts Aimée, as she has wanted to shout every single day since her aunt came home.

Julienne opens her eyes wide, momentarily stunned, then howls back at her, "The stain will never come out! Where is my baby?"

"Your baby's dead!" shouts Aimée. "Pomponne, tell me what happened!"

"That man—from the Azor plantation." Pomponne shuts her eyes again.

"Monsieur Azor?"

"His son," sobs Pomponne. She curls up again and scrunches herself into the smallest ball, one that can never be unfolded and one that will keep all her shame and pain safely hidden inside.

"What did he do?" Aimée says, still looking at her friend's skirt, bunched high, barely covering that dirty place where animals rut at, that men seek to pry in and tear apart.

"He touched me," wails Pomponne, finally reaching out for comfort. She pulls Aimée down beside her, blood and mud now on the front of Aimée's white dress. "He hit me and got on top of me and Mama is going to be so angry."

"That colored boy? How dare he!" Aimée struggles free of her friend. "We'll tell Mama and she'll punish him!"

"No, please, don't tell her," begs Pomponne, the weight of her shame smothering her. "No one must know."

"I'll get Brac to whip him!" decides Aimée. "I must tell Mama."

"No," sobs Pomponne. "Please."

"I don't know," says Aimée, standing up now and unsure. "I'll get you... some water."

Aimée leaves the room, her feet unsteady. Henri hurt Pomponne in that way. *Ravished* her. What men do to the slaves in the pigpen but Pomponne doesn't belong in the pigpen. And he hurt her—all that blood. The blankness in her eyes. Aimée stands still on the veranda, the last echoes of light illuminating the flower garden, the world unsteady around her and the floors seeming to slope away.

Soon everything will be in darkness, only the flickering candles to fight the night.

Aimée tries to pass through into the dining room without her mother noticing but Rose sees and is instantly on her feet. Aimée stops, caught; she wants to sink through the floor into the cellar below with spiders and the nasty things that crawl in crevices. She follows her mother's horrified eyes and realizes she has blood—Pomponne's blood? Henri's blood?—on her hands and some on her skirt. Oh.

Rose hustles her daughter away from the eyes of the men. Aimée lets herself be propelled back onto the veranda and down the steps, Jeannette following behind.

"Aimée, what's wrong? What happened to your skirt?"

"I…" says Aimée, staring down at the blood.

"What is going on?" asks Rose, grabbing her daughter by the shoulders. "Are you hurt?"

Aimée tears her eyes away from the stain and gazes up at her mother.

"Aimée!" says her mother, squeezing her shoulders, urgency in her grasp. "You're scaring me! Are you all right?"

"Is it Pomponne?" asks Jeannette, coming up beside them.

"Yes, Pomponne," chokes Aimée.

Jeannette pulls Aimée her away from her mother. "What did he do?"

Rose takes her daughter back. "What do you mean? What happened to Pomponne?"

"That colored man… he…"

"Where is she?" cries Jeannette.

"In my room."

Jeannette flies up the steps and Rose turns back to her daughter, her relief bright and apparent. "Darling, you are fine. You are not hurt?"

"No, Mama, but Pomponne… she is bleeding. That man…"

"Oh, that foolish girl," says Rose sadly, wetting her thumb and rubbing a spot off her daughter's cheek. "But thank goodness you're all right. Just in shock. You'll need to change."

"What?"

"You need to change your dress before dinner."

"No—what did you call Pomponne?"

"Never mind her," says her mother. "Besides, why was she with that man and not at her chores? Supper for eight and the table to be set!"

"But she didn't do anything, he was the… he hit her."

"Oh, Aimée," says her mother, sounding tired. "I am sorry for what happened to Pomponne and I will express my displeasure to the young man, but right now this is not our concern. You go change and I shall get back to our guests."

"But it is our concern! Pomponne is *mine*." Aimée searches her mother's face for a sign that she is joking or hasn't quite understood, but all she sees is the familiar crossness and her mother closing off again. Nothing makes sense, least of all her mother's reaction—relief, but no care at all for Pomponne.

"Yes, darling but she will be fine. These little mulatto girls…"

"What?" cries Aimée, unable to believe that her mother is being so callous. And wrong! "Pomponne is not like that!" Aimée knows the stories about beautiful colored women, sirens who entice white men from their wives and cause so many ills. But not *Pomponne*.

Rose gives her daughter an awkward hug, kisses her on the forehead. "Don't fret. I'm sorry about Pomponne but we have more important matters to deal with—the constable coming and that man, murdered. And we have guests! Monsieur Azor has been very kind today and is sending us slaves to help with the harvest."

"We don't need his stupid slaves! I want Brac to whip his son!"

Rose laughs dryly, and shakes her head. "No. Tell Pomponne she may stay in bed for the evening and if the doctor is required, we will send for him tomorrow."

"You are horrible!"

Her mother slaps her with surprising force. "Pull yourself together—if you wish to join us in the dining room, get out of that filthy skirt; otherwise stay with Pomponne and your aunt. Do as you wish but I am going back to our guests."

Aimée reels back, grasping her cheek, her world turned

firmly upside down. Her mother starts up the steps but finds her way blocked by Jeannette.

The Gardens
7 pm

Jeannette stands on the stone steps, rigid. She heard everything and knows all she needs to know. Madame Rose looks up at her, annoyed, and a terrible anger courses through Jeannette as she looks down on her mistress. On *benevolent* Madame Rose.

Rose pauses, frowns, then makes the slightest of movements to the right. So does Jeannette.

"I am very sorry," says Rose, her voice stiff and displeased. "Aimée told me what happened. We will take care of Pomponne tomorrow."

"I heard everything," Jeannette says quietly. "You called her a foolish girl."

"I also said we will take care of her," snaps Rose. "Get out of my way."

"Take care of her now," says Jeannette.

"You do not tell me what to do! I will deal with this in the morning."

"No," says Jeannette softly. She comes down the steps and closes the distance between them, glaring at the woman she has lived her life around. The woman who is now treating her daughter as a cast-off.

"What would you have me do?" says Rose, throwing up her hands. "Whip that boy, as my daughter is so foolishly suggesting, or kick his father out when his generosity has been without reproach?"

"Yes."

"Nonsense!" says Rose. "Besides, we do not know what really happened and we cannot rely on the words of a young girl."

Jeannette steps closer to Rose; she wants to push the white woman down on her knees and force her take back her words. "I know what happened." Jeannette raises her voice, to imprint her words in the air and make them true. "That boy took Pomponne in a foul way. She is in the room, bleeding. Punish him!"

"Be quiet," says Rose, backing away from the anger she can feel pulsing off her cook. "And I will not take the word of a slave girl against a man such as Master Azor."

"Pomponne wouldn't lie," cries Aimée.

"This is ridiculous," Rose snaps. "We are ready to eat—go to the kitchens and bring the food."

I could kill her, thinks Jeannette in mute fury, staring at the pinched features of her mistress. I know every line, every wrinkle, and I hate every one. And how ugly she is—her skin so dull, the pale eyes with nothing behind them. When she was young she was so pretty, but now... so ugly.

"I want that boy punished," Jeannette repeats.

"I apologize if I have caused any concern," laughs Henri from the veranda where the men have emerged, drawn by the scene below. Jeannette whirls around and sees them gathered up there: Henri, smirking; his father beside him, a warning hand on his son's arm; the rooster Thoreau, and the man Mercier.

"The girl was quite hungry for it, you know they often are," Henri adds and Mercier chuckles in agreement.

"You lie!" cries Jeannette to the wall of unbearable male smugness. "You took her by force!"

"It's true!" sobs Aimée. "She's hurt, badly."

"He raped my daughter," says Jeannette, looking between Rose and the men, searching for a safe landing place but finding none.

"Madame Rose, I cannot countenance the way this woman is talking to my son," protests Azor, his hand still on his son's arm. "Why do you let a slave talk to you thus?"

Something inside Jeannette falters and she feels the world shift, as though a great earthquake is coming. This can't be happening. She stumbles then pulls herself back up again.

"Please, Madame, help us." Her daughter, wounded. The bloody dress and the vacant eyes. The terrible cry of that bird warning her. She should have listened but she didn't. "Please, Madame, I beg of you, for all the fondness you bear Pomponne. Do not let that man get away. Come with me and see her."

Jeannette grabs Rose by the arm, the first time they have touched over the long years since they laughed together in the kitchens. When Rose recoils and tries to shake herself free, Jeannette knows she has made a mistake but she cannot stop. Not now, not ever and not for her daughter, broken by that man.

"Get off of me! How dare you! I'll send you to the fields!"

"Or the penal gangs," suggests Henri from above.

"Please, Madame Rose, please," Jeannette is now wildly grasping at her mistress, going further down the road into the rising darkness and the place of no return. "What if it was Aimée? Your own daughter?"

Mercier strides down the steps and pulls Jeannette away. He strikes her across the face, the heavy blow sending her spinning down to the ground. Rose steps back with shock on her face, rubbing her arm. Aimée rushes in rage at Mercier, who turns around and swats her off with a vicious slap. She too falls back, her face scarlet.

"I hate you! Why won't you help her?" screams Aimée, then stumbles off into the darkness.

Rose takes a deep breath and stares at Jeannette, motionless on the ground. What a mess. The hate on Jeannette's face. Sadness seeps through her, but why? *Almost as if,* comes a voice from long ago, *almost as if she were affected with maternal instinct, that noble devotion I may credit my wife with but would scarcely expect in a savage.* Rose shakes her head, aware of the men up on the veranda, waiting and watching.

"Jeannette," says Rose. "Jeannette! I know you are upset." Her voice is wobbly and thin but she wills herself to sound stern—this slave just attacked her. "We will take care of Pomponne. But tonight... Go and get the supper, please. Laurine or another may help you."

"Ah, Madame Rose, this evidence of your laxness is not to be borne!" cries Mercier. "Allowing a slave to attack you like that, then pleading with her!" He kicks Jeannette, crumpled on the ground. "The whipping post can be used again. Or throw her in the cellar and keep her for the constable."

"No. Thank you," Rose says shakily, still rubbing her arm where Jeannette grabbed her. She looks for her daughter but Aimée has run off into the night. What to do next? From the veranda Azor moves forward. Ignoring Mercier, she walks shakily up the steps and at the top Azor takes her arm and leads her back into the salon.

Over the water the setting sun is suddenly gone, leaving behind only faint streaks of purple and pink in the ever-deepening pitch. In the garden at the bottom of the stairs, the last of the sun slips away and casts the garden and the whole of the coast into gray darkness.

Jeannette sits up.

The Beach
8 pm

Slowly Jeannette lifts herself away from the embrace of the soft earth. She rises with difficulty but when she stands her legs do not shake; she is held aloft by anger. She touches her lip where Mercier punched and is surprised to find blood. He will regret that, she thinks, but only slightly more than Henri will regret what he did to her daughter. Jeannette picks the leaves from her sleeves and smooths her skirt, winds her scarf back on her head.

She ignores Madame Rose's injunction to go to the kitchen and finish preparing the meal. No—things cannot go back to how they were. Instead she creeps up the steps and skirts the veranda to the bedroom where her daughter lies.

"She's asleep," says Julienne, stroking her head. "Poor girl."

Jeannette peels the sheet back to reveal her daughter, still curled up like a snail.

"You'll never get the blood out."

"I know that," says Jeannette, covering Pomponne again. She stares curiously at the white woman who lies with her arms around her daughter. She has heard many stories of this woman—and of her mad, repetitive incantations—but rarely saw her and certainly not this close. She's younger than expected, her skin smooth and flushed as though she has a fever, her eyes open wide to let the horrors in.

"Blood never comes out."

"I know."

"They took my baby," continues Julienne fearfully. "Nurse tried to stop them but they smashed him on the floor. Are you a nurse?"

"Of course," says Jeannette, her hand on Pomponne's brow. Pomponne doesn't stir and appears to be sleeping. There is blood but the worst wounds may not be physical. Jeannette bites back the horrible guilt that rises inside her. She sent Pomponne to Henri, but how was she to know he was a beast in white with a scarlet cravat?

"I couldn't save him and now we can't get the blood out. Will you try? Can you get it out?"

"I cannot," replies Jeannette kindly, now stroking the mad woman's face. "No one can get the blood out." She leans closer and whispers: "But you won't suffer long. You are all going to die tonight."

*

Appollon sits beside one of the half-walls flanking the entrance gates to the Bayardel plantation. In front of him is the swamp and then further out, separated by the white ribbon of the beach, lies the curve of the bay. From the swamp comes the croaking of toads and the gentle calls of birds roosting for the night. Peaceful. Appollon lies back and tries to still the restless nerves that have carried him through the day.

"How's your leg?" he asks the old watchman, lying on the ground beside his dog.

"Fire as always," Joseph replies; his leg was so eaten by yaws it had to be cut off some twenty years ago. "The only peace is when I sleep." Joseph closes his eyes. "You look out for that carriage."

"I will."

The dog barks suddenly and splashes off into the swamp. Appollon doesn't like the swamp, with its mosquitoes and marshy depths, the twisted roots of the half-dead mangrove trees. Capidon caught a giant turtle there a few days ago and promised a feast of turtle meat. Before Friday, I hope, thinks Appollon, and chuckles at his own joke.

Appollon gets up; he is as restless as Joseph's dog. So much happened today yet they are further behind. Mixed messages, changed plans, sticks broken one by one before they can be united. He leaves the lantern with Joseph and walks down the road, the white limestone lighting his way. He stares at the far rise of the hill that separates this bay from the next, dark in the distance against the indigo sky. No lantern light from a carriage; all is silent and black. Appollon smells a faint fire but no blaze comes from Belleville's promontory that was to announce the start of everything.

Appollon leans his head back and stares up at the great black yonder, dense and heavy and so far away. He remembers how he looked to the night sky when he first arrived, and how the stars comforted him; wherever they are, there I am. He killed a man today. Well, half-killed, for he only finished what Milord began. But all the same he helped send La Fleur off from this life, launched him into eternity and the great unknown.

Out in the bay are two boats, one of them dark, the other lit and with faint voices. Appollon squints but the night reveals nothing more. Once Appollon used to be like that man who asked Milord where the boat would be, the boat that would take him home after they had thrown all the whites into the sea. Gradually those dreams receded. Not because of Milord and the revolution that was coming; no, Appollon lost those dreams years before.

Even as he toiled in captivity, he grew to love this land, so different from the extremes of fortune regularly visited upon the delta of Whydah: the flooding rains, the parched months, the famines and general hardness of life. By contrast, this island feels blessed by the gods, fruits hanging from trees, tubers and vegetables sprouting with little help from human hand. The seas full of fish, the rivers awash with life. Appollon will never go back to Whydah to that squalid life of dealing in men; he will never throw his lot in with the white man again.

Saint Domingue is where he will stay.

Appollon settles himself against a thicket of wild sugarcane at the edge of the road and allows himself to daydream. He imagines the coast around here purged of plantations, theirs for the taking. He would raise livestock; catch feral pigs and tend them to multiply, find a goat and do the same. Jeannette could dry the meat, make sausages, grow vegetables and all those herbs and spices she so delights in. Or he might pull his living from the sea, carve a canoe and make a net of palm fibers.

Life would be hard but anything is better than what it is now. Even if they eat only cassava every day and have not even a coin to rub together, at least they will do it themselves and not under the whip and wiles of the hated whites.

Appollon looks up the hill to where the big house sits, lights faintly visible through the trees. He imagines a room there for him and Jeannette, with Pomponne and then their own children. He would tell them about Whydah and their ancestors but they won't care so much; they will be like Jeannette, born here, this island their one and true home. Who would ever have thought, even a year ago, that such a life might be possible, that dreams of freedom would creep so close they could almost be touched?

Joseph's dog barks and splashes out of the swamp. Appollon sees a light bobbing and hears horses descending the road from the north. Coming from the billiards hall at Dame Marie, no doubt, and one of the men calls out a cheery, drunken greeting to Joseph. Appollon sinks into the shadows and watches them pass, unobserved. Good, go back to your plantations and be there on Friday. The two men disappear into the night, their solitary lantern floating in the darkness, chatting eagerly about their evening and their wins. Sport and game, still going on while the world is about to explode.

Appollon walks back to the plantation gates and sits awhile with Joseph. He pats the mangy dog, proudly holding a half dead crab in its jaws. Then the sound of someone coming down the hill, stumbling over the gravel.

"Who is it?" grumbles Joseph. "A regular come-and-go tonight!"

"Who's there?" Appollon calls out and holds up the lantern as a figure in white emerges. "Jeannette?" She runs towards him and throws herself into his arms. "What is it?"

She doesn't answer and he holds her, waiting for her to calm and speak.

"What is it?" Appollon asks again and raises her face to the light. He sees her split lip and the blood on her chin. "Who? What?"

"We must do it," she whispers. She drags him away from where Joseph is lying. "Tonight."

"Do what, Jeannie?"

"The plan! We must kill them all. Tonight."

"Friday," says Appollon. Her arms are gripping him, fingernails cutting their way through the thin fabric of his shirt. "Keep your voice low! It can't happen tonight. But who hit you? What happened?"

"It must!" Jeannette cries. "They must die! We have to start it."

"No! The plan has changed!" Appollon's voice is low and nervous; he doesn't fear Joseph but he fears the shadows and what they hide, and the way sounds carry through the night air. Brac's house by the beach, the boats anchored in the bay. "Love, what happened?"

Jeannette crumples at his feet, sobbing, and he crouches down beside her.

"Pomponne," she finally gulps out. "He took Pomponne."

"Who?"

"That colored boy, he raped her and then—" Jeannette pauses, looks at him and hisses, "The bitch told me to be quiet. And he was standing there, laughing."

"That young Azor boy?" says Appollon, comprehension dawning. "But where?"

"In the garden. I sent her to him."

"Oh, Jeannie." He folds her in his arms. "Is Pomponne all right?"

"The bleeding has stopped," sobs Jeannette. "She is sleeping in the white girl's bed."

"I am so sorry." Appollon holds her tightly. He thinks of the young man whose horse he tried to saddle; the white trousers and the scarlet cravat, the sneering voice. They sit in silence and he can feel Jeannette growing calmer in his arms.

"That boy laughed and the bitch called Pomponne a foolish girl and she doesn't care." Jeannette's voice breaks slightly but her tears are done.

"No surprise," says Appollon. It worries him how much Jeannette cares for the white madam, always defending her and admiring how well she treats Pomponne. But some things never

334

change: rivers only flow one way and the love is never returned. We are all the same for them, just black bodies to be worked and disposed of.

"I thought she loved Pomponne as a daughter. I thought she cared for *me*," says Jeannette quietly.

"Never," says Appollon. "I doubt she even loves her own daughter. They don't know how."

Jeannette takes a deep breath. "I want her dead."

"Soon enough," murmurs Appollon, caressing her cheek. "Friday."

"No! Tonight! The boy is here now and I want him killed too! They'll be gone by Friday."

"But the Azor plantation is also targeted," lies Appollon; in truth he doesn't know. "We will have our revenge then."

"It's not. I know when you lie."

"I can't give the signal," says Appollon. "It's not tonight. We all have to act together. One stick—"

"Oh, shut up about your sticks!" cries Jeannette, standing up and scrambling away from him. "It doesn't matter how many you are, you will not succeed! You will kill some, yes, but then they will kill all of you, every single one of you six times over. So why does it matter if it starts now or Friday?"

Appollon stares at her, her words unknown to him. "You don't believe?"

"Of course I don't. Who believes?" answers Jeannette scornfully.

"We all do."

"Only because you're under the spell of that witch-man Milord," she snaps. "You have been here for many years—have you not learned? We cannot defeat the whites."

"But we will succeed!" says Appollon angrily, getting up. "You don't understand."

"I understand. But I can't stop you. It kills me too, to see you run straight to your death."

Appollon is silent a while, then looks back at the plantation gates. Joseph has heard but it doesn't matter. The old man is one of the lucky ones, he thinks sadly; he has already lived his life. But I—I need to fight.

"It may be," Appollon says softly. "Maybe we are running

to our deaths, but we still have to try." That boat sailing across the ocean, carrying him and his destiny with it. "A single termite cannot take down a house, but thousands, chipping away, eating—"

Jeannette shakes her head in impatience. "Will you set the fire?"

"No."

"Will you set the fire for my daughter?" she repeats in a tone he hasn't heard before: cold and flat, build on a formidable foundation of anger.

"Friday," he pleads. "You know I love Pomponne like my own daughter. What is two days?"

They stare at each other for a few minutes, the golden orb of the lantern separating them from the rest of the world but not bringing them any closer.

"Then I will set the fire," says Jeannette.

"No, you won't! If you set it, the messages will be confused," Appollon says, unsure who this woman is. Jeannette, usually so calm and practical, the palm tree that sways but never breaks. "More will die, we have to—"

"You're a coward," shouts Jeannette. She runs past him into the darkness and he hears her start up towards the big house, her feet scrambling over the loose stones.

Appollon stares after her, absorbing the sting of her words. She is not thinking straight. Friday will give us the best chance we have and I cannot change that. But she doesn't believe, in me or in what we are planning.

Then I will set the fire, Jeannette said in a voice so flat. Would she carry through her threat? Setting fire to sugarcane or cotton is easy and tempting but coffee is more resistant; even if she lit one bush, it might not catch beyond the quincunx. The Jeannette he knows would never try such a thing but now—her mind muddled with grief and anger, her daughter raped by that colored boy, the mistress she once loved betraying her...

Appollon looks south down the road but there is no carriage on the horizon, only the bobbing light of the two men and their horses, ascending the cliffs to the south. This is foolish; no one is coming tonight. And what do I care now if I abandon my post? He picks up the lantern and heads for the plantation gates.

"Your woman giving you trouble?" asks Joseph, still lying down.

Appollon pauses; he knows what Joseph heard. "Look, if the carriage comes, don't stop it. Let it pass by."

Joseph grunts.

Appollon makes his way up the hill, past the big house— vibrantly lit, the murmur of white voices floating into the night. He hurries to the kitchens, skirting the clearing around the apricot tree and avoiding the few men and women who are still chatting in front of their fires. To his immense relief Jeannette is in the kitchen, working busily. Flore, snoring in the corner.

Of course. She is a sensible, practical woman; she knows they have to wait for Friday. He watches her lay strips of pastry on top of the pie, weaving them in a lattice fashion. All appears normal.

Finally, she looks at him, her face blank, only her swollen lip hinting at the drama of the recent hour.

"Are you all right?" Appollon asks.

"Yes. I have to finish the supper. Eight are eating tonight." The lattice complete, she looks dully down at the pie. "You'll put it in the oven? And find Laurine to help me with the dishes."

"Of course." Appollon carries the pie outside to the brick oven and places it inside, the heat singeing the hair on his hands. Back inside, he watches Jeannette shred a dried carp. The wild woman from the road is almost completely gone, but Appollon can see, almost imperceptibly, her slight struggle to control her breathing.

"You are calmer now," he says cautiously.

"I am," agrees Jeannette in a dead voice.

Appollon goes to embrace her, to whisper again that he will take care of both her and Pomponne. She ducks away.

"I love you," says Appollon, searching her face. Don't think there are no crocodiles just because the water is calm, his mother used to say, and he remembers the sharks that lay in wait for the canoes as they set off for the slave ships.

"I love you too," Jeannette replies without looking at him. She starts to chop a pile of carrots. "Please get Laurine. And Samedi or Dimanche too, if they are not asleep."

Appollon leaves, uneasy. Has he broken something that

cannot be fixed? Words once spoken never die and Jeannette might think him as cold and uncaring as Madame Rose. But the world cannot stop over Pomponne; even the love of a child cannot compete with what is coming. Surely Jeannette will understand that and forgive him?

The Dining Room
8 pm

Azor helps Madame Rose back to the salon, then grabs his son and pulls him outside.

"Truthfully—did you go to Dame Marie and speak with Bassompierre?" Azor says, voicing his earlier suspicions. "Or did you stay here and whore around with the girl?"

"No," confesses Henri, not meeting his father's eyes. "I started but I didn't get to Dame Marie. A man told me Bassompierre wasn't there, that he went to Les Irois."

"You never made it to Dame Marie!" says Azor, his anger rising. "Who told you Bassompierre went to Les Irois? Reliable information?"

"A man at a rum stand," whines Henri. "Next bay over. What reason would he have to lie?"

"Lazy cur!" Azor cuffs Henri on the head.

"Ow! Why do you care? And as Mercier says, we don't even need the constable."

"We are trying to do the right thing here," says Azor grimly. He wants to shake his boy, rattle the nonchalance right out of him. "Unlike you. Always messing things up. That incident with the girl—could you not keep it in your—whatever those things are—keep it in your *trousers* for just one day? This is the last thing that Madame Rose needs, with all the other troubles."

Henri moves a safe distance away from his father. "*Oh, poor Madame Rose,*" he mimics.

Azor stares with something like hate at the foppish youth in front. All of his fears for his son are confirmed: a liar, a philanderer and above all, a boy who does not think of the consequences of his actions. A trait that Azor deplores. In this country and in this time, every action has consequences, and to think that his boy does not understand that is terrifying. He grabs Henri by the ear and drags him back into the salon.

"Ow, Father, let go! I'm not six!"

"Messieurs and Madame," Azor announces, his grip still on Henri's ear. "I confess to this room of adults that my son is in many ways still a child. Apparently, he did not get to Dame Marie—on the road he received information that Bassompierre was at Les Irois, information we do not know to be true or not."

"Oh, for goodness sake," says Mercier in irritation. "Give it a rest with Bassompierre. The matter is done. Plunkett is buried, the culprit taken care of. What does it matter now? Madame Rose can make a deposition at her leisure."

Azor releases his son and turns to Madame Rose. Her face is still pale and her lace sleeve ripped where the slave woman grabbed her. "And furthermore, I must apologize, Madame Rose, for the unpleasantness you were subjected to. I am distressed that my son was a catalyst, real or imagined, for that dreadful scene. We will of course compensate you in the amount required for any damage to your property."

"Hardly damaged," protests Henri. "Like I said, she wanted it." He dodges away to avoid a blow from his father.

"No, Noel, you have been more than helpful. The slaves you promised for tomorrow—that is recompense enough. I am grateful for your assistance." Rose pauses and Azor is aware of something, stronger and more solid, beneath her fragile exterior. "Now please, everyone to the dining room—the table is set and supper should be with us shortly."

Azor seats himself at one end of the table, Mercier taking the other master's chair before Thoreau can sidle in. Now Azor sits opposite the man responsible for the murder of his son. By God, how he would like to expose the man, right here and now and spare everyone the agony of this meal. If he could be sure of better back-up—he glances at Thoreau, then at Henri—he would risk bringing the denouement of this day forward!

*

Mathilde enters the dining room and everyone realizes she has been missing.

"Ah, sister," says Thoreau in surprise. "How nice of you to join us. You… enjoyed your nap?"

Mathilde ignores her brother and seats herself, smiling around broadly and rubbing her belly. Her cap is askew and one of her sleeves is stained, as though with grass or mud.

"Where have you been, Madame Mathilde?" Rose asks.

"I have seen the darkness," Mathilde says brightly, nodding at her hostess.

"Indeed, night falls very quickly on the equator. Unlike in France," says Thoreau. "Here dusk is but a fleeting hour."

Mathilde smiles and repeats, to no one in particular, that she has seen the darkness.

"*A la française*, Messieurs, Madame," Rose says, turning away from the oddness of Mathilde and gesturing to the bottles laid on the table. "Please, serve yourselves."

"How very modern!" enthuses Thoreau. "A style quite fashionable in France and how forward of you to espouse it here!" As if to show his approval he reaches over and proudly pours himself a generous glass of wine.

"Well done, Monsieur," says Henri, with an edge of sarcasm. "Not a drop on your cuffs or the table cloth."

Rose ignores Henri and smiles at Thoreau. What is wrong with a little enthusiasm? A light breeze, harbinger of the night rains, wafts across the room and the candles flicker. Rose pours herself a glass and looks around at her guests. Before tonight she didn't know Azor and regarded Thoreau as more of a nuisance than a man, but now, what comfort they offer! Azor especially; Rose thinks of how his hand felt on her arm, steadying her as he led her away from the dreadfulness in the garden. Azor fair radiated calm, even in the midst of such passion and confusion.

Rose glances briefly at Henri, sitting opposite, then looks away. How dare he? Despite her harsh words earlier, she feels disgusted with him and sorry for Pomponne. But there are bigger things at stake, she reminds herself. The survival of her plantation, and how can one little slave girl even set herself close to that?

Rose looks at the two empty place settings where Aimée and Charles should be. They ran away as they are always running away, hiding in the indigo vats or down by the beach, off in their own world without her. She failed them both today: her son forced to do something he couldn't, her daughter witnessing that scene with Jeannette. But not only today, Rose realizes. She failed them both by bringing them up here in this ugly, ugly world. That woman, attacking her. The hate in her eyes, the hate all around, constant and never-ending, draining the life out of her. The strength that it takes to pretend it doesn't exist.

Why are we not back in France? Rose remembers the peace of her aunt's garden in Nantes, the strictness of life and its secure routines that now seem to her wonderful things. Was the grayness of France so bad? Rose imagines opening the curtains, tending the flowers, transforming the house with the happiness of family. Aimée, stitching beside her on the sofa, Charles busy with scholarly pursuits. Both of them free of the vileness of life here. How did she ever let Marcel convince her this was normal?

We're leaving this cursed island, Rose thinks suddenly. She finishes her wine, the deep red liquid as bold as her thoughts. We'll all take passage with Charles on the *Esprit*. I'll bring Marcel with me, dig up his bones and those of my baby as well. Then without wanting to, Rose looks at Azor, already looking at her. They stare at each other until she blushes and turns away, wishing the wine would never end and reveal the hollowness of her dreams.

A noise on the back steps. Jeannette and Laurine come through, followed by the twins Samedi and Dimanche. All of them bearing food. Oh, thank goodness. Rose smiles gratefully at her cook. Despite her swollen lip, Jeannette looks as she always does, beautiful and calm.

"Excellent, Jeannette, what do we have here?"

Jeannette lists the food in a voice devoid of emotion. She doesn't look at Rose as she speaks but rather down at her hands in a posture of perfect slavely contrition.

Too calm and contrite, thinks Rose, but instead she says: "Wonderful! Well done." Everything will be fine. Rose can feel her world, like an overburdened boat, slowly righting itself on calm seas.

"It all looks very delicious!" agrees Thoreau with enthusiasm.

The guests watch in silence as the two slave women lay the food on the table: the enormous latticed chicken pie, steaming and succulent; a tureen of carp stew; a hearty omelet and a mound of seasoned green peas. Bread, butter, cream cheese.

Jeannette, despite her extraordinary outburst this evening, is an excellent cook. It would be a pity to let her go and perhaps after a suitable punishment—nothing like Bridget's, Rose thinks with a shudder—they can resume their earlier, easier relationship.

Rose has always liked her, maybe even loved her. Though their earlier intimacy is gone—where and how that happened, Rose can't remember—there is no doubt that Jeannette is a valuable cook and someone to rely on. And I do, thinks Rose in surprise, watching Jeannette supervise Samedi or Dimanche as they solemnly lay out the cruets and spices. She wouldn't think one could be dependent on a slave but now she realizes that Jeannette is the keystone without which all the walls at Bayardel would fall down.

And she has been a good mistress, Rose thinks, wanting to explain herself to the look of dead indifference from Jeannette. The favor she has shown Pomponne! Raising her in the big house with her own children, even educating her.

Rose winces. No, she won't think about Pomponne right now.

She will send for the doctor tomorrow, spare one of the mules. Perhaps the harvest and the coffee doesn't matter so much. There will be another ship. Jeannette didn't mean to attack her, she was just mad with grief; perhaps what happened to her daughter is punishment enough. Rose imagines how she would feel if something similar happened to Aimée. Those words from long ago: *Almost as if she were affected with maternal devotion…*

And Rose knows it to be true, no mere supposition or hunch. They have the same emotions, the same cares, dreams… It doesn't bear thinking about and Rose has made a life of ignoring it. To acknowledge it is to drown in horror, and in the end it doesn't matter. They—the slaves—make this life and all these riches possible and so it has to be; all one can do is treat them kindly and not think on it too much.

"Thank you, Jeannette. Please, more wine for our guests," says Rose, taking a key from the little pocket around her waist. "And some bottles of champagne—it is not often we have such company," she says, looking at Azor.

Wordlessly Jeannette takes the key and the women exit, Samedi and Dimanche barely into the salon before they break out in excited babble; this was their first time in the big house.

"*A la française* again, Messieurs, Mathilde," Rose says when the slaves are gone. She lets out a little giggle and realizes her words are too bright and her glass is too empty. Azor pours her more wine and she smiles at him gratefully. I could smile at him all day, she thinks, then remembers Marcel, down in the graveyard at Jérémie.

*

Thoreau helps himself to a generous portion of the pie, steaming enticingly in the middle of the table. He delves into his food and finds happiness there. Good food, fine wine (for it is a surprisingly good Gamay, that had hitherto not graced the table) and somewhat good company—what more could a man ask for? And what an extraordinary day! The mystery solved, the murderer found, and of course his own critical role in finding and fingering him. Thoreau watches as Mercier serves himself some pie and omelet. He imagines denouncing Mercier in front of the constable; one of Bassompierre's men might even bind the ignoble knave in chains!

A satisfactory end to a most vexing, incredible, and perplexing day. Perhaps the strangest day he has ever encountered. Thoreau chuckles; in reality, there is no comparison. While he is not of general disposition to read novels, it cannot be denied that this day has had many elements of a one, particularly those of the dark mystery genre known as *gothic*.

Perhaps he might even venture to write a novel himself! While Thoreau feels keenly that novelists occupy the bottom rung of the ladder of literary ability, there was a certain excitement and rhythm to the events of the day that might compel him to put pen to paper. Thoreau remembers one novel in particular: *The Castle of Otranto*, a book of Mathilde's that he had chanced upon in a fit of boredom. That tale had all the elements of this day: mystery, murder, hidden identities, ancient family secrets, mad relations in cupboards, or at least in bedrooms. Here, the supernatural element could be provided by the *Vaudun* of the slaves and their superstitions. The romance angle was perhaps the only element not adequately covered, despite the ravishment of the pretty colored girl by the villain. One of the villains. Thoreau glances at Rose, sitting next to Azor. What a... Well. Perhaps that type of romance, if it could even be called that, would best be omitted from even the most fantastical novel.

Thoreau partakes heartily of the pie then butters himself some bread and, given that no one else is talking, feels his usual compunction to fill the void and impart his views; silence always beckons.

"That was indeed an extraordinary scene," Thoreau remarks. "The passion of that slave woman was most elucidating; the maternal instinct can occur in the most unexpected of places! Love, concern, shame: I could have sworn I saw all those emotions in her." Thoreau is aware his voice is troubled, and pauses. "If I sound vexed on this matter, it is because I am. The premise of enslavement must rest on more than the savagery of the Africans; it must rest on the Negro being a separate *species* from ourselves. But the emotion..." Thoreau catches himself, annoyed at his doubts but feeling a compunction to honesty. "Yes, it was all quite amazing. Such concern over her daughter's chastity and the rightful shame she felt!"

"I agree!" says Rose. "I mean, about their emotions."

"Monsieur Azor," says Thoreau, emboldened by the wine and an acute misinterpretation of the level of camaraderie at the table, "what are your thoughts on this matter? You are perhaps in a special position, between the two camps as we say—you might speak of your mother?"

"What of her, Monsieur?" replies Azor, his voice neutral but with a hint of wariness, his gray eyes fixed on Thoreau.

"Well, about her emotions and maternal instincts. The level thereof? She was a slave...?" offers Thoreau. Henri snorts and helps himself to more wine. Despite the tolerance of the average colonist, everyone at the table is getting rather drunk; even Mathilde is sipping, a faint circle of pink appearing on each cheek.

Azor smiles, thin and painful. "My mother, Monsieur

Thoreau, was the daughter of a mulatto and a white man. She counts but one grandparent as a Negro, her African blood as diluted as a drop of coffee in a washbasin. She was raised in great style in Jacmel where her father was a merchant and her uncle the owner of six—six, I stress!—plantations. My mother was also an accomplished pianist and in her youth played often at the Cap-Français theater, under proper chaperone of course."

"Ah, indeed," says Thoreau, vaguely aware he has blundered into something he doesn't quite understand, and afraid his foolish remark has undermined their earlier rapport. "I am so sorry. I misspoke! Your mother was not a slave! Of course, you—"

"No offense taken, Monsieur, but I would prefer to change the conversation."

"One drop," says Mercier darkly. "One drop is all it takes." His voice catches on the last word and he slams down his glass and stares darkly into the carp stew swimming on his plate.

"I would wager the refinements of my ancestors, their education and wealth, against any Frenchman in this colony," says Azor to Mercier.

"It's not a question of lineage!" Mercier practically shouts.

"This pie really is superb," Rose says brightly, though she has scarcely taken a bite.

Azor smiles at her. "I am most sorry, Rose, we must endeavor to keep our conversation light and civil."

"*Rose*?!" explodes Henri. "Is no one going to say anything? What about you, eh, what is your Christian name?"

"Ah—Philiberte," says Thoreau, taken aback at the sudden outburst and the fork pointing at him. Though the young man does have a good point: Why are Azor and Madame Rose speaking to each other so intimately?

"Good, well, *Philiberte*, how do you like your pie?"

"Ah, yes, yes, it is good."

"I think it tastes funny," observes Mathilde.

"Remember your manners," reproves Thoreau and to oblige himself in front of his hostess he takes a few bites in rapid succession. Yes, there is a faint sour taste but not overly so. Odd, but then most things taste slightly odd here.

Are slightly odd here.

The Indigo Vats
8 pm

Aimée runs into the night, the world made blurry through her tears. She runs along a familiar path back to childhood and safety, away from the house and her mother and all those evil men and the misery of Pomponne. She reaches the indigo fields and stops short; someone is sitting on the steps of a vat, a dark purple outline against the darkness.

The feeling of danger that has been suffocating her all day squeezes tighter before she realizes who it is.

"Charles!"

He stands up and she clings to him, still whimpering and shaking, but oh! how glad she is to see him. "Charles! Why weren't you there?"

"Where? What's the matter?"

"It's Pomponne," Aimée says. She wipes her face and rubs her cheek, still smarting where Mercier slapped her. "That colored boy, he took Pomponne," she whispers, then louder: "And Mercier smacked me and punched Jeannette but she was just worried about Pomponne and Mama didn't care!"

Charles stares at her, confused. "Oh, Aimée. It all sounds terrible. Mercier hit you?" They sit down together on one of the steps and she leans against him, sniffing.

"He should be punished, Charles."

Charles puts his arm around her and strokes her hair. "Even if he is our neighbor, we'll never invite him here again."

"What? No, not Mercier. I hate him,"—Aimée realizes Charles doesn't know about Mercier killing Plunkett—"but it's Henri. That colored boy. He's the one who... who did it to Pomponne." Aimée can't bring herself to say the awful word out loud, not even to her brother. It's a word that belongs only in locked boxes, kept down dark holes that let up no secrets.

Charles thinks back to the Azors' arrival and remembers the young cocky boy—man?—with his strange white pantaloons and knotted scarlet scarf. "Henri Azor?"

"Yes, him! Please, Charles, help us," his sister pleads. "Pomponne's hurt."

"Well, I don't know how we could punish him," says Charles cautiously, still struggling to understand what had happened while he was hiding here, away from his fears and from what he did to Bridget. "His father is very rich and—"

"But they are just coloreds!" says Aimée. "We can whip him if we want. Brac? If you won't?"

"The laws, I think they have changed," says Charles uncertainly. The idea of him—or Brac for that matter—whipping the well-dressed young man is patently ridiculous. And his father is a formidable man. Besides, Charles isn't touching that rawhide again; that was the vow he made to himself this afternoon. A vow he will keep, but secretly.

"Please, Charles! For Pomponne. She's our friend." Aimée pulls herself away from her brother's arms. "You get a whip and I'll pretend I want to talk to Henri and I'll bring him outside!"

"No, Aimée."

"But you whipped that slave this afternoon!"

"Well, I—" If he says it isn't true, perhaps it won't be. "No, I never whipped her," Charles says firmly. "And I won't whip that boy."

Aimée stares at him. "It's because you are a man," she says finally, bitterly. "Because you do it too!"

"Aimée!"

"I know you've done it and now you don't care."

"No, that's not—"

"It's true," Aimée says. "You've changed."

Charles doesn't answer; he can't. He remembers what his sister said in the boat about the pigpen. Why did he follow Brac there? Why had he wanted that? And with Bridget...

They sit in silence awhile longer.

"I'm sorry Mercier hit you," Charles says eventually. "And why are they still here? The Azors—why didn't Mama just send them away?"

"Oh! They have to stay, Charles," Aimée explains. "We found Plunkett's murderer!"

"Really? Who?"

"Monsieur Mercier! Plunkett was blackmailing him so he came and killed him last night. And Monsieur Azor has to stay, to protect Mama."

"Oh. Goodness." Charles sees Mercier's twisted face, his shining eyes, the way he taunted him. The cruelty, the sheer horribleness of the man! The knife that he used to slit Bridget's blouse. "I think he killed Bridget as well," Charles says carefully, trying out the words. He needs this to be true, needs a story for the events of the afternoon or everything will shatter.

"Oh—he's an evil man. Poor Madame Nathalie," says Aimée. "Married to such a monster."

The darkness deepens around them, and from the bushes the last of the night birds and insects quiet.

"Do you remember we used to play out here, Charles?"

"Of course. This was our place."

"But we never come here anymore," Aimée says, lightly accusing. "I still come, sometimes, but we never play here."

"I don't know why we don't," Charles says. "Maybe because I am leaving soon."

"What are you doing out here, not back at the house? Is that blood on your shirt?"

"I wanted to get away." From myself, Charles thinks. He needs a potion, like Flore claims she can make, some magic to erase his memories. Something to make him forget the sound of the whip through the air and the dreadful crack when it hit her body, the screams that turned to whimpers and then to silence.

"I don't want to go back to the house," Aimée whispers. "Everything is wrong back there. The drums... I can't bear to hear them tonight. Can we sleep here?"

"Mama will be worried," Charles says but he doesn't want to go back either. "Come." He stands up and takes his sister's hand. They climb into the vat and lie down, the sky a tapestry of black and silver above them, the old weeded walls around them comforting and protective. Everything is quiet. Maybe Aimée won't hear the drums out here and Charles wonders if he has heard them too.

"Do you remember how we used to play hide and seek?" says Charles, seeing his father's tousled, sweaty head popping up over the vat. A scream that was half-terror and half-laughter, then a scramble up and out, his father running after him and bringing him down amidst the flowers. Her mother there, laughing as well.

"Of course."

Silence.

"I miss him so much," says Charles, fighting back tears. "Everything went wrong after he died."

"I don't want you to go," Aimée whispers, reaching for his hand and twining her fingers in his.

"I don't want to go either. I can't leave you and Mama here." Why is he going to France? To study and learn and grow into a man, then come back and be like Mercier? Live his life full of hate and surrounded by it too?

"I wish we could come too," says Aimée. "I'm scared. Something bad is coming. Don't laugh!"

"I won't. I believe you about the drums. But don't be scared, I'll…" Charles searches for the words to comfort, but can't find any. And so they lie, two children under the vast night sky, sheltered from the hurricane of hate about to thrash through the plantation.

The Dining Room
9 pm

"Though I hate to leave your fair abode, Madame, the future beckons!"

Thoreau and Azor are discussing a visit to La Fraternité as the next stop on his tour.

"Oh, no Monsieur," Rose says warmly, aware her voice is too loud; she must stop drinking. "I am sure La Fraternité will offer you extensive opportunities for your study." How wonderful to have that tiresome man out of her house and for life to return to normal. And perhaps… his presence at the Azor plantation might give her an excuse to visit, even as early as next week?

Rose casts a sideways glance at Azor. He returns a small half-smile, secret and intimate. The memory of Marcel fades, just a bit, allowing room for someone else in her heart. Thank you, she mouths, both to Azor and to the universe.

"I don't feel well," says Mathilde.

Rose giggles; the two pink spots on Mathilde's cheeks have grown larger.

"I must confess my mouth salivates—or perhaps I should say my heart, though can a heart salivate? I salivate, regardless, at the library that Monsieur Azor has painted such a fair picture of!" says Thoreau. "How I have lacked books on my travels and I think I will—oh my goodness! Who is that?"

"Sister!" exclaims Rose. Julienne in her white nightgown, framed in the doorway. Rose stands up, her legs watery with wine.

351

"Julie—what are you doing? You cannot come like this…"

Thoreau also rises. "And might you be Madame du Choiseul?" he inquires as the other guests drink in her uncombed hair and bare ankles.

Mathilde giggles.

"Tush," scolds Thoreau, frowning. "Madame du Choiseul is unwell."

Walking unsteadily, Julienne approaches the table and sits in one of the places set for the children. She looks around, her eyes blank and unfocused.

"We don't have much time," she finally announces to the gawking guests. "We are all going to die."

"I know," chirps Mathilde breathlessly. "The darkness is here!"

Oh God, thinks Rose. Not now, not on top of everything else.

"Madame du Choiseul, you are unwell," says Thoreau. He goes to Julienne's side and takes her arm gently. "Come with me, perhaps back to your room?"

Julienne shakes her head. "We are all going to die tonight," she repeats in her high, girlish voice.

"That woman is completely unhinged," says Mercier. "Disgusting. Given what happened to her, it would have been better if she died at Limbé."

"What happened at Limbé?" asks Mathilde, leaning forward. "Did the darkness get inside her too?"

Julienne's unfocused eyes fasten on Mathilde: "We're all going to die tonight."

"Madame," Thoreau repeats helplessly, tugging gently on her arm.

"What's she babbling on about?" says Henri. "And she's wearing a nightgown!"

"Where's your baby?" says Rose, the bud of an idea forming in her mind. She feels the reassuring pressure of Azor's hand on the curve of her back, steadying her and giving her strength.

Julienne swivels to look at her.

"I've found your baby. This way…" Rose points out into the salon. With reluctance she steps away from Azor and the comfort of his hand on her waist. She takes Julienne's arm, as thin as a sparrow's wing and ready to snap. "Come, dearest, we'll find your baby."

"Oh." Julienne bites her lip, comprehension forming beneath the fuddled surface. "My baby—is he all right?"

"Of course he is," says Rose and to her relief Julienne rises, again exposing her bare ankles. "He's coming but we have to go to your room so he can find you. Come with me." Rose leads Julienne, docile now, out through to the salon. She takes a lantern and brings her to Aimée's bedchamber and settles her back in the bed where Pomponne still lies.

Julienne sighs. "I knew it wasn't real," she whispers, smiling up at Rose. "None of it was real."

Rose strokes her brow. "None of this is real."

Beside Julienne, Pomponne is lying with her eyes closed, so still she doesn't appear to be breathing. Rose touches the girl's forehead but Pomponne doesn't stir; at least her brow is cool. She pulls back the sheet and peers at the mess around the girl's legs. The thing about blood, it always looks so plentiful, a teaspoon resembling a quart. Rose covers Pomponne again. Poor girl, what a rude awakening to the world of men that would surely define her life. Rose knows well what beauty means in this place; no, not just beauty but extraordinary beauty. In slumber, Pomponne appears to be an angel, cherubic and unmarred.

Rose looks around her daughter's room—it has been a while since she was here. She used to visit Julienne every day but the low keening or incessant questions about her son and the stains never stopped. *Time*, the doctor said, but it's been almost a year. Rose sees a statue on the table.

How curious. She picks it up and its placid amber eyes stare back at her.

"When is he coming?" asks Julienne eagerly from the bed.

"Soon. Is this yours?"

Julienne shakes her head. "No, it's Aimée's. But it's not hers."

Rose sighs; the girl makes no sense and never did. But perhaps this new development—getting out of bed and even appearing to understand some of what is going on around her—is to be praised? There is a new doctor in Jérémie; he can come tomorrow for Pomponne and look at Julienne as well. Help the two broken females in her care.

"Go to sleep, dearest, and in the morning your baby will be here."

To Rose's relief, Julienne sighs and closes her eyes. Tomorrow before the doctor comes Laurine can wash her, get her dressed and do her hair. Rose hesitates, then tucks the statue into her pocket, unaware that Pomponne's eyes are now open and watching.

Rose goes outside and leans over the railing, looking down over the flower gardens. Grief comes careening through the half light of the veranda and flattens her. She falls into a hammock, exhaustion and misery engulfing her in physical form. The darkness that was circling the house has now come up on the veranda and it is as near as it has ever been.

It is not beginning, for it began so long ago.

Rose starts sobbing. She can't breathe. Everyone is hurting, they are all suffering and what are they doing? No one is innocent. The dreadful lassitude and defeat that has walked alongside her these last few years catches her in its dismal embrace. Everyone and everything ruined, the sheer misery draped over their days. Her son become a monster, her daughter so delicate yet wild, Julie… Oh poor Julie. And Pomponne, taken by that odious boy. Jeannette… Rose sobs and sinks further into the hammock.

"I'm sorry," she whispers. "I'm sorry for everything. I want to go back to France." She can't stop crying. She wants her children back, all of them. She wants her husband back and she wants to howl in rage at the gods with their awful rules that say that Marcel will never live again or hold her one last time, no matter how much she cries and prays.

The rocking of the hammock like the rocking of the boat, the one Rose boarded last week when she bought those six Aradas. She made the mistake of looking at one, directly, and though she turned away quickly it was not soon enough: she had seen it. Then two of them died and in the morning, she kicked the bodies and cursed them. Would God forgive her? They feel the same sorrows, Rose thinks with a giant sob and clutches herself, rocking more furiously now. Those poor souls, what have I done?

She needs to get out of this evil place but she has nowhere

to go and no money, only foolish dreams of boats taking her to a better life. Would Azor run away with her? To America, to a place where anything is possible. But perhaps there is no such place on earth, no sanctuary or reprieve from the misery. And she can't leave, this is where her children are and her husband is and all she wants to do is curl up and stop breathing.

*

In the dining room the guests sit in awkward limbo until Mercier grunts and starts eating again. No use waiting for their hostess. He cleans his plate and reaches over to fetch more pie and omelet. The other guests follow, the stunned tableau gradually returning to life.

"Who was that?" asks Henri curiously. "That woman—did you see her skirt? And bare ankles?"

"Her ankles, young man," says Thoreau, disliking the undertone of salaciousness in the boy's voice, "are not appropriate to comment on. That woman has suffered greatly and we should offer her the politeness of not mentioning what we have seen."

Henri rolls his eyes. "Oh! That's the mad whore of Limbé! And I heard none of them were wearing stockings when they were rescued, either."

"Do not talk of a white woman like that!" Mercier hisses, then reconsiders. "Can they even be considered white, after that taint?"

"What taint?" says Mathilde, rubbing her belly, her face bright pink and flushed. "The darkness? Inside her?"

Thoreau tells Mathilde to be quiet but then realizes he has a certain prurient—nay, scientific—interest in the question himself. But only in the facts, of course. And they are amongst men here, his sister excepted, and perhaps quickly before Madame Rose returns… "Were there any… ah… pregnancies? Infants? Resulting from their unfortunate captivity?"

Mercier laughs. "Such a thing is hardly possible—you with your scientific pretensions should know that."

"Certainly, yes, but the more one considers, if progeny is possible between a white man and a black woman, then surely—"

"It's against nature, that's why!" shouts Mercier. "Such a thing has never been countenanced or observed!"

355

"A woman in our village once gave birth to a hare," chips in Mathilde. "I don't feel well," she adds, still rubbing her belly.

"If it can go one way, then why not the other?" inquires Azor in a lightly baiting tone. "Simply because we have never seen such a child, surely that is due more to the natural restraint of the white female than to any biological imperative?"

Mercier glares at him, his face almost as red as Mathilde's.

"And don't we find this preoccupation with the mixing of white and black to be sorely time consuming and quite beside the main point?" Azor asks, looking at Mercier. Oh, to stand up and denounce the man!

"Not beside the point, not at all," shouts Mercier. "It is precisely the point! All of you," he says, pointing with his fork at Thoreau, Henri and Azor, "pretending these things don't matter. But things *must* be black and white. There has to be master and a slave and nothing in between! If things change—as they are changing now—then it is all over and there can be no more Saint Domingue!"

Mercier looks around for support but finds only disdain from Azor, shocked silence from Thoreau, and a shrug from Henri. Exasperated, he finishes his wine and attacks the rum. "Fools, all of you!"

"So you insist that things must be black and white?" says Azor. "That the very foundation of our society rests on that duality?"

"Yes, and that is why you people disgust me—you are in between, muddying all waters!"

Thoreau gobbles his omelet greedily as he watches the two men. Azor is baiting Mercier and might even be on the verge of exposing his secret. Thoreau decides he shall allow Azor to be the one to cast the first blow. The insults that Mercier has been throwing at him all day—*fop of no sound judgement* rings particularly harsh—pale before the insults Mercier has flung at his new friend. More excitement!

Thoreau's head is spinning and he feels slightly unwell. Goodness, has he really drunk so much wine? And hadn't Madame Rose promised champagne?

Mercier's face has gone from flushed to ashen. He is looking at Azor with wide eyes, rocking slightly.

"It would seem to me," says Azor, also looking rather pale; he lets out a discrete belch. "A thousand pardons, fellow guests, but it would seem to me that this single-minded insistence on purity might have unfortunate repercussions for you, Monsieur Mercier."

"This pie tastes funny," says Mathilde and she is the first to collapse. A small sigh and a thin bubble of drool runs down her cheek as her head falls onto her plate. Thoreau leaps up before he too collapses and rolls onto the floor.

"Poison!" shouts Mercier wildly, spitting out a mouthful of omelet. He tries to stand but a great wave of pain hits him and he doubles over. The pie, the greens, the drink, what? He sticks his finger down his throat to retch but collapses on the floor, his body contorting in an awful squeezing, breath trapped in his swelling throat.

Mathilde's words and her quick collapse fill Azor with dread. It cannot be! Hysteria of the mind, he thinks as Thoreau falls over but then he too feels a strangling at his throat. Bile rises and his chest compresses. Surely this is not how it ends, he thinks in amazement as the toxins course through his body and stop his heart, mercifully and quickly.

Henri ate the least of the pie and he fights the most. He manages to get up and stagger away, trying to flee the horror inside him. He reaches the salon. I don't want to die, he thinks in terror, and not like this. Someone has to help him. He falls over a small table and smashes to the floor alongside a chair, his world reduced to the bright orange of the velvet cover before him.

*

Her work done, Jeannette makes her way slowly back to the kitchens through the darkness. She walked these paths as a child and she feels the warmth of the night surrounding her, the soft cooing of the poultry drawing her home. She used to run back and forth and Cunette, and old Madame Francine... Between the kitchen and the big house, the kitchen and my house. This is where she belongs.

"What have you done, child?" breathes Flore, smelling death on Jeannette's fingers.

"Only what was needed," says Jeannette. Her voice feels faint, as though coming from far away. Am I dead? Is this heaven? She sits down by the wooden table, flour still littered over it, stray pieces of crust being carried away by ants. She traces a line in the flour. The line, that separates all things.

Flore starts keening loudly, summoning help.

"Shut up," says Jeannette listlessly. Should she have stayed to watch that boy and Madame Rose as they fell off their chairs in agony? Standing in the shadows as she always stands?

From his lookout, Appollon hears the cries coming from the kitchen hut. He has been searching the hills—it is not impossible that Jeannette bribed some of the men to start a fire. Flore's cries draw him down and a terrible suspicion grows in his heart.

"Jeannette!" he cries, bursting into the kitchen, the shock of sudden understanding when he sees her listless yet curiously satisfied face. "What have you done?"

"Only what was needed. What you would not," she says quietly. "Coward."

"I smell death on her fingers," cries Flore from the corner. "How did I not smell it before?"

"Oh, Jeannie, what have you done?" Appollon is holding her, cradling her, pulling her to him.

"Get off me! Coward." Jeannette's voice is flat but triumphant; she has won.

"The pie," rasps Flore. "It was in the pie."

Appollon runs out of the kitchen, Jeannette laughing softly behind him. What did she do? But that is a stupid question—he knows what she has done. Appollon runs to the storehouse and finds the shovels Louis left outside. He grabs one and hurries towards the house, his heart beating in a strange rhythm he doesn't understand. Please, Jeannette, no. Don't let me find what I think I will.

Don't let it be Jeannette who chooses my destiny.

The big house rises ahead of him, ablaze with candles. Appollon hesitates at the bottom of the steps. All is quiet, except for the low grunting of someone gasping for breath. Cautiously he makes his way up the back steps, holding the shovel in front of him. He peers in, hesitates, then enters the fortress—he has never been inside. A big room with tufted sofas and tables, the paintings on the walls, all glass and glossy wood but he can smell the rottenness underneath.

Appollon sees the mulatto boy on the floor, crawling towards the front of the room. He follows the rest of the low moaning through a set of doors and into a room with a table. Yes— here they are. The old white woman he scared earlier and the fancy Frenchman, fallen together in death. Mercier gurgling, but the foaming at his mouth says the end is near. An older mulatto man slumped over the table. The remains of the dinner—eggs, vegetables, bread. And the pie, mostly eaten. Appollon sniffs at it cautiously but it only releases a rich odor of meat and herbs.

Mercier looks at him with a flicker of recognition. Appollon smiles back until the man's eyes finally close in one last flutter of agony. How wonderful that this white, representing all of the evil of this earth, should see what it was that killed him.

But this triumph is no triumph. It was not supposed to happen like this.

Appollon prods the colored man, pushes him back in his chair and the body falls heavily to the floor. He pulls off the man's fine jacket—blue and orange stripes—and feels something in the pockets. A yellowed paper in one, a wad of bills bound with ribbons in the other. Appollon can't count or read but he knows what money looks like and the thickness of the bundle bodes well. Money, and lots of it. He places the jacket on a side table, away from what is coming.

Appollon looks at the half-eaten plate beside where the colored man was sitting. Where is Madame Rose? He sits down in her place, on the softness of the padded chair. He runs his hands across the tablecloth, lifts a knife and touches a china plate, as white and translucent as a shell. All these fineries that he has heard of but rarely seen. *Those two thousand livres will buy a most handsome china set*, he hears Chalumette saying, so many years ago in a different life.

Appollon takes a wine glass and finishes it; he is sure the poison is not in the drink. The liquid courses through him, odd and tart. He remembers how the men would terrify the new ones by telling them the red liquid the whites drank was really African blood. Appollon downs another glass to give him the courage and heart for what he has to do.

He stands up.

Oh, Jeannette, he thinks sadly. In a plan so broad and complicated, with so many things that could go wrong, surely something would. But like this? Who would have predicted such a turn?

Appollon takes up his shovel and starts to methodically chop at the inert bodies, one by one, bashing their faces with the heavy iron edge to erase their wild eyes and bubbling mouths— sure signs of poison. Like hoeing the ground, thwack, thwack, erasing Jeannette's guilt and transferring it to himself. Finished, he goes into the salon and finds Henri half out the door, still gasping. He flips him over and leans close, happy to see the boy's eyes register him and the bloody shovel.

"Not dead yet, eh, young master?" This is the boy who violated Pomponne, the one who set off this terrible chain of events. "Look at you, with your fine coat and fancy trousers, lying on the floor. At my mercy. You know what I mean?"

The head moves slightly and the eyes flicker.

"I didn't plan it like this," says Appollon, crouching down. "If you care—it was supposed to happen Friday."

A gurgle.

Appollon stands back up and smiles. "You are rotten to me. You have the blood of the whites in you and that is a stain that can never be erased. Never, like indigo on the skin, only yours is within you."

Henri closes his eyes. Appollon deals the death blow, nearly severing his head.

Right.

Appollon is breathing heavily now, his head light from the unaccustomed wine. He goes back and drains one of the rum bottles, puts on the fine blue and orange jacket. There is not much left of the pie to throw away, so he leaves it on the table. Where is Madame Rose and the children? I must go quickly. I will leave and everyone—the whites and the slaves—can blame me and then… Will Milord have him killed, for messing things up so badly?

You're all going to die anyways, Jeannette screamed at him on the beach road.

He finds Rose in one of the hammocks.

"Please, don't," she says, opening her eyes. Her body is curled in fetal terror; she heard the noises from the dining room and knows the evil has breached the false safety of the house. She stares up at the slave with the bloody shovel, wearing Azor's fine coat. Appollon from the stables. Then she thinks: Why not? I don't want to live and be like Julienne. But—"Where are my children?" she asks but Appollon doesn't answer. A movement behind and Pomponne comes out of the bedchamber.

"Child, are you all right?" asks Appollon.

"I'm fine," says Pomponne. She looks composed and tidy but somehow smaller. So much power, thinks Appollon; he has always respected this strange girl of Jeannette's, with her bright mind and blue eyes that see everything. She has more fire in her than a hundred men, more iron in that small body than in the largest cauldron for boiling sugar. But what her future will be in this new world, Appollon cannot say; will there be a place for her at Les Platons? Or perhaps women as beautiful as Pomponne need never fear for their future, no matter what color they are.

Pomponne looks down at Madame Rose in the hammock, her eyes closed now and looking almost peaceful. Carefully Pomponne reaches in and takes the statue from Rose's pocket. "Look," she says to Appollon and holds it up high, then dashes it against the floor where it breaks into a hundred pieces of terracotta and evil. Pomponne goes to the window and looks into the dining room.

"What happened?"

"I killed them," says Appollon, trying out the words. "I killed them all! Everything is beginning."

Pomponne nods, still staring through the window. "Where's the colored boy?"

"In the big room."

She finds Henri just at the entry, almost headless.

"Good," she says, then turns back to Appollon. "But you killed them all? They are so many. Four men," she counts. "And the old hen."

"I killed them all," replies Appollon. "This is... how everything is supposed to start. Don't be afraid."

"But I thought it was delayed?"

"It's not."

Rose whimpers from the hammock.

Pomponne looks at Henri again and remembers his hands on her, the moment he caught her in the dark wood and took so much from her. "But—how did you do it. Four men?"

Appollon remains silent. She knows, he thinks, as she knows everything. Pomponne comes back to stand by him. Rose's eyes are still closed and she is breathing heavily.

"Are you going to kill her?"

"Let the Aradas out," murmurs Rose.

"I don't know," says Appollon. "And what about your friends? The white girl and her brother?"

"What about them?"

"I don't know where they are."

Pomponne shrugs, still staring down at Rose. "Probably in the indigo fields, that's where they go to hide."

"Do you...?" He has asked before what was to happen to them but Jeannette always refused to answer.

Pomponne hesitates and Rose whimpers, her eyelids fluttering. "I don't know," Pomponne says and realizes in surprise she doesn't.

They both stare down at Rose, still whimpering. *Aimée*, Pomponne hears her whisper. "If you let this one live, it might be worse for her," suggests Pomponne. "She'll become mad like the aunt. Or Lubin."

Appollon nods. The wind whips up and the light in one of the lanterns flutters then flickers out, never to be re-lit.

"I have to go," he says. They are talking so slowly, as if time has stopped but he must remember the urgency. "Tell everyone that it was me. Me and La Fleur! We surprised them at supper. No uprising, no plan or rebellion. Just this plantation, just us two. You understand me?"

"Yes."

"Go back and take care of your mother. Put her to bed, keep her quiet."

"I know what to do, Appollon," says Pomponne calmly. "You go. We will see you soon."

Appollon sprints down the steps and runs past the carriage then hesitates—one path leads to the indigo vats, the other off into the hills towards the Pellegrin plantation where he will find Milord and tell him that the revolution came early to Bayardel.

Either path will eventually lead to Milord. Appollon pauses in indecision and thinks once more how incredible it is that everything that happened today was already foretold, as is everything that will happen in the future.

My destiny is a ship that has already sailed, and Jeannette steered it for me.

Then he takes the path straight to the hills.

Epilogue
New Orleans, 1810

The windows are closed and draped with black curtains. Heavy cloth swathes the walls and a garland of dark flowers adorns the door of the house on the Rue Royale. Death has come and the streets outside are quiet and subdued as though in sympathy for the passing in their midst.

Inside the house is also silent. The family sit around the coffin, lying on a bed of ice on the dining table. Henceforth it might not be used as such; Monsieur Christian will doubtless have it moved, perhaps into his office. They can scarcely eat off it now.

I see all this from the doorway where I stand in the shadows. Madame Rose is dead. She was fifty-three—not a great age but not a poor one either and there are so many that don't have that many years of God's grace. She was ailing since our arrival in New Orleans last year and Monsieur Christian—Aimée's husband and a surgeon— predicted she would not last many months.

I like to think she was ailing for much longer though I shouldn't say that—it sounds as though I wished her ill, when in reality I never did. I think she stopped living when her husband died, though God still kept her on this earth and gave her so many trials: the deaths of her children and all the struggles of the next decade as the chaos on the island— bloodier and more frightful with each passing year—swirled ever closer. And that night in October 1792. That night didn't bring the revolution to the Grand'Anse but it almost destroyed Bayardel and everything I loved. Henri killed something in me that day and now I can only skirt around my memories of it, never look it directly in the face.

Aimée is crying, her eyes red and her hair unpinned and disheveled. She leans against her husband, sobbing.

"She was always kind," I hear her say and then she is talking swiftly through her tears as though to imprint on everyone the life of this woman who will soon be but a marble gravestone in the cemetery of Saint Louis. We have one portrait of Madame Rose, done a few years before her death when all her sorrows had already cast her down. I wish they had painted her when she was younger, because my earliest memories are of a pretty woman, soft and delicate.

"She was kind. And she would comfort me," sobs Aimée. "She loved me. And my brother."

"A strong woman," murmurs her husband Christian and I think: but it is true. There was a strength to Madame Rose, of an uncommon sort, perhaps like the strength of a thin vine that climbs and clings with force and eventually covers a whole wall.

"Pomponne!" cries Aimée, calling to me; she can't see me in the shadows but she knows I am never far. I step into the dining room, my face impassive as always. "Pomponne, you loved her too. Tell me about her—talk!"

Aimée thinks us close but we are not, and never were. I have been wearing a mask for years—perhaps all my life— and now I am so used to being what others want me to be that the mask is now like my own skin. It is now *me*.

"I loved her," I say softly and run my hand up and down Aimée's arm to comfort her. "She was kind. *Benevolent.* And yes, Monsieur Christian, she was strong in her own way."

Aimée sniffs and nods. "I remember she always cared and once when Charles—" As Aimée continues telling the world about her mother, I slip back into the shadows where I belong and make my way to the kitchens. There I find the cook preparing cinnamon and nutmeg cakes; the whites of this country treat funerals like weddings and the house will be full of people all week long.

"Have a bite," says the cook, offering me a slice. "You must be upset."

"I am," I say, pretending as I have been pretending all my life. Pretending I have a heart, which perhaps I do. I take the plate from the cook. Not my mother but a woman Madame Rose bought in Cuba who came with us to Louisiana. Also in the kitchen are Babichon and Susie, sitting at the table and shelling a great mound of pecans. We are all slaves, though many in town now prefer to hire Irish girls because they are cheaper and their masters aren't responsible for their burial costs. But not Madame Rose; she remains true to the old ways.

I take my cake and go outside to the courtyard. It's July and too hot in the house—after the burial we will go up country, stay with the Gaultiers at their plantation in Trois Rivières. I sit on a bench and enjoy the faint night breeze and the perfume from the jasmine trees. I want to be alone with the confusion of my thoughts but in truth I am not upset as I told the cook. Instead, I am free.

Free from the dirty burden of fear that struck me whenever Madame Rose turned to me. Sometimes she looked at me with blank eyes that told me she had forgotten, but other times she looked slightly puzzled, as though there was a memory there that she was trying to find. She either forgot the words that passed between Appollon and I that night, or chose to do so. Regardless, she never said anything and neither did I, and as the years passed the fear lessened, the burden sprinkled out and dispersed like clouds after a storm until only faint white traces remained.

And now Madame Rose is dead and the secrets of that horrible night are truly only with me. Or with Appollon and my mother, if they are still alive.

*

After Appollon left, I ran back to the kitchens to be with my mother. I found her sitting amongst the remnants of her life, weeping. When she saw me, she started talking, apologizing, pleading, telling me she only did it for me, telling me all about the pie and the poison and the hatred she had for everyone and everything and how very sorry she was for sending me to that beast called Henri.

I held her and comforted her. Come to bed, I pleaded and Flore tried to quiet her too, but nothing would stop her mad ramblings or wild eyes; I don't know what she was looking at but it wasn't us. The rest of the plantation was quiet—everyone asleep, Brac down in his house by the beach, all of them unaware of the horror at the big house.

I saw what Appollon had not: my mother could not stay here. He might have physically erased all signs of the poison but my mother's mind and words would still betray her guilt. When she started to giggle about soft fruit puddings running all over creation, I knew I had to get her away. Bring her to Appollon.

I hugged Flore goodbye then took my mother by the hand and set off towards where I knew the Pellegrin plantation to be. We followed a stream high into the mountains and my mother gradually fell quiet as we picked our way through the night. The moon was big and bright, the same moon that was supposed to guide the rebellion but now only overlooked us, two small players in a greater tragedy. After a few hours we lay down, and before we slept my mother whispered to me about cakes and pies and fruit puddings. As she talked, I saw that she had slipped away to an earlier time, perhaps when she was happy.

In the morning we crossed a field of slaves working a coffee field high in the hills. I asked one for directions and soon we arrived at the abandoned gates of the Pellegrin place.

All was quiet but I knew they were there, watching. I shouted for Appollon and for Milord, as I knew his name to be, but for a long time the only answer came from birds chirping in the trees. As the sun rose, I started to panic. What would I do if no one came? But no—it was not possible that they had already gone, despite the aborted plan; someone must still be here. I called out again and again, stubbornly.

Finally, a man appeared. "I need Appollon!" I cried.

The man laughed. He was tall, with a wandering eye and scarifications.

"You are Milord," I said, my arms around my mother, protecting her.

"What are you doing here?" demanded the man.

"Please," I faltered, summoning my words and guile through all the fear. "My mother. She is not right in her mind, she was talking too much. I had to get her away. Please, she needs to be with Appollon."

Milord nodded. "Appollon told us what happened." His face was stone and I could not tell if he was angry or not. All those weeks of planning and surely everything was now aborted; with all that had happened at Bayardel, the entire district would soon be on high alert and swarming with militia. I feared for Appollon: The whites had won again, and who would Milord blame?

On hearing Appollon's name, my mother began to shriek. I hugged her and held her until she calmed, Milord watching us and the thicket behind with his roving eye.

Finally, he said, "And what about you?"

"I will return and say it was Appollon and La Fleur, that they plotted alone."

Milord nodded and something joined us: here was a man who could see into souls and here was I who could do the same. An understanding passed between us and I hoped he could trust me.

"Go," he said finally. "We will take care of her." His words neither chilled nor comforted, and there was nothing in his blank eyes to tell me which way I should fear. Should I have left my mother with him? Remember I was only twelve and trying to save her. Back at Bayardel, my mother would die. Here... I wasn't sure what her fate would be, but is not a thing with a small chance of success better than the certainty of nothing?

I hugged my mother then relinquished her to Milord and her destiny.

I ran back down to Bayardel and reached the house in

the afternoon. By then the district militia was there, confronting the horror and looking for the missing slaves: La Fleur, Appollon, Jeannette, and of course me.

A man in uniform grabbed me and threw me on my knees in front of the white captain.

"I was hiding by the indigo vats!" I protested, at the same time wondering what his sword would feel like, cold and slicing through me.

"Liar!" shrieked Aimée and I knew then that that was where she had been. Her mother was nowhere to be seen—Madame Rose was the only keeper of the truth and it was her that I feared the most.

"I was there, watching over you and Charles in the vat!" and with that lie and lucky guess, I gained back Aimée's trust and saved my life. Aimée dragged me away from the constable and hugged me until Bassompierre pulled me back to continue the interrogation. Brac was standing beside him, but I never looked in his eyes.

Appollon and La Fleur, in league against the world, I said. I talked quickly, aware that the lives of all the slaves at Bayardel hung on my words. A fiendish plot and no one trusted Appollon. Everyone hated him, everyone knew he was plotting something with La Fleur. The other slaves said it was true, even as they suffered the whip: they all swore they mistrusted Appollon from the moment he arrived, and La Fleur as well. Capidon and Pierre babbled easily and gave many details while Bassompierre and his men nodded and wrote it all down.

Only Brac was suspicious and kept urging the men to search the mountains again for the rebels he was convinced were hiding there.

They buried them all—Thoreau and his sister, Azor and his son—in one grave under one tombstone, down at the family plot where Henri raped me. I never went back there or saw the grave.

I don't know if anyone missed Mercier; they sent what was left of him back to his wife.

Madame Suzette, Azor's wife, came to cry at the grave of her husband and son. When she saw me, she shrieked like she had seen a ghost. I was glad about Henri, of course, but sad for his father; every war has battles and he was an early casualty.

I held my breath for weeks but though the militia combed the mountains behind us, and Desombrages, the Intendant from Jérémie, even had government troops come to assist, they never found anyone. Not Milord nor any trace of him and his men; they must have left for the higher mountains, back towards Les Platons.

My dream is that Milord led my mother to Appollon and in his arms she became whole again. That Milord forgave my mother and Appollon, and that he accepted the inevitable gracefully, as all great leaders must, and abandoned his plans for the Grand'Anse.

The next year we heard the news that the stronghold at Les Platons was taken by French forces and all the rebels massacred, women and children included. I didn't care; I knew in my heart, the same heart that deceives and pretends and comforts, that Appollon and my mother were not among them. They had left long before, going deeper and deeper into the mountains and making a home for themselves alone and together. In the future I made for them, they built a house and had a son and lived a true love story, high above the war that was tearing the foothills and plains apart. There, they are alive still, because they live in my heart and this is my story. Sometimes I even think about my half-brother, the one I created, and wonder if I will ever meet him.

Back at Bayardel life eventually returned to normal. After Bassompierre and the authorities left, Brac killed Pierre and Capidon, as well as two other slaves he never liked. He refused to believe the story about La Fleur. Madame Rose fired him and he left with Ernestine; I don't know what became of them.

Though Madame Rose was more of a ghost than before, she never said anything. I tiptoed around her until it became clear that her mind had neatly erased all of the horrors of that night and what we had talked about as she lay in the hammock. Charles emerged as the true hero of the story. He remained at Bayardel, forwent his chance for a

French education to stay by his mother's side and gradually took over the running of the plantation.

In 1793, not a year after the horror of October, the Jacobins in France abolished slavery in Saint Domingue but it did nothing for any of us at Bayardel; the British invaded the Grand'Anse the next month and reinstated it. Life went on as before. We slaves had no freedom but we lived, and in the stories we heard of the bloody fight between the French and the slaves and the coloreds elsewhere in the colony, sometimes our little hollow of peace seemed like the best sort of life as everything else disintegrated.

We struggled on through the next decade, the coffee still growing and providing enough money to survive. Aimée married a handsome German surgeon, posted with the English barracks at Dame Marie. Christian Miltenberger was his name and he stayed behind after the British left in 1798, helped Charles with Bayardel and our coffee. All around us plantations were being attacked by small bands of rebels, and that year Charles was killed in a skirmish on the Belleville plantation.

In 1803 the beast finally came to the Grand'Anse. The French forces that had taken over after the British left, retreated and left the countryside open. The Grand'Anse had held out for so long but it couldn't keep the revolution away forever. We knew it was all over and we were told as much: the colored General Rigaud, coming from the south with an army, sent word that any whites found on their plantations would be killed.

We immediately fled to Jérémie, leaving behind most of the slaves; only myself and Samedi went with the family. Madame Rose gave us a choice and I can't pretend she didn't. And I chose to go with them. I would have scoffed if you ever told me I would ever be like my mother, choosing security over freedom and an uncertain future. But there I was. Don't judge me; I could not stay behind and live off the land as most of the slaves were able to do, with the cities burning and the country a shattered hull of what it once had been.

All I had for protection in the world was Madame

Rose, Monsieur Christian and Aimée. And so rather than be cast out into a cold world, I chose to remain a slave, tied to the whites who were now my only family. And what is a slave, I sometimes think, but a person whose owner must feed and shelter them? The sweetest way of looking at it, and the foulest.

In Jérémie we were fortunate to get out on one of the last ships. The day we left, Dame Marie and all the countryside around, including Bayardel, fell to Rigaud's army. When the black general Dessalines' forces arrived the following month in Jérémie, all the white men left in town were rounded up and executed in the main square.

We sailed to Cuba along with thousands of other whites from the Grand'Anse and there we spent six years in poverty. Cuba was hotter and more fetid than Saint Domingue, a rough place of new Africans and coarse Spaniards where coffee cultivation was just beginning. Our family was more fortunate than most, for only a few had the means to buy or rent land, but Christian was a doctor and his earnings gave us a modest life.

Then the Spanish expelled all the French from Cuba and we were forced to leave again. We came to New Orleans, and though many things here are strange, more is familiar. Already Monsieur Christian has a thriving practice and his experience with the dreaded yellow fever, so common in Saint Domingue and Cuba, is welcome and valuable. Here, life is vibrant and disorderly and energetic; there is a freedom here, even for one enslaved. Sometimes I think the city like a giant, pulsating stew of discordant vegetables, that nonetheless tastes quite pleasant, and I have long ceased to try and make sense of all its contradictions and sights.

*

I stand up, smooth my skirts and return to the house, fleeing the ghosts of memory that have consumed me. I rarely think about that night these days; I can't. Back inside I walk on soft-slippered feet to the dining room and look in. The room is empty now. It's late, almost midnight, and the house is

Apricots

asleep. I take a candle to the coffin and look down at Madame Rose. I stay like that a while, the only sounds my breathing and the steady ticking of the grandfather clock, drawing dawn closer.

Free, I think, free of the truth of what happened that night in October. Madame Rose is dead and I am free from fear and betrayal. And the next week, when the lawyer comes to read the will, I learn that Madame Rose has also freed me.

I am now a free person of color, and my home is New Orleans.

AFTERWORD

The Haitian Revolution is generally agreed to have begun in August 1791 with the slave uprising on the northern plains, though antecedents include the armed struggle between the coloreds and the whites that erupted shortly after the start of the French Revolution in 1789.

After the events of this book in October 1792, for another eleven years the colony of Saint Domingue would be consumed by rebellions, insurrections, legal challenges, invasions, monstrous violence and shifting alliances between whites, coloreds and blacks; a dizzying kaleidoscope of events that is well beyond the scope of a simple explanation. As one historian noted, the Haitian Revolution was actually several revolutions in one: Each of the three main demographics (black, colored, white) had three different goals (freedom, equality, independence), and in each of the three provinces, those groups suffered vastly different experiences.

For a long time the Grand'Anse, the remote region of the South Province where this story takes place, remained relatively free of the troubles engulfing the rest of the island. In 1793 British forces occupied the district at the invitation of the planter elite—an event I foreshadow in this story—and remained there until 1798.

After defeating Napoleonic forces, on January 1, 1804 the black General Dessalines declared the creation of the Haitian Republic. Myth tells us the Haitian flag was made by tearing out the white center of the French tricolor, symbolically removing the whites, and leaving behind the red (blacks) and the blue (coloreds) stripes. After 1804 any remaining whites were massacred, and the blacks and coloreds remained in an uneasy alliance that has lasted to this day.

The thirteen-year struggle, bloody and vicious, left a crippled country, its population more than halved from 450,000 in 1789 down to less than 200,000 in 1804. A country born in turmoil and in turmoil it continued. For daring to overturn the established order, the world punished Haiti and it remained a pariah among nations, a potent symbol that struck fear into the heart of every slave-owning country, including the United States.

Stripped of its place in the world and of any international support, Haiti's history since independence has been troubled. In the middle of the 19th century and in return for sovereign recognition, Haiti agreed to pay "reparations" to the French colonists who lost their plantations. It was an enormous and odious payment that financially crippled the country and which to this day has not—incredibly—been repaid by the French government.

Today, Haiti is a vibrant, unsettled and exuberant country, where issues of race and slavery still linger in the national consciousness. Long plagued by poverty, the country is nonetheless a fascinating place and filled with compelling contradictions. Coffee is still one of the main exports, the beans mostly of the *Bourbon Arabica* variety, the same as grown by French planters and their slaves in the 18th century.

*

All of the history in this book—events and people—that take place *off* the Bayardel plantation are based on fact: the slave revolts; the incidents at Jérémie, Les Cayes, and Les Platons; people like Jean Kina; the white female hostages up north; the plans for slave genocide in the Grand'Anse, etc. They are factual, but subject to the limitations and unreliability of eyewitness accounts. The South Province in general, and the Grand'Anse in particular, remain the most unexplored part of the colony with regards to the history of the Haitian Revolution.

The main characters and events in this book, including the murder of Plunkett and the planned slave uprising for the

Grand'Anse, are fictional but I used the plantation records of the
Fongravier/Mercier family that lived at the Bayardel plantation
through the years 1771-1803 to ground my story and develop my
characters. In 1803, that family left with hundreds of other whites
from the Grand'Anse, spending six years in Cuba then onward to
New Orleans where they eventually settled. They took with them
some of their slaves, presumably mostly house slaves, including
one young girl called Pomponne.

I was able to visit the hill where old maps indicate that in
1780 a large house existed on the Bayardel plantation. Today
nothing remains of that plantation and that is true of the country in
general: more than 8,000 18th century plantations, often with
massive stone infrastructure—big houses, wells, aqueducts, mills,
granaries, warehouses, basins, drying platforms—have mostly,
with very few exceptions, been erased from the landscape by a
complex mixture of time, indifference and poverty.

Today the Grand'Anse—now a *departement* of Haiti—is
perhaps even more isolated than it was in the 18th century when it
played a small but vital role in the overall Saint Domingue export
machine. It is a beautiful region of hills and remote mountains,
bays and limestone cliffs, terrible roads and lush vegetation.
Wooden boats and dugout canoes still ply the coast, carrying on
trade just as they did 200 years ago.

At the bottom of the hill where the "big house" of the
Bayardel plantation might have stood is the small village of
Baryadel (as it is known in Creole), nestled at one end of the Bay
D'Airdelles. Amongst its few hundred inhabitants are surely some
of the descendants of the eighty-six slaves that were inventoried on
the Bayardel plantation in the 1790s, and from which I took the
names of all the slave men and women in this book.

Please visit my website for more information on my
sources, research process and the events that inspired this story, as
well as photographs, maps and portraits.

ABOUT THE AUTHOR

Sally Christie is the author of the *Mistresses of Versailles* trilogy (Atria/Simon&Schuster) about the many mistresses of Louis XV of France (1715-1774): *The Sisters of Versailles*, focusing on the four Mailly Nesle sisters; *The Rivals of Versailles*, about Madame de Pompadour, and *The Enemies of Versailles* with the Comtesse du Barry. *Apricots* is her fourth novel. Sally was born in England and grew up around the world in England, Canada, Argentina, and Lesotho, attending eight schools in three languages. She received her undergraduate degree in anthropology from McGill University and an MBA from the Wharton School in Philadelphia. A life-long history buff, most of her career was spent working in international development. Visit her website at www.sallychristieauthor.com to learn more.

Apricots

Made in the USA
Coppell, TX
22 November 2020